About the author

Sharon Booth writes uplifting won
laughter, and happy ever after. Happy endings are guaranteed
for her main characters, though she likes to make them work
for it.

Sharon is a member of the Society of Authors and the
Romantic Novelists' Association, and an Authorpreneur
member of the Alliance of Independent Authors.

She loves Yorkshire Tea, Doctor Who, and Cary Grant movies
— not necessarily in that order — and admits to being
shamefully prone to crushes on fictional heroes.

Sharon grew up in the East Riding of Yorkshire, and the
Yorkshire coast and countryside feature strongly in her novels.
Her stories are set in pretty villages and quirky market towns,
by the sea or in the countryside, and feature lots of humour,
romance, and friendship.

If you love stories with gorgeous, *kind* heroes, and heroines
who have far more important things on their minds than
buying shoes, you'll love her books.

Books by Sharon Booth

There Must Be an Angel
A Kiss from a Rose
Once Upon a Long Ago
The Whole of the Moon

Summer Secrets at Wildflower Farm
Summer Wedding at Wildflower Farm

Resisting Mr Rochester
Saving Mr Scrooge

Baxter's Christmas Wish
The Other Side of Christmas
Christmas with Cary

New Doctor at Chestnut House
Christmas at the Country Practice
Fresh Starts at Folly Farm
A Merry Bramblewick Christmas
Summer at the Country Practice
Christmas at Cuckoo Nest Cottage

Belle, Book and Christmas Candle
My Favourite Witch
To Catch a Witch

The Whole of The Moon

A Kearton Bay Novel

Sharon Booth

Green Ginger
Publishing

Published in 2021 by:
Green Ginger Publishing
Yorkshire, England

Copyright © 2021 Sharon Booth.

Cover design by Berni Stevens. www.bernistevenscoverdesign.com

ISBN: 978-1-8384242-2-0

For all the readers who have journeyed with me to Kearton Bay.
Thank you for being part of the adventure.
I hope you enjoy this final catch-up with our friends.

SAMHAIN

1

'Well, I must say, this all smells divine.'
I leaned against the kitchen door frame and inhaled the delicious aromas emanating from the ovens and several pans on the hob. Jack had come up with tonight's special menu himself, with little input from me. He was familiar enough with the different sabbats to know exactly what was required of him. He'd done me proud, as I'd known he would. It had never been in doubt. Jack's cooking was legendary in Kearton Bay.

'Roast lamb and rosemary.' I sighed with pleasure. 'That will go down a treat. Even Sophie won't be able to find fault in this.'

Jack, still a handsome man in his mid-seventies, straightened and gave me a wry look. 'It won't stop her trying though will it, Rhiannon? We all know Sophie.'

I smiled. 'We do indeed.'

Bossy, opinionated, and blunt, with a heart of gold and a fierce love for her family, we wouldn't have her any other way. Though I rather suspected members of said family had, at various times in their lives, fantasised about the possibility.

'I expect she'll be too busy talking about her wedding vows renewal,' I said hopefully. 'It seems to be her latest obsession. Anyone would think she was actually getting married for the first time, she's so excited.'

'Never does things by half does she?' Jack said. 'I don't know how Archie copes.'

'Oh, he loves her to bits,' I assured him. 'He'd be lost without her, however much he pretends otherwise.'

'Well, she can gabble on about her ceremony all she likes tonight, as long as she doesn't criticise my food.'

'Remind me again,' I said. 'What's the vegetarian option?'

'Pumpkin and chickpea curry.' Jack beamed. 'It's so tasty even non-vegetarians might plump for it, instead of the lamb.'

'And the soup is—?'

Jack sighed. 'I've told you all this. I think you're stressing too much again. You need to calm down.'

'I'm perfectly calm,' I assured him. 'I don't know what you mean about stressing. I never stress.'

'You never used to. You seem to have a bit more difficulty staying positive these days.'

'Nonsense!' Hearing the kindness in his tone almost undid me. I gave him what I hoped was a convincing smile, even though I knew I could never fool Jack. 'So, you were saying about the soup?'

Jack shook his head slightly, but thankfully didn't pursue that topic of conversation.

'Winter vegetable or wild mushroom, both served with crusty bread, either white or granary. Then there's roast lamb with all the trimmings, or the pumpkin and chickpea curry, followed by either apple crumble or poached pears. Should be enough to fill anyone up.'

'And we have muller cider, mulled wine, and seasonal fruit ciders on offer, too,' I said, more to myself than to Jack. I grinned at him. 'Those toffee apples you made went down a treat with the little ones. Little Violet Pennington-Rhys ate two. Flynn was over the moon when I told him because they can't get her to eat any fruit normally. I told him, just dip it all in toffee, she'll eat anything then.'

'Can't see Flynn going for that,' he said, laughing. 'Although Rose probably would. Anything for a quiet life.'

'Oh, Rose is such a good mum!' The smile slipped from my face. 'At least *her* children still want to be around her.'

Jack placed a spatula in the sink and walked over to where I was now slumped in the doorway.

'Come on, Rhiannon. None of that,' he murmured, putting his arms around me. 'You're blaming yourself again, and there's no need.'

'There's every need, Jack, and I think we both know it.' I nestled in the safety of his embrace, feeling the sadness wash over me once more. 'He's not coming back, is he?'

Jack kissed the top of my forehead. 'Of course he is. Just be patient. Give it time.'

My bitter laughter was smothered against his chest. 'Give it time! It's been three-and-a-half years! I think if he were coming home, he'd have done so by now.'

'He sends postcards, and he texts you.'

'He *used* to send postcards,' I reminded him. 'During the last year I've had the grand total of two of them, and he rarely texts me these days. It's hardly an enthusiastic correspondence, is it? Face it, my father's done his job. Derry hates me now, probably almost as much as his grandfather does.'

Jack was quiet for a moment, as if trying to decide how best to answer without upsetting me even more. 'Derry could never hate you. And as for your father — well, he's more to be pitied, if you ask me.'

'You don't know him,' I said, shivering. 'He never wanted me, and after I got pregnant with Derry that was it as far as he was concerned. He loathes me, and the feeling's mutual.'

'Like I said. More to be pitied. Look what he's missed out on all this time.'

I pulled away from him and stared into his dark eyes. 'I can't pity him! All these years and not a word from him. No interest in Derry at all. Suddenly they're best friends and I'm out in the cold. Oh!' I shook my head, the emotions too powerful to put into words.

Jack clearly felt helpless to reassure me. I reached for his hand, ashamed that I'd put him in that position. 'I'm sorry. Let's forget it, shall we?'

'Things will work out, my darling,' he said kindly. 'Don't give up hope. What is it you're always telling everyone? *The universe unfolds just as it should.* Let it do its job without worrying how it does it, eh?'

He was quite correct. I did always say that. Funny how it was so much easier to apply that philosophy to other people's troubles.

'You're absolutely right,' I said. 'Sorry, Jack.'

'Never apologise to me,' he said, turning back to the hob. 'You can say anything you like to me, and well you know it. I'm going nowhere.'

I gazed fondly at him as he gave the contents of a saucepan a gentle stir. I was so lucky to have found Jack. Although, come to think of it, he'd found me. He'd turned up at The Hare and Moon the day before my grand opening, twenty-eight years ago, and informed me that I was going to need a chef, and he was the best around.

I hadn't even thought about serving food. I don't think I'd given enough thought at all to what I was going to do with the pub. I was twenty-two, and naïve, not to mention pregnant. In retrospect, I was amazed at the optimism and courage I'd had then. Sir Paul, the father of my child, had offered to pay me an allowance, but I didn't want that. Instead, he gave me The Hare and Moon, one of the properties owned by the Kearton Estate, and I determined to make my own way from that point on.

I was going to run a traditional pub, with simple bar snacks on offer. Jack had persuaded me that I'd be missing a trick if I didn't provide good hearty meals.

'Think about it,' he'd said. 'It's a long walk down that hill to the seafront. Don't tell me people aren't going to be ready for some food when they get here. Then there'll be all those people on the beach, running about, swimming, playing rounders... They're going to be starving when they're done, and they'll turn up on your doorstep expecting to be fed. A bag of cheese and onion crisps just won't cut it. Think about it, Miss Bone.'

So I did think about it and decided he was quite right. Jack had agreed to a month's trial and I soon discovered he was worth every penny, despite my initial misgivings about the extra expense of hiring a chef. He was excellent at his job, and food quickly became an important part of my trade. Initially, I'd only been able to pay him an extremely low wage, so for the first five years he lived in at the pub, and was a huge help to me, especially after I had Derry. After that, he rented his own flat in Helmston, and our relationship continued to flourish. He was like the father I wished I'd had, and despite our frequent skirmishes over the menu, we got on exceptionally well, once I'd acknowledged that, when it came to food, he was usually right, and I was nearly always wrong.

He'd always been close to my son, and I knew he missed Derry deeply. Almost as much as I did. Almost.

I pushed the grief away, determined not to let anything spoil the sabbat. Samhain was always such a special time of year. Most people celebrated it as Halloween, but to me, and to many others, it was the Feast of the Dead, and the Celtic New Year.

'It's going to be a wonderful night,' I said, as if to convince myself as much as Jack.

'It is. All the usual suspects coming, I suppose?'

'I should think so. Even Will and Lexi have said they'll be here, although I'll be amazed if they actually make it,' I mused. 'After all, the baby only arrived last week, and I expect they're both shattered. Not to mention the difficulties of getting a babysitter for such a young child, and Milo, of course.'

'Will Charlie and Joe be coming?' Jack asked hopefully. 'Oh, they do make me laugh, those two.'

I shook my head. 'Sorry, Jack. They're babysitting for Eliza and Gabriel's children. But Rose and Flynn will be here, and Rose is always good fun. And I believe Fuchsia and Pandora are coming, too.'

'And Tally?'

We exchanged knowing looks. The youngest of Sophie and Archie Crook's three children, Tally was a darling, but she was far too nice for her own good, constantly trying to please people — especially her mother. Tally never seemed to think about what she wanted from her life. It was always about what other people

11

wanted her to do. I suspected that was why she'd ended up working for Will and Lexi at Kearton Hall, as the wedding and events co-ordinator.

Sophie had always been extraordinarily proud of the fact that her husband, Archie, was Sir Paul's, and then Will's personal solicitor, so when Archie retired, she'd been quite deflated. Of course, once her niece Lexi married Will and became Lady Boden-Kean, Sophie's spirits had lifted, and she'd nudged Tally into accepting the job offer even though her daughter had never shown the slightest interest in that sort of employment.

Only today she'd been more-or-less cajoled into stepping in at the last minute to host the Halloween story time for local children at the pub. My barmaid, Kerry, was supposed to do it, but she'd called me that morning to say she'd lost a filling in her tooth, was in agony, and couldn't get an emergency appointment with her dentist until the following day. Reading to a bunch of excited primary and nursery-age children was quite out of the question.

Unfortunately for Tally, Sophie had been in the pub having lunch with Eliza when I took the call, and she'd immediately volunteered her daughter for the job, despite both Eliza's and my words of caution.

Tally had duly arrived at The Hare and Moon, having been allowed to leave Kearton Hall early, and had valiantly tried to hide her dismay when she set eyes on the pumpkin costume that Kerry had volunteered to wear.

'You don't have to wear it,' I'd said hastily. 'It was merely something Kerry thought would amuse the children, but honestly, it doesn't matter.'

'No, no, if the children are expecting it...' Tally took the costume from me and gave a watery smile. 'It's not a problem, honestly.'

Poor Tally. One day, I was convinced she would snap and rebel, and lord help Sophie when she did.

'Well, everything's simmering away nicely,' Jack announced. He glanced at the clock on the wall. 'Should be arriving any time soon, shouldn't they?'

12

'They should,' I agreed. 'I expect the visitors from Whitby will be here first. They usually are. I have no idea how I'm going to manage behind the bar tonight, though. With Kerry absent, it's going to be a nightmare.'

'You can borrow young Harriet if you like,' Jack offered. 'She'd probably enjoy working behind the bar for a change.'

'Absolutely not. I hired Harriet to wait on tables. You can't manage that, as well as the cooking. Don't worry, Jack. I'll cope. We both will.'

'We always do,' he said, giving me an affectionate smile. 'I don't see why tonight should be any different.'

I kissed him lightly on the cheek then headed back to the bar. As I gazed around the room, I felt a swell of love for this beautiful old inn that had been my home for so many years.

The Hare and Moon stood on the seafront of Kearton Bay, with breath-taking views of the North Sea. Apart from the Elizabethan Kearton Hall it was the oldest building in the village, and I loved it heart and soul.

For my Samhain celebration I'd lit the fire in the hearth, and the bar looked warm, cosy and inviting on this dark October night. I'd dotted around bunches of rosemary, and their delicious scent suffused the room. Candles flickered in carved pumpkins on the window ledges, and trays of gingerbread, bowls of apples and pears and dishes of nuts lined the bar counter, especially for the sabbat.

On the mantelpiece above the fireplace, candles flickered: black ones, representing the god and the old year, and white ones which signified the goddess and the new year. Between them, propped up against the wall, stood a faded black and white photograph of a beautiful young woman. My mother.

I stared at it for a moment, wondering what she would make of everything that had happened recently. Would she have approved of Derry moving in with my father? Or would she have felt my pain, understood why I couldn't bear the situation? I supposed I would never know. My mother had died years ago, and she'd never even met her grandson, thanks to my father's domineering nature. It was just one more thing he'd done to hurt me.

I pushed the thought away and forced myself to think more positively. Tonight was going to be busy, and I would be rushed off my feet, but it was going to be fun, too. My friends and neighbours would have a good time. I would make sure of it.

****

Harry Jarvis felt his stomach flutter with dread as he knocked on the door of Wychwood. A hundred scenarios ran through his mind as he waited on the step, each one worse than the next. Who would answer, he wondered? He couldn't decide who he'd prefer. He'd probably get a punch on the nose from Eliza's new husband, for a start.

He tutted impatiently. He was hardly her *new* husband, was he? In fact, he was fairly sure that she and Gabriel had been married longer than he and Eliza had been. Even so, he still saw Gabriel Bailey as some sort of interloper, which he knew deep down was ridiculous, but he couldn't help it.

Would it be any better, though, if Eliza herself answered the door? He could well imagine the look of dismay on her face as she realised he was in Kearton Bay — her territory. He remembered the last time he'd been here. So many years ago now, and so much had happened since. He could only hope things went a little better this time than they had then.

It occurred to him suddenly that it might be Amy herself who answered. That thought was enough to cause a sickening lurch in his stomach, and he took a deep breath. She would be, what, ten and a half now.

He felt a sudden shame. She'd been seven when he last saw her in person. He'd sent her birthday and Christmas cards, of course, and money. Lots of money. But he hadn't actually set eyes on her. Living on the other side of the Atlantic had made things tricky.

But no. He mentally shook his head. He could have made more of an effort. He could even have video called her if he'd wanted to, but there was always something else to do, something else to think about, to take up his time, and then with everything that had happened... To be fair, she'd never suggested it either, and nor had Eliza. Oh well.

He frowned. Where were they? Surely they must be in at this time? They had children, didn't they? Other children, that is, younger than Amy. Twins, he thought. He wondered how Amy had taken to having younger siblings. She already had a half-brother through him, of course, but she'd only met Rufus once, and he'd been very young then. He doubted she'd given him much thought since.

He sighed and crouched down to peer through the letter box.

'Hello! Anyone at home?'

All was silent. Harry straightened and stepped back, looking up at the windows. There was a lamp on in the living room, but other than that the house seemed to be in darkness. He wasn't sure what to do next.

Damn! He'd come all this way, psyched himself up for a confrontation, and no one was home. Now what? He glanced at his watch. Ten past nine. Too late to go to the house, and he supposed he may as well go back to The Kearton Arms. He'd booked a room there for the night, and a glass of wine and some food sounded good to him after the long drive to North Yorkshire. He had no idea where Eliza and her family were, and not a clue where to start. What an anti-climax.

As he crunched down the drive to his car, he remembered that Eliza's uncle, Joe, lived not far away. He'd been to Whisperwood Farm before, the last time he was in Kearton Bay, when Eliza's grandmother, Hannah, had owned it. Not that he'd known she was Eliza's grandmother then. Neither had Eliza, come to that, or at least he didn't think she had. It had been a fraught time and his memory was clouded on the subject. He'd had other things on his mind, as he recalled, not least the imminent publication of a terrible kiss-and-tell story in the newspapers by some girl he'd once slept with, and the incandescent rage of his then-mistress Melody Bird.

He blew out his cheeks, suddenly worn out. It had been a long and tiring day, and at the memory of Melody he felt deflated and weary. Never mind a long and tiring day, it had been a long and tiring year. Two years, really. He dropped into the seat of his car and stared unseeingly out of the window.

Had he ever been happy since the day he'd moved to the US permanently? It had seemed like an exciting adventure at the time, but it had turned sour quickly. For him at least. For Melody, the new life had got better and better.

Sod it, he'd go to Whisperwood Farm and see if Eliza was there. He'd probably get short shrift from Joe, of course. Her uncle had never liked him, and in all honesty, he couldn't say he blamed him. Joe idolised Eliza, and Harry had to admit he'd hardly been a model husband. If any husband of Amy's treated her the way he'd treated her mother…

Harry backed out of the drive onto the lane. Whisperwood Farm, if he remembered correctly, wasn't far away from here. He drove slowly out of Daisyfield Walk and down Clover Lane, not even bothering to turn on any music, his usual driving companion. Memories flooded back to him of the last time he'd driven in this direction, heading towards a reunion with his then wife, convincing himself that she'd be putty in his hands, despite his appalling behaviour. He'd always been able to persuade her to believe him before. It hadn't occurred to him that she wouldn't fall over herself to make it up with him.

Well, that had gone a bit pear-shaped, hadn't it?

He scowled at the memory. Gabriel bloody Bailey had been there, and he hadn't stood a chance with him in the picture. His jaw tightened with anger, aimed mostly at himself. He'd been a fool, throwing Eliza away for Melody. He'd got what he deserved in the end. No doubt Eliza and Gabriel would say it was karma, and perhaps they'd be right. He still wasn't ready to hear it from them, though. He hoped they'd not gloat about it, at least to his face.

The gate to Whisperwood Farm was closed. Harry pulled over at the side of the lane and crossed the road to open it. It was padlocked. Bugger!

He hesitated a moment, then shrugged and climbed over. No doubt there were security cameras everywhere and he was being spied upon at this very moment, but he didn't much care. He'd come this far, and he wanted at least *some* sort of resolution to today's adrenaline-fuelled adventures. Anything else would be unacceptable. Even if it ended on a row, he had to see *someone*, talk to *someone* about his plans. He'd never sleep tonight if he didn't let them know he was back.

He blinked as security lights came on and dazzled him momentarily. The farmyard was lit up brighter than a summer's day. Harry wondered what the electricity bill was for Whisperwood. Whatever, he supposed Charlie and Joe could afford it, being *celebrities*.

He realised the bitterness was back and pushed it away, focusing instead on the farmhouse. It had certainly improved one hundred per cent since he'd last visited. It had been a bit of a shack back then, with peeling paint and loose tiles and an unloved look about it. As someone who'd spent his entire working life in property it had deeply offended him. Now, though, it looked amazing. A new front door and windows, clearly a new roof, and a freshly painted exterior. Joe had really improved it; he'd give him that.

He gave a nervous gulp as he walked towards the door, preparing himself mentally to knock. He needn't have bothered. The door flew open as he got within a few yards of it, and Harry found himself staring at not only Joe Hollingsworth, but his husband, comedian Charlie Hope, too.

'Well!' Charlie seemed to recover his voice first which, when he thought about it later, didn't surprise Harry in the slightest. 'It *is* you! Talk about the bad penny. What are you doing here then? Got a nerve ain't you?'

'Harry Jarvis was never short of confidence,' Joe said grimly. He folded his arms and fixed Harry with a cold stare. 'What do you want?'

Harry jutted out his chin. There was no way in hell he was going to let them talk to him like dirt. Okay, he'd made mistakes in the past, but hadn't everyone? Besides, what was it to do with them? Time to bring out his inner bastard.

'Well, I should think it's perfectly obvious what I want,' he said calmly. 'It certainly wouldn't be you now, would it? I went to Wychwood, but no one was home, so I came to see if Eliza is here.'

'What you wanna see Eliza for?' Charlie demanded, his eyes narrowing behind his glasses.

'I doubt very much she'll want to see you,' Joe added. His lip was practically curling, Harry observed indignantly. Honestly, the cheek of it! Eliza was a grown woman. It was for her to decide who she wanted to see, not Laurel and Hardy here.

'Whether she wants to see me or not is irrelevant,' he said, with a great deal more confidence than he felt.

'Oh, you think so?' Joe scowled at him and Charlie laid a hand on his arm.

'Now, Joe, remember your 'eart. You wanna watch it,' he told Harry. 'He's a tiger when he gets going, trust me.'

Harry almost laughed at the idea, but mindful of his cool demeanour he merely said, 'I'll take your word for it. Now, is Eliza here or not?'

'Why do you wanna see her?' Charlie asked again. 'She never said you were coming. Does she know?'

'Well,' Harry said, 'if she'd known she would have been at home, wouldn't she?'

'You keep telling yourself that,' Joe said. 'Personally, I think she'd have been on the first plane to New Zealand to get away from you. But as Charlie has now asked you twice, what do you want to see her about?'

'For fuck's sake,' Harry snapped, beginning to lose patience, 'I rather think that's between me and her, don't you?'

'Oh, there's plenty between you and her,' Joe told him. 'Me and Charlie for a start.'

Harry fought valiantly to keep his cool. 'Is Amy here then?' he managed between gritted teeth.

Joe's eyebrows knitted together. 'Wherever Amy is has got nothing to do with you. Now go away before I set the dog on you.'

'He will, too,' Charlie assured him. 'I'd make a run for it if I were you.'

Harry had never been a big fan of dogs, having been bitten by one when he was a small boy. He cast a nervous glance into the hallway behind the two men, listening intently for the sound of paws on the slate floor.

'You don't believe us?' Charlie stood aside and indicated for him to enter the house. 'Be our guest. Come and meet the dog for yourself.'

'I sincerely hope you're insured,' Joe murmured.

Harry decided, on balance, that hanging around Whisperwood Farm was a waste of time. 'Fine, I'll go. But when you see Eliza, tell her I'm looking for her, will you? I'll try again at her house tomorrow.'

'You do that,' Joe said. 'I'm sure she'll be thrilled.'

Harry glared at him. 'You know, it's been years since our divorce, Joe. Surely it's time to put what happened behind us?'

'Like hell it is,' Joe said. 'You think I'll ever forget or forgive what you put that girl through? Think again.'

After a moment's hesitation, Harry turned and headed back to the gate, realising it was pointless arguing with them.

Behind him he heard Charlie yell, 'And stay out!' before the front door slammed.

Feeling humiliated and not a little lost, he climbed back over the gate and got in his car, just as the security lighting switched off and the farmyard was plunged into darkness. Now what?

The Kearton Arms, he supposed. God knows, he was hungry and tired, and an early night would probably be his best bet.

He managed a U-turn with some difficulty in the narrow lane and drove back along Clover Lane towards the main road. Parking a few minutes later in The Kearton Arms' car park, he sat for a moment, staring out of the windscreen into the darkness at the black shape of the large, Victorian pub in front of him. He felt worn out, miserable, and generally defeated by life.

He'd known it was probably best to wait to speak to Eliza until the morning, when he'd had a good sleep and was feeling refreshed and more like himself, but his natural impatience had overtaken common sense. Quite honestly, he'd worried that his nerve might fail him if he didn't get it over with immediately. Now he wasn't sure how he felt. Maybe coming to Kearton Bay had been a big mistake after all. Bit late now, though. He'd put all his eggs in one basket. No going back.

It was as Harry entered the lobby of The Kearton Arms that he noticed the poster. He thought it extraordinary that one pub would allow an advert for another to be pinned to the corkboard, but there it was, plain as day.

CELEBRATE SAMHAIN AT
THE HARE AND MOON PUB
THE SLIPWAY
KEARTON BAY
CHILDREN'S HALLOWEEN STORY TIME 4.00PM
SAMHAIN CEREMONY
WITH SPECIAL MENU AND SEASONAL DRINKS
FROM 7.00PM
ALL WELCOME!

He eyed it curiously. What the hell was a Samhain ceremony?

'Thinking of going, mate?' An elderly man peered over his shoulder and nodded at the poster. 'Reckon you'll have to hurry if you want to get some grub. Most likely be finished serving by now. It's not a normal night, is it? And you know what Rhiannon's like with her sabbats.'

Harry had no idea what he was talking about. 'What is this? What's a Samhain ceremony?'

'Sow-een it's pronounced.' The man grinned. 'See, she's trained us all. One of them witchy events Rhiannon likes to hold.'

'Rhiannon?'

'Landlady of The Hare and Moon. Not been here before then?'

'Many years ago,' Harry murmured. 'Good of the landlord to advertise another pub's events in here.'

'Oh, it won't impact his trade,' the man said comfortably. 'Besides, it's like that around here. We all help each other out. As it should be.'

Harry's mind was working fast. If there was a special event this evening, complete with children's stories and food and drink, it was probable that Eliza and Gabriel and the children were there.

'Where is this Hare and Moon place?' he enquired.

The old man shrugged. 'Can't miss it. Go straight down the bottom of the hill and it's right on the seafront.'

Harry nodded his appreciation. 'Am I right in thinking you can't take your car down there?'

'That's right. Long walk it is an' all. Mind you,' the man added, laughing, 'it feels a hell of a lot longer when you're walking back up the bugger.'

'Thanks.'

Harry realised, ten minutes later, that the man hadn't been joking. Bay Street, as the hill was named, was quite a walk. He kept to the left-hand side, which had broad steps with a handrail separating them from the road. Maybe cars weren't allowed down here, but it was dark, despite the street lights, and he wasn't taking any chances.

The hill twisted its way down the cliff side toward the sea, edged on either side with quaint buildings — some stone, others rendered and whitewashed. He noted the red pantile roofs and crooked chimneys, and the narrow strips of cobbles at the sides of the road, which he guessed were what was left of the original road and wondered how old this part of Kearton Bay was.

Rounding a bend he spotted an outdoor clothing shop, and to his left, tucked into a corner, a five-storey building — The Mermaid Inn. Standing some five storeys high, it was a whitewashed building, very narrow, and the welcoming light fixed on its side wall revealed an intriguing passageway behind it, with a flight of wooden steps leading to the first-floor rooms. Next to the pub a fish and chip shop was packed with customers, and Harry's nose twitched at the delicious smells wafting out of the open doorway. He was half-tempted to join the queue.

Nobly he resisted temptation and headed over a little stone

bridge which crossed a stream, and passed a large stone house, which had apparently once been the village police station, according to a sign over the door, illuminated by an old-fashioned lamp fixed above it.

Then the road twisted once more, and the sea finally came into view. He hurried down the final stretch of the hill, past another row of shops and cafés, a fossil and dinosaur museum and an art gallery. In front of him was a slipway to the beach, where two boats waited for their next adventure on the seas. To the right of the slope was a long, low building which proclaimed itself to be a museum. To the left stood The Hare and Moon.

Harry paused for a moment and took a deep breath. It had been a long walk, and while he didn't mind that, it had given him more time to run through all the possible scenarios that might play out when he finally came face to face with his ex-wife. None of them, unfortunately, were pleasant.

Oh, well, he'd come this far.

He eyed the pub curiously. In its leaded windows, he could see lanterns glowing, and frowned as he noticed the pumpkin lanterns glowing on each picnic table outside. It seemed that The Hare and Moon was not your average seaside pub. He wondered about the person who ran it — this Rhiannon woman. She sounded a real odd bod. Even so, the building itself was beautiful, even in the lamplight. He took a moment to appreciate its obvious age and character, then took a deep breath to steady his nerves.

He had no way of knowing what he was walking into, he realised suddenly. They might be there with friends and neighbours. Gabriel Bailey's family all lived in the area. He would be surrounded by hostile natives. Was this such a good idea?

'Bollocks,' he muttered to himself. 'You're here now. Just deal with it, you bloody wimp.'

He climbed the steps, ignoring the hollow feeling in his legs, then pushed open the door. Whatever reaction he got hell would freeze over before he'd let them know he was intimidated. He'd been humiliated enough recently. His life had come tumbling down around his ears in the most degrading and cruel way. It was time to start rebuilding it. And for that, like it or not, he needed Eliza.

2

Whatever Harry had been expecting inside The Hare and Moon, this wasn't it. The bar was in darkness except for the lanterns glowing in the windows and a fire blazing in the hearth. There was a strong smell in the air. Harry sniffed it, wondering what it was. He caught the scent of rosemary, but there was something else, too. He thought, maybe cinnamon.

He was relieved that no one seemed to have noticed his arrival. They were all focused on a petite brunette, standing in the centre of the room. She looked like something from a gothic romance, with dark tumbling curls, a long black skirt and Victorian style blouse, and black ankle boots.

Harry quickly cast a glance around, looking for Eliza. His gaze fell on a group of people dressed in the most extraordinary costumes, wearing makeup that transformed their faces into something quite otherworldly. He remembered the notices he'd seen around the village advertising the nearby Whitby Goth Festival, and guessed they were something to do with that.

He wrinkled his nose in disapproval as he noticed Gabriel Bailey sitting at a table, his attention fixed on the brunette. Well, Eliza couldn't be far away then. He wished someone would switch the sodding light on.

His gaze returned to the centre of the room as the brunette began to speak.

'Samhain is the third harvest, summer's end. It's also the night when the veil between the worlds is at its thinnest.'

Her voice wasn't at all as he'd expected. Instead of a broad Yorkshire accent, she sounded like a BBC announcer from the early days of television. He had a fleeting thought that perhaps she wasn't of this time at all. Was she even real?

Harry suddenly wondered if he would be wiser to leave. Whatever was going on in this place, it wasn't your average night at the pub. He recalled the scene in *An American Werewolf in London*, when the two hitchhikers arrived at the pub in Yorkshire, and it was immediately clear that something bad was going to happen. What the hell had he walked in on?

He took a step back, half hoping to edge his way out of the pub and jumped in fright as he bumped into someone. He turned round and muttered an apology to a bearded man and a smartly dressed woman. He hadn't even heard them come in, but now his way out was blocked and he daren't ask them to move in case it drew attention to him. Not that he was afraid, obviously, but one never knew with these strange village pubs. And they clearly didn't come much stranger than this one.

The brunette took a tall black candle from the mantelpiece and lit the central candle in a tray full of small, white candles that she'd placed on the bar.

'It's the night for remembering those who have gone before us. Each of you who wishes to do so may light one of these candles in remembrance of a loved one, and state something about them — some much-loved quality that you remember about them. If you have a photograph of your loved one, place it on the alter on the mantelpiece.'

A middle-aged woman with a blonde bob, sitting just in front of him, tutted loudly.

'She gets dafter every year,' she whispered, not so quietly that Harry couldn't hear her perfectly well. She received a quick nudge from the grey-haired man sitting next to her, who clearly didn't approve of her comment. For Harry, though, it had been a reassurance. At least he wasn't the only one who thought this was weird.

Evidently, though, they were in the minority. He watched, amazed, as people queued to light a candle for someone they'd lost, and the collection of photographs on the mantelpiece grew quickly.

His heart rate quickened as he spotted Eliza at last. She took the black candle from the brunette and lit a small candle in the tray.

Harry strained to hear what she was saying, and realised she was lighting it for her mother.

'You were always patient and kind, and never spoke ill of anyone.'

Harry had never met her mother, but he knew how much Eliza missed her, and felt a pang of sadness for her. He rather suspected his own behaviour towards her daughter might have tested Ms Hollingsworth's famed patience and kindness to breaking point.

A long-legged redhead was right behind Eliza. 'For Hannah, whose open heart and generosity brought my family together.'

'For Father.' The man holding the redhead's hand lit another candle. 'He sometimes struggled to fit into today's world, but he always did what he thought was right.'

Together, they placed photographs of their loved ones beside the ones already on the mantelpiece.

The stream of people lighting candles seemed never ending. Harry thought fleetingly of his own father and thought he ought to light one in his memory. He mentally shook himself. What the hell was he thinking? His father would have howled with laughter at the thought of it and would most certainly have dismissed this entire ceremony as mumbo-jumbo. Besides, Harry wasn't about to draw attention to himself. God knows what was going to happen next. For all he knew, it could be a human sacrifice. He'd seen *The Wicker Man*.

He noticed the queue had dispersed and watched as the brunette lit a candle and stared into the flame. He could see the sense of loss in her face, and his anxiety left him. There was no harm in this woman, he was sure of that. She looked small and vulnerable, and he could almost feel her sadness.

'For my mother,' she said softly. 'For all she bravely bore, and for loving me. Wherever she is now, I hope she's found the peace that eluded her in life.'

The blonde bob woman had given up pretending to be uncaring and was dabbing her eyes with a tissue.

'You never speak much about your mother,' she said tearfully. 'Who was she exactly, Rhiannon?'

Ah, so the brunette was Rhiannon. He should have guessed.

'Now's not the time, Sophe,' the grey-haired man said gently.

'Tonight,' Rhiannon continued, having obviously decided the best course of action was to pretend she hadn't heard this Sophie woman, 'we have lit these candles to remember those we loved and lost, and the lanterns in the windows are to reassure them they are always welcome, and always loved.'

'Oh, I'm not so sure about that,' Sophie said, shivering. 'This is all a bit scary, Archie.'

Rhiannon gave her a reassuring smile. 'These are the people we've loved, who loved us,' she reminded her. 'There's nothing to be afraid of. Now,' she added, addressing everyone, 'with the ceremony complete, please feel free to enjoy what's left of the evening. And do help yourselves to the gingerbread. It needs eating, and there's only half an hour to closing time.'

And just like that, The Hare and Moon was a normal place again. People took their seats, or milled around in groups, chatting, and a queue formed for drinks at the bar before last orders.

Harry hadn't realised how tense he'd been. He closed his eyes, dropped his shoulders and forced himself to relax. Everything was fine. There was no cause for anxiety.

'I don't bloody believe it! What the hell are you doing here?'

Harry's eyes snapped open, and he found himself face to face with Gabriel Bailey, of all people. Okay, maybe he'd relaxed too soon.

****

27

My sociable and peaceful Samhain celebration seemed to have deteriorated somewhat.

Harry Jarvis sauntered over to the bar where Tally was serving, having been — almost inevitably — volunteered for the job by Sophie earlier in the evening, when it became apparent that I was struggling on my own. Cerise had also volunteered, and it was a good job I had them both as I certainly wouldn't have managed without them. As Rose had reminded me, I should have taken on permanent bar staff after Derry left, but I hadn't. To do so would be like admitting to myself that he wasn't coming back, and I still wasn't ready to do that. Would I ever be?

'White wine please,' Harry said.

Tally glanced nervously at Eliza before pouring the drink. She pushed the glass towards him, and he passed her a ten-pound note.

'Keep the change,' he said, giving her a wink, then turned to us and raised his glass in a silent toast. Really, one would think he hadn't a care in the world as he leaned casually against the bar, glass in hand, surveying us all with a sardonic smile on his lips.

Eliza stood by Gabriel's side, while Gabriel's daughter, Lexi, Sophie and Rose stood behind them, like bodyguards.

'Harry, why are you here?'

I heard the tremor in Eliza's voice and realised how shaken she was to see her ex-husband in The Hare and Moon, of all places. I'd never seen him in the flesh before, nor had I ever watched any of his programmes. My only images of him had been in the tabloids, when his affair with his co-presenter Melody Bird was big news, much to Eliza's distress.

He looked older now, his short brown hair peppered with grey, and fine lines feathering his turquoise-coloured eyes. He was wearing a well-cut suit that looked far too formal for the occasion. I wondered what had brought him to Kearton Bay after all this time.

'Well,' Harry said, 'I'm sure you'll be delighted to know that I've moved back to Britain permanently — to Yorkshire actually. Kearton Bay to be exact. Surprise! I'm your new neighbour.'

There was a stunned silence.

Gabriel found his voice first. 'You can't be serious!'

'Perfectly serious.' Harry gave him a brief smile. 'Aren't you pleased?'

'Where?' Eliza demanded. 'Whereabouts in Kearton Bay have you moved to?'

'Well,' Harry said, 'I don't know if you've heard of it. It's a little place up on the cliff top called Eight Bells.'

'Eight Bells!' Eliza sounded astonished, as well she might. 'Eight Bells is in an awful state! It's not fit to live in, surely?'

She had a point. Eight Bells was a large, Georgian house that had once been run as an inn, before being turned into a hotel. By the time it passed to Matthew Reynolds, its last owner, it had already become a bit run down and was no more than a second-rate guest house.

Matthew had moved to Sandsend to live with his daughter around seven years ago, and since then the house had stood empty. I could well imagine the condition it must be in.

'Matthew won't sell it,' Gabriel challenged. 'He's had loads of offers, but he's always turned them down. His granddaughter is a patient of mine and she once told me he'd been inundated with enquiries about it over the years, but he wouldn't budge, as he always said he'd go back there one day.'

'Yes, well he won't be going back there now,' Harry said with a shrug. 'He passed away a few months ago, and the daughter apparently couldn't wait to be shot of it.'

'Oh,' I said, feeling a pang of sadness, 'did he? I never even knew. Bless him, how awful.'

Harry shot me a look of surprise. 'Er, yes. Awful.'

'Awful for him,' Sophie said sharply. 'Bit of an opportunity for you.'

'And you are?'

Sophie drew herself up to her full five feet two inches and glared at Harry. 'I'm Sophie Crook, Gabriel's sister.'

'Ah.' It was one word, but it spoke volumes.

'Harry, you haven't really bought Eight Bells,' Eliza said weakly. 'Tell me you haven't.'

'All right,' he said. 'I haven't.'

29

'But have you?'

'For goodness' sake, Eliza, make up your mind. Do you want me to tell you the truth or don't you?'

Gabriel gave a short laugh. 'As if you'd know the truth!'

Eliza sank into a nearby chair, looking dazed. 'You have, haven't you? You've moved to Kearton Bay.'

'Yes,' Harry said. He sounded a little more gentle, less aggressive. 'I know it must have come as a bit of a shock to you—'

'That's one way of putting it,' Rose muttered.

'Why?' Eliza asked. 'Why here? Why now?'

'Amy,' Harry said simply. 'I want to rebuild my relationship with my daughter. I want to see her on a regular basis, and I can't do that from California, can I?'

'Over my dead body!' Gabriel was clearly having none of it.

'You've got a bloody nerve,' Sophie snapped, giving Harry a look that dripped pure poison. 'How long is it since you last saw her? My brother's been more of a father to her than you've ever been, and if you think you can swan in here—'

'Mum,' Tally said urgently, 'stay out of it. It's nothing to do with anyone else. This is between the three of them.'

Harry beamed at her. 'Well said, that girl. Brains as well as beauty.'

Tally glared back. 'Keep your patronising comments to yourself.'

'Well,' Harry said, looking nonplussed by her about turn. 'That told me, didn't it?'

'You can't just turn up here and announce you want to see Amy,' Eliza said. 'It doesn't work that way.'

'I don't see why not. She's my daughter as much as yours. *We* made her.' Harry's gaze flickered briefly towards Gabriel. '*He's* nothing to do with it.'

'Nothing to do with it?' Eliza seemed close to tears. 'If it hadn't been for Gabriel—'

'I think,' I said hastily, 'that this is a private matter, and you need to discuss it alone. You're very welcome to use my living room.'

'Absolutely,' Sophie agreed, picking up her bag. 'Come on, let's go upstairs.'

'Not you, Sophe.' Archie's tone was firm. 'We're going home.'

Rose, who was Eliza's best friend as well as her business partner, folded her arms. 'I'm going nowhere unless Eliza tells me to. That little shit may need a punch on the nose.'

'If he does,' her husband Flynn said firmly, 'I'm sure Gabriel will want to be the one to give it to him.'

'What? A man of healing? Surely not.'

Harry smirked, and I thought he must be either terribly brave or terribly stupid to provoke such hostilities. I watched him closely as he took a sip of wine and, very briefly, saw something else beneath the surface. There was a definite tremor to his hand, and now that I looked deeper into his eyes, there was the faintest flicker of anxiety. Hmm. He was playing to an audience. He'd no doubt get much further if he'd reason with them — be a bit humbler, apologetic even. Though it probably wasn't Harry Jarvis's style. I had a feeling he didn't do humble.

I switched on the lights as the visitors from Whitby took their leave, assuring me they'd had a wonderful evening, and tactfully not mentioning its descent into anarchy. I smiled at them and thanked them for coming and told them I'd be delighted to see them at Beltane.

Archie handed a reluctant Sophie her coat. 'Come on, love. Time for home. Let's leave them to it.'

'Rose?' Flynn handed his wife her coat, too.

She wrinkled her nose. 'Really?'

'Really,' he said firmly.

Sophie clearly didn't want to go. 'But what about Gabriel and Eliza? We can't just—'

'They can manage,' Archie said, pulling her arms through her coat sleeves as if she were a helpless child. 'Let's leave these people in peace, okay?'

'Do you need a hand to clear up, Rhiannon?'

I blinked, dragging my attention away from Sophie and Archie as I realised Tally was talking to me.

'What? Oh, no, darling, that's fine. Jack and I will manage perfectly well. Get yourself off home and thank you so much. I'll arrange payment tomorrow for you and Cerise.'

They both held up their hands, insisting they didn't need paying, but I was adamant. 'No arguments,' I told them. 'I'll see you tomorrow.'

'I'm going now,' Sophie told Gabriel as she passed him. 'If you need me, you ring me, and I'll be straight over.'

Gabriel nodded. 'Thanks, Sophie,' he said, 'but I think I can deal with this.'

'Well if you can't,' Rose said loudly, 'let me know and I'll come round and thump him one.'

'You'll do no such thing,' Flynn said. He put a hand on Gabriel's shoulder. 'Good luck. Stay calm, okay?'

Gabriel nodded and Flynn bundled Rose out of the bar, followed by Fuchsia, Pandora and Cerise. Archie nodded at me, then took a clearly reluctant Sophie's hand and led her outside. Tally gave me a weak smile and followed behind them.

Lexi shot Harry a warning glance, then she and Will left the pub, arm in arm.

Within minutes, my other customers had left for home, until only Eliza, Gabriel, Harry and I remained.

'Please, feel free to go upstairs,' I said. 'I'll be helping Jack in the kitchen anyway, so I won't disturb you.'

'It hardly seems appropriate to have this conversation in a pub,' Harry objected. 'Can't we go back to your house, Eliza?'

'No we can't,' she snapped. 'You're not going anywhere near our home. That's *our* place. You're having no part of it.'

'I don't *want* any part of it,' Harry assured her. 'Really, darling, you do need to get some perspective.'

Eliza's mouth dropped open. 'I can't believe the cheek of you! Look, just say what you have to say and go home.'

'Unfortunately,' Harry said, 'I can't go home yet, not in the darkness. I'm staying at The Kearton Arms tonight and I'll be going to Eight Bells tomorrow to see what needs doing. I must say, Joe inspired me earlier this evening. He's done a sterling job with Whisperwood Farm, hasn't he?'

'You saw Joe?'

'You went to Whisperwood?' Gabriel glared at him. 'Did you speak to Amy?'

'So she *was* there!' Harry tutted. 'I should have known Joe was lying. He knows how to hold a grudge, doesn't he?'

I saw the look on my friends' faces and decided things needed moving on.

'You can make tea or coffee,' I said, practically shooing them all towards the door. Sadly, they took no notice of me whatsoever.

'I don't know how you dare say that,' Eliza said. 'Of course he holds a grudge. Look what you did!'

'I don't get it.' Harry shook his head. 'What's the problem? You and I reached an understanding, didn't we? Our divorce went ahead smoothly. I didn't cause trouble for you, even though you were shacked up with another man.'

'Your bit on the side was pregnant!' Eliza gasped at the nerve of him. 'You'd been in the papers for months with your affairs! What trouble could you possibly cause for me? Oh!' she shook her head, clearly exasperated. 'I'm not going through this again. It was years ago.'

'Exactly,' Harry said, 'so what's your problem? We've both surely moved on from our marriage by now?' He smirked suddenly. 'Unless you're still carrying a torch for me, that is.'

Gabriel's jaw clenched and I laid a restraining hand on his arm. 'I do think you need to talk this out in private,' I said desperately. 'I have a bar to clean up, and I need to start now. Take this upstairs, and please, no fighting. It would quite ruin the karma of this building, and I won't have it.'

'I should think,' Harry said, glancing around the room, 'that there's been plenty of fighting in here over the years. But don't worry. I'm not a man of violence. I shall be perfectly reasonable.'

'Just get upstairs,' Eliza snapped. 'Rhiannon's right. We're in her way. Go up to her room, say what you have to say and get lost.'

Gabriel's face was pinched as he led the way through the door to my private quarters, and I wondered what I'd let herself in for. I had breakables up there, after all. I did hope they'd deal with things calmly and rationally, though judging by Gabriel's quiet fury, Eliza's clear anxiety and Harry's smirk, I wasn't convinced there was going to be much progress made tonight. Not at all.

3

Harry pushed open the heavy oak door and sighed as it rocked on its hinges. He'd need a new door. This one was rotten. He'd suspected as much. He glanced around the central entrance hall and pulled a face, wondering what exactly had possessed him to purchase the dilapidated Eight Bells Hotel, without so much as checking it over first.

He'd bought it while staying at his mother's house in London. He'd been scouring the internet for properties for sale in the Kearton Bay area and had been dismayed to discover there were very few available. The ones that were for sale were tiny little cottages, and he couldn't bear the thought of being cooped up in one of those. It would drive him insane.

He'd thought back to the beach front property he'd shared with Melody in California and could have cried. If he were being honest with himself, he'd miss that house more than he'd miss her. It had been his dream home, and he'd poured all his love and experience and attention on it, creating the perfect environment for his new family. Or so he'd thought.

Harry scowled and kicked at the pile of junk mail that lay on the mat. He supposed, thinking about it now, that he'd fallen for this shack of a building purely because it overlooked the sea. He could have bought a more modern house on a new estate in the neighbouring village of Farthingdale, but there was no ocean view from there, and he wanted something that was in walking distance for Amy, should she choose to visit him one day. Not being familiar with Kearton Bay or its neighbour, he'd not realised that this house on the cliff top was further away from Wychwood than Farthingdale. It would have been quicker for Amy to walk to the estate.

Even so, he didn't think he could have settled in one of those houses. He didn't much fancy being surrounded by other people. This house may be a bit remote, but it was an escape, a bolthole from the villagers who would, he'd realised even then, not want him around. He thought he'd probably need that bit of distance from them, and it was likely a bonus that he was at the very opposite end of Kearton Bay to Gabriel and Eliza.

He'd bought the house without giving it much thought. Compared with the price of the Californian house, Eight Bells had cost peanuts. He'd rashly decided not to worry what state it was in. Houses could be fixed. He'd had years of experience with property, and it didn't faze him. He could always hire tradesmen for the stuff he couldn't manage alone. He wondered now where that bravado had come from.

Harry entered the living room on the left-hand side of the hallway. It was a decent size, at least, although there wasn't much else he could say in its favour. He looked dubiously at the peeling flock wallpaper on the walls. Damp. He was sure of it. He could smell it.

The trouble was, he needed this house to look perfect. It had to be the best house in Kearton Bay, bar none. Whatever the cost. Because he didn't want the Baileys — including Amy — to guess at the truth. He'd never live it down.

He made his way through to the back room, rolling his eyes at the dated decor and grimy windows. Still, it didn't look too bad in here. Like the living room, it was a good size, and probably just needed cleaning and decorating. He didn't think there was any structural problem. Of course, it would be his own bloody fault if there were. What was it he'd drummed into his clients for years? Get a survey done! It was the cardinal rule, and he'd broken it. He'd been too impatient, desperate to secure a property in this village, and the price had been too tempting. He'd convinced himself someone else would snap it up if he didn't move fast. It wasn't like him, not at all. When had he got so reckless when it came to buying houses?

His mother had told him he was a fool, but then again, her advice had always been his green light to do the opposite. She'd told him Eliza was slovenly and that with an uncle like hers and a background like the one she had he should run a mile. That had convinced him Eliza was the one for him. Of course, his mother had adored Melody, and gushed over her glamorous looks and thriving career. He should have listened to his gut over that one.

The right-hand side rooms proved to be similar, although with a less attractive fireplace, and the addition of a kitchen at the back, which was a shambles: tiny, grubby, and hopelessly impractical. Harry guessed that *hotel* was rather a misnomer. This looked like a shabby bed and breakfast at best. What on earth had he let himself in for? He stuck his hands in his pockets and headed back out through the living room into the hallway.

The central staircase was broad and rather grand, with a curved handrail that would probably need replacing. Following the bend in the stairs, Harry reached the landing, where his investigations revealed six double bedrooms, each containing a hand basin, a couple of smaller rooms that would just about fit a single bed and a wardrobe, a bathroom that looked as if it had been installed fifty years ago, with a separate toilet next door, and another bathroom with a more modern bath, shower, and toilet. Harry noticed that one of the toilets was leaking and realised it was probably what was causing the damp in the living room downstairs. Well, in a way that was cheering. Easily solved.

He couldn't smell any damp upstairs, apart from a horrible musty smell in one of the bathrooms, and thought the roof was probably sound. He knew he should climb the second set of stairs and inspect the attic rooms, but he didn't have the stomach for it today. He had to brave the bloody annexe at the side of the house next. God knows what he'd find in there. It had once apparently been used as a games room for the "hotel". Hotel!

Harry pulled out his mobile phone and checked his messages. His architect was coming up to Kearton Bay to look around the place in the next couple of days. This was no time to lose heart or courage. Obviously, there was a lot of work to be done, but it wasn't *too* bad. There was nothing that couldn't be fixed with some time, effort, and a bit of money. Or a lot of money.

And therein lay the problem.

He needed a job. He walked over to the window and gazed out over the overgrown garden below. The estate agent's blurb had said there were extensive gardens with glorious sea views, and in his mind's eye he'd visualised the most beautiful outdoor space where he could sit and relax and listen to the ocean, as he had in Malibu, but his heart sank looking down at this tangle of weeds and overgrown bushes. He caught a glimpse of a fence between shrubs, but had no idea what condition it was in.

Even so... his heart lifted as he caught sight of the sea. Not looking its best on this gloomy November morning, but still, it was an ocean. He missed the sea, which was strange really. Until he'd moved to California, he hadn't been that bothered about it at all. He supposed living there for the last few years had given him a taste for the life. Kearton Bay wasn't exactly Malibu, but it was quaint in its own way, and it would be good to wake up each morning to the sound of rolling waves and the cry of seagulls.

He found himself suddenly feeling considerably lighter. Things would pan out, somehow. He'd had a horrible time of it lately, but he could turn it all around. He would make this house a palace and settle into his new life. He would make friends, win over the villagers. Eliza would come round. He knew that, deep down, all she wanted was for Amy to be happy. She would see that it was better for their daughter to have her father in her life full-time. He would make amends with her, make his little girl love him again. And he'd get a job. Put out feelers. Contact his old pals. There would be something, surely? He was an experienced television presenter, after all, and property was always popular.

If all else failed, he could always sell this place when it was done and buy another. Start a property portfolio from scratch if he had to. Anyway, there was plenty of time. He wasn't exactly destitute, despite the catastrophic couple of years he'd had. His priority was getting this place straight, so he had somewhere to invite Amy to stay.

Harry shoved his mobile phone back in his pocket and leaned against the wall, gazing out over the North Sea. An uncomplicated life, that's all he wanted. He'd had enough of drama, arguments and lies. He wanted peace and quiet and a chance to get to know his daughter. It was all possible. He just had to be patient.

****

When I called Tally the following day to remind her to collect her wages, she informed me that she was already on her way.

'Not for the money,' she added hastily. 'We're all coming. Fuchsia and Pandora have asked us to meet them there, so we should be with you in about ten minutes.'

Sure enough, the door to The Hare and Moon was pushed open around ten minutes later, and Tally entered the bar along with her mum and dad.

Sophie dropped her bag on the counter and sighed. 'Afternoon, Rhiannon. Here we are again then.'

'Indeed you are,' I said. 'And to what do I owe this unexpected pleasure?'

'I have no idea,' she confessed. 'We've been ordered here by Fuchsia, but what for is anyone's guess.'

'Hardly ordered, love,' Archie said, rolling his eyes at me. 'The girls asked us politely if we'd meet them here, that's all. Don't be so dramatic.'

'Well, why not come to our house instead of dragging us all the way here?' Sophie demanded. 'Take a seat, both of you. I'll get the drinks.'

Archie and Tally headed off to find a table and Sophie leaned over the bar and whispered, 'So what went on last night after we left then?'

I suppressed a smile. 'Didn't Gabriel fill you in?'

She tutted. 'Oh, you know Gabriel. He didn't tell me anything I didn't already know. Harry Jarvis wants regular access to Amy.

39

But what else happened? Was there a row? Was there a punch up?'

Her eyes were bright with eagerness, and I was almost reluctant to disappoint her.

'I'm sorry,' I said, 'but I honestly don't know. They went upstairs and Jack and I got on with cleaning up the pub. I couldn't tell you what was said, although I doubt there was any violence. There was no blood anyway.'

Sophie sighed. 'Fat lot of use you are.'

'I'm terribly sorry,' I said, amused. 'Now, what can I get you to drink?'

'Three orange juices,' she said firmly. 'We had more than enough Lightweights units last night, thank you very much, what with the drinks and all that delicious food. No one does a roast lamb quite like Jack, although I come a pretty close second, if I say so myself. Oh!' She nodded towards the door. 'Here we go.'

As I poured the orange juice, I smiled a welcome at Rose, Flynn, Cerise, Violet, Fuchsia and Pandora.

'Goodness,' I said. 'It's quite the family gathering.'

'I didn't realise you were invited, too,' Sophie said to Rose.

'Well, we *are* family you know,' Rose pointed out.

'Only by marriage,' Sophie said, giving her daughter Pandora a resentful look, as if she still hadn't forgiven her for linking the Crooks with Rose by marrying her daughter, Fuchsia.

'Don't worry, Sophe. I don't know any more than you do about why we're here. You haven't missed anything.'

Sophie hooked her bag over her arm and took the glasses of orange juice from the counter. 'I'll be sitting with your dad when you finally decide to let us in on the mystery,' she informed Pandora, before heading over to the table in the corner, where Archie and Tally were sitting, deep in conversation.

Fuchsia and Pandora exchanged knowing looks.

'I think we've upset your mum,' Fuchsia said.

Pan shrugged. 'What's new?'

'What do you all want to drink?' Flynn asked, but Rose wasn't having that.

'No, the drinks are on me today,' she insisted. 'You all go and sit down.'

'Really?' Flynn looked bemused. 'Well, all right. Half a pint for me, please.'

'Just Coke for us, Mum,' Fuchsia said.

'And me,' Cerise added.

'Can I have a lemonade?' Violet asked, and I smiled at her sweet little face. It wasn't very often I saw her, as she was rarely brought into the pub. With her dark hair and deep blue eyes, she was looking more like Flynn every day.

'You *have* grown,' I told her. 'Of course you can have a lemonade. Would you like some crisps, too?'

She nodded eagerly and I began to sort the order as Flynn led his family to the table next to the Crooks.

As I'd known she would, Rose immediately leaned over the counter as I poured Flynn's beer.

'So go on,' she hissed. 'What went on last night? Spill the beans.'

'As I've already told Sophie,' I said patiently, 'I have no idea what went on. I was far too busy clearing the bar after the Samhain ceremony to eavesdrop on what was happening upstairs, even if I'd wanted to. Which,' I added pointedly, 'I didn't.'

'You're no use at all,' Rose complained.

'Which is exactly what Sophie said,' I admitted. 'Terribly sorry.'

'Oh well, I expect Eliza will fill me in on it when I see her,' she said glumly. 'Honestly, can you believe the nerve of that man? As if he can just waltz in here and lay claim to Amy!'

'He *is* her father,' I reminded her. 'I expect he has rights.'

'Rights? I think he gave up those when he swanned off with Melody Bird, don't you?'

'I should think Amy would want to see him,' I said. 'Surely it's better for a child to have her father in her life if he wants to be?'

Rose gave me a hard stare and I could tell what she was thinking. She had a point. I had, after all, not even told Derry who his father was until he was a grown man, and only then because I'd been forced to, due to the death of Sir Paul and the legacy he'd bequeathed his son.

'Well,' I said uncomfortably, 'you know what I mean.'

'Harry Jarvis doesn't deserve a second chance,' she stated flatly. 'I bloody hope Eliza isn't soft enough to give him one.'

Flynn arrived at her side to help her carry the drinks to the table. She gave me a rueful look.

'God knows what this is about,' she said, nodding over at her family. 'It had better not be more drama, that's all. Not when things are finally on an even keel for us. Oh well, only one way to find out.'

'Don't forget I have your wages here, girls,' I called to Cerise and Tally, who nodded and smiled at me, as Kerry arrived, bang on time for her shift.

'Wages?' she asked, taking off her coat. 'Did you hire them for last night's do? I'm ever so sorry, Rhiannon. I hated to let you down—'

'Think no more of it,' I said. 'I know you would never have called in sick if you didn't have to.'

'Well, at least you managed to get help,' she said, sounding relieved. 'I was so worried about you managing on your own last night. I know how busy it gets on the sabbat nights. How did it go anyway? Did I miss anything exciting?'

I laughed. 'Er, you could say that. It depends on your definition of exciting. Harry Jarvis turned up.'

She frowned. 'Harry Jarvis? Oh! *That* Harry Jarvis! Bloody hell, what did he want?'

'It seems he's moved here to Kearton Bay. He's bought Eight Bells and he wants access to Amy.'

'Oh well, fair play to him. He is her dad, after all.'

I smiled at her affectionately. 'Go and make yourself a cup of tea, Kerry. I can cope down here for another ten minutes.'

She grinned. 'Okay, so I'm guessing you want a cuppa, too? Consider it done.'

She headed through the door to my private quarters, and I leaned on the bar, thinking it was a good thing that Fuchsia and Pandora had called a family meeting, or the room would be empty. Customers were thin on the ground on cold, grey November afternoons.

I blinked, realising my name was being called.

'Sorry? What did you say?'

'I said you may as well listen to this, too,' Fuchsia said. 'Seeing as you're the only other person in the bar.'

I headed over to the table and sat down next to Rose. 'It sounds terribly exciting,' I said, feeling honoured to be included. 'What's the news?'

'That's what I want to know,' Rose said suspiciously.

'Well, if you'll give us a minute, we'll tell you,' Fuchsia said.

She and Pandora linked hands and beamed round at us all. 'We're pregnant.'

There was a stunned silence for a moment, then a chorus of congratulations as both girls were hugged and kissed.

I noticed, however, that Rose and Sophie hadn't moved. They were both sitting in silence, clearly stunned as they stared at their respective daughters.

Before too long, Fuchsia folded her arms and said, in a rather challenging tone, 'Well, aren't you going to say anything?'

Rose shook her head slightly. 'How the hell did you manage that?' she said at last.

Flynn rolled his eyes. 'Oh, Rose.'

'IVF,' Pandora said promptly. 'We were lucky because it worked first time.'

'How on earth did you afford that?' Sophie managed. She looked as shocked as Rose, and I thought it amazing that, finally, they both seemed to be having the same reaction to something.

Pan looked irritated. 'What a question! If you must know, Flynn gave us some money for our wedding, and we used that.'

Everyone looked at Flynn who, as usual, looked mortified at the attention.

'Well, that's great!' Rose nudged her husband crossly. 'I told you not to give them money. We'd already bought them a new fridge freezer and a cooker, and we're renting the flat above the shop to them at bargain basement rates. Why did you have to give them cash?'

'You know why,' Flynn mumbled. 'For a deposit on a house when the time was right.'

'Well, that worked out well, didn't it?' Rose said. 'You should have got it in writing that it was only to be used for that.'

'Charming,' Pandora muttered.

Fuchsia glared at her mother. 'Thanks for that, Mam. Is that all you can say? You're going to be a grandma.' She looked at Sophie. 'You're both going to be grandmas. Does that mean nothing to you?'

'Who— I mean, which one of you…'

'Me,' Fuchsia said. 'I'm pregnant.'

'Why you?' Sophie questioned immediately.

'Does it matter?' Cerise asked. 'Point is, they're having a baby. It's great news,' she told Fuchsia and Pandora, smiling at them warmly. 'I'm going to be an auntie. Can't wait.'

'Me neither,' Tally said firmly. 'Congratulations.'

'But what I mean is…' Sophie's voice trailed off and she shrugged.

'Well, I'm over the moon,' Archie said firmly. He put his arm around Sophie's shoulders. 'And I know your mum will be too as soon as the shock wears off.'

'I somehow doubt that,' Fuchsia said, giving Sophie a reproachful stare.

'I expect Lexi will have lots of baby clothes and bits and bobs you'll be able to have,' I said quickly, hoping to break the awkward silence. 'Ellie will have grown out of them by the time your baby arrives, and it will be a few years before they're needed again as she and Will want a gap before they have another one. When's the baby due, by the way?'

'The end of April,' Pandora said. 'We've had the twelve-week scan and everything's fine, so we thought we'd tell you all while we're here together.'

'You could have told us in private first,' Rose said. 'Fancy springing it on us in public like this.'

Sophie evidently had other pressing concerns. 'Our ceremony's in the middle of April,' she gasped. 'That's cutting it a bit fine, isn't it?'

'Sorry.' Pan shrugged. 'We could hardly postpone treatment on the off chance the birth would clash with your wedding vows renewal. It will be fine.'

Archie cleared his throat. 'What a time we're having, eh, Sophe? You and I are renewing our vows, and now we have our first grandchild to look forward to. Brilliant.'

He was rewarded with smiles that were as full of affection as his own, and I thought it was a shame that Rose and Sophie hadn't reacted in a more positive way to the news. I was surprised they hadn't. A grandchild was a grandchild, and I couldn't imagine how it could be seen as anything other than a blessing. Maybe they both needed time to get over the shock.

'How are you all going to fit in that flat?' Rose demanded.

'We can work all that out later,' Flynn said hurriedly.

'You've got a short memory,' Fuchsia said. 'Have you forgotten that me, you and Cerise used to live in that flat? And we managed perfectly fine. We even had Gran living with us one year.'

'Yes, and I had to sleep on the sofa!' Rose snapped.

'But that was four adults!' Fuchsia gave an exasperated sigh. 'Look, we've plenty of time to think about that. Babies don't take up much room, and there are two bedrooms. It will be okay.'

'Well, let's hope so,' Rose said. 'Because how you're ever going to afford a new place to live now you've blown Flynn's wedding money on IVF I don't know.'

'Drinks all round!' Flynn got to his feet, clearly determined that no one was going to spoil this day for Fuchsia and Pandora. 'What can I get you all?'

'Second round's on me then,' Archie said, rather too heartily. 'I'll help you carry them all, Flynn.'

They both followed me to the bar, and my heart went out to them for the valiant effort they were making to compensate for their respective wives' less-than-enthusiastic reaction to the news.

****

45

It was half an hour later when the Crooks and the MacLeans bid me farewell and headed out of The Hare and Moon.

'Tally, your wages!' I called, remembering just in time.

'I'll catch you up, Mum,' Tally said, and returned to the bar.

'I forgot to give Cerise hers,' I said, handing her two envelopes containing the cash I owed them. 'Would you be a poppet and pass it to her?'

'Of course.' Tally glanced at the door, as if making sure no one was coming back in, then she climbed onto a stool and rested her elbows on the bar. 'Could I have half of that mulled cider you were serving last night please?'

'Of course,' I said, surprised. 'Coming right up.'

Tally muttered a thank you as I handed her the drink, and I watched as she gulped half of it down in a manner that was most unlike her.

'I bloody needed that,' she announced. 'Honestly, mothers! How embarrassing was that? I was mortified for Fuchsia and Pan.'

'Oh dear.' I opened a bottle of fruit juice and poured it into a glass, deciding I needed a drink myself. It had got very stuffy in the bar. I glanced outside and saw the dark clouds gathering on the horizon. A storm was on its way, I reckoned. 'I'm sure this is all borne out of love, you know. I think, with Rose, it's because she's been there herself. She knows how tough it is to raise children when you have no money.'

'It's *their* decision though, surely?' Tally sounded more cross than I'd ever seen her. 'I'm so sick of people thinking they can live other people's lives for them, tell them what's best for them. How can they possibly know?'

'I know, Tally, but a mother always worries about her children. I must admit, though, I am surprised at Sophie's reaction. She's such a family-oriented person.'

Tally took another long gulp of cider and gave me a knowing look. 'She seemed obsessed with the fact that it's Fuchsia who's having the baby and not Pandora. I mean, what difference does it make? And of course, that's wound Rose up, because she thinks Mum's insinuating that MacLean genes aren't as good as

46

Crook genes. You know what they're like when they start.' She sighed. 'So much for our celebration.'

'Never a dull moment,' I said.

'You can say that again.'

'Are you all right, Tally?'

Tally looked surprised. 'Me? Of course. Why shouldn't I be?'

'How are things at work?'

She shrugged. 'Fine. It's calming down a bit now that summer's over. We've got a flurry of weddings coming up in December but there's only one booked for November.'

'Still enjoying the job?'

'It's okay.' Tally gave me a wry smile. 'When Mum's not hovering around, demanding extra meetings about her flipping wedding vows renewal. Honestly, you'd think it was the Royal Wedding the way she goes on about it. Poor Dad. He only agreed to it to shut her up. Still, at least she's keeping me busy. Let's face it, it's the perfect job for me, isn't it? Making sure other people have the perfect day.'

'Nat's not giving you a hard time?' I asked, knowing what Will's cousin could be like. He'd mellowed an awful lot since falling in love with Lexi's best friend, Georgia, but he could be a bit tactless and insensitive. As Events Manager at Kearton Hall, he was Tally's direct boss, and I could imagine that he'd be able to steamroller her into agreeing with anything he wanted if he chose.

To my relief, Tally dismissed my fears. 'Nat? No, not at all. We get on well.' She managed a smile at last. 'Georgia would never let him get away with being rude to me anyway. And you know he'd never do anything to annoy Georgia.'

'Well, that's true enough.' I laughed, relieved to see humour in her eyes. There was the old Tally I knew and loved.

'This cider's lovely,' she said. 'I could get quite addicted to the stuff.'

'You definitely don't want to do that,' I said lightly. 'Not a good idea to develop too much of a fondness for cider, or any other alcoholic drink.'

47

'Fancy saying that when you run a pub!' She laughed. 'Maybe you're in the wrong job!'

'Maybe you're right,' I said, without thinking.

Tally looked almost as shocked as I felt. Where on earth had that come from?

'What do you mean? You love it here. You know you do. This pub, it *is* you. You're so perfect for each other.'

'We are,' I said, smiling around at the bar I loved so much. 'I adore this building. I wanted it from the first moment I saw it. But it's not all plain sailing, you know. Running a pub is hard work, and while I've never been afraid of that, it does mean that there's much less time to do other things in one's life. Hobbies, socialising — it's all out of the question while I have this place to see to. I'm not saying I made the wrong decision when I took it on, because I didn't. It was exactly what I needed at that time in my life. It's just…'

'Just what?' Tally asked, clearly stunned that I could even contemplate leaving The Hare and Moon. 'This is the most beautiful building in Kearton Bay. You can't seriously be thinking of moving on?'

'I don't think I could bear to hand this place over to strangers,' I admitted. 'And I do love this village so much. But I wish I had time to enjoy other things in my life instead of always being on call here. Maybe I'm feeling my age. It sometimes feels like I've sacrificed a lot of time to my job. And of course, it meant I never gave Derry the attention he needed. I was always on duty. Always behind the bar. The nights he spent alone upstairs while I worked down here…' I broke off as I remembered, and my heart contracted with grief.

Tally was quiet for a moment. She traced the rim of her glass with her index finger then said hesitantly, 'Have you heard from him? From Derry?'

I shook my head. 'The last time was my birthday in August. He sent me a card, and some flowers arrived later in the day. Just said, "Love Derry" on them.'

'But it's something,' she said kindly. 'Obviously, he was thinking of you.'

'It felt very much like a token gesture,' I admitted. 'Still, we are where we are. No use dwelling on the matter.'

'Families, eh?' Tally gave me a sympathetic grin and I squeezed her hand.

'Indeed. Have you heard from Oliver lately?'

Oliver, her brother and Pan's twin, lived and worked in Bristol, and I knew Sophie missed him dreadfully.

Tally shook her head. 'Nope. Out of sight out of mind with Olly. You know what he's like. Mummy's angel, even though in reality he's a selfish, irresponsible idiot.'

'Maybe he's matured,' I ventured. 'After all, he's a solicitor now. I'm sure he has some sense of responsibility these days.'

'It would be nice to think so,' she said. 'I just wish he'd come home. It would mean the world to Mum. Not like that would matter to him.' She tutted. 'Honestly, him and Pan — you can tell they're twins. Peas in a pod. Both doing whatever they want to do, whether Mum likes it or not. Never caring if they upset her. What a way to live.'

She sounded wistful.

'Have you ever thought that maybe it's time you stood up for yourself more?' I asked her.

'Have you tried standing up to Mum?' she said, eyes wide. 'It's not worth the hassle. The thing is, with Pan and Olly doing whatever they like, I feel like I owe it to her to be the good one, and it's not fair. If she only knew what I'd given up for her...' She shook her head. 'It's just, it upset Mum when Oliver left Kearton Bay and moved to Bristol, but he didn't care about that, so how could I ever leave here?'

'Did you *want* to leave here?' I asked, surprised.

She blushed. 'Well, maybe. One day. But that's out of the question now. It was the same with university. When Pan quit her course, Mum was devastated, which meant that I had to stay on and finish my degree, even though I hadn't even wanted to go to uni in the first place, and only applied to please her. And now this baby...'

'But the baby's a good thing. Sophie will love it when it's here,' I said. 'She'll be the world's best grandma; you wait and see.'

49

'I thought she'd be over the moon,' Tally confessed, 'but she's surprised me. She doesn't seem happy about it at all. So guess who's going to have to be the one to listen to her moaning and will have to try to cheer her up somehow. Muggins here. It never ends.'

It *could* end, I thought, as I watched her taking a sip of cider, but for that to happen, Tally would have to decide what she wanted and go for it. Right now, I couldn't see her standing up to her mother and moving out of The Old Vicarage any time soon.

It was as Derry had repeatedly told me. Tally was far too nice for her own good.

4

Harry felt his guts twist in dread as he heard the knock on the door.

Eliza looked pale when he opened it, and he thought maybe she was as nervous as he was, which was some comfort. He peered over her shoulder. No Bailey. So she'd kept her promise. That was something. He hadn't been sure she would, although thinking about it, he should have trusted her. Eliza had always been the honest and decent half of his first marriage. He shouldn't judge her by his own standards.

'You came alone then.'

'That's what we agreed at the pub the other night,' she reminded him, her voice rather brittle.

'I know, but I wasn't sure it would work out that way. I didn't think *he'd* allow it,' Harry admitted.

Eliza folded her arms. 'Gabriel's not like that. He lets me make my own decisions and supports me whatever I decide to do.'

'What an angel,' Harry said, feeling his hackles rise already. Bloody hell, she'd not even got over the doorstep yet and she was already winding him up about her perfect second husband.

'He *is* an angel,' Eliza confirmed. 'He understands Amy needs a relationship with her father, however unreliable he may be, and he's not putting any obstacles in the way of that. It's me you've got to convince, Harry. Now, are you going to invite me in or are we going to stand here for the next half hour?'

'Sorry, sorry.' Harry stepped aside to let her in, dreading her response when she saw the state of the place. He'd rather optimistically hoped that a few bottles of bleach and a dozen scented candles would make a difference. They hadn't. As expected, she looked appalled.

'You're living here? Seriously?'

'Not here exactly,' he said hastily. 'The back of the house is where I spend most of my time. It's a lot nicer than it is in here.'

'It would have to be,' she responded, wrinkling her nose at the state of the place, something for which Harry couldn't, in all honesty, blame her. The damp problem had been fixed but that terrible flock wallpaper was enough to give anyone a headache.

'Shall we go through?'

'After you,' she murmured.

He led the way into the back room, hearing Eliza's footsteps behind him and sensing reluctance in every step. This was going to be tricky. He was relieved Gabriel Bailey had done the decent thing and kept away. He was sure Eliza would be more amenable to him seeing Amy if that bloody interloper wasn't breathing down her neck.

'Tea, coffee?' He'd led her into the kitchen, such as it was, and indicated the kettle.

Eliza's eyes were wide as she looked around. 'Seriously? You're living in here? Why?'

'What do you mean, why? I'm renovating it, obviously. Well, right now I'm working on cleaning it up. My architect will be visiting to draw up plans to make it more suitable as a residential dwelling, but until then there's a lot I can be getting on with. Obviously.'

'Obviously,' she said. 'But even so, why live here while you're doing it? Why don't you move into a hotel, or a rental cottage?'

Harry shrugged. 'I did look for a rental cottage, but they all seemed to be taken. Besides, it's easier to live on site, don't you think?'

She looked unconvinced. 'No tea or coffee for me, thank you.'

He tried not to be offended. 'It's safe, you know. I thoroughly scrubbed the cupboards, and the cups are mine. Brand new.'

She eyed him warily. 'What's going on, Harry?'

'What do you mean, what's going on?'

'This!' She waved a hand around the kitchen, looking disgusted. 'You don't do this sort of thing. Why did you even buy it? Don't tell me you couldn't have bought something ready to move into because I know for a fact that there are houses on that new estate in Farthingdale still for sale, and I'm sure there are plenty of other places you could have found somewhere.'

'But nothing much in Kearton Bay,' he told her. 'At least, nothing that wasn't absolutely tiny.'

'Why did it have to be Kearton Bay? You could have moved to one of the neighbouring villages. Moreton Cross might have suited you better, or you could have gone to Whitby. Helmston even. You're not a village person. And anyway,' she added, a touch tartly, 'last time you were here you said it was the back of beyond. You clearly hated it, so why would you want to live here?'

Harry remembered all too well how he'd reacted to Kearton Bay when he'd last been here, but he'd learned a lot since then. Age and experience had a way of making you look at things from a different perspective. The long, lonely nights in Malibu had left him dreaming of this village. He wanted what Eliza had, but how could he possibly tell her that without looking a total loser?

'Amy's here,' he said simply.

'But what does that matter?' she said, clearly exasperated. 'You've got a car. You can drive. You wouldn't be far away from her even if you chose Whitby! It didn't have to be Kearton Bay, of all places.'

'Why does it bother you so much?' he demanded.

She stared at him, her eyes showing incredulity. 'You're kidding, right? Why do you think it bothers me? This is Kearton Bay, my home. It's the place I escaped to after you — after you and Melody — oh, you know what I mean! This is where I found my family. My grandmother. Gabriel. This is where Joe found peace and love at last. This is our home, and now you're here, infecting it all with — with you.'

'Infecting it? Bloody charming. Don't hold back, will you?'

53

'What did you expect, Harry? That I'd hang out the bunting? You're part of my past, and I wanted you to stay that way.'

Harry flinched inwardly but did his best not to betray how much that stung. He deserved it, he supposed. Well, no suppose about it. But even so, it hurt like hell to hear her say it.

'Look, I'm perfectly aware that you and I are in the past, and I fully accept that you'll probably never be my biggest fan. But can't we at least try to be civil to each other? Our marriage may be over, Eliza, but we still have Amy, and surely we owe it to her to make this work?'

'Don't you dare!' Eliza's face twisted with rage. 'Don't you dare tell me what I owe Amy, as if this is all down to me! What about what *you* owe Amy? Where have you been? What happened to all your promises to keep her in your life? How long is it since you last saw her, Harry? Answer me that!'

He hung his head, staring at the lino flooring and thinking how hideous it was.

'Well? Do you even know?'

'Three and a half years, or thereabouts,' he muttered, realising as he said it how awfully long three and a half years must seem to a little girl. 'I'm sorry.'

'You're sorry.' Eliza gave a short laugh. 'Well, that's all right then, isn't it? Harry's sorry.'

'Why are you being like this?' he burst out. 'I thought we'd reached an understanding at the pub the other night?'

'An understanding? We barely scraped the surface!'

'Only because you spent most of the time listing all the ways I'd failed as a husband, a father and a human being,' he said sulkily. 'Look, I know, all too well, that I let Amy down. You don't have to go on about it, you know. But life hasn't been all fun and games for me, either. Did you ever once think to ask me how *I* was doing? What was going on in *my* life during that time?'

Eliza's eyes were cold, her expression unforgiving. He'd never seen her like this before. She'd always been so pliant, so easy to placate. She'd changed.

'To be honest,' she said, 'I don't care what you were doing. All I know is you've waltzed into my life, spoiling it all, ruining everything I've built over the last few years, and now you want to do the same to Amy.'

'I don't want to spoil anything! Not for you or Amy. Why would I do that?'

'Because it's what you do,' she ground out. 'You can't help yourself. You lie and you cheat, and you break promises. It's all you know. And I won't have you tearing Amy's life apart like that. She's happy now. She's got security, a safe home, a family that loves her, two sisters and a brother, Joe and Charlie just up the lane—'

'And the Angel Gabriel as her father, I suppose.' He knew he sounded petulant, but he couldn't help himself. She was painting a picture of his little girl's life, a life that didn't feature him at all. It was a sharp reminder of the past couple of years, and he couldn't bear it. He couldn't lose two children. He just couldn't. A sudden thought struck him, and he stared at her in horror. 'She doesn't call him Dad, does she?'

Eliza squirmed. 'Well…'

'My God!' He felt sick at the thought of it. 'Why did you encourage her to do that?'

'I didn't!' She was clearly stung at the suggestion. 'We never, ever asked her to call him Dad. She started doing it of her own accord. Probably around the time that the twins started calling him Daddy. It honestly wasn't a deliberate act, Harry. And she doesn't always call him Dad. Sometimes she calls him Gabriel. It depends on her mood.'

'Wonderful,' Harry said. 'At least there's some hope then.'

Eliza waved her arm impatiently. 'Oh, don't be so immature! And stop acting the victim. It's your own fault. You're the one who left her to be with Melody Bird.'

'I left you, not Amy,' Harry blurted. 'There's a difference.'

'Try explaining that difference to a little girl, Eliza said. 'And thanks for that, by the way.'

'Well, what do you want me to say? You know as well as I do what happened.'

'Oh, I remember it all too well,' she said, harshly. 'You behaved like a total swine and left me and Amy to it so you could swan off with your bit on the side.'

'Yes, yes, all right. It worked out well for you, though, didn't it? I mean, look at you! Married to a doctor, your own business, and twins, too. You always wanted more children, didn't you? You can't say it wasn't for the best.'

'It was definitely for the best,' Eliza snapped. 'I just don't think Amy saw it that way at the time. Have you any idea how hurt she was by the whole thing? Not at first. She was too young to understand, and you'd never been around much anyway. But as she got a bit older, and you kept making and breaking promises, that got to her. In the end, she pushed you out of her mind so you wouldn't be able to hurt her again. What does that say about your relationship?'

'I got a lot of things wrong,' Harry admitted. 'I never intended to mess her around like that. I wanted to see her, really I did. But — but it wasn't a good place for her to be.'

'What? A luxury beach house in Malibu? No, terrible place,' Eliza said.

'Not the house. The situation.'

'All couples argue. Just because you and Melody had problems, so what? Amy should have come first.'

'I always thought about her,' Harry said.

'I'm sure that was a big comfort to her,' she told him.

'For God's sake! Are we going to talk this out like reasonable adults, or shall we stand here exchanging insults all day? I thought the whole point of you coming here today was so that we could discuss this properly, without anyone else butting in and clouding the issue. That's what you agreed after our fruitless argument at the pub. If you don't intend to listen to me or give me a chance, why come here?'

Eliza didn't respond, and for a moment he thought she was going to ignore him completely, or maybe walk out of the door. Instead, she looked around the kitchen and sighed.

'Okay, point taken. Maybe a coffee would be okay.'

His heart lifted a little. 'No problem,' he said. 'There's a sofa in the next room if you want to sit down while I make it?'

'Is it safe? I mean, I'm not going to be sitting on a nest of rats or anything?'

'It's a new sofa! It's not a grand one, I admit. Didn't seem much point in buying a good one while the house is in this state, but it will do for now and it's completely safe, thank you very much.'

'Where's your coffee machine?' she asked suddenly.

He flushed slightly. 'Er, there isn't one. Is instant okay? And it's decaf I'm afraid. All they had left at the shop.'

Now he'd really surprised her. Her mouth fell open and she stared at him.

'Harry Jarvis, drinking instant coffee? Has the world gone mad?'

'You know what they say,' he said, with a light shrug. 'How the mighty have fallen.'

For the first time he saw the hostility leave her face, and she looked at him with an expression that reminded him of the old Eliza.

He gave her a slight grin and she smiled back.

Harry's heart leapt as she said, 'I'll be in the next room. Not too much milk.'

He slapped his forehead, furious with himself. 'Fuck! The milk. I haven't got any milk!'

To his relief, she laughed. 'It's okay. I can drink it black.'

'Coming right up,' he promised her.

Eliza turned and headed out into the hallway.

'First on the left,' he called.

'Got it!'

He hurriedly boiled the kettle and sought out his best two mugs.

She was sitting on the sofa when he entered the living room, such as it was, carrying the coffees. She looked pensive and was clearly ill-at-ease. He thought she probably regretted her earlier good humour toward him and sighed inwardly, wondering if it was always going to be a case of one step forward, two steps back.

'Coffee,' he said, handing one to her. 'Sorry about the milk. I haven't got round to buying a fridge yet.'

'Looks like you haven't got round to buying very much yet,' she ventured. 'Which makes me wonder what on earth you're doing here. It doesn't make sense.'

'It makes perfect sense.' Harry sat down on the chair opposite her, not wanting to push his luck by being too close. 'You can see how much work needs doing. Why waste time going backwards and forwards to some other house while I get on with it? Much simpler to be here, on the job, so to speak.'

'Hmm.' Eliza peered into her cup as if she were expecting to see something nasty lurking in her drink. 'It doesn't seem like the sort of thing you'd do, that's all. You were never one for getting your hands dirty. I thought you'd be directing operations from afar and hiring a ton of workers to do the heavy stuff for you.'

'That was the old me,' Harry said lightly. 'I've changed a lot since then.'

'Have you?' She sounded doubtful, and he squirmed inwardly as she scrutinised him. 'Well,' she said eventually, 'you've certainly aged.'

'Thanks very much,' he said, offended. 'Fancy saying that to me. How would you feel if I said the same to you? *Hi, Eliza, great to see you again. God, you look old. Can't believe how many crow's feet and wrinkles you have now.*'

She touched her face, clearly rattled. 'Really? Have I?'

Harry hesitated then sighed. 'No. To be honest, you don't look much older than you did when we — when you lived in Chiswick.'

'Thanks.' She took a sip of coffee. 'I'm not saying you look bad, Harry. If anything, I think you look better. You've aged, but you've aged well. Men can carry it off so much better anyway, can't they? It's ever so annoying. Like, I dye my hair at the first sign of a grey hair, whereas your hair is—' She leaned forward, peering at him, '—peppered with grey throughout. I didn't notice before. I'm impressed.'

'Impressed?' He laughed. 'That I've gone grey? Doesn't take much to impress you, does it?'

'That you haven't succumbed to the dye bottle. To be honest, I always thought you would go the whole hog. I had visions of you having the works done while you were living in Malibu: Botox, fillers, a face lift.'

'So, you did think about me then?'

She scowled. 'Not in a good way, trust me.'

'I can well imagine.' He took a mouthful of coffee and managed not to pull a face. God, he missed his espresso machine. He supposed Melody was making full use of that little beauty.

'You've lost weight, though,' she remarked, sounding thoughtful. 'I expect that's down to the Malibu lifestyle. They're all health freaks out there, aren't they? I suppose you were out running every day and living off fruit juice and protein shakes.'

He wrinkled his nose. 'You must be joking.'

'Really?' She sounded surprised. 'You were so picky about your diet when we were together. You practically lived off rice cakes from what I remember. Coffee was your only vice. Well,' she added quickly, 'not your *only* vice.'

'I try to be healthy. I always did. But I suppose when you're living with someone who monitors every calorie you're eating, it becomes a bit boring,' he admitted.

'You're telling me,' she said wryly.

He felt a sudden shame, remembering how he used to tell her off for eating cake, constantly reminding her how many calories were in the foods she most enjoyed. What a waste of time that had been. She looked great now and, in his opinion, she'd aged better than he had. And not a trace of Botox.

'So Melody finally cured you of your weight loss obsession,' she said. 'How ironic that you're now thinner than you were then.'

'I was thinking the same about you,' he confessed. 'Look, can we not talk about Melody?'

She leaned back in the sofa and eyed him thoughtfully. 'Still hurts?'

'What?'

'Your break-up?'

He shrugged. 'If it did, would you care?'

Eliza hesitated. 'I know how it feels to have your heart broken,' she said at last. 'I wouldn't wish it on anyone. Even you.'

Harry felt a lump in his throat and swallowed it down. 'Good job I'm not heartbroken then,' he said lightly. 'You know me. I'm like Teflon. Nothing sticks.'

'Lucky you. It must be wonderful to go through life like that,' she said. She took another sip of coffee. 'Actually, scrap that. It's sad. I'd rather risk having my heart broken and really love someone than spend my entire time on this earth not feeling anything.'

'Can we talk about Amy?' Harry said, feeling desperate to change the subject. This was all getting frighteningly painful, and he wasn't sure he could keep up the act much longer. 'Have you told her I'm here?'

Eliza went to put the mug on the floor, but noticing there was no carpet, and seeing the state of the floorboards, she evidently changed her mind and rested it carefully in her lap instead, keeping a tight grip on the handle. 'Yes,' she said simply.

'And?'

'And what?'

'Well, how did she react? Was she pleased? Does she want to see me?'

Eliza looked as if she were searching for the right words. 'She didn't say much, to be honest.'

Harry frowned. 'But she must have said something, surely? After all this time?'

'I think that's the problem,' Eliza admitted. 'It's been ages since she last saw you. You're not that important to her any more.'

He felt his throat tighten and was horrified to find his vision blurring. He took a large gulp of coffee and snapped, 'Well, that's bloody charming. I suppose Gabriel had plenty to say to her on the subject?'

Eliza's mouth tightened. 'For your information, he wasn't there. He stayed downstairs while I went to her room and broke it to her alone.'

'Broke it to her? You make it sound like bad news.'

'Well, it's hardly good news, is it? Bloody hell, Harry, you don't get it, do you? Amy got used to being let down by you, and she's grown accustomed to not having you in her life, to feeling like she doesn't matter to you. She's got her life sorted now, and whether that annoys you or not, the fact is she sees Gabriel as her father, and you barely figure. But that's not Gabriel's fault, and it's certainly not Amy's. If you want to be angry at someone, be angry at yourself, because this is all your doing.'

There was an uncomfortable silence. Harry wanted to fight back, defend his corner, but he couldn't think of a single thing he could say in his own defence. She was right, after all. He'd let Amy down badly. He deserved everything he got. But, by God, it was galling to hear that Amy considered Gabriel her father. Did Rufus call Chuck Dad, too? It was an unbearable thought on both counts. Well, he might not be able to do much about Rufus, for now at least, but somehow, he had to change Amy's mindset. But how?

As he tried to work things out, he realised Eliza was watching him closely.

'What?' he said gruffly.

'You didn't argue back,' she said, clearly surprised. 'I thought you'd be rude and aggressive.'

'Not a lot to argue about,' he said wearily, then pulled himself together. 'Anyway, I'm sure Amy will change her mind once we meet up again.'

Eliza shook her head slightly. 'So what are your plans for this place?' she asked

Harry glanced around the room and fought the temptation to suggest demolition. 'Oh, I'll soon lick it into shape. My priority,' he said thoughtfully, 'is to get the internet connected. Please tell me you can get broadband round here.'

She gave him a look of disgust. 'That's your priority? Obviously. God forbid you should lose any Instagram followers.'

Harry was about to explain that he needed the internet to video call his son, but then he realised how bad that would look, since he hadn't video called his daughter the entire time they'd been apart. Eliza would be furious. Better she thought he was missing social media than Rufus.

'Do you have a job? I mean, now you're back in England I'm presuming your contract with the American network is over. So what are you going to do for a living?'

It was a good question. Harry shrugged. 'Oh, I don't know. Easy come, easy go.'

Eliza banged her cup on the floor, clearly having had enough. 'You see, this is what I mean. This is why I can't trust you because you never make a commitment. Everything's always free and easy with you. Promises are made and broken without any thought. You don't even have a job, and what if you get offered one in London? Or another one back in the States? Will you clear off and leave Amy like you did before? How can I let her get involved with you again? You're not going to break her heart a second time, Harry.'

'I wouldn't do that!'

'Why not? You've abandoned Rufus, haven't you? What's to stop you doing it to Amy again?'

'Because I've said I wouldn't! I promise—'

'You promise?' Eliza gave a short laugh. 'Like your promises ever meant anything.'

'Eliza, please listen,' he said, beginning to feel desperate. 'All I'm asking for is the chance to make amends to my daughter. I know I messed up spectacularly last time, but she's still my little girl. My baby.'

'But that's just it, Harry,' Eliza said. 'She's not your little girl any more, and she's certainly not your baby. She's eleven on her next birthday. Next summer she'll be going to high school. She's got friends and interests that you have no idea about, and she's not the Amy you remember. The truth is you don't know her. You don't know her at all.'

Feeling utterly wretched, Harry stared into his coffee cup as her words sank in. He didn't know what he could say to convince Eliza that he was sincere in his wish to be part of his daughter's life.

'Maybe I don't know her,' he managed at last. 'But don't you see? That's what I need to change. It's what I *want* to change. I want to get to know her, and I want her to know me.'

Eliza sighed. 'I'm not saying I don't sympathise,' she said at last. 'And I do think Amy needs to know her father. It's just — it's just trusting you not to hurt her, Harry. That's the problem.'

'I know,' he said miserably. 'And I get it. I really do. But how do I make it up to her if I can't even see her?'

They sat quietly for a few minutes, each lost in their own thoughts. Then Eliza said, almost reluctantly, 'Maybe you could see her after school one night this week.'

Harry's heart leapt. 'Really? Fantastic. You tell me the address of the school and I'll pick her up. I'll make her tea and she can—'

Eliza shook her head. 'You can't just turn up at the school to collect her. The staff don't know you. They won't let her go with you anyway. Besides,' she added, casting a disparaging glance around the room, 'you can't seriously expect to bring her back here? It's awful!'

Harry supposed she was right, as galling as it was to admit it.

'Well, what then?' he said, cursing himself as he realised how sulky he sounded.

'You can take her out for tea somewhere,' Eliza suggested. 'I'll collect her from school and drop her off at a café and you can meet her there.'

'Great. No problem,' he said. 'Just tell me where and when.'

Eliza got to her feet. 'I'll text you tomorrow and let you know. Have you got a new number?'

Harry nodded. 'I'll text you now, then you've got it.'

He quickly tapped out a message.

✉ Thank you, Eliza. I really appreciate it. H. xx

Eliza glanced up from the screen and gave him a wry smile. 'Got it. Just don't let me down, Harry. And more importantly, don't let Amy down. Because I swear to you, if you do, you'll never get another chance.'

5

'This is a surprise,' I said, seeing Tally entering The Hare and Moon with Pandora and Fuchsia. 'I assumed the booking was for you, your mum and dad.'

'It was,' Tally said. She and Pan exchanged looks. 'The booking's changed, is that okay? It's the three of us for dinner now. Dad's paying, so we thought, why not?'

'Of course. I'll show you to your table,' I said, and led them through to the dining room, where I'd reserved a window table with a view over the sea. 'Would you like a drink before you order?'

'I'd kill for half a lager,' Fuchsia admitted. 'Guess a lemonade will have to do.'

'How are you, Fuchsia?' I asked. 'Any morning sickness?'

'No, I'm over that. It didn't last long, thank God,' she said. 'I was dreading it, remembering what Mum was like with Violet.'

'When she threw up in church over your gran's fiancé's shoes,' Pandora giggled. 'What a day that was.'

'No wonder the wedding never went ahead,' Tally said, smiling. 'It still makes me laugh when I think of it.'

'Can I have a lemonade, too?' Pandora asked. 'I don't think it's fair that I drink when Fuchsia can't.'

'Don't be daft,' Fuchsia said. 'I don't expect you to—'

Pandora squeezed her hand. 'It's the least I can do.'

Fuchsia smiled at her, and I thought what a lovely couple they were, and what a shame it was that Rose and Sophie weren't more excited about such an amazing time in their lives, for some misguided reason or other.

'I'll fetch the drinks,' Tally said. 'Save you bringing them, Rhiannon.'

'I really don't mind,' I assured her, but she was insistent, so I gave in.

'Are your mum and dad all right?' I asked her, as I poured two lemonades and a Coke for Tally. 'I've never known them cancel a booking for dinner before.'

Tally put her head in her hands. 'It's another family drama,' she confessed, as I put the drinks on the counter. 'We've had some big news. Mum's so upset she wouldn't even contemplate coming here tonight, so Dad said to take Pan and Fuchsia instead and gave me his credit card to cover it. I think he's going to spend the evening trying to calm Mum down.'

'Good heavens,' I said, alarmed. 'I hope it's nothing serious.'

'Serious enough,' she told me, giving me a wry look. 'Oliver's got married.'

I stared at her in astonishment. 'Oliver? I didn't even know he was dating.'

'Neither did we,' she said grimly. 'Mum got a postcard from him this morning. He and his new wife are currently honeymooning in Mauritius. She was beside herself. Honestly, the way she screamed I thought someone had died.'

'So you don't know his bride?' I asked, imagining all too well Sophie's shock.

'Nope. Never heard of her. And Mum's adamant that Uncle Gordon and Auntie Caroline must have known.'

'Uncle Gordon? Ah, Archie's brother.'

'Yeah. They took Olly in when he decided to finish his legal training in Bristol. He moved out of theirs a year ago, but Mum's sure they must have met this girl and that they've conspired to keep it all a secret. Dad keeps telling her that Uncle Gordon would never do that, but she won't have it.'

'Your poor mother,' I murmured.

'She's had a good cry,' Tally admitted.

'I'm not surprised.'

'But the thing is,' she added, taking a quick sip of her Coke, 'she's doing the same thing again. You should have heard her going on about Uncle Gordon and Auntie Caroline, as if they're the most devious people ever, when all they've ever actually done is to be kind and take Oliver in as a favour to Mum and Dad. There's nothing to suggest that they've ever met Oliver's new wife or knew anything about the wedding. And when she'd done ranting about their deceit, she started on at his new wife. Stephanie, I think her name is. Mum's adamant that she must have plotted to keep Oliver from coming back here. She's got it in her head that this Stephanie wants to keep him all to herself, and that he'll be sucked into her family and forget all about his own.'

She scowled and took another sip of Coke.

'She's hurt and upset,' I said. 'She'll come round and start seeing things more calmly soon.'

'But she'll still blame everyone but Oliver,' Tally said grimly. 'It's always the same. It's like with this baby.' She cast a surreptitious look in the direction of the dining room, making sure that Pan and Fuchsia were nowhere near. 'She's blaming Fuchsia for the whole thing. Says Pandora's been pushed into letting her have the baby, so that Fuchsia can give up her job, and she says Pan's life is ruined, and she'll have to work twice as hard to support Fuchsia and the baby now. Honestly, it's as if Pan hasn't got a mind of her own. Can you really see my sister letting anyone make any sort of decisions for her?'

I had to agree that I couldn't. Pandora knew what she wanted and went for it, much like her twin.

'It annoys me,' Tally grumbled. 'Nothing's ever Pan's fault, or Oliver's fault. It's always down to someone else. They run rings around Mum and always have, and she lets them get away with it. Yet here I am, doing everything I can to keep the peace, to make her happy, to do what she wants, and what do I get out of it? Oh!' She shook her head in clear exasperation. 'Let's not go over this again. I'd better take these drinks to the table before they go flat.'

'Let me know when you're ready to order,' I said, feeling sorry for her. I could see she was getting herself worked up again, and really, I couldn't blame her. She did, after all, have a point.

'I will.' Tally hesitated then said, 'You know what's even worse, Rhiannon?'

I shook my head, waiting.

'Pan knew.'

'Pan—'

'Oliver told her he was getting married. Even invited her to the wedding. I only found out when I called at the flat on the way here, and they both admitted it to me. He'd asked her to keep it quiet, so she had. Even to me.'

Her eyes filled with tears. 'He didn't even tell me! His own sister. I get why he'd keep Mum in the dark, because he'd probably be worried about her taking over the wedding. You know what she's like. But me! What did I ever do to him? Selfish pig. Honestly, I'm sick to death of the whole bloody lot of them.'

She sounded it, too. I could only watch her in sympathy as she scooped up the glasses and carried them carefully into the dining room.

****

'Well, you've certainly taken on a project,' Gareth said, shaking his head at Harry. 'Can't believe you're living in it while the work gets done, though. It's not like you.'

'Needs must,' Harry mumbled. He wondered if he should be so honest with Gareth, but then, he'd known his architect for many, many years, and trusted him. Gareth wasn't interested in gossip. He turned up, did the job, and kept his opinions on people's personal lives to himself, which was something Harry had always appreciated. 'The fact is, I'm trying to save money. I'm — I'm not working now, after all.'

Gareth raised an eyebrow. 'Nothing in the pipeline?'

Harry hesitated, then shook his head. 'Nope, not really.'

'What happened in America?' Gareth shifted in his chair to get more comfortable. Having spent the last few hours going over

Eight Bells and showing Harry his ideas, the two of them were now sitting in what passed for a living room, sipping instant decaffeinated coffee, and eating custard creams. 'I thought maybe you'd left because you'd had a better offer over here.'

Harry bit into a biscuit and crunched dolefully. 'I wish. I left because I couldn't stand it over there any longer. Long story,' he added as Gareth looked intrigued. 'Very dull story, too. Not worth going over. But the point is, my contract over there had ended and there was nothing else on the table, so it seemed a good point to return to England and try to build bridges with my daughter.'

'Ah yes. I remember you had a little girl. Emma, was it?'

'Amy.'

'Amy. That's right. She lives in this village then?'

'Yes, she does.'

'So, her mother lives here, too?'

Harry nodded and Gareth whistled. 'Complicated indeed. Small village and I remember what happened at the time of your break-up. You're a brave man, Harry.'

'Not brave at all,' Harry confessed. 'Just desperate to make it up to my daughter.'

'And how's that working out?'

Harry stared at his custard cream, thinking he shouldn't be eating biscuits. He dropped what was left of it onto the tea plate on his lap.

'It's challenging. I met up with her the other night for the first time in ages. Eliza — that's her mother — let me take her to tea after school. We spent a couple of hours talking. Well,' he added, 'she talked. I mostly listened.'

Hadn't he just! Not as if he'd had any choice in the matter. Amy was, he'd discovered, an opinionated little girl who wasn't shy about telling her father exactly what she thought of him.

They'd met outside a small tea shop in Farthingdale, because Eliza didn't want them to be disturbed by anyone who knew Amy — or Harry. She'd left, making Harry promise that he'd drop Amy at the gates of Wychwood by six, which he'd considered a bit mean of her as it didn't give him much time with his daughter.

As it turned out, it was plenty of time. Amy had metaphorically shone a light in his eyes and interrogated him, and it had been a deeply uncomfortable meal.

The tea shop was okay, though a bit twee for his taste. All frilly tablecloths and cutesy animal pictures on the walls. Amy had got out of the car, said goodbye to Eliza, then greeted Harry with an accusing stare and not much else. She'd led the way to a table by the window, sat down and immediately picked up a menu, ignoring him.

Harry felt nonplussed. He'd — perhaps foolishly in retrospect — expected at the very least a hug. If he were being honest with himself, he'd imagined many times that she would jump out of the car and run towards him, he'd throw his arms around her and spin her around in a joyful embrace, and she'd cling to him and tell him how much she'd missed her daddy, and how happy she was to see him again.

The reality proved distressingly different, and Harry realised, as he surveyed his daughter — or at least the part of her that wasn't hidden by the large, laminated menu — that he was going to have his work cut out.

He removed his coat and draped it over the back of his chair. 'Do you want to take your coat off?'

Amy lowered the menu and gave him a disdainful look. 'If I did, I would have done, wouldn't I?'

When did she get so cheeky? Harry blinked. 'Well, you won't—'

Amy dropped the menu and held up one hand. 'Don't say it! Don't say *you won't feel the benefit* because Mum says that all the time and it drives me mad. What does it mean anyway?'

Harry shrugged, having never thought about it much. 'Well, I suppose it means that if you keep your coat on indoors, you'll feel colder when you go outside.'

'See? It doesn't even make sense.' Amy pulled a face and resumed scanning her menu.

Harry picked up his own and tried to focus on it, but his mind was racing. Who was this child? Where was his sweet, gentle little girl?

'Have you had a nice day at school?' he asked, wincing at how feeble that sounded. Nice day at school indeed! It reminded him of his maiden great-aunt who'd never asked him anything else. He'd loathed her. Mind you, her beard had been scary to a six-year-old child, so it wasn't surprising.

Amy gave him a withering look. 'Really?'

He sighed. 'No, not really. I can see you're angry with me.'

He'd half hoped she'd deny it, but she folded her arms, stared at him with gleaming turquoise eyes that were touchingly like his own, and said, 'Yes I am, and do you blame me?'

His mouth twitched with amusement. Little madam! But she was right, no one could blame her.

'No I don't,' he assured her. 'I behaved very badly and I'm sorry, Amy. I really am.'

She looked suspicious. 'Hmm. So you say.'

Harry bit his lip to stop himself from smiling. That would never do. But there was something about her that reminded her of him, and yet also of Eliza. The new, bolder Eliza. He couldn't help but feel a teensy bit proud of his daughter.

'I don't expect you to forgive me straightaway,' he said carefully, 'but I really do want us to get to know each other again, and I want to make it up to you for all the time we've lost.'

Amy said nothing. She studied the menu for a moment then said, 'I want sausage and chips, but I don't want peas or beans. I hate them both.'

Harry nodded. 'Right, right.' He stared at his own menu for a moment. 'Er, are these the children's meals we're looking at?'

'Well, what do you think?' Amy tilted her head and waited for his answer.

'I honestly don't know,' he admitted.

'No, you don't. Well, Mum would know, wouldn't she?'

'I suppose she would.'

Amy watched him through narrow eyes. 'And Gabriel would know.'

Harry fought down an unfurling anger at the mention of that man's name. 'Hmm.'

'I never have children's portions. You do know I'm ten and a half?'

'Yes, I know that.'

'Well then, why would I be having children's portions?'

'I — I suppose…'

'And I want bread and butter with that,' Amy added. 'And a banana milkshake.'

'Fair enough,' Harry said.

The waitress had arrived at their table and she gave them a pleasant smile. 'Ready to order?'

'Er, sausage and chips for my daughter please,' Harry began.

'With no peas or beans,' Amy interrupted.

The waitress nodded. 'Is that a children's portion?'

'Definitely not,' Harry said hastily.

'Would you like salad with your sausage and chips instead of beans or peas?' the waitress suggested to Amy.

Harry gave his daughter a conspiratorial smile and a wink. As if!

'That would be great,' Amy said. 'I love salad.'

Harry sighed inwardly. 'And a banana milkshake for her too, please.'

'And for you?'

'Er, the dressed crab. Oh, and a double espresso.' Sod it, he thought. He deserved that at the very least.

'I'm ever so sorry. Our coffee machine's developed a fault,' the waitress said. 'We have instant?'

Harry sighed. It was one of those days, obviously. Fucking karma.

'Instant will be fine,' he said heavily. 'Make it a decaf, will you?'

She gave him a cheery smile and headed behind the counter, and Amy collected up both the menus and put them back in the little stand on the table.

'Okay, now what?' she said.

Harry wasn't sure what she meant.

'Are you going to ask me loads of boring questions about what I've been up to for the last three years?'

'Do you want to tell me?'

'Not really.'

'Then there's not much point is there?'

'S'pose not.' Amy stuck her elbows on the table, propped her face in her hands and surveyed Harry with beady eyes. 'What have you been doing anyway?'

'Me? Well, er, working mostly.'

'In America?'

'Yes, in America.'

'Doing that programme about posh houses like Kearton Hall?'

'Kearton Hall?'

'Will and Lexi live there. It's massive and old and there are secret passages there. Will teaches me riding. He's ace. He's my brother-in-law, 'cos he's married to my sister.'

Harry's jaw tightened. He wanted to say, *she's not your sister!* but sensed that if he did, he'd have a riot on his hands. Now wasn't the time.

'That's nice.'

'So is that what you've been doing? Telling Americans about places like Kearton Hall?'

'Among other things.'

'What other things?'

'Just bits and bobs. A few other shows. Nothing worth talking about really.' He could say that again. Disasters, every one.

Amy didn't blink. 'And what about Melody? What's she doing?'

He didn't want to think about what Melody was doing right now. He could imagine it all too well and the thought made his stomach churn with anger.

'Did she do that programme with you? The one about posh houses?'

'No. Melody did another show.' And then another, and then another. Each one more successful than the last, and all of them infinitely more popular than his own.

'Mum says you're divorced now.'

Harry carefully unwrapped the cutlery that was nestled in a paper napkin on the table and examined it closely. He could imagine that Eliza had said quite a lot on that subject, too. Luckily, he'd told her little about the divorce so she wouldn't have much to gloat about.

'Mum says Melody's got a new boyfriend. She said he's gorgeous and rich and plays sport. Is that right?'

Harry almost dropped the knife and fork. How the hell—? He took a deep breath. Obviously, it had all been reported in the papers over here, too. So much for keeping his humiliation quiet.

'Yes. Yes, she's got a new — boyfriend.' *Boy* being the operative word. How old was Chuck anyway? Bloody Chuck! Seriously? Twenty-seven years old. Twenty fucking seven. It was obscene. Melody was making a total fool of herself. She'd always been too vain to see her faults.

'That's karma for you,' Amy said.

'What? Where on earth did you get that from?'

'It's what Joe said. He was talking to Mum about you and Melody. They were discussing your divorce and Joe said it was karma, and it had bitten you on the arse at last and about bloody time.'

Harry swallowed down his anger. 'You shouldn't swear.'

'I didn't. I just repeated what Joe said. It doesn't count.'

'It does count.'

'Gabriel lets me swear.'

Harry gave her a smile that nearly killed him. 'I'm sure he doesn't.'

'He does. He lets me do anything I like. Do you think Chuck will let Rufus do what he likes?'

She was a demon child! How could a kid of ten and a half be so aware, and so bloody brutal? *Because she's like you?* He shifted uncomfortably, realising that Amy had more of his genes in her than he'd realised.

'It's not up to Chuck. It's up to Melody. She's his mum.'

'Hmm.' Amy gave him a sly grin and he couldn't have been more relieved to see the waitress when she returned, bearing food and drinks.

The next quarter of an hour brought virtual silence and a blissful respite from Amy's interrogation, as every time she started to talk, he admonished her with, 'Don't speak with your mouth full.' He had an uncomfortable feeling, though, that she was saving it all up for the end.

After eating less than half her sausage and chips, Amy announced she'd had enough, but was ready for dessert.

'If you're full up, you won't need dessert,' he said.

'That's got nothing to do with it,' she protested. 'I'm full up for normal food, but I've got room in my pudding tummy.'

'In your what?'

Amy grinned, for the first time that evening. 'Pudding tummy. That's what Mum calls it. She says it's why, no matter how full we are, we can always fit in a pudding.'

'Okay, okay. You can have a pudding.'

'Aren't you having one?'

'I'm not hungry.'

'Didn't you like your crab?' Amy asked, staring meaningfully at his half-full plate. 'Not that I blame you. Who could eat crab? It's like eating a big spider. Yuck!'

Normally, Harry enjoyed crab, and there was certainly nothing wrong with the food at this café. Lately, though, his appetite had deserted him. No wonder all his clothes were loose on him. And it wasn't only his appetite for food that had vanished. He had no interest in work either, or even the opposite sex. And that worried him as much as anything. Work and women had always been the things he loved most in the world. With no desire for either, what was left for him?

'What do you want for dessert then?'

Amy considered the menu and announced she wanted chocolate fudge cake with cream, so Harry ordered that when the waitress collected the plates, along with another coffee for himself, then leaned back in the chair and wondered what on earth to talk to his daughter about.

'Is Rufus coming over?' she asked suddenly.

The stab of pain that shot through him surprised him for a moment, and he shook his head. 'Not yet. Maybe one day.'

'Does he like having a stepdad then?'
'Chuck's not his stepdad,' Harry managed, through gritted teeth. 'He's Melody's boyfriend.'
'Don't they live together?'
'He lives at her house,' Harry said. *In my sodding home.*
'So they live together.' Amy shrugged 'Bet you anything he thinks Chuck's his stepdad.'
'No he doesn't,' Harry insisted. 'Anyway, Chuck won't last long. He's far too young to settle down. They'll be over by Christmas.'
'And then what will happen?' Amy enquired.
'What do you mean?'
'I mean, if Melody and her boyfriend break up, will you and Melody get back together?'
Harry held up his hands. 'No way! No, it's definitely over between me and Melody.'
'So it's a shame you left Mum for her then, isn't it?'
My God, who is this child?
'Things are complicated, Amy. It's not always as simple as it seems.'
'It *is* simple though,' Amy insisted. 'You left me and Mum because you loved Melody more. But Mum is much nicer than Melody, so you were a bit daft, weren't you? And now Melody's got another boyfriend so you'd have been better off staying with us, wouldn't you?'
Harry didn't know how to respond to that, so he stared dumbly at her and gave a silent prayer of thanks when the waitress handed Amy her chocolate fudge cake.
'Good?' he asked, as she scooped up her fifth mouthful, having not said a word since it arrived.
She nodded. 'Mm.'
He sipped his coffee and gazed out of the window at the narrow street outside. It was mostly empty now. The other shops had shut. This place would be shutting at six, too. Despite his earlier protests about not seeing his daughter for long, he was rather glad of the fact now. He felt wrung out. Amy wasn't who he'd imagined she'd be, and things hadn't gone at all as expected. She'd clearly moved on and didn't want or need him around. He

slumped, more depressed than ever. What was the point of any of it really?

'Dad?'

His heart leapt and he turned his gaze on his daughter, who was eyeing him warily, empty spoon in one hand. She'd called him Dad, and even though it was a small victory it felt like something huge. He would never have believed that one little word would give him so much hope.

'Yes, Amy?'

'Are you really staying in Kearton Bay?'

He smiled. 'Yes, I am.'

'What about if Melody and Chuck break up?'

'Even then.'

'But what about Rufus?'

'I want to see Rufus, of course. But I'm hoping he'll come over to stay in the holidays.'

'What if he wants you to move back to America?'

'I—I don't think…'

'Because you left here before, and how do I know you won't leave here again?' She tossed back her hair and gave him a defiant stare. 'I don't care if you do. I just want to know.'

He saw the faint wobble in her bottom lip and his heart contracted with shame and grief. 'I won't leave you again, Amy. I promise you.'

'Well — anyway.' Amy resumed eating her chocolate fudge cake. 'We'll see.'

As he dropped her off at the gates of Wychwood and waited to make sure she got safely inside the house, Harry had reflected that he'd done a great deal of damage to his daughter, and behind that confident, cheeky facade was a very hurt little girl. He had so much to make up for, and he only hoped he was up to it. He didn't have a great deal of confidence in himself, to be honest. He seemed to make bad decisions at every turn and messed up other people's lives as much as his own. Maybe Joe was right. Maybe karma *had* come for him, and if it had, how could he deny it served him right?

'Have you thought of turning this place back into a hotel? Or a bed and breakfast at least?'

Harry blinked back into awareness as Gareth's voice cut through his thoughts. 'What? Not really, why would I?'

'I was thinking what you said about needing an income. This is in a prime location. I mean, look at those views. You could make it a good quality guest house and it would buy you some time while you re-establish a career in the UK.'

Harry wrinkled his nose. 'But having strangers in the place?'

'Just bed and breakfast. I could make sure you got lots of privacy and your own space here. It's certainly big enough. It's worth considering, surely?'

'I don't know…'

'Well, have a think about it before we progress any further. Place could bring you in a steady income, and there'd be no problem with planning permission since it was run as a guest house before.'

'Yeah, I'll think it over.'

Gareth gave him a sympathetic smile. 'You know what you need, old chap? A bloody good drink. What say we head to the nearest pub and toast your new beginning?'

Or drown my sorrows. But Gareth was right about one thing. Harry needed a drink.

6

Harry decided he quite liked The Hare and Moon pub, especially when Gabriel Bailey's awful family wasn't in it. The barmaid, a cheerful brunette, probably in her early thirties, served him with a smile, and he and Gareth found a cosy table near the fire and sat for an hour, putting the world to rights, and agreed that this place was probably a goldmine, especially with the summer trade.

'See, this is what I mean,' Gareth said. 'It's a pretty little village and I'll bet there's huge demand for holiday accommodation. You should really consider taking in guests.'

Harry wrinkled his nose. 'But strangers in my home? It wouldn't feel right. They'd get on my nerves.'

'Not if you do bed and breakfast, surely? You could throw them out by half ten and wouldn't see them again until the early evening. And look, I could make you separate living accommodation with no trouble. The loft, for example. I could easily incorporate a large master suite up there. It's huge. A whole other floor.'

'But Amy?'

'What about her?'

'If she's coming to stay with me, I wouldn't feel safe having her on another floor with strangers.'

'That's not a problem. I could put another bedroom or even two up on the second floor. See, what I was visualising was maybe four or five en suite guest rooms on the first floor, and then downstairs, expand that tiny kitchen by knocking it through to the middle room, so you'd have a good-sized kitchen diner that was strictly off limits to guests. The front room off the central hallway would be for you to use as an office or study, or your own living room, whatever you wanted. On the other side of the hallway, I could open the living room and back room, making one big open plan space, with sofas and dining tables for the guests, and French doors into the garden. I could put French doors in your kitchen diner, too, if you like.'

Harry nodded. 'I sort of see how that would work,' he agreed. 'I'd have one side of the ground floor, the guests would have the other side and the first floor, and I'd have the second floor, right?'

'Right. What do you think?'

'It's not what I was imagining for myself when I moved here, that's all.'

'You could make enough during the summer to see you through the rest of the year,' Gareth said. 'I doubt you'd have to take in guests all year round. You could do up that old annexe, too. Turn it into a self-contained holiday let. It's up to you, of course. I was thinking if you need the income—'

'I'm not destitute,' Harry said hastily. 'I do have money, you know.' Just not as much as he used to have, and with all the work needed on the house and no new money flowing into his bank account, he supposed he'd have to get serious about his finances at some point. It was a bit of a shock, given that he'd spent years not thinking much about money at all. As for the annexe, that would have to wait. He had to focus on the main house first.

'Ah well, it's your call.' Gareth glanced at his watch. 'I'd better get off, old chap. Early train back to London tomorrow and I've got to get back to the hotel in Whitby. I'd better ring for a taxi.'

'Of course. Fair enough. I'll finish this drink and I'll be heading home, too.'

But when Gareth finally said his goodbyes, leaving Harry sitting alone, he realised he didn't particularly want to go back to Eight Bells yet. It was good to have people around him. Besides, it was warm and cosy in the pub, and a hell of a lot more appealing than the dump he'd left behind. He decided to order another drink and stay on for a while and headed over to the bar to order another glass of wine.

A rather attractive young woman with dark hair and large, dark eyes was standing at the bar. He vaguely recognised her and thought she might be the person who'd served him that first night he'd arrived. He smirked to himself. Ah yes, the one who'd told him not to patronise her. Well, whoever she was, she seemed to be having some difficulty getting served, judging by the barmaid's pursed lips as she surveyed her.

'What's wrong with that?' The young woman sounded annoyed, but the barmaid looked worried.

'Another pint? Are you sure, Tally?'

'What do you mean, am I sure? Why wouldn't I be sure?'

'It's just, you've had two already, and you don't usually drink that much. It's potent stuff, you know, and you downed that one quick enough. Are you certain you wouldn't like a soft drink now, just to break it up before you have another cider?'

'Definitely not. I'm not a kid, you know, Kerry.'

'I know that, but like I said, this stuff is potent, and you don't usually drink.'

'Well, keep your opinions to yourself.'

'God, Tally, what's got into you?'

'Two pints of cider, and now I wish to make it three.'

Kerry glanced around, as if looking for help. 'I don't know...'

Tally was clearly livid. 'What do you mean, you don't know? I'm an adult for God's sake. I have money. I can pay. What's your problem?'

'I was going to ask you the same thing,' Kerry admitted. 'This isn't you, Tally. Why don't you get yourself home, eh? Do you want me to ring your mum and dad?'

'What?' Tally sounded as if she couldn't believe it, and Harry couldn't blame her. He frowned, feeling a tad impatient as she snapped, 'Are you seriously telling me I'm not allowed a third drink?'

Kirsty squirmed. 'I just don't think you should—'

'Fuck me!' Harry simply couldn't stand it any longer. 'How old is she? Twelve? Just get her a bloody drink, for God's sake.'

Tally turned her head to face him then winced. Two pints of cider had clearly already had an effect. 'I can speak for myself,' she said haughtily. 'I certainly don't need your help.'

'Well, bloody hurry up about it then,' Harry said. 'Some of us are gasping for a glass of wine, and since there only seems to be one barmaid in this God-forsaken place, I'd love it if you'd stop hogging her.'

'Hogging her!'

Kerry scowled. 'What did you want?'

'Large white wine please,' Harry said. 'House white will do. I'm learning not to be so fussy living here, *oop north*.'

'Just a minute,' Tally protested, 'I was here first, and I haven't been served yet.'

'You must learn to be more assertive,' Harry told her. 'People will walk all over you if you don't.'

'Like you just did, you mean?'

'Not just me,' he pointed out, waving a hand in the direction of Kerry who was now pouring his wine. 'Look at that. I mean, how rude. She should have served you. Unless you're a known alcoholic. Are you a known alcoholic?'

'No I'm not!'

'Well, are you a secret alcoholic then? Maybe she's particularly good at spotting those and I've done her a grave disservice.'

Tally stared at him. 'I'm not an alcoholic at all. I just want a bloody cider.'

'Fair enough.' As Kerry handed Harry the wine, he said, 'And a pint of cider for my friend here.'

Kerry looked at Tally, clearly rattled. Tally gave what sounded like a cross between a giggle and a snort.

'Tally?'

'You heard the man,' Tally said, beaming at Kerry. 'Pear cider, remember.'

'Surprised *you* remember,' Kerry muttered, but she fulfilled the order and handed the drink over, then held out her hand to Harry for the payment.

He passed her a note and told her to keep the change, wondering if he was meant to hear her mutter, 'Flash git,' under her breath as she opened the till. Charming. What was flash about that? He noticed her drop a ten-pound note and some change in the tip jar on the counter and groaned inwardly. He must have given her a twenty-pound note instead of a bloody tenner! He would have to learn to be more careful with his money. If he was going to spend twenty pounds each time he fancied a drink he'd be bankrupt in no time, and it wasn't as if anyone around here appreciated his generosity — intentional or otherwise.

'Would you care to join me?' He wasn't sure why he'd asked Tally the question. Somewhere in the back of his mind he thought it was probably to annoy the barmaid even more.

Tally blinked at him. 'Are you talking to me?'

'Unless there are any other raging alcoholics in the bar,' he said. 'I'm sitting over there, by the fireplace.'

She glanced over at his table and her eyes narrowed. 'You're on your own?'

'My business associate had to leave. He's staying at a hotel in Whitby, and he's got a long journey back home tomorrow, so it's going to be an early start. He's not as young as he was.' He gave a heavy sigh. 'None of us is.'

'Speak for yourself,' Tally said lightly. 'I'm still twelve apparently.'

Harry grinned, and Tally grinned back, which cheered him up enormously for some reason.

'Oh, go on then,' she said. 'But don't think for a minute that means I'm on your side about Amy, because I'm not.'

So she remembered him then. He wasn't sure whether to be flattered or worried.

'Heaven forbid,' Harry said, rolling his eyes.

Tally followed him over to his table, making a slight detour to collect her coat and scarf from the chair she'd previously been sitting in.

'It's a nice place, isn't it?' he asked, as she plonked herself in a chair. He was already wondering what on earth he was going to talk to her about and regretting his impetuous offer to her to sit with him.

Tally glanced around and her expression softened. 'It is. I can never decide when I love it most. I love it how it is right now in winter, with the fairy lights and the fire roaring away, and this gorgeous cosy feel. But in the summer, when the windows are open and there's that fantastic view over the sea, and fresh flowers in the cauldron—'

Harry gulped down his wine and stared at her. 'Excuse me?'

'Rhiannon's cauldron.' Tally smirked at him. 'Did you not know she's a witch? Didn't you notice the broomstick?'

'Are you mad?'

'I'm not joking. Look.' She nodded at the wall behind him, and he turned in his chair, his eyes widening in astonishment as he saw the broomstick propped up near the fireplace.

'Well, that explains that weird ceremony I walked in on at Halloween,' he said. 'Once I'd got over the shock of finding myself in a Hammer Horror set, I thought maybe it was a gimmick — you know, for tourists. So she actually *is* a fruit loop? What is this place? The meeting place for the local coven?'

'Rhiannon doesn't belong to a coven, and she doesn't label herself.' Tally pursed her lips. 'Other people are quick enough to do that for her. All I know is, she's some sort of pagan. We have regular celebrations — something to do with the Wheel of the Year.'

Harry remembered Samhain and nodded. 'What's the difference between a witch and a pagan then? Or is a witch a pagan? I'm confused.'

Tally considered the matter. 'Not sure to be honest. Does it matter?'

'Probably not. She sounds completely off her tree whatever she is.'

'I don't see why. It's a belief system, like any other. Don't you believe in anything, Harry?'

Harry thought about the shabby house he'd left behind and the mammoth task that lay ahead of him, making it presentable. 'I believe flock wallpaper is the work of the devil,' he said with feeling.

'The devil, eh? So do you believe in God then?'

'Do I fuck. But I never say that out loud in case it pisses Him off.'

Tally laughed. 'Idiot!'

'It's all too deep for me. I'm as shallow as a puddle, ask my ex-wives.'

'Both of them?'

'Without doubt. It's hard to say which one of them would give me the worst reference.'

Tally sipped her cider, watching him thoughtfully. 'I think I should tell you, here and now, that Gabriel's my uncle,' she said at last. 'I'm very fond of Eliza, so I'll have no truck with you badmouthing either of them. Just in case you were thinking of doing so.'

Harry looked at her, amused. 'Why would I badmouth either of them? You're making wild assumptions there. I know it would delight you all to believe it, but I'm not here to cause trouble. I want to see my daughter. Is that so wrong?'

'It probably wouldn't be a concern if you hadn't abandoned her for years,' Tally admonished him, rather unfairly he thought.

Then again, she sounded a little slurry, so drink had probably made her more belligerent than she would normally be. Alcohol had that effect on some people. Melody could be an absolute bitch when she'd had a few, he remembered with a shudder. Then again, she had a mean turn of phrase when she was sober, too.

'I mean, what sort of a father are you?'

'A crap one, evidently.' Harry took a slow drink from his wine glass and gazed into the middle distance, his mood sinking as he thought about the mess he'd made of everything.

'Are you having me on?' Tally waved her pint glass at him. 'Because I'm not in the mood, so be warned.'

He pulled a face. 'Watch it, you're slopping cider all over the table. And no, I'm not having you on. About what anyway?'

'About…' Tally stopped, her face blank, and he thought she'd probably forgotten what they'd been talking about. 'Anyway, I'm Tally.'

He raised a glass to her, trying his best to hide his amusement. 'How lovely to meet you, Tally. I'm Harry.'

'I know you are. You're Harry Jarvis. I'm Gabriel's niece.'

'You don't say.'

'I do say, so don't be saying anything bad about him, okay?'

'The thought never entered my head.'

Tally nodded, evidently satisfied, and took another drink of her cider. Suddenly she started to giggle and clapped a hand over her mouth as if to drown the sound.

'What's so funny?' Harry queried.

Tally hiccupped, then giggled again. 'Just picturing what my mum would say if she saw me here with you.'

'And what would she say?'

'That I ought to be ashamed of myself, and did I have no common sense, and hadn't she brought me up better than this?'

Tally's laughter died and she gave a heavy sigh.

'You sound as if you have the weight of the world on your shoulders,' Harry said.

'I'm a bit fed up,' she confessed.

Harry leaned back in his chair. 'You and me both,' he said heavily. 'I've had a bloody awful time of it lately.'

'You probably brought it all on yourself,' she replied.

'Quite right, and don't I know it,' he said gloomily.

Tally's mouth fell open in surprise and she peered at him closely.

'What?' he said.

'I wasn't expecting you to admit it,' she told him. 'I expected a tirade of reasons why nothing was your fault, and everything was everyone else's fault, not this defeated confession.' She frowned and stared at him even more closely.

Harry shuffled in his chair. 'I do wish you'd stop staring,' he said. 'It's terribly off-putting, you know.'

Tally's face crumpled, and for one awful minute he thought she was going to cry.

'What on earth's the matter?' he asked her.

'You're sad!' Tally shook her head. 'Harry Jarvis is sad.'

'I'm not sad,' he said, taken aback by her bluntness. 'Why on earth would you say such a thing?'

She wasn't even listening. She'd gone off into her own little world. 'You poor thing. I mean, what have you done that was so bad? Okay, you messed up your marriage to Eliza, but loads of people have affairs, and it doesn't make them bad people. And it all worked out for the best anyway because look how much Eliza and Gabriel love each other, and how happy they are. You did her a favour.'

'Thanks for pointing that out,' he said, somewhat tetchily. 'You're right, of course. I should have got a medal.'

'Have you seen Amy yet?' she asked tentatively.

He nodded. 'We had tea. It didn't go quite as planned, I must say. She's not my little girl any more, really. She certainly let me know what she thought of me.'

'She *is* still your little girl,' Tally said, sounding rather sympathetic, which annoyed him slightly. 'She's hurt, that's all. She's protecting herself. We all do that, don't we?'

Harry eyed her uncertainly. 'You think so?'

'Absolutely. Don't you put a tough face on to show the world? I know I do.'

He leaned forward, resting his elbows on the table as he surveyed her. 'So, Tally, what's your problem?'

'My problem?' She laughed and took another swig of cider. 'I have no problems. Life is perfect.'

'Which most definitely means it isn't.' Harry shook his head slightly. 'Boyfriend troubles?'

'I haven't got a boyfriend,' she said dully.

'I don't believe it. Someone as beautiful as you, single?'

They stared at each other and both burst out laughing. Harry clapped his hand to his forehead and groaned. 'God, sorry. That sounded so bloody corny. It wasn't a come-on, I promise you. I was genuinely surprised, but feel free to mock.'

'Was that taken from the *Harry Jarvis Big Book of Chat-Up Lines*?' Tally giggled. 'Honestly, it's like something from the 1970s.'

'I know, I know. God I'm embarrassed.'

'So you should be, trying to chat up a woman of my age at your time of life.'

Harry reared back, offended. 'What do you mean, *my time of life?* I'm not that bloody old.'

'How old are you?'

He cleared his throat. 'Really? Well, er, forty-seven.'

'And the rest,' she said, laughing.

His eyes widened. 'I am! I swear it.'

'Oh well, you've had a rough time of it lately so…' She giggled again and Harry found himself laughing with her.

'How old are you then?'

'Twenty-four.'

Harry groaned. 'Oh, God. Nearly half my age. How obscene.'

'Good job we're not about to hook up then, isn't it?'

'I guess it is. It would be an outrage. The villagers would be after me with flaming torches and pitchforks.'

'And my mother would be leading the mob.'

'I expect she would, and quite right, too.'

Tally circled the top of her glass thoughtfully. She stared into his eyes and he saw a sudden gleam in hers that sparked a feeling of excitement that he hadn't felt for a long time. He was reasonably sure she was attracted to him, and he had to admit, putting aside who she was, and the difference in their ages, he found her jolly attractive, too. She had the most beautiful dark eyes, and a stunning smile, and there was something else, a glint of mischief and naughtiness that quite extinguished his sadness, along with any common sense he had left.

'Of course, I've never been one to care what the rest of the world thinks,' she said, which he was quite sure was an outright lie.

'Are you sure?' he said. 'Because I get the feeling, from the way you speak about your mother, that you care very much what other people think.'

Tally hesitated then shrugged. 'Maybe I have done in the past. But isn't it time that changed? Oh, how freeing it felt, to say those words. As if, by saying it out loud, I could make it true.'

Harry wasn't sure where all this was going, and he was reasonably certain he should put a halt to it right here and now, but Tally seemed to be talking to herself, rather than to him.

'How wonderful would it feel to go off and do something that everyone in my family would thoroughly disapprove of, and not care a damn about doing it? To do something, because I want to, no matter how outrageous or unwise or stupid it is. Just once.'

'That would make you a very wicked woman,' Harry said awkwardly. Was she saying what he thought she was saying? And how did he feel about that anyway? Why would someone like her want someone like him?

She reached out and gently touched his face.

Harry covered her hand with his own. 'You shouldn't do things like that, you know. It can lead to places you really shouldn't go.'

'But suppose I want to go there?'

He laughed, though he was no longer feeling amused. Terrified, yes. Intrigued, yes. Amused, absolutely not. 'I don't think you do.'

'But I do. For God's sake, I'm not a kid, and I'm sick of being treated like one. Believe it or not, I know my own mind.'

'But your family—'

'Stuff my family. This isn't about my family. It's about you and me, and the moment. Can't we do something totally crazy for the sheer hell of it? What's the harm?'

She had talked herself into it, he could tell. Wise or not, she wanted this. Thoughts of Melody and her toy boy lover sprang into his mind. If it was good enough for her, why not for him? She'd mocked him, ridiculed him, called him an old man, said he was finished. Chuck, her new boyfriend, was young, virile. If Melody could attract someone so much younger than she was, why couldn't he? Why *shouldn't* he?

He felt a stab of disappointment as she began to shrug on her coat.

'Are you leaving?' he asked, wondering what he'd done wrong.

'Yes, I am. With you. Take me back to Eight Bells, Harry. Let's have one night where we say screw the world. This is for us.'

Harry got to his feet. 'I want it on record that I met a wanton woman and she led me astray.'

Tally beamed. 'Brilliant. I've always wanted to be a wanton woman.'

Arm in arm, they left The Hare and Moon.

7

The cold night air had a sobering effect on Harry, in more ways than one. As he unlocked the door to Eight Bells, he asked himself for the hundredth time what on earth he thought he was doing. This was one of the worst ideas he'd ever had, and God knows, he'd had some real humdingers in his time.

But he'd been so low, and she'd been so appealing, and yes, she was pretty, and it was flattering, and hell, he needed *someone* to make him feel better.

Tally didn't seem to notice the state of the place when he flicked the light switch on. She clearly only had eyes for him. She launched herself at him the moment he closed the door behind them, and to his amazement he found himself responding. It was good to be held, to be kissed. It was good to feel wanted again, to feel attractive. He'd almost forgotten how that felt.

And did it matter? She said herself it was just one night, one night for themselves and screw the rest of the world. That appealed to him. One night to put all that pain and misery behind him and remember how wonderful it could feel to be part of another human being again. He deserved that, didn't he?

He locked the door and led her upstairs, painfully aware, as he switched on the bedside lamp, of how shabby the place looked, and hoped it wouldn't turn her off completely. The room he was using for a bedroom was hardly a seducer's lair, but at least the bed was new, and the sheets were clean. Maybe she wouldn't care.

She didn't. Harry almost fell over as she threw herself on him, kissing him furiously as if she were trying to devour him. *Bloody hell, steady on!*

She opened her eyes and he saw her gaze slide over to the bed. She pulled away from him and began to unbutton her coat.

Harry took her hands in his. 'Tally, are you sure about this? Are you sure it's what you want?'

"Course it is! Get your clothes off. Hurry up!'

He told himself her voice wasn't that slurry, and removed his coat, then began to unbutton his shirt. His hands were shaking, and he wondered why. He'd only had three glasses of wine, hardly enough to have that sort of effect. He realised he was strangely reluctant to look at her, and his usual seduction techniques seemed to have gone out of the window. This was possibly the least romantic he'd ever felt in his life.

He thought of Eliza's reaction if she found out. What would she say? How could he tell her he was serious about rebuilding his relationship with Amy if he'd jumped into bed with Gabriel's niece five minutes after moving to the village? What the hell was he playing at?

Almost against his will, he glanced up at her and his fingers stilled on his shirt button. She was down to her underwear, her clothes strewn on the bare floorboards, her dark hair tumbling over her shoulders as she watched him through large brown eyes that were trying so hard to express confidence. They weren't succeeding.

Harry wondered what had happened to him and considered the worrying possibility that he was growing up. He sighed and hastily fastened up his shirt again.

Tally looked alarmed. 'What are you doing?'

'Getting dressed, and you should, too.'

'But — but aren't we going to—?'

'No, Tally. We're not.'

To his dismay, she crumpled and sat down heavily on the bed, tears spilling onto her cheeks.

'Even you don't want me! I just wanted one night, just one night.'

'I know you want something, Tally,' he said gently, 'but I don't think this is it.'

Her trembling fingers plucked at the strap of her bra, and he hastily scooped up her clothes and handed them to her.

'Here you go. You get dressed and I'll make us both some coffee,' he said.

She was fully dressed when he returned to the bedroom, but she was still sitting on the bed. She looked dazed, shell-shocked. Harry handed her a mug and sat down on a chair in a corner of the room.

'Drink that,' he told her. 'You'll feel better.'

She gave a bitter laugh. 'I don't think a coffee will make up for this humiliation,' she said.

'You'd be surprised,' he told her. 'Trust me, you'll thank me for this tomorrow.'

'I won't,' she muttered. 'How low can a woman go? Being rejected by Harry Jarvis, of all people. I mean, you'll shag anything.'

Harry puffed out his cheeks. 'Wow. Thanks for that.'

'Well, don't you?' She sounded challenging. She was clearly hurt and angry, and he couldn't blame her, but he had no doubt she'd be glad it had worked out this way tomorrow. He wasn't what she wanted, whatever she thought. And he didn't want her either, as incredible as that sounded.

Even in his own head it was a surprise to form the words. Tally was pretty, no question. It had been hugely flattering to have someone as young and beautiful as she was throwing themselves at him, especially after the year he'd had. He'd needed that assurance that he was still attractive, and he had to admit, it had been a relief to discover he could still respond to a woman physically. He hadn't known he was capable these days. Well, he knew now that he could. His new worry was that he wouldn't sustain that feeling, but that must wait for another day. Right now, he had Tally to console.

The trouble was, looking at her he'd realised, all too clearly, that she wasn't the answer. And she was so young, so vulnerable, that sleeping with her would be an act of cruelty. Why should she suffer because he needed his ego soothing? She would have regretted it the next day, and it would have been too late. He couldn't do that to her.

'Drink your coffee,' he told her. 'And no, for your information I don't. It may surprise you to know that I haven't had sex with anyone for over a year. And if you tell anyone that I will take you to court and sue you for slander.'

She sniffed. 'You're just saying that to make me feel better.'

'And make me look like a total loser in the process? Does that sound like the sort of thing I'd do?' he said.

She narrowed her eyes. 'I'm not sure any more, to be honest. You're a lot nicer than I thought you'd be.'

'I think that's a compliment,' he mused. 'I'll take it as one anyway.'

'I feel such a fool,' she said, cradling her mug of coffee. 'You must think I'm such a slapper.'

'Don't be ridiculous.' Harry gave her a reassuring smile. 'If you're a slapper then I'm one, too. Or the male equivalent. Let's face it, we both made an error of judgment, but we realised it in time and there's no harm done.'

'Except my pride,' she muttered. 'I don't make a habit of this, you know. It's only the second time…'

Harry swallowed hard. Thank God he'd not gone through with it. He'd never have forgiven himself.

'Bloody hell,' was all he could manage.

'Yeah, things haven't been too good in that department,' Tally admitted. She gave a strangled sob. 'The only time I went with someone, he cleared off a few days later. I mean, literally. He left the village. How bad's that?'

'I'm sure that had nothing to do with you,' Harry said, thinking what a swine this man was, and then realising with shame that it was probably the sort of thing he'd have done once, without even thinking about it. 'It's his loss anyway. Don't waste your time fretting over him. Young men are — well idiots, to be honest. It's rarely the woman's fault. It's genetic.'

Tally spluttered with laughter. 'Nice try. Thanks.' She drank her coffee, staring into the distance, clearly lost in thought.

Harry sipped his own coffee, not sure what to say to her. He was afraid whatever he said would make her feel worse, so he decided to keep his mouth shut.

'I'm sorry,' she said eventually.

He hadn't expected an apology, of all things. 'What are you sorry for? You've done nothing wrong.'

'This!' She waved a hand around the room. 'It's completely messed up. I don't know what I was thinking. You must think I'm such a child.'

'I don't think that at all,' he said softly. 'I think you're a bit sad today, that's all. Something's upsetting you, and you wanted to feel better.'

'You're absolutely right,' she admitted. 'That's exactly it. But I shouldn't have used you to do it.'

'You didn't,' he pointed out. 'Nothing happened, remember?'

'Thanks to you,' she said. She drained the last of her coffee and stood up. 'I'd better be going. I've taken up enough of your time.'

'No you haven't.' He realised he didn't want her to go. It wasn't that he wanted anything to happen between them because he didn't. But she was a nice young woman, and something was clearly getting her down, and to be truthful it was good to have some company. Harry hadn't realised how lonely he'd felt, and now that he had he didn't want to be alone again. Not yet. He was enjoying having someone around, someone to take his mind off his own troubles. 'Honestly, stay as long as you want. Tell me what's on your mind or say nothing at all. It's up to you. But you don't have to rush off.'

Tally put her cup on the floor and looked around, as if seeing the room for the first time.

'Wow,' she said. 'This is much worse than I thought. But it's a good-sized room. It could be lovely. I expect it will be stunning when you've finished.'

'Hmm.'

'Must be exciting when money's no object.'

'Who said money was no object?'

She widened her eyes in surprise. 'Well, is it? I mean, you're a famous television star. I expect you're planning on turning it into a proper show house.'

'Just a home would be nice,' he said quietly.

Tally leaned forward. 'You're not at all what I imagined,' she said. 'You're actually okay, you know. Why do you pretend to be an arsehole?'

He grinned. 'No, that's the real me. One hundred per cent. I'm acting now.'

'No you're not, I can tell.' She sighed. 'I really don't want to go home, you know.'

'Well don't then. At least, not yet. Like I said, I'm glad to have the company.'

'But it's nearly midnight,' she pointed out, glancing at the clock on his bedside table. 'Don't you have to be up early tomorrow?'

'What for? I'm not working, remember. Then again, I suppose you are. Sorry, I never thought. Do you want me to call you a taxi?'

'Not really. I'd rather stay here and talk,' she admitted.

'Tally, tell me if I'm speaking out of turn here,' he said, 'but something's weighing you down, and making you act out of character. I don't think this is the sort of thing you do on a regular basis, and I'd like to help if I can. If you want to talk, whatever you say won't go any further.'

'And I can trust you because…?'

He shrugged. 'You're right. You don't know me, except by reputation, and I suppose that's pretty awful. Forget I asked.'

'No.' She reached out a hand and laid it on his. 'I'm sorry. I think you've proved I can trust you after the way you've behaved tonight. You're quite a gentleman. Who'd have thought it?'

'Not me,' he confessed. 'There's hope for us all. So, you know, if you want to talk…'

'How about another coffee?' she asked.

He stood. 'Sure, coming right up.'

'I'll come with you,' she said. 'And I'll tell you my tale of woe while you make it.'

She wasn't kidding. Two hours later, sitting by her side on the sofa, sipping his fourth cup of coffee, Harry thought he knew just about everything that had ever happened to her during the last few years of her life. When the floodgates had opened, it had all poured out. Years of hurt and sadness and anger and a strong sense of injustice. From what Harry could gather, her mother was a total control freak, her father was a gutless doormat, and her sister and brother were selfish, thoughtless gits who took advantage of Tally's nice nature to go off and do whatever they wanted, leaving her to pick up the pieces. Then there was the boyfriend who'd turned out not to be a boyfriend at all, just a user who was still hung up on his ex. No wonder she was fed up.

'I'm ever so sorry,' she said, as he stifled a yawn. 'Have I bored you to death? Oh, my God! It's gone two o'clock in the morning. You must be sick of me.'

'Not at all,' he assured her. 'It made a pleasant change to listen to someone else's problems.'

'Even so,' she said, 'I shouldn't have gone on so much. I'm not usually like this, you know. I don't know what's wrong with me lately. I feel so angry and frustrated all the time.'

'We all have a breaking point.'

'I suppose… Look, I really should be going. Would you mind ringing me that taxi?'

'Of course not.' Harry took out his mobile phone. 'Do you know the number of a local firm?'

Tally reeled a number off, and he quickly made the call.

'It will be here in ten minutes,' he promised her, putting the phone back in his pocket.

'Thanks so much, Harry. You know, I've enjoyed tonight, despite the terrible beginning.'

'Me, too. And look, if you ever want to pop round to chat, or complain, or have a cup of coffee, you're always welcome,' he said, surprised at how much he meant it. He'd genuinely enjoyed talking to her, and he certainly could use a friend around here.

Tally smiled, and he thought again how pretty she was, and wondered what the hell had got into him that he hadn't wanted to sleep with her. Then again, he knew the answer to that really, but if anyone could have helped him get over it surely it would be someone as young and attractive as Tally? Evidently not. Curse his new-found morals.

'I'd like that,' she said. 'But be warned, I may take you up on it.'

'Please do.' He mentally crossed his fingers. Life seemed a little less lonely right now. He hoped she would visit again, though once her family found out where she'd been, he had a feeling that any budding friendship with Harry Jarvis, enemy of the people, would be firmly nipped in the bud.

YULE

8

'Have you got your Christmas tree up yet?'

Harry handed the young woman behind the counter the exact amount of money needed, picked up the tray and turned to look down on Amy.

'Not yet no.' *Not yet?* He'd not even thought about it. It seemed rather pointless putting a Christmas tree up in that hovel. 'I thought I told you to find a table.'

'You did, but there are plenty spare, so I thought I'd wait for you.'

'Okay, so where do you want to sit?'

Amy put her hands on her hips and surveyed the little café thoughtfully. Harry couldn't imagine what was taking her so long.

'Make a decision,' he said, feeling the tray growing heavier in his hands. 'It's hardly life or death, is it?'

Amy glared up at him. 'Are you getting cross?' she demanded.

'No, no, of course I'm not. But these burgers are getting cold, and we don't want that, do we?'

Hell no. They would taste disgusting enough hot. The things he did for Amy. He'd never had a cheeseburger in his life, and now here he was, standing in a seafront café in Scarborough, about to force down a lump of gristly meat and processed cheese, not to mention a banana milkshake, of all things. He'd seen more appealing looking meals on a Bush Tucker Challenge. There was, he thought, a heavy price to pay for redeeming himself with his daughter.

Amy slipped into a seat by the window and Harry settled in the seat opposite her. It took him a good five minutes and a lot of coaxing to begin eating.

Amy chewed happily on her own burger, watching him with laughter in her eyes.

'Well? What do you think?' she asked eventually.

Harry wiped his chin with a paper napkin and sighed. 'As I suspected. Utterly vile. I might ask if I can drink the washing up water to take away the taste.'

'Don't be silly.' Amy giggled and Harry reached over and dabbed at her chin with the napkin.

'Ketchup,' he explained.

'Yummy,' she responded. 'So why haven't you got your Christmas tree up yet?'

'It's early yet,' he pointed out. 'Have you got yours up?'

'Yes. Mum and Joe put it up on the first of December. They always do them together, first at Whisperwood and then at Wychwood. It's a lovely tree. We got it from Will and Lexi's estate. They grow Christmas trees there, you know. They have a full forest. And we got a wreath from there, too, and holly and mistletoe.'

'So, Lexi's married to some sort of lord, is she?'

'He's a baronet,' Amy said. 'He's ever so nice. He gives me riding lessons. Can you ride?'

'Afraid not,' he admitted. 'You like riding then?'

'I love riding,' she said, her eyes shining. 'All I've ever wanted is a pony of my own, and I always put one on my Christmas list, but Mum says they're expensive, and cost too much to keep.'

'I expect she's right,' Harry said. 'And Father Christmas probably doesn't deal in livestock.'

'Da-d!' Amy rolled her eyes. 'I'm not a kid. I know about Father Christmas.'

'Oh.' Harry felt bitterly disappointed. What a shame. He supposed he shouldn't be surprised, though. He'd figured out the truth way before Amy's age. Still, it seemed like another milestone had been passed that he'd missed out on. 'I'm sorry.'

'Mum nearly cried when I told her,' Amy admitted. 'She gave me a big hug and said I was growing up too fast.'

'I know how she felt,' he said, with feeling.

'It worked out for the best for me though,' she continued. 'I got a laptop out of it.'

'How did you get a laptop out of it?' Harry eyed her, confused.

'It was guilt, I think,' she said happily. 'I wasn't excited about Christmas any more because you know, it's not the same, is it? Once you know, I mean.'

'No,' Harry agreed. 'It never is.'

'Well, I was a bit fed up. I was going to pretend to Mum and Gabriel that I still believed in Father Christmas, because they were working hard to fool me and I didn't want to spoil it for them, but then I thought I'd better tell them the truth because, honestly, it was getting embarrassing. So I told them, and Mum got really upset like I said, and then they asked me if I could pretend to be excited at least, because Hannah and Mikey still believe in Father Christmas, you see. They're only four. So I was really good and made a lot of fuss and helped them write their lists to Santa and everything, and then on Christmas morning, when I thought it would be all dull and boring, I got a laptop. It was all I'd ever wanted.'

Harry stared at her. 'I thought a pony was all you'd ever wanted?'

She rolled her eyes. 'Well, obviously. But apart from a pony, a laptop was all I'd ever wanted, and I got one, just because I didn't believe in Father Christmas.'

Harry thought it had probably taught Amy a valuable lesson — parental guilt was the key to riches. She'd learned the lesson well.

'So what's Father Christmas bringing you this year?' he enquired, prodding listlessly at the burger, as if hoping it would somehow disintegrate beneath his fingers.

Amy took a long drink of her milkshake before answering him. 'You didn't listen to a word I said, did you? I don't believe in Father Christmas any longer. You can stop pretending.'

'I know, I know. I didn't mean it literally. It's just something people say,' he assured her.

'Are you eating that?'

'Of course.'

'Well, go on then, and while you're eating it, I'll tell you what I want for Christmas.'

'Super.'

Harry closed his eyes, took a deep breath then went for it. God, he should win some sort of parent of the year prize for this ordeal.

'I really, really want a dog,' Amy told him. 'It's all I've ever wanted. I've been asking for one for ages, but Mum and Da— Gabriel keep saying no.'

Harry couldn't, in all honesty, blame them. 'Shame,' he managed. 'So, when you said a pony was all you ever wanted, you mean it was one of a long list of things you want?'

'No! A pony's absolutely top of the list. In fact, it has a list all its own. But I'm never going to get one, am I? So on my other list, a dog is top. Joe and Charlie have got a dog, but I don't want one like Honoria Glossop.'

Harry rolled his eyes. Trust those two to call their dog something so pretentious. Then a thought occurred to him. Honoria Glossop didn't sound much like the name of a guard dog.

'What sort of dog is Honoria Glossop?' he asked suspiciously.

'A Yorkshire terrier,' Amy informed him.

Oh, the humiliation! Those two had tricked him into believing he was about to be savaged by a bloody Yorkie! They must have laughed their heads off that night he arrived at Whisperwood. God, he hoped they hadn't mentioned it to anyone else.

'Will and Lexi have got a dog, too,' Amy continued, oblivious to his embarrassment. 'He's a gorgeous chocolate Labrador called Buttons. I want a Labrador, too. Or a spaniel.' She tilted her head, thinking. 'Yes, I'd like a spaniel. A black cocker spaniel girl. I'd call her Lyra.'

'Why Lyra?'

'I like that name. I wish you'd called me Lyra instead of Amy. There are three other Amys in my school, but not a single Lyra.'

'Sorry,' Harry said. 'So your mum and Gabriel won't let you have a dog?'

'No. They say I've had enough money spent on me, what with the bike and the laptop.'

'Do you have a bike, too?'

Amy shrugged. 'Obvs.'

He couldn't imagine what else she'd need. He had to admit that his daughter seemed to lack for nothing.

'Second hand though,' Amy added. 'The bike was Tally's. Mum thinks I don't know that, but I heard her talking to Sophie about it. And Gabriel was clear that I was only allowed a — a — reconditioned laptop,' she said, with some difficulty. 'And then only because of schoolwork. They say a dog is a big responsibility and takes a lot more looking after than I realise. As if I don't know that! I can read. Besides, if Joe and Charlie can have a dog, I don't see why I can't, but Mum and Gabriel say it's not happening. They're ever so mean. They won't even let me go on TikTok.'

'I should hope not!'

'My friends are all on TikTok. I'm the talk of the school,' she said dramatically.

'I'm sure you'll cope,' Harry said.

'Hmm. I thought you'd understand at least.' Amy sounded betrayed by his indifference.

'Well...' Harry, having swilled his mouth with banana milkshake, and feeling a little queasy again, geared himself up for the last bite of the cheeseburger and said, 'it seems you have everything you could possibly want. I can't imagine what I'm going to get you for Christmas.'

'A mobile phone,' Amy said immediately. 'I really, really want a mobile phone. It's all I've ever wanted.'

'I thought a pony, a laptop and a dog were all you'd ever wanted.'

'They are. But a mobile phone's allowed, too.'

'Right. Fair enough.'

'The thing is, they won't let me have one.'

'Why not?'

Amy tutted. 'They give me a different reason every time. They're too expensive. They're not safe. They're not for children. I'm too young. Blah, blah, blah.'

Harry's lips twitched. 'Do any of your friends have a mobile phone?'

'They *all* have a mobile phone!' Amy propped her chin in her hands and gave a big sigh. 'I'm the only one in the class who hasn't got one. And when you think about it,' she added, as if the thought had just occurred to her, 'it would be useful, wouldn't it? Because then we could keep in touch, couldn't we? I could talk to you whenever I wanted, and you wouldn't have to go through Mum all the time.'

She had a point.

'Well, I suppose…'

'The thing is, round here the signal's not very good,' she continued. 'Da— Gabriel's always complaining about it. You have to have a decent phone to get through to anyone.'

'Oh, really?' Harry could see where this conversation was heading.

'Really. Those old, cheap ones don't work round here.'

'Of course they don't,' Harry said. 'Well, they wouldn't, would they?'

'No. So it would have to be a good phone. Like an iPhone, say. The new one. My friend's got one, and she never loses the signal.'

'I expect it depends a lot on the network,' Harry said gravely. 'That's extremely important.'

Amy looked bemused. 'Er, yeah. Anyway, do you think I could have an iPhone for Christmas?'

Harry frowned. 'Are you asking me to get one for you?'

'Well, der!' Amy rolled her eyes. 'Obviously.'

'I don't know, Amy,' Harry said nervously. 'If your mum says no…'

Amy leaned forward, her voice taking on a conspiratorial tone. 'I think she says no because Gabriel says no. She wouldn't mind really. In fact, she's always saying it would be better because then she'd know I was safe if I was out anywhere. I think,' she added, picking off bits of her cheeseburger, 'that it's money that's the problem. Gabriel hasn't been on the telly after all. He's just a doctor. I don't suppose they earn much money.'

Harry laughed. 'I think they do okay.'

'But he's got three children to support,' she pointed out. 'That probably costs a lot of money. He's always moaning about bills and how much Mum spends at Sainsbury's.'

Three children to support! Harry scowled for a moment, then forced himself to smile. 'Well, not really, darling, because *I* support *you*. I send your mum money for you every month. I always have.'

Amy stared at him. 'Have you?' She tilted her head to one side, thinking. 'I wonder where that all goes then? I only get two pounds a week pocket money.'

'Are you going to finish that burger?' he asked her.

Amy shook her head. 'No, it's horrible.'

Harry's mouth dropped open. 'What? Are you joking?'

'Nope. I've never had one from here before, and I didn't know it would taste so bad. Next time, you can take me to the burger place in Moreton Cross. That's my favourite. You'll like that.'

'Never again,' he promised. 'That was my first and last burger.'

'But you enjoyed it, didn't you?' she said, her eyes gleaming. 'You ate it all.'

'You *made* me eat it all!' My God! She could run rings around him.

'So, about this phone,' she said. 'What do you think?'

'I don't know, Amy. I'll have to think about it.'

'I'd like to be able to text you,' she said wistfully. 'It would be nice to talk to you every day, like I can Dad.'

Dad!

'I mean,' she continued, 'I see him every single day, and we chat all the time, but I can't tell *you* things, can I? Like, if I come home from school and something's happened that I want to talk about, I can tell Dad, because he's always around. But it would be great if I could tell you instead, and if I had a phone, I could do that, couldn't I?'

'Yes,' he said. 'You could. Maybe a phone is a good idea.'

She beamed at him. 'But it has to be a good phone, like my friend's,' she warned him. 'Otherwise there's no point.'

'Message received and understood,' he promised.

Bloody hell, how much was that going to cost him? Still, she was worth every penny. He wanted to start rebuilding his relationship with her, and if she had a phone, it would be so much easier. She was right about that. He would go into Helmston tomorrow and see what he could find. And while he was at it, he'd have to push Eliza about access to Amy over Christmas. It was time she saw Eight Bells. He supposed he'd better get a Christmas tree.

9

I woke up on Christmas morning to the sound of rain pattering on my bedroom window. No white Christmas for us this year then, sadly. I got out of bed and wandered over to open the curtains, then stared out across the North Sea. The landscape was painted in shades of grey today. The clouds hung low and heavy over water the colour of slate, and there didn't appear to be much to inspire festive cheer.

I rested my forehead on the glass, contemplating another Christmas Day without Derry. What was he doing now, I wondered? I imagined him exchanging gifts with my father, and the jealousy twisted my guts, catching me by surprise with its ferocity. Derry should be with me, not with that man. He was mine, not his!

Tears blurred my eyes and I blinked them away, knowing they would be a waste of time. I had a lot to get through today, and now wasn't the time for wallowing.

I quickly showered and dressed and made myself a cup of tea to start the day. Jack would be here soon to start prepping for the Christmas lunches, so I didn't want to hang around up here for long. I skipped breakfast, telling myself I'd eat later, and made my way downstairs, thinking I could at least start peeling and chopping vegetables.

As I made my way downstairs, I could hear the faint sound of music. It sounded like some jolly, festive pop song, and I

106

hesitated. Surely… Then I shook my head. It wouldn't be Derry. Of course it wouldn't.

I pushed open the kitchen door and smiled as Jack turned to face me, vegetable peeler in one hand, potato in another.

'What are you doing here so early?' I said, as he beamed at me.

'I didn't see any point in staying at home when I was up and awake, and there's so much to be done,' he said. He put down the peeler and the potato and hurried over to hug me. 'Merry Christmas, Rhiannon.'

'Merry Christmas, Jack,' I said. 'You do know you're a saint?'

'Don't be silly. Just doing my job.' He tilted my chin and scrutinised my face. 'How are you doing? No tears this morning?'

I wanted to laugh and deny there'd even been a possibility of such a thing, but I'd broken down in front of him the first Christmas that Derry wasn't there, and he'd caught me in tears a couple of times in the intervening years, so I knew there was no point.

'Maybe a hint of a tear,' I admitted cautiously. 'Don't worry. I'm in control.'

'I'm not worried, my darling,' he said. 'I just hurt when you hurt, that's all.'

I put my arms around his waist and rested my head against his chest as he stroked my hair. I seriously don't know what I'd have done without him. He'd been my rock, not just since Derry left, but since before my son was even born. Other than Derry himself, he was my only real family. My father certainly didn't count and, sadly, even my mother had apparently forsaken me when I got pregnant, although I sort of understood why. Standing up to my father wasn't easy to do. He was such an aggressive, bombastic man. I simply couldn't understand how Derry had stood him so long. All I could think was that either my father had mellowed astonishingly over the years, or he was a competent actor.

'Right,' I said, deciding I wasn't going to let my mind wander down that path again, 'enough of this. I have something for you.'

'I've got something for you, too,' he said, letting me go and heading over to the larder. 'Close your eyes.'

I did as I was told, smiling as I heard him opening the larder door and moving around inside it. The door closed and I heard his voice in front of me. 'Hold out your hands.'

I held them out and Jack lowered them slightly and folded them around a parcel that seemed surprisingly large. It felt like...

'Is it a painting?'

'Open your eyes,' he said, and I did.

'Sorry I didn't wrap it,' he said. 'I only managed to collect it last night and I didn't have the time or energy by then, to be honest. An artist from Whitby painted it. Do you like it? He did it from a photo but added a few additional touches. I think he's done an amazing job personally.'

I tilted the painting so I could get a better look at it and he tutted impatiently.

'I am stupid sometimes. Hang on.' He took it from me, held it in front of him and stepped back so I could see it properly.

It was a landscape painting of The Hare and Moon and, as Jack had said, the artist had added a few of his own touches. Instead of electric lights, lanterns glowed in the windows. We didn't have a wooden pub sign, but there was one in the portrait, swinging from a hook near the door. A moonlit sky and a brown hare gazing up at it sat beneath the name on the shabby wooden board, making the pub look even more like the ancient seafront inn it was. Above the red roof and crooked chimneys, starry skies glittered, and a sliver of moon reflected its light onto a midnight sea. Beside the whitewashed walls, two old rowing boats lay, oars lying within them as if they'd been left ready to be pulled down the slipway and into the water at any moment. It looked like the old smugglers' haunt it had once been, and there was a real magical feel to it that took my breath away.

'Do you like it?' He sounded anxious and I raised my eyes to his, hardly able to put into words how much I loved it.

'Oh, Jack. It's perfect!'

He smiled, obviously relieved. 'I'm so glad. I hoped you would.'

'Jack, you're amazing.' Tears welled up in my eyes again and I blinked them away, not wanting to upset him. 'It's the loveliest present I've ever had. Honestly, I don't know what to say.'

'You don't have to say anything,' he told me. 'Your face says it all, and that's thanks enough for me.'

'It's not going in the bar,' I decided. 'It's too personal and too precious for that. I'll put it upstairs in the living room. Pride of place. Oh, thank you so much.'

'No worries,' he said. 'Now, I'll just lean it against the wall a minute while I give you something else.'

'Not another present!' This was embarrassing. I'd got him a CD player and some audio stories — discs of his favourite crime books. Jack loved reading, but he'd struggled badly with his eyesight during the last couple of years, finding paperbacks difficult to read. He wouldn't contemplate getting the internet, so an e-reader was out of the question. I'd thought audio books might be the way to go, but it seemed a poor exchange for such a beautiful and thoughtful painting, and now he was telling me there was another present.

'Not from me,' he said. He handed me a small package. 'This arrived at my flat last week. It's for you. I just had to keep it safe.'

I looked down at the package and saw the label, and my heart thudded.

To Mum
Merry Christmas and a happy New Year
Lots of love
Derry xx

Lots of love! Well, that was an improvement. Usually, any card or gift I received from him simply read, *Love Derry* on it. This message was practically *War and Peace* in comparison.

I tore open the wrapping paper, lifted the lid on a cardboard box which bore the name of a well-known Cornish jewellery company, and carefully removed a black velvet bag. Inside were two items. The first was a Celtic design hair slide, fashioned from pewter, with a walnut pin on the back, perfect for holding back my thick, dark hair. The second item was a brooch. Openwork pewter formed a crescent moon, and in the curve of the moon sat a hare, gazing upwards.

'How lovely,' I breathed. I reached into the bag and brought out two little cards, which explained the meaning of the gifts. The one for the brooch gave me a brief outline of the meaning of the hare and the moon and its connection with femininity, rebirth, and the goddesses Ostara and Oestra. But it was the one for the hair slide that reduced me to tears yet again.

'Jack, look!'

He took the card from my shaking fingers and read it, then looked up at me and smiled. I could see by his expression that he realised how much this meant to me, and that it meant a lot to him, too.

'The Eternal Bond,' he said, glancing back at the card. 'This stunning Celtic design depicts in knotwork a mother holding her child. An eternal bond that can never be broken. Well,' he said heavily, 'I think that says all you need to know, don't you?'

'You think it means he's forgiven me?'

Jack sighed. 'Honestly, Rhiannon, I don't think there was anything to forgive you for. I keep telling you this. But since you and Derry seem to believe you did something dreadful, then in that context, yes, I would say he's forgiven you. And about time if he has,' he added. 'I'll give him a piece of my mind one day.'

'No! Please don't,' I begged. 'I don't want him to fall out with you, too. And anyway, if he's coming round, if he's ready to forgive…'

His eyes crinkled in the corners and he said gently, 'Why don't you call him? Wish him a merry Christmas.'

'I should, shouldn't I?' I stared down at the brooch and the hair slide, thinking. 'I ought to thank him for these lovely gifts if nothing else.'

'Well, go on then,' he said. 'I'm going to get on with the veggies now, so I'll leave you to it.'

'I won't be a minute,' I promised him.

'Take your time, darling. Nothing more important than the bond between parent and child.'

I gave him a grateful smile for being so understanding and hurried into the hall to call Derry.

My nerves jangled as the phone rang and rang and bit by bit my new-found optimism drained away. He wasn't going to answer, was he? Eventually the messaging service switched on, and I trembled with nerves as I heard Derry's voice.

'Hi, this is Derry. Sorry I can't take your call right now. If you leave a message, I'll get back to you when I can. Cheers!'

'Derry?' I gripped my phone tightly. 'It's your mum. Just wanted to say, thank you so much for the lovely presents. They're beautiful and I love them so much. I hope you got the package I sent you. Anyway, I just — I just want to wish you a happy Christmas and I hope you're having a great time, and I love you so much. Bye. Love you. Bye.'

'That was short and sweet,' Jack said, raising an eyebrow as I returned to the kitchen, feeling somewhat subdued.

'He didn't answer. I left a message.'

'Probably still in bed,' Jack said reassuringly. 'Never was much of an early riser, was he? And it is still early you know.'

I glanced at the clock, realising he was right. It was only seven-thirty and Derry might well still be asleep.

'Tell you what,' Jack said. 'Let's have a cup of tea before we do anything else. Kerry will be here around nine and we've plenty of time.'

I nodded. 'A cup of tea would be just the ticket. I'll put the kettle on. Would you like something to eat? A bacon sandwich perhaps?'

He wrinkled his nose, which surprised me. Jack loved a bacon sandwich.

'Not today,' he said. 'Feel a bit off and I don't fancy any food. Just tea would be fine.'

'What do you mean, you feel a bit off?' I asked. 'Do you want to have a lie down for a while?"

'I'm fine. Probably a bit tired. I'm sure I'll buck up soon. Now, I've got three turkeys cooking in the ovens, and everything's in hand, so don't worry.'

'I'm not worried,' I said. 'I have complete faith in you.'

He picked up the peeler and turned back to the pile of potatoes waiting for him. 'I'm glad to hear it. Between you, me, and Kerry, we'll manage beautifully. This Christmas is going to run like clockwork. You'll see.'

I believed him. Jack was an expert when it came to events like this. Before long, Kerry had arrived, and after exchanging token gifts and hugs and Christmas greetings, the three of us got on with our tasks. We had a lot to get through, and soon the pub was a hive of activity. The smells coming from the oven were enough to make our stomachs growl, and I had to admit I was looking forward to my own Christmas lunch as soon as the guests had been served.

'I'll start laying the tables,' I told Jack, who nodded without replying.

Kerry and I were soon hard at work in the dining room, making sure each table wore a crisp, white tablecloth, sparkling cutlery wrapped in crisp napkins, and rather attractive festive floral displays that I'd bought from Helmston market a few days before, and which I'd thought would provide a pretty finishing touch.

'I'll go and get the condiments,' Kerry announced, and hurried out of the dining room.

I glanced at the clock. We were in plenty of time. It would be another hour or so before the guests started to arrive. I was quite sure we were on schedule.

'Rhiannon!'

I heard Kerry's call and something in her tone turned my blood to ice. I dropped a bundle of cutlery on the nearest table and ran out of the dining room into the kitchen. Jack was slumped on the floor, his eyes half closed, his face pale.

'What is it?' I crouched on the floor beside him and took his hand. 'Jack! Jack, can you hear me?'

When he didn't respond, I glanced up at Kerry, terrified. 'What happened?'

'He said his head hurt, then he started being slurry and weird, and saying stuff that made no sense. Next thing I knew he'd sort of slid down the units onto the floor. He terrified me.'

'Call an ambulance,' I instructed. 'Tell them it's an emergency.'

I tried to make Jack as comfortable as I could by putting cushions behind his head. He didn't seem to be aware of where he was, and certainly couldn't answer my increasingly frantic questions. He didn't look like Jack at all. There was something different in his expression, and his eyes seemed to be staring at nothing. I'd never been more afraid in my life.

As the paramedics bundled him into the ambulance, some thirty minutes later, one of them asked for Jack's next of kin.

My mind was blank as I gazed at the man I loved dearly, lying so helpless on a stretcher in the ambulance.

'I don't know,' I said, feeling useless. 'He's never told me.'

'You're his employer, aren't you?' she asked, surprised. 'Don't you have contact details for him? He must have someone.'

Tears rolled down my cheeks.

'Me,' I murmured. 'He's got me.'

****

Harry hated Christmas Day. In fact, if he had his way, he'd ban the damn thing, like Oliver Cromwell had, back in the dim and distant past. Well, someone like Oliver Cromwell anyway. He wasn't that sure about history, but he had a feeling it had something to do with those Roundhead chaps. Anyway, whoever had done away with Christmas had had the right idea, in his opinion.

He woke up that morning to rain, which didn't make him feel any better. At least it wasn't snowing, which would have been even worse. He knew, by the sick feeling in his stomach, that it was here — the day he'd been dreading. Christmas Day without either of his children.

'Right,' he said out loud to himself, as he clambered out of bed. 'No way am I going to sit here and wallow. Time to get on with some work.'

Eight Bells was beginning to take shape, thanks to the work of Gareth, and the enthusiasm of Tally, who seemed to have become a permanent fixture in his life. When she'd said she might take him up on his offer to visit whenever she liked, she hadn't been joking. She turned up most evenings and, although it had irritated him at first, as time passed he found he was glad of her company. Despite their inauspicious start, they'd already become good friends.

It was one such evening, as they sat together watching some romcom she liked on the television, that Tally suggested he ought to think about turning the place back into a hotel.

'Oh, don't you start,' he'd groaned.

She turned to him, surprised. 'Why, who else has suggested it?'

'My architect pal, Gareth. He thinks it would be a good idea to consider it anyway. If not a proper hotel, then at least a guest house.'

Tally folded her arms. 'Well, don't you agree? This place is far too big for one person, Harry. You'll be rattling around in here, completely lost.'

'But Amy will be able to stay here one day,' he said. 'And maybe even Rufus, too. Eventually.'

'But even so, there's loads of room. And it would give you something to do. You don't seem to have done much on the job-hunting front.'

Harry had stayed silent for a while, not wanting to be drawn into a conversation about his employment prospects. He'd pretended to focus on the dismal film instead, but Tally hadn't let it drop. She'd brought it up again a day or two later, and when Gareth called him to ask if he'd done any more thinking on the subject, Harry had given in and accepted the inevitable.

Really, he thought, it did make sense. The house was too big for him, even if his dream of both his children staying with him at times came true. And it was in such a lovely spot, with those sea views, that it was likely to be a popular holiday location.

Tally had done some digging around and had told him he could make a sizeable income from it, especially in the summer.

'And all you need do is offer bed and breakfast. It's not like you'd have people hanging around you all day, and you won't be at anyone's beck and call. Do you think you could manage to cook all those breakfasts?'

Harry had been indignant at her doubtful expression. 'Manage breakfast? I'll have you know my breakfasts are legendary. In fact, I'm quite nifty in the kitchen. I make a mean roast dinner.'

He would prove it to her by taking photos of the Christmas feast he intended to cook for Amy. He'd pulled out all the stops, determined that she would enjoy her second Christmas Day with him as much as she'd enjoy the real deal with Eliza and that man. He'd made the decision to ignore Christmas Day on the twenty-fifth and celebrate on Boxing Day with his daughter instead.

He'd given Amy her main present but had a whole stack of gifts for her to open tomorrow. He'd also sent some gifts and money to Melody to give to Rufus and intended to call him to speak to him in person, but that would obviously have to wait until later in the day, given the time difference. What would Melody think to him running a guest house? He could almost hear her laughter and felt a sinking sensation in the pit of his stomach.

He knew he had to take his mind off his troubles, so after making himself a decaffeinated coffee and forcing himself to eat a bowl of bran cereal, he set to work stripping off the dreadful flock paper in the lounge downstairs. He'd hired a steamer and was glad he'd had the foresight to do so, since the wallpaper seemed to have little intention of loosening its vice like grip on the walls.

By the time he'd done one wall it was already lunchtime, and Harry was starving, which was when he realised that all he had in stock were the ingredients for Amy's Christmas feast tomorrow. He should have done some shopping, but he'd wanted to avoid the supermarket and the crowds and the whole *Jingle Bells* vibe that he so hated.

'Well,' Harry said to himself, sinking into the sofa, 'this is a lovely predicament, isn't it? Happy Christmas, Harry.'

He put his head in his hands, staring gloomily at the bare floorboards beneath his feet. They weren't in bad condition, he thought distractedly. Maybe, instead of carpeting the lounge, he should polish and varnish the boards and scatter a few rugs around. He'd see what Tally thought.

He sat up straight in alarm. Where had that come from? What did it matter what Tally thought? He realised suddenly that he'd grown worryingly dependent on her. She was the only person who came to Eight Bells, and it occurred to him how much he looked forward to her visits. Tally had undoubtedly made the last month or so more bearable. He had no one else in the village apart from Eliza and Amy, and even they were erratic, being sometimes pleasant and warm, and other times distinctly frosty, often for no reason that he could fathom.

He had a feeling that Tally got as much from their friendship as he did, if not more. She seemed to need someone who would listen to her without judging, as she poured out her worries and troubles. Being honest with himself, Harry recognised it was good for him to acknowledge that other people had their problems, too. It had been easy, throughout the last couple of years, for him to wallow and believe that bad things only happened to him, and everyone else's life was perfect. Tally had been a welcome distraction, but he hadn't grasped how much he'd come to rely on her for companionship until now.

This wasn't good. If anyone in her family found out, it could cause real problems for him with access to Amy. Besides, he didn't want Tally getting the wrong idea about their relationship. He liked her. She was a nice girl, and very kind-hearted. They'd had some great chats and a few laughs, and she'd brightened up his days considerably, but there was nothing more to it than that. At least, not from his point of view. He hoped she understood that.

Oh, God, he was fit to drop, and he'd only done one bloody wall. Harry glanced at his watch and sighed, hearing the rumblings in his stomach. Fuck it. He was going to the pub. There was bound to be something on offer there, even if it was only a packet of salted peanuts.

10

The Hare and Moon seemed busy at first, and Harry could smell something delicious cooking in the kitchen. His stomach growled in appreciation, and he thought maybe a packet of peanuts wouldn't cut it. But he had no doubt that Christmas lunches were pre-booked, and there'd be nothing going spare for the likes of him.

The bar looked like half a forest had been moved in. Apart from a Christmas tree in one corner, there was greenery everywhere. Sprigs of mistletoe and boughs of holly hung from every ivy-trailed beam, and evergreen garlands and wreaths were plentiful enough to make Harry feel as if he'd wandered into a Christmas shop by mistake. Except, maybe not. There were no gaudy glittery decorations in here. No flashing lights or tinsel. The light in the room came from the roaring fire in the grate, and candles and lanterns placed at a safe distance from the greenery and careless elbows.

He waited at the bar, gradually aware of the rising level of conversation coming from the dining room. He wandered in and glanced round, half hoping there was an empty table, and someone would take pity and allow him to place an order. He noted that none of the people were eating, and that the tables were bare of food. He looked at his watch again. Nearly half past two. Surely lunch should have been served by now.

The young woman who'd refused to serve Tally that fateful night — Kerry? — hurried into the room behind him, clearly flustered. Immediately one or two of the customers stood and began calling to her for her attention.

She threw up her hands. 'Please, can you be patient? I'm afraid we've had an unforeseen problem in the kitchen.'

'Maybe so, love,' someone said, 'but this is our Christmas lunch and we've paid good money for it. Now, are we going to get fed or not?'

The young woman nodded. 'I promise, you'll get your lunch, but it may be delayed a while.'

'For God's sake!'

There was a general muttering that sounded far from understanding.

Harry leaned towards the barmaid, who looked close to tears.

'Don't let them upset you. If it's late, it's late. They'll have to lump it, won't they?'

Kerry shook her head. 'Thing is, they might not get it at all at this rate. Rhiannon's doing her best, but she's no cook.'

'Then why offer Christmas lunches?' Harry asked, perplexed.

'How were we to know our chef would be taken ill?' she said stroppily. She cast a wary look at the diners, obviously worried she'd been overheard.

'You're telling me there's no one to cook the dinners?'

'Like I said,' she repeated, 'Rhiannon's doing her best.'

Harry saw the anxiety in her eyes and knew he had no choice.

'I can cook a roast dinner,' he said. 'Do you think she'd like a hand?'

Kerry's eyes widened. 'Are you serious?'

'Of course. Happy to help.'

She bit her lip, thinking about it. 'Not sure… I'll have to ask her.'

'Well, go on then,' Harry said. 'I don't think now's the time to procrastinate, do you?'

Kerry needed no second bidding. She shot out of the room, and Harry wandered back into the bar, wondering what on earth he thought he was doing. That was all he needed, wasn't it? Spending an afternoon ankle deep in gravy for the benefit of loads of ungrateful customers, who had absolutely nothing to do with him anyway. He must be mad. Oh well, maybe Rhiannon would say no. Anyway, she was a witch, wasn't she? Perhaps, he thought with some amusement, she was casting a spell to whip up Christmas lunch at that very moment.

When Kerry rushed into the bar and beckoned to him. Harry gave an inward sigh at his own folly and followed her through the door marked private, finding himself in a large, functional kitchen that looked out of place in this old building. It was all splashbacks and white tiles and stainless steel, and lacked the character of the rest of the pub. Although, he mused, that was probably a good thing. It was reassuring that it was so modern and clean. There was nothing worse than an old, shabby kitchen — as well he knew. Ugh!

'He's here, Rhiannon.'

'Thank you, Kerry.'

A vision of beauty turned to face Harry and he caught his breath. He'd seen her that night he first arrived in the village, obviously, but the place had been in semi-darkness then, and besides, he'd been far too stressed and anxious, and too busy trying to cover those feelings up, to pay her much attention, beyond noticing her old-fashioned clothes and lack of a Yorkshire accent.

Faced with her now, though, he thought he'd never seen anyone so utterly stunning. She was small and slender, with a heart-shaped face, large dark eyes, and a rosebud mouth. Long, dark curls fell to her shoulders; she wore a wine-coloured top with lace sleeves, and a long black skirt, with black lace-up boots. She was unusual and gothic and romantic and totally exquisite.

'You're Harry, aren't you.'

It wasn't a question.

'That's right. But don't let that put you off.'

'If you can cook, I don't care if you're Rasputin. Just tell me now, do you think you can manage twenty-four Christmas lunches?'

'Twenty-four…' Harry blew out his cheeks. 'Bloody hell.'

'Jack — he's my chef…' Rhiannon's voice wobbled, and her eyes filled with tears.

'Are you okay?'

Kerry patted Rhiannon's arm. 'He'll be all right, Rhiannon. He's in the best place.'

'And I should be with him.' Rhiannon gazed up at Harry. 'They gave him aspirin. I think they must suspect a stroke. He seemed fine this morning, that's the thing. He said he was tired, that's all. If I'd had any idea that he wasn't well...'

'But you didn't,' Kerry said. 'And you know Jack. He wouldn't want to let you down.'

'He cooked all the turkeys,' Rhiannon told Harry. 'I took them out about twenty minutes ago, but I haven't even started on the rest of the stuff. My mind's gone blank, and I'm so stressed about Jack.'

'Right.' Harry took off his coat and began to roll up his sleeves. 'I'll wash my hands and we'll get started, shall we? You need to tie your hair up,' he told her. 'Kerry, can you go back to the dining room and try to keep the customers happy with drinks for now?'

'On the house,' Rhiannon added. She gave Harry a tentative smile. 'Are you sure you're up for this?'

'Of course. No problem.' The fact that he'd never cooked for more than four people before was neither here nor there. Harry had a job to do, and besides, it was a relief to have something to take his mind off his own disastrous relationship with Christmas. This could turn out to be a godsend.

****

'Well,' Harry said, leaning back in his chair, 'that was exceptionally tasty, if I do say so myself.'

Kerry laughed. 'Nothing like blowing your own trumpet. Mind you, you're right. It was good grub; I'll give you that.'

'Have you saved some for Rhiannon?'

'Of course. Keeping warm in the oven.' Kerry lifted her phone and peered at the screen. 'Nearly six. She should be back soon, I reckon.'

'Do you think she'll mind that we closed the pub after the lunches were finished?'

Kerry shook her head. 'She'll understand. Besides, we deserved a break and something to eat after all that. Well, you did, especially. You worked really hard.'

'We all worked really hard,' he insisted. 'You were backwards and forwards all day, and Rhiannon worked flat out, too, and when you think how worried she was…'

'Thank you,' Kerry said, clearly meaning it.

Harry swallowed, quite touched by her thanks. 'You're welcome.'

'We'd never have done it without your help,' she admitted. 'It would have been a catastrophe, and Rhiannon's got enough on her plate.'

'I gather Jack's more than her chef,' Harry said tentatively. 'Are they — involved?'

Kerry laughed. 'Involved? You mean, are they shagging? God, no! Ugh! Jack's been here forever. He's like an old uncle to her or something.'

'Ah.' He wondered why he was so relieved to hear it. 'What did she say when she rang?'

'Not much. Just that he was comfortable, and she'd tell me more when she got back. She should be here soon. She was going to get a taxi.'

'Is it true that she's a witch?' Hell, why had he said that? He sounded like a frightened five-year-old. 'Not a real witch, obviously, but you know.'

Kerry grinned. 'Didn't take long for the gossip to reach you, did it?'

'Is that all it is? Gossip?'

She shrugged. 'She doesn't run naked under the moonlight or anything like that. Some of the blokes in this village would be selling tickets if she did.' She rolled her eyes. 'She finds her own way. Does her own thing. That's Rhiannon for you. I'm not sure she'd label herself in any way. She just believes what she believes.'

'I couldn't help noticing the bar looks like Sherwood Forest,' he said. 'Is that part of it?'

'Yeah. That was for Yule. She tends to celebrate her own special days. Sabbats, she calls them. So for her, Yule is the biggie, rather than Christmas. She'll be doing stuff for Easter for the local kids, but to her Ostara is the sacred celebration. Then there was Samhain on Halloween.' She grinned. 'You'll remember that one.'

'And she includes the locals in these things?'

'She never forces her beliefs on anyone, and some things she keeps private. But if events coincide, like with Samhain and Halloween, or Beltane and May Day, she loves to get everyone involved in ways that won't scare them off. Beltane's great. We have a May Queen and a Green Man, and there's always a bonfire and a big feast at the pub afterwards. Some of the villagers laugh at her, and she knows it, but she doesn't mind so long as people are happy. Oh!' She glanced up at a knock on the door. 'That may be her now.'

'Or an irate customer, wanting to know why he can't have a Christmas drink here,' Harry pointed out. 'I'll take these empty plates into the kitchen. Call me if you need help with that irate customer.'

He strode into the kitchen, plates in hand, reflecting that what had been a nightmare for Rhiannon and Kerry had proved to be a welcome distraction for him. Not that he wished any harm to Jack, of course. Far from it. It was just that, as it turned out, working flat out in the kitchen, preparing Christmas lunch for a bar full of hungry and rather disgruntled guests, had been exactly what he needed to take his mind off the fact that he was alone at Christmas, with both his son and daughter spending the day with their respective mothers' partners instead of with him.

He and Kerry had decided that, after the last of the guests left, they'd close the pub, have a well-deserved drink in the bar, and eat their own Christmas lunch at last.

Now that was over and he finally had a minute to himself, he decided it was time to call his son. He felt hugely optimistic and excited, but it didn't take long for Melody, who was clearly in a bad mood with him, to change all that.

'You're late,' she snapped, and he cringed at the fake American accent she'd adopted recently.

'It couldn't be helped,' he explained. 'I was dealing with an emergency.'

'Sure you were. Well, if you're hoping to speak to Rufus, you're gonna be disappointed.'

'What? What do you mean? Where is he?'

'Delivering presents to Chuck's family.'

'Are you serious?'

'Of course I'm serious. He gets on great with them all and they love seeing him. Chuck was going to go alone, but Rufus begged to go with him, and we couldn't say no, just because you couldn't be bothered to ring when you said you would. He's been up hours. You know what he's like at Christmas. You could have rung him two hours ago and it would have been fine, but no, you had to wait until nine when obviously we'd be doing other things.'

'I told you, I had an emergency.'

'Well, there you go. What can you do?'

Harry stared at the screen, noting the Botoxed forehead and lips plump with filler, and wondered what he'd ever seen in Melody Bird. He'd loved her hair, which was blonde and curly and wild, but it was scraped back into a ponytail right now, focusing his attention on her mannequin-like face, and he saw the coldness in her blue eyes and thought he must have been mad to leave Eliza and Amy for her. You reaped what you sowed, and there was no doubt he'd got what he deserved. Even so, it seemed desperately cruel to him that he should have to battle for every precious bit of contact with his son.

'When will he be back?'

'He's not coming back here. We're all going to church. I'm meeting them there, and then we're going to Chuck's mom's for lunch.'

'Church?' Harry could hardly believe his ears. 'Since when do you go to church?'

'I have a lot to thank God for,' she said. 'Getting rid of you, for a start.'

'Thanks, Melody.'

'Oh, what do you care? You're back in Yorkshire, aren't you? Back with your precious first family. You never really left them in your heart anyway and you know it. It was always bloody Eliza and her saintly ways that did it for you, and Rufus never mattered half as much as your darling Amy.'

The injustice left him breathless.

'I left Eliza for you!' he reminded her. 'I gave up everything to be with you. And don't ever say that Rufus didn't matter as much as Amy. I loved him just as much and you know it.'

'I'm sure I know no such thing,' Melody snapped, apparently forgetting she had an American accent these days. 'At least Chuck gives him his undivided attention. It's made all the difference. Rufus is thriving. Stop trying to spoil things. We're a family here, whether you like it or not, so concentrate on your English life now and leave us alone.'

'But what about Rufus? I need to talk to him, to wish him a merry Christmas.'

'I'll tell him you said hello,' she said, rather grudgingly.

'Did he get the presents I sent him?' Harry asked desperately.

'They were okay. He's a bit obsessed with basketball right now. He and Chuck were out shooting hoops first thing this morning. He was more interested in the sporty stuff we got him.'

Harry slumped. 'Right. Well, can I call him later or not?'

'There wouldn't be much point. He can hardly talk to you in church, and it would be rude to call us when we're at Chuck's family home. We'll be there until bedtime. In fact, we may stay overnight. They have a huge house with lots of spare rooms so... Really, it might be best if you called again tomorrow.'

'I have Amy tomorrow,' Harry murmured, more to himself than to her, but Melody had ears like radar sets when it suited her.

'Oh, well, there you are! Amy first again. Nothing new under the sun. Bye, Harry.'

The call ended, leaving Harry staring at a blank screen, wondering how it had come to this.

He scraped the leftovers in the bin, rinsed the plates under a tap and stacked them in the dishwasher, a sinking feeling in the pit of his stomach as he realised he probably wasn't going to get to talk to Rufus over Christmas at all. Melody would find a way to prevent it, no doubt about it. And the worst of it was, he was sure that Rufus either wouldn't notice, or if he did, he wouldn't care. He was too besotted with pretty-boy Chuck these days.

'Fuck it!' He slammed the dishwasher door shut and thumped it for good measure.

'Having a bad day?'

Harry spun round and gulped as he saw Rhiannon standing in the doorway, looking small and rather vulnerable as she clutched her coat in her hands and stared at him with large, dark eyes.

'God, I'm so sorry. I didn't damage it. At least, I don't think I did...' He turned his head to check, but thankfully couldn't see any dents in the dishwasher. That would have been typical, and all he needed.

She gave him a rueful smile. 'It's okay. I think you've earned an outlet for your frustration. It must have been a tough afternoon. I can't thank you enough.'

'Oh, no. No! You don't understand. It wasn't because of — this. It was my son, you see. Well, my ex-wife more than my son. Christmas Day. And I don't get to see him or even speak to him, and it's hard...' His voice trailed off and he shrugged. 'Sorry.'

She threw her coat on the table and walked towards him. 'You don't have to be sorry,' she said. 'I understand, really I do. I haven't seen or heard from my son today either. It breaks my heart.'

She stopped close to him, and he saw her eyes wet with unshed tears and had a sudden incredibly powerful urge to wrap his arms around her and hold her. He blinked and turned away slightly, knowing it was best not to go down that road.

'Jack.' God, his voice was so gruff! He cleared his throat. 'Er, how is Jack?'

Rhiannon leaned against the dishwasher and ran a hand through her dark hair. 'Much better than he was, thank goodness.'

'Have they said what it was?'

'I think they suspect a mini stroke. He's seeing a specialist tomorrow anyway, so we should know for certain then.'

'Try not to worry too much,' Harry said, hearing the anxiety in her voice. 'I'm sure he'll be okay. He'll no doubt be home tomorrow. You know how they like to throw people out at the earliest opportunity these days.'

'He's not going home. He's coming here, whether he likes it or not.'

'Does he know that?' Harry smiled, hearing the determination in her voice.

'Oh, he will do. He'll insist he'll be fine alone, of course, but there's no way I'm letting that happen. I need to be able to keep an eye on him.' She sighed. 'We need to talk about his job. He shouldn't be working full-time now anyway. We've had the conversation before, but he's always managed to wriggle out of it somehow. He's terribly stubborn.'

'Is he old enough to retire?'

She laughed. 'Old enough to retire? He should have retired years ago. He's seventy-five!'

'Wow!' Harry puffed out his cheeks. 'I'm impressed. This afternoon just about knackered me. How does a bloke of that age manage it every single day?'

'He's a miracle,' Rhiannon said, and he heard the fondness in her tone. 'I'd be lost without him.'

'Maybe he knows that,' Harry suggested. 'Maybe he doesn't want to let you down.'

'No doubt about it,' she said sadly. 'But he's going to have to come to terms with that, because I can't go through all this again. He needs to slow down and enjoy life more. It can't all be about work, and I'm afraid that's what his life has been. All work.'

'What about his family? Doesn't he spend time with them?'

Rhiannon twisted a lock of her hair around one of her fingers. 'I'm sorry to say he hasn't got any family. That's why he fills his days with this pub and his job. It's such a shame. He's such a lovely man and he deserves better.'

Harry couldn't help but think that, one day, this could happen to him. What if he reached Jack's age and spent every day alone, with no family to be there for him? Was this his future? He thought it a scary prospect indeed, and his mood plunged even further.

'I'm so sorry,' she said. 'I'm rambling on when you probably want to get off home.'

'Oh, no, it's fine. I'm in no hurry, honestly. We saved you a plate of Christmas lunch, you know. It's in the oven, keeping warm.'

'Yes, Kerry said. It's so kind of you. Maybe later. I need a bath I think.'

He realised he was being dismissed. 'Okay, well, I'll get off then.'

'Money!'

'I'm sorry?'

'I haven't paid you.'

Harry held up his hands. 'God, no! I don't want paying.'

'Oh, but you must take something. You've worked all afternoon and it's Christmas Day.'

'Season of goodwill,' he said with a slight shrug. 'Let's just say, I owed the universe something. I'm hoping karma's taking notes.'

She stared at him for a moment then gave him an understanding smile. 'Thank you, Harry.'

Harry's knees trembled as she said his name, and he wondered if he'd gone completely mad. Rhiannon may be an eccentric, with some strange beliefs, but my God she was beautiful, and there was something so different about her that she left him feeling quite weak. He couldn't remember ever having such a strong and immediate reaction to any woman before. Even Melody had been the one to do the chasing in the early days, hard though that was to imagine now. Maybe the villagers were right. Maybe Rhiannon was a witch after all.

'You're welcome,' he said. Because, after all, what else was there to say? This wasn't supposed to happen. How very unexpected.

11

Amy's eyes were like saucers as she gazed around the living room. 'Wow.'

'Wow good, or wow bad?' Harry asked nervously.

Amy looked up at him, her brow furrowed. 'Well, what do you think?'

He glanced around at the walls that had been stripped of the flock wallpaper but hadn't yet been skimmed and painted. 'This isn't the room I use,' he said quickly. 'Come through to the back. It's much nicer there.'

The back room was in a much better state already, the walls painted in a soft mushroom colour. He'd put a large rug on the floor to soften the starkness of bare floorboards, and there was a Christmas tree in the corner that dazzled with bright, shiny baubles and fairy lights, all hurriedly purchased the previous weekend so she wouldn't be disappointed.

Amy exchanged looks with Eliza.

'All right, it's not great,' Harry admitted.

'You said it,' Amy said.

'But look, we're starting work on it after Christmas. It's going to be fabulous when it's done, and you'll be getting your own room. Anyway, never mind all that. Would you like something to drink?'

'I don't know,' Amy said cautiously. 'Is it safe to drink here?'

'What do you mean, safe to drink here?'

'She watched a film about a Victorian family who died of cholera,' Eliza explained. 'Gabriel told her that it was caused by contaminated water, so you can hardly blame her for being wary.'

'There's nothing wrong with my water supply,' Harry protested. 'It's no different to yours or anyone else's in this village. Good God, can someone give me a break please?'

'All right, keep your hair on,' Amy said, rolling her eyes. 'What have you got?'

'What do you mean?'

'To drink,' she said sarcastically. 'What have you got to drink?'

'I have some cans of cola for you,' he said hopefully.

'Gabriel says cola's bad for you,' she informed him.

Eliza gave him an apologetic smile. 'I'm sure one can won't hurt, Amy,' she said.

Harry thought Gabriel sounded like an insufferable prig and that he'd quite like to throttle him one of these days. He pictured both Gabriel and Chuck meeting grisly deaths and the thought cheered him up immensely.

'What are you smirking at?' asked Eliza, suspicion in her tone.

'What? Oh, nothing. I have a bottle of banana milkshake if she'd prefer that?'

'Well, why don't you ask her?'

'Amy, would you—'

'I heard,' Amy said. 'I'll have that later. I'll have the cola first.'

'Please,' Eliza reminded her.

Amy tutted. 'Pur-lease.'

She threw herself onto the sofa and patted it. 'This isn't off a rubbish tip, is it?'

'No it isn't,' he said crossly. 'It's new.'

'It doesn't look new.'

'It was cheap, but it is new.'

'Why did you get a cheap sofa?'

'Because when this house is done, I'll be buying all new furniture.'

'Oh. Fair enough.'

Eliza raised her eyebrows at Harry. 'Nightmare, isn't she?'

He grinned. 'Just a bit.'

'Can I have a word with you?'

He groaned inwardly. What had he done now?

'Come through to the kitchen,' he said. 'I'm making a coffee and getting Amy's drink anyway.' Since she was clearly going to tell him off, like some naughty kid, at least she could do it away from Amy's mocking gaze.

He led her through, filled the kettle under the tap and flicked the switch. 'Do you want to get Amy's can out of the fridge? And do you want a coffee?'

She shook her head. 'I'm not staying. I — hang on.'

She took the can of cola through to Amy, then returned to the kitchen and folded her arms, clearly contemplating what to say.

'Go on then.' Harry spooned decaf into his mug and turned to face her. 'What now?'

She nibbled at her thumbnail for a moment then burst out, 'Why the hell did you get Amy an iPhone?'

Harry sighed. 'I thought it would be about this.'

'Well, if you were expecting a reprimand, why did you do it?'

'Because she asked me to.'

'She asked us to get her a puppy!'

'Did you get her one?'

'No! You don't have to get her everything she wants you know. You can't buy children.'

'But you bought her a bike and a laptop. No different to buying her an iPhone, I'd have thought.'

She glared at him. 'That's different.'

'Why is it?'

'Because – because she needed a laptop for school, and all her friends had bikes. And they were second hand, too. Anyway, that's not the point. The point is, she's ten years old and doesn't need an iPhone. In fact, she doesn't need a phone at all.'

'But she said you wanted her to have one,' Harry said, bemused. 'She said you'd feel safer so you could keep in touch with her when she's out.'

'When she's out? She only goes to Joe's or Lexi's or Sophie's. If she goes to her friend's house, she stays there, and her friend's mother has a phone. I drop her off and pick her up everywhere she goes. Or Gabriel does.'

'Oh.' Harry sighed. 'Well, maybe she misled me.'

'Wrapped you round her little finger more like,' Eliza said. 'And did it have to be an iPhone? Any cheap phone would have done.' She shook her head slightly and her shoulders dropped, her stance softened. 'Look, Harry, I get it okay? I get that you want to be able to keep in touch with her, without having to call me first, and that's understandable. I even get that you want to please her, and if she asked you for a phone, you'd want to buy her one. But it could have been something a bit less showy.'

'She said it had to be an iPhone,' he admitted sheepishly. 'She said her friends had one, and she'd be the only girl in the class without a decent phone. Also, the signal only works on good phones.'

'She said what?'

They stared at each other, then burst out laughing.

'What's she like?' Eliza said, pushing a strand of hair away from her eyes. 'Honestly, the devious little madam.'

'You can't blame her for trying. I expect she thinks it's no more than I owe her.'

'Well…' Eliza tucked the annoying strand behind her ear. 'Anyway, don't go falling for it all again. She's clever, you know. You have to watch her like a hawk.'

'I see that,' he said. 'But really, does it matter that much? I just want her to like me.'

'She does like you, Harry,' Eliza said softly. 'It's trusting you that's the problem. I think you're going to be tested for a while, so be wary, okay?'

'Got it.'

He poured boiling water into his mug and stirred the coffee slowly.

'Did you hear from Rufus yesterday?' she asked.

He straightened. 'No. I tried, but he was busy.'

'I see.'

He heard the sympathy in her voice, and it rankled. 'It was okay. I had a busy day anyway.'

'Oh? Doing what?'

'I went to the pub—' he began, but she dismissed him with a wave of her hand.

'Brilliant,' she said sarcastically. 'Well, as long as you enjoyed yourself.' She glanced at her phone screen. 'I'd better be getting back. Hannah and Mikey will be demanding lunch.'

'Can't Gabriel cook them something?' he asked sulkily.

'He could, but I'd still like to be there to eat with them.' She hesitated at the door. 'You have got food for Amy's lunch I take it?'

'Of course! I'm cooking a full Christmas lunch actually.'

'I can't smell anything cooking.'

'I did the turkey last night — well, chicken actually. But the rest of it won't take long.'

'Are you up to cooking a full Christmas lunch?'

He narrowed his eyes. 'You'd be surprised.'

'I would indeed. You *have* changed, if that's the case, Harry. You could barely boil an egg when we were married.'

'I could,' he protested. 'I just chose not to.'

She gave him a knowing look and he crumbled. 'I know. I was a crap husband. You don't have to tell me.'

'See you later, Harry.'

Amy handed him the empty can as he and Eliza headed back into the living room. Harry put down his coffee, crumpled the cola can and put it on the coffee table beside his mug.

'I hope you recycle,' Amy said primly.

'Of course,' he said. 'Doesn't everyone?'

'I'm going, Amy,' Eliza said. 'Behave yourself for your father. No more trying to hoodwink him, okay?'

'What do you mean?' Amy asked.

'Oh, I think you know what I mean,' Eliza said sternly. 'Be good, and I'll pick you up at six, okay?'

'Okay.'

Harry showed Eliza to the door.

'Remember what I said,' she told him. 'If you're serious about sticking around in Kearton Bay, you're going to have to learn not to give in to her all the time. Be a real father to her, not Father Christmas.'

'I know, I know,' he said.

But as he closed the door, he knew, deep down that he would give Amy anything she wanted. He'd lost his son already. He could feel it in his gut. He couldn't lose Amy, too. Not now, when he had a real chance of winning her back. He would do anything for her. He hoped, for the sake of his ever-dwindling bank balance, that she wouldn't take advantage of that too often.

****

To my relief, Jack looked much better when I visited him the following evening, bearing grapes, his CD player, and a couple of audio books to cheer him up.

'I won't be needing all that,' he said cheerfully. 'I can go home tomorrow.'

'So soon?'

Obviously, it was wonderful that he wasn't so seriously ill that he needed to stay in, but it worried me that the same thing could happen to him again.

'So soon?' Jack shook his head. 'Not soon enough, if you ask me.'

'What was it? Have they said yet?' They must surely know by now. Jack had, after all, had a barrage of tests, including blood tests, an ECG, and an ultrasound. If they didn't know by now, they never would.

'A TIA — transient ischaemic attack,' he said. 'Sort of a mini stroke.'

'Well, what are they going to do about it?' I demanded. 'Surely you're not going to be released into the wild to fend for yourself?'

Jack wrinkled his nose. 'I've had a long chat with the doctor,' he assured me. 'I'm going to be put on medication — blood pressure and cholesterol tablets. It was quite an easy conversation. He told me to stop smoking.'

'You don't smoke.'

133

'Exactly, so that was an easy promise. Also told me to cut down on drinking.'

'You rarely drink.'

'I know! It gets better, doesn't it? He also told me to walk every day, and I told him I get off the Helmston bus in Farthingdale and walk from there to work and back every day, including up that steep hill, so I get a good cardiac workout regularly. He seemed at a bit of a loss after that, so he's decided the culprit's my penchant for bacon sandwiches — too salty, you see — and I'd better cut those out.'

I laughed. 'Well, as long as you know. Did he say anything about work?'

Jack looked cagey. 'Why would he?'

'Well,' I said carefully, 'if he's so concerned about your lifestyle, he must surely have had an opinion on the fact that you work such long hours at your age?'

'Never said a thing about it,' Jack said gruffly. 'Keeps me young, doesn't it?'

'Jack,' I said, 'we need to talk.'

He rearranged his pillows and folded his arms, his mouth pursed. I could see he'd already dug his heels in.

'You know you can't carry on working full time,' I said gently. 'It just isn't practical. I've been so selfish, wanting to keep you around for as long as I could. I should have put a stop to this ages ago. I'm so sorry.'

'Don't, Rhiannon,' he said.

I saw the anxiety in his eyes and my heart broke for him.

'Don't say you're firing me!'

'Of course I'm not firing you,' I soothed. 'But surely you're ready to retire? Think about it. You could have time to yourself for once, instead of having your entire life revolve around The Hare and Moon.'

'And what exactly am I supposed to do with all this time?' he asked. 'I haven't got any hobbies.'

'You could take up hobbies,' I suggested. 'It's never too late. The only reason you haven't got any is because of work, because of me. I'm so sorry, Jack.' I felt tears bubbling up as I realised how much of his life my own life had drained from him. 'All these years, all you've done is slave away in that kitchen, and supported Derry and me. We've robbed you of your free time and this is how you're repaid. It's so wrong. I can't tell you how bad I feel.'

'Rhiannon, don't! Don't cry, my darling.' Jack reached out and grasped my hand. 'You're not to blame. I chose this life. There was nothing else I wanted or needed. You've been my family all these years — you and Derry. What man could ask for more than to spend time with his family every day, eh?'

I wiped my eyes. 'Jack, is there anyone…? I mean, I know you said you had no family, but surely there's someone? When you went off in that ambulance and Kerry told me she'd had to give my name as your next of kin, it seemed so wrong. You must have relatives somewhere?'

'None I have any contact with,' he murmured. 'I think Kerry got it right, putting your name down. There's no one I've been closer to for the past twenty-nine years or thereabouts.'

Twenty-nine years. How had so much time gone by so fast? I thought back to those early days of our friendship and tried to remember what he'd told me. He'd trained in a London restaurant, I remembered, when he was young. His references had been impeccable, but I didn't recall him mentioning any family, even then.

I'd once asked him if he'd ever been married, and he'd said he'd never even come close. He'd sounded sad, and I'd felt rather sorry for him, without being entirely sure why. After all, I'd never come close to marrying either and it certainly didn't bother me. He said he'd come to North Yorkshire, looking for a fresh start, and had heard about the old pub on the seafront in Kearton Bay reopening under new management, and thought he'd chance his arm. Really, that was about as much as I knew. He was an extremely private man, and I'd always respected that. But looking back, it did seem a terrible shame that he'd been so isolated all these years. So cut off from those he'd once known and, presumably, loved.

'You're not going back to your house anyway,' I said, determined that there was at least one thing I could do for him. 'You're staying with me. Just until you're fully recovered,' I added as he started to protest. 'You can have my room. It's by far the nicest. I'll have one of the old guest rooms.'

'Don't be so daft,' he said. 'If you want me to stay with you, I will, but I can have the guest room.'

'No you won't. My room has an en suite bathroom for a start. I absolutely insist you take it.'

The truth was, I wanted Jack to have as much comfort as he could, so that he didn't rush to go home. My room was the largest in the pub, and I thought Jack would love the views out over the sea. If I could make him as welcome as possible, he would more likely stay longer, and I'd feel a lot easier, knowing there was someone around to keep an eye on him. The thought of him having another TIA, or worse, alone at his flat in Helmston filled me with dread. I wanted him under my roof where he'd be safer.

'All right. If you say so,' he said with a sigh.

'And about the job, Jack—'

'Please, Rhiannon, don't. It's all I've got. It's everything to me.'

I plucked nervously at my skirt, wondering what to do for the best. He shouldn't be working so hard, not at seventy-five. Running a pub restaurant was such hard work, and it was asking far too much of him.

'Okay,' I said. 'How about a compromise? I won't hire a new chef, but I will look for an assistant chef to help you. That way you won't be alone, and you can have a day off when you need it, too. What do you think?'

He pulled a face. 'Have someone else working in my kitchen?'

'It's that or nothing,' I said firmly. 'I'm not budging on this.'

'Do I get to interview them?' he asked. 'Only, I think I should since I'm the one who's going to be working with them.'

'Of course,' I promised. 'You can manage the whole thing if you like. You can place the advert, make a shortlist, do the interviews, the lot.'

He looked a bit more cheerful at that. 'Well, okay,' he said grudgingly. 'I suppose it will be bearable if we find the right person.' He managed a grin. 'I was worried you were going to replace me with Harry Jarvis, after he stepped in for me on Christmas Day.'

I laughed. 'No, I can't see him wanting to do the job full time. He looked ready for bed by the time he'd finished. It was extraordinarily kind of him to volunteer, though. Not at all what I'd have expected from him.'

'I'm sorry about leaving you in the lurch,' Jack said miserably. 'I feel so bad about that. You must have been frantic. Thank goodness for Harry. I suppose, when I think about it from that perspective, it's probably best that we have a deputy chef on hand.'

I squeezed his hand. 'It is, Jack. Thank you. You do know I'm only doing this for your own good, don't you? You mean the world to me, you really do.'

He didn't answer, but nodded his head, staring steadfastly at me as he gripped my hand.

'And now we've sorted that out,' he said, 'perhaps you can tell me what else is on your mind?'

'What on earth do you mean?' I asked, unnerved at his perception. I thought I'd done an amazing job at covering up my anxiety, but clearly not.

'I think I've known you long enough by now to realise when you're hiding something. What is it? Don't say you don't want to worry me, because if you don't tell me what it is, I'll imagine all sorts and worry even more.'

He had a point.

'All right, there *is* something,' I said. 'But it's nothing bad. At least, I don't think it is.'

'Go on,' he said quietly.

'Will came to see me this morning — he and Lexi send their love by the way.'

'That's nice of them. What did he want?'

'It was about Eleanor's christening. He was worried about telling me, but he thought I should know that they'd written to Derry to ask him if he'd be her godfather.'

Jack nodded. 'Right. Well, I suppose that makes sense. Derry is her uncle, after all. Having said that, he didn't come back for Milo's christening, did he? Don't get your hopes up, my darling. He may not return to Kearton Bay, even for such a special occasion.'

I hesitated, hardly believing what I was about to say. 'The thing is, Jack, he's already accepted. That's why Will told me. Derry's coming home.'

Jack took my hand. 'Well now,' he said.

'Indeed.'

I felt a slight tremor in his hand and squeezed it tightly. 'It will be all right, won't it, Jack? That is, it has to mean something, doesn't it?'

'I think it does. And after those presents he got you for Christmas...'

'That's what I thought,' I said eagerly. 'I just don't want to make any assumptions. I couldn't bear it if I'd got it all wrong.'

'If you have, my darling, then so have I.'

We smiled at each other, recognising that we might well be on the cusp of a breakthrough at last.

After a few moments, seeing the weariness in his eyes, I got up to leave.

'As soon as they say you can go home, call me and I'll come and fetch you in a taxi,' I told him.

'Will do,' he confirmed.

I dropped a kiss on his cheek, told him I'd see him tomorrow and headed for the door.

'Rhiannon!'

I turned and saw him looking at me, a strange expression on his face. For a long moment, we stared at each other, then I smiled.

'I know, Jack. I love you, too.'

12

Jack settled in at The Hare and Moon quite easily. Of course, he protested about having my room, insisting he would be happy in a guest room, but I wasn't having that, and he soon realised he was fighting a losing battle. I was quite contented with a smaller room. It still looked out over the sea, which was all I cared about, and I spent so little time in it anyway it hardly mattered.

Maybe I was getting old. I still loved this building with all my heart but being a pub landlady was losing its appeal. I was beginning to feel chained to my job. It had been creeping up on me for a while — the realisation that my life revolved around bar work and all it entailed. Lately it had begun to rankle that I was never free to go out to the cinema for an evening, or for a daytime jaunt to Whitby.

I only saw my friends and neighbours when they came into the pub for a drink. Life had become all work and no play, and I realised it had been that way for far too long. I suppose it hit home when I couldn't leave the place to be with Jack at the hospital after his illness. Seeing him driven away in an ambulance, knowing I couldn't be with him because I had a pub to run and customers to see to, had made me distraught, and it felt like too much suddenly.

But without The Hare and Moon, what would I do? Where would I go? And how could I bear to part with this beautiful building? There seemed to be no solution, as I confided to Jack one bitterly cold January morning while we sat together in the kitchen, and I waited for a load of tea towels and cloths to dry.

'The trouble is,' Jack said, with no trace of irony, 'the pub business is a young person's game.'

I lowered my cup of tea and stared at him, wondering if he'd realised what he said.

'It's different for me,' he said, shuffling on his chair, revealing that it had just dawned on him.

'Why is it different for you?' I tried to hide my amusement as I waited for his excuse.

'Because I turn up and cook,' he said firmly. 'You've got it all to deal with — not only the serving part, but the admin, too. Everything that comes with running this place. I have to say, though, I can't imagine you anywhere else. You've got the name of this pub running right through you, like Whitby through a stick of rock.'

'I know.' I sighed. 'I'm being silly, I suppose. I don't know anything else, after all. And I do love part of the job. I like serving drinks to my customers. I like standing behind the bar and chatting to them. It's the rest of it that's starting to get to me. And the hours, of course.'

'Thing is, you used to have Derry working alongside Kerry full time, and then young Lexi used to cover whenever you needed extra help, but Derry's no longer here, and Lexi's far too busy at the Hall with her babies, as well as helping to run the place. Have you thought about hiring someone to help? An assistant bar manager perhaps?'

'I don't need that,' I said immediately, then stopped as I saw the twinkle in his eye. 'Okay, so maybe I'm as much of a control freak as you are. What can I say?'

He laughed. 'It's not as bad as it seems, you know. I thought I'd be furious, having an assistant chef dogging my footsteps and trying to take over in my kitchen, but young Aidan's a nice lad, and he's doing well. Learning fast.'

'He is doing well,' I admitted. 'And we were so lucky to find him, although it was an awful shame for The Black Swan, obviously.'

The Black Swan in Starfish Sands, further down the coast, had gone into administration, and all its staff had been made redundant. Awful for them, but lucky for us and for Aidan. He'd seen our advertisement and had been able to start work immediately. The fact that he was keen to do so spoke volumes about him. I could see him being quite an asset to The Hare and Moon.

'What you need,' Jack said, settling back in his chair now that he felt on safer ground, 'is a bit of fun. A break from this place.'

'Well, wouldn't that be nice?' I said lightly. 'A fortnight in the Maldives sounds perfect.'

He tutted. 'That's not what I meant, and you know it.' He nodded at the washing machine. 'Door's clicked. Think they're done.'

I opened the door of the washer/dryer and took out the tea towels and cloths. 'What did you mean then?' I asked, folding them up and placing them on the table.

'I don't know. Just go out somewhere, anywhere. Go to a friend's for coffee. Meet someone for lunch. Go to the cinema. Anything that doesn't revolve around this place.'

It was a tempting thought. I really wanted to go into Whitby. There were a couple of shops there that I loved to browse. They sold the most divine incense sticks, and I was almost out of mine. I loved to wander around, picking up crystals, breathing in the heady, musky fragrance of incense and candles, examining the latest artwork on the walls. It had been ages since I'd last been. A walk along the seafront would do me good, too.

'But it would mean leaving Kerry on her own,' I said. 'I'm not sure that would be fair.'

'It's January,' he reminded me. 'Not exactly heaving in here most days. Best chance you have, I reckon. Don't waste it.'

'I'll think about it,' I promised him. 'Now, would you like some lunch before I go downstairs?'

'If I fancy anything, I'll make it myself,' he said. 'You don't have to run around after me. I can manage fine. In fact, I feel a complete fraud, being here like this. There's nothing wrong with me. I'm taking my medication like a good boy and I feel perfectly well.'

'Even so, I feel better having you here where I can keep an eye on you.'

'Maybe another week or so,' he said, 'but then I do have to go home. It's not fair on you. You need your room back, and I need to go back to normal life.'

'But Jack—'

He held up his hand. 'No arguments, my darling. You've been very kind, but I'm not an invalid. Now, have *you* had anything to eat, never mind me? Do you want me to cook something for you?'

'I'm not hungry,' I admitted.

'You didn't have breakfast,' he reminded me. 'Right, that's it. The bar can wait a while. I'm making us both a sandwich and no arguments.'

I smiled. 'But not bacon.'

'I can promise you that,' he said. 'Definitely not bacon.'

In the event, Jack had tuna and I had cheese. After I'd eaten my sandwich, and managed to drink yet another cup of tea, I gathered up the tea towels and cloths and headed downstairs to start work.

Kerry was leaning on the bar, scrolling through her phone. There were a handful of customers, sitting at various tables, drinking and chatting. It was a relaxed day, typical of mid-January.

'Not too busy for you then,' I teased, as she hurriedly tucked her phone under the counter.

'Sorry, I was just—'

'Oh, don't worry about it. Honestly, it's fine.' Kerry was a good and reliable worker. I had no issue with her catching up on social media when she had a spare minute.

'I sent a friend request to Aidan,' she confessed in a whisper. 'He mentioned he was on Facebook, so I did a search for him. Do you think he'll mind?'

'He can only refuse it if he does,' I pointed out. 'And I don't see why he should. A lot of people have work colleagues as Facebook friends, don't they?'

Not that I'd know, having never been anywhere near social media. I couldn't imagine anything worse, frankly, but I seemed to be in a minority there.

'If he does refuse it will make things ever so awkward,' she agonised. 'Oh, I wish I hadn't sent it now.'

'Do I take it you're rather enamoured of young Aidan?' I said, amused.

She raised an eyebrow. 'You mean, do I fancy him? Yeah, you could say that. He's hot, right?'

I hadn't given the matter much thought, but I smiled and said, 'Extremely cute.'

'Cute? God, Rhiannon, you're so out of the loop. When was the last time you had a bloke?'

I stared at her as the question sank in. When *was* the last time? I hadn't had a relationship since a brief affair with Cyril Goodall, who ran the art gallery, and that was — when was that? I tried to remember. It had been a few months before Rose and Flynn got together, I recalled, because Rose had suspected the man I was seeing was Flynn and she wasn't best pleased about it, having already fallen in love with him. Goodness, that was a long time ago. Their daughter, Violet, would be six in March! Before that, there had been Will, of course and then... well no real relationships at all. After I'd had Derry, it had been a string of short-lived affairs and one-night stands. I hadn't wanted anything else, which was possibly why I'd frequently chosen men who were already married.

It hadn't been a conscious choice, but thinking about it now, I suspected that deep down it *had* been deliberate on some level. I didn't want a relationship. I never had. I'd never met a man yet who could persuade me otherwise, though many had tried. I doubted such a man existed.

'I knew it,' Kerry said. 'You can't even remember. Time you got back in the saddle, Rhiannon. You're not that old.'

'Well, thank you very much for the glowing compliment, Kerry.'

143

'Sorry. I didn't mean that the way it sounded. Oh, you know what I mean. But seriously, it's time you went on a date.'

'I don't think so. I'm perfectly happy the way I am thanks.'

The bar door pushed open, and Harry strolled in. Kerry giggled and nudged me, and I was rather surprised to find that my face heated up with embarrassment. That rarely happened. I wasn't one for blushing.

'What about him? He rode to your rescue on Christmas Day, didn't he? What more could you want from a knight in shining armour?'

'Kerry, hush!' Mortified, I turned to face Harry. 'Good afternoon, Harry. What can I get you?'

'Just a white wine please, Rhiannon. I don't suppose you're serving food?'

'We don't have a full lunchtime menu right now, but we have a selection of sandwiches to choose from, or there's soup of the day.'

Harry nodded. 'A sandwich would do fine. I haven't got anything in at home, and I only realised when I stopped work to eat because I was ravenous, and the cupboard was bare.'

'What sandwich would you like?' I asked him. 'There's cheese, ham, prawn, egg mayonnaise and tuna. All served with salad and crisps.'

Harry considered. 'Cheese sounds good,' he said.

I beamed at him. 'It is good. I've just had one myself. Kerry, could you let Aidan know, please?'

She nodded and disappeared into the kitchen.

Harry sighed. 'I must get more organised. Really, I have to learn how to do a food shop but I'm hopeless at it.'

'There are some good supermarkets in Whitby,' I said. 'You could get everything you need there.'

'I loathe supermarkets. They bring me out in hives. Maybe,' Harry said slowly, 'you could come with me one day. Show me what to buy. I only nip into local shops and get what I need each day and I'm sure it would make more sense to buy enough for the week. It would certainly save me time.'

144

'And money,' I added, suddenly becoming uncomfortably aware that Kerry had returned and was listening to our conversation. 'Although I do try to support the local shops as much as I can. We must all do our bit, after all.'

'So, would you?' Harry asked. 'Come with me one day?'

'I, er, don't see why not,' I said. 'If I can ever get time away from this place. Now, let me get you that drink.'

I poured him a glass of wine, shooting a warning look at Kerry who was wiping down the counter and had an unmistakable smirk on her face.

'On the house,' I told Harry firmly as he held out a ten-pound note.

'Why?' he asked, looking puzzled as I pushed his hand away.

'Are you serious? You worked here all Christmas Day, slaving away in the kitchen for me, and you refused payment. The very least I can do is give you a free drink. In fact, you can have free drinks for the next month. I insist.'

'Certainly not,' he said. 'You have a business to run, don't you? You can't go around giving away free drinks.'

'If it hadn't been for you, my business would have been swamped with vile reviews on Trip Adviser. You saved me from a fate worse than death. I owe you.'

'Proper knight in shining armour, wasn't he, Rhiannon?'

Kerry giggled and headed back into the kitchen. I rolled my eyes and turned back to Harry, who was frowning.

'What's she laughing at? Have I said something funny?'

I patted his hand, deciding the time for schoolgirl games was well behind me.

'Ignore her,' I said. 'Kerry has decided that it's time I had a man, and she seems to think you fit the bill.'

Harry spluttered on his wine, and I laughed. 'It's okay, calm down. I'm not looking for a man, and your marriage has just ended. I hardly think we're going to jump into bed with each other.'

I was surprised to see him looking distinctly uncomfortable. No doubt he'd heard all about my reputation.

'Goodness, Harry, don't worry. I won't pounce on you.'

'I — I know that. I was, er, surprised, that's all.'

'Oh, you know what young girls are like,' I said airily. 'Always trying to matchmake.'

Kerry came through, carrying a plate with Harry's sandwich, and a set of cutlery wrapped in a napkin. 'Here you go,' she said, placing it on the counter in front of him. 'You need to find a table, though. You're not supposed to eat here.'

'Oh, sorry.' He slipped off the stool and glanced around, looking for a table. Not difficult to spot one really, since there was hardly anyone in the pub. 'Do I have to go in the dining room?'

'No, it's fine. Just sit wherever you like.'

Harry wandered over to a table and sat down, unwrapping his knife and fork.

'Aw, Rhiannon, he's all by himself,' Kerry said. 'Don't be mean. Go and sit with him.'

'Kerry, will you be quiet? Honestly, you're acting like a teenager. Harry's a kind man who did me a huge favour, that's all.'

'From what I've heard,' Kerry said, 'he's a bit of a player, that one. I wouldn't go near him if you want a relationship, but if you're looking for a quick bunk-up, I reckon he's your man.'

'Kerry!'

She laughed. 'You're blushing! Oh my God! I've never seen you blush before. And since when did you get so prudish?' Her eyes widened suddenly. 'Do you fancy him? Bloody hell, you do, don't you?'

'He's an extremely attractive man,' I said honestly, 'but he comes with a whole heap of baggage. He's certainly not someone I should get involved with.'

'I suppose you're right,' she said. 'Eliza and Sophie think he's the devil. Sophie said he's practically a gigolo, whatever that means.'

'Sophie tends to exaggerate,' I said. 'And I hardly think he's the devil. Not that I believe in the devil. But even so, he would hardly have helped on Christmas Day if he were such a bad person, would he? I'm a firm believer in taking people as I find them, not as others tell me to.'

'Well, if you think that, why don't you go shopping with him then? Are you worried what Sophie and Eliza would say?'

'Of course not. I'd be helping him out, that's all. Returning the favour.'

'Well then?'

I hesitated, wondering what it was, exactly, that was making me hold back. Harry had done me a favour and I owed him. If he needed help with his shopping, surely it was the least I could do? Besides, it could kill two birds with one stone.

I wandered over to his table and said, 'Would you mind if I sat down for a moment?'

He looked surprised but indicated the chair opposite him. 'Please do.'

'I've been thinking about your supermarket problem.'

'My supermarket phobia,' he said with a shudder. 'I hate them.'

'Well, okay, your supermarket phobia then,' I said with a smile. 'I'll go with you to help you do your shopping.'

He looked delighted. 'You will? Brilliant. Thank you.'

'There's a condition,' I said.

He gave me a wary look. 'Go on.'

'I've been wanting to go to Whitby to browse the shops for ages, and I also feel what you did merits more than a supermarket shop. So, I propose we go to Whitby, and I buy you lunch as a thank you.'

'You've thanked me enough,' he protested. 'Honestly—'

'That's the deal, Harry,' I said firmly. 'Take it or leave it.'

He eyed me for a moment, and I saw him thinking it over and wondered if I was so scary a prospect.

'Okay. Deal.'

'After lunch,' I continued, 'I'll help you with your shopping, then you can drive it all home and I'll have a wander around the shops in Whitby and catch a bus back.'

'You don't have to do that,' he said. 'I haven't seen much of Whitby at all, but I've heard great things about it. So, I propose this. We go into Whitby, and you can browse the shops and show me around the town, then we have lunch, then we go to the supermarket. What say you?'

'Goodness, we'll be there for hours,' I said.

'I think we both deserve a break,' he said comfortably, prodding at some of the crisps on his plate. 'After all, you're constantly working here, and I'm up to my neck in plaster and paint at Eight Bells. So?'

'I browse some strange shops,' I said. 'And you might get bored. I could be in there some time.'

'If I get bored, I'll wander off and look elsewhere,' he said. 'I'm sure there are plenty of other things to look at.'

'Are you sure about this, Harry?' I asked. 'I wouldn't want to upset Eliza.'

His eyebrows shot up. 'Upset Eliza? Why on earth would it upset Eliza if I went into Whitby with you?'

I felt suddenly incredibly stupid, like I'd read far too much into all this, even though I hadn't. I was sure I hadn't. But by mentioning Eliza it looked as if I were making more of our trip than it was. He was right, of course. Why would Eliza care if we did a bit of shopping and had some lunch? I felt my face burning and thought how odd it was that I'd taken to blushing. Maybe I was reaching the menopause?

'Fine,' I said. 'That's okay then. Just wanted to be clear.'

'Great. When should we go?'

I stared at him blankly. I hadn't even thought of that.

'Nothing wrong with tomorrow,' Kerry called.

We both whipped round and saw her grinning at us from behind the bar.

'Good God. She has good hearing,' Harry said. 'Who is she? Batwoman?'

'Just your friendly neighbourhood superhero trying to do you both a good deed,' Kerry said. 'Go tomorrow. It's not forecast rain, and we won't be busy.'

I looked at Harry.

He shrugged. 'Fine by me.'

'There you go,' Kerry said. 'All sorted. Happy to help.'

'Goodness, I'll have to have words with her,' I murmured.

Harry grinned. 'Crisp?'

13

Whitby was as charming as Harry had been led to believe. A quaint coastal town, with the added attraction of a ruined abbey perched high on a cliff top overlooking the harbour and sea, a pier, and some rather lovely old, red-roofed buildings that had a charm all their own.

Rhiannon seemed to know her way around easily, pointing out various streets and shops and the marketplace to him as they walked. She told him random facts about the Whitby whaling industry, as they looked up at the whalebones that formed an arch on the cliff top opposite the abbey and gave him a condensed history of the life and times of Captain Cook, whose statue stood not far from the bones.

She even showed him the Captain Cook Memorial Museum, a seventeenth century house down a little alleyway called Grape Lane, where the man himself had apparently once lodged when he'd been an apprentice. Sadly, it wasn't open, so they couldn't go in, but it didn't stop Rhiannon reeling off all sorts of facts about him. She amazed him with her knowledge. Clearly, she loved Whitby and its history.

She insisted they climb the hundred and ninety-nine steps up to the abbey, even though Harry warned her it would probably kill him. She didn't make him go inside the abbey grounds, but they had a good look at it from the outside, and at the church, with its extensive cliff top graveyard, and large cross dedicated to Caedmon, "the first English poet", apparently.

She wasn't joking either about loving to browse the shops. She led him down a passageway that reminded him of something from a Dickens novel, into a rather dark and mysterious sort of building, and his nose twitched at the overpowering smell of heavy incense.

Rhiannon took a deep breath, inhaling the scent with evident delight.

'Doesn't it smell divine?' she whispered, as if they were in church. He noticed that she was very hushed inside the shop, moving slowly and carefully around, examining various items with exaggerated care and a look of awe on her face. Now and then she'd murmur something approving, and nod to herself. He watched her with a mixture of curiosity and amusement. She evidently believed in all this tosh. You only had to look at her face to see that.

'Rhiannon, love!'

A thin, middle-aged man wearing a multi-coloured waistcoat and brown corduroy trousers, his long, straggly grey hair scraped into a ponytail, stepped out from the back of the shop. 'It's been ages. Smashing to see you.'

'Robert!' Rhiannon sounded genuinely delighted to see him, and Harry surveyed them curiously as they hugged each other.

'You're looking well,' Robert said, stepping back and eyeing her with what Harry thought looked suspiciously like lust.

'Thank you. As are you. How's your mother doing?'

'Oh, she's not too bad. Did I tell you she's retired from the cards?'

Evidently, this came as a surprise to Rhiannon.

'She hasn't! I never thought she'd give up the readings. What brought that on?'

Robert sighed. 'She met a fella and her hormones all flooded back from retirement. He doesn't approve of the cards. Thinks it's all mumbo jumbo, and Mum wants to please him, so that's that. Can you believe it?'

Rhiannon looked genuinely shocked. 'How dreadful! Fancy giving up such a gift for the sake of a man. And what sort of man would expect her to?'

'Well exactly,' Robert said. 'Non-believers. They ruin everything.'

He gave Harry a discerning look, and Harry gave him a defiant glare in return.

'I expect her clients are missing her,' Rhiannon said.

'Well, obviously. They keep asking me if there's anyone else I can recommend, but no one had the gift like my mother. Present company excepted of course.'

Rhiannon laughed. 'Oh, I never had the gift that your mother had. She taught me everything I know, after all.'

'And that's another thing,' Robert said. 'All the classes have stopped. Not only will she not give readings, but she won't teach anyone how to read the cards either. I've got a list as long as my arm of people who want to learn, and I'm sick of telling them how sorry I am. I mean, how do you tell people you're sorry your mum can't help them, but she's rediscovered the joys of sex at the age of seventy-nine?'

Harry's eyes widened. Lucky Robert's mum!

'I don't suppose,' Robert said, his voice taking on a wheedling tone, 'you'd be interested, would you? Just a few classes a week,' he said quickly, as she started to protest. 'One a week even. For me?'

'I'd love to, Robert,' Rhiannon said. 'I really would, but the truth is I don't have the time. The pub takes up every waking moment. Why do you think it's been so long since I last came here?'

He sighed. 'I know, I know. It was worth asking. Oh well, I'm sure I'll find someone eventually. Or the customers will. There's a high demand for it, you know. I wish I could get the hang of it, but I've never had my mother's knack.'

Rhiannon patted his arm. 'Never mind, darling. I'm sure you have other gifts.'

Other gifts! Harry dreaded to think what they were. Honestly, what a weird conversation. He presumed they were talking about tarot cards. More mumbo jumbo. How could grown adults seriously believe that a pack of cards could tell them the future? Talk about deluded. He felt sorry for them really.

Yet, moments later, as he saw Rhiannon examining a selection of incense sticks, closing her eyes as she breathed in the fragrance, he felt something else, too. An unfurling wonder. There was something about her delight and her almost childlike faith in what was, essentially, the stuff of fairy tales, that touched something within him.

He was used to the hard-bitten cynicism of Melody. Rhiannon couldn't be more different. She seemed to find something to love in everything. He found it astonishing that she could reach middle age and still be so enchanted by life. Still believe in something. Anything. He had little faith in the world, but she made him want to believe again.

His throat felt full, and he blinked away tears, wondering where the hell they'd sprung from. He motioned to Rhiannon that he was going to wait outside, and she nodded and smiled at him, unaware of the seismic effect she was having on him.

'What the actual fuck?' He leaned against the wall and took a gulp of fresh, cold air. His heart was pounding, and he put his hand on his chest, as if to slow it down somewhat. He took deep breaths to calm himself. He was fine. It was just…

Just what? He had no idea because he'd never felt that way before in his life. Like he was looking at the woman who could save him. But he hadn't even known he needed saving.

He shook his head as if to banish his thoughts. What did they put in that incense? It had clearly had a weird effect on him. He tried to think about paint samples and door handles, but all he could picture was Rhiannon's huge dark eyes, wide with wonder as she gazed around the shop, like it was some fairy tale realm.

'It's nothing,' he said out loud. 'It's because you've been lonely.'

But he hadn't been too lonely, because he'd had Tally coming over almost every night, seeking refuge at Eight Bells. She was good company, and they chatted easily. And she was attractive and fun, too. But she hadn't sparked anything within him. She hadn't made him feel as if he were starting to come alive again for the first time in years. As if suddenly, there was hope, that all things were possible…

'All done.' Rhiannon's voice beside him made him jump, and he stared at her guiltily, as if she knew what he was thinking.

She frowned. 'Are you all right? You look a bit shaken. The shop didn't scare you, did it?'

He managed a smile. 'As if! Did you get what you wanted?'

'Yes, lots of incense sticks and a few more candles. One can never have too many candles. I absolutely love them, don't you?'

He shrugged. 'I guess.'

She patted his arm, sending what felt like an electric current shooting through his body. 'You're hungry,' she said. 'I can tell by your face. You're getting that grouchy look that men get when all they can think about is food.'

Who the hell could think about food around her, Harry wondered? He nodded. 'You're probably right.'

'I know just the place,' she said.

They cut through the marketplace into Church Street, and she led him into a cosy double-fronted café, with two bay windows at either side of a heavy, wooden door. It was another old building, but inside was bright and contemporary.

Rhiannon ushered him to a table in the corner by the window, so they had a good view of Church Street. She passed him a menu and he briefly scanned it, pleasantly surprised by the wide variety of dishes, even though his appetite appeared to have deserted him, despite what he'd told her earlier.

He couldn't decide what to eat and Rhiannon put down the menu and surveyed him, her eyes shining. 'I know! Let's go all traditional and have Whitby fish and chips. I can't remember the last time I ate that, and it really is tasty. Let's go the whole hog, with mushy peas and bread and butter and a pot of tea. What do you say?'

Since Harry suspected that anything he ate would taste pretty much like cardboard anyway, he saw no harm in agreeing to it. Besides, she looked so thrilled at the prospect that he wouldn't have said no, even if he'd been allergic to fish. How could anyone get so excited about fish and chips? And yet, there she was, beaming at him as if they were on some amazing adventure. He envied her. He admired her. She was like a bright, flickering flame, and he was the helpless moth being drawn towards her, quite unable to free himself of the desire to fly to the light — whatever the consequences.

The waitress took their order, and Rhiannon sat back in her chair, gazing out over Church Street.

'You love it here, don't you?' he said affectionately.

'I do. It's an amazing place. The trouble is, I rarely get the chance to visit, even though it's only a few miles from home. Sad really.'

'I suppose running a pub takes up a lot of time.'

She folded her arms and rested them on the table, her expression suddenly wistful. 'I don't think I realised how much until recently. I seem to be hankering after all the things I can't do instead of appreciating what I have. I've been thinking about how much of my life has been spent standing behind a bar, while all around me life went on.' She sighed. ' I don't know. Maybe it's my age.'

'You're hardly old,' he said laughing.

'I'm fifty,' she told him.

He struggled to hide his surprise. She didn't look fifty.

'It's okay,' she said. 'You can blurt it out.'

'Blurt what out?'

'All the usual comments about fifty not being old, and how good I look for my age.'

'Well,' he said, rather uncomfortably, 'it's not, and you do.'

'Yes, I know.'

Her disarming honesty made her more intriguing. He peered closely at her, taking in every detail of her beautiful face.

'No I haven't,' she said.

'I'm sorry?'

'Had work done. I haven't.'

'Oh my God, I wasn't looking for that!' He hadn't been either. It hadn't even occurred to him.

'I embrace the crone,' she said lightly. 'I've had my day in the sun as the maiden, I've been the mother, now it's the crone's time, and I'm okay with that.'

He wasn't sure what on earth she was talking about, and his face must have shown his bewilderment because she laughed. 'The triple goddess: maiden, mother and crone. Aspects of the one. Woman.'

'O-kay.'

'Do I scare you, Harry?'

Hell, you have no idea.

'Of course not. Why should you?'

'I think I scare some people. I have a bit of a reputation as a witch. Some think I'm spooky. Others are kinder and call me eccentric.'

'Are you a witch?'

'Of course.'

'Fuck me!' He hadn't meant to say that out loud, but to his relief she laughed again.

'Don't worry. I'm exceedingly kind.'

'You mean, you cast spells and stuff?'

'Yes, I do. Don't look so worried. It's a belief system — a faith like any other. I don't see casting a spell as anything different to saying a prayer. It's still a way of communicating a desire to the universe. Stating your intention out loud. Do you believe in God, Harry?'

Hadn't he had this conversation once with Tally? Was the universe trying to tell him something?

'I don't know,' he said honestly. 'I've never given it much thought.'

'So what do you believe in? You must believe in something?'

You. It was on the tip of his tongue, and he only just stopped himself from saying it out loud. He rubbed his forehead, thinking that, whether she was a real witch or not, she certainly had some power over him. It was terrifying.

'Well?'

He shrugged, not wanting to give too much away. 'I believe there's nothing better in life than a glass of champagne, apart from two glasses of champagne. Other than that, the jury's still out.'

'Oh, Harry!' Rhiannon gave him a knowing look. 'I don't believe it you know.'

'What? Okay, you've got me. I don't particularly like champagne. But you forced me into a corner.'

'I mean this devil-may-care attitude of yours. I think there's an awful lot more to you than you reveal. I sense hidden depths in you, Harry.'

'Oh, trust me. I'm boring as hell.'

'I sincerely doubt that.'

His skin prickled in anticipation. Was she flirting with him?

'Ooh, the food's here!'

Harry blinked, hardly knowing where he was. Rhiannon was smiling at the waitress who'd just arrived at the table, plates were being laid down, cups and saucers and a teapot were being placed in the middle of them, and all was normal and well with the world. Except his had rocked on its axis, and he had no idea which way was up any more.

'Doesn't it look gorgeous?' she said eagerly as she eyed the large, crispy haddock and golden chips on her plate. 'Ooh, I think I'll put salt and vinegar on mine. Would you like anything, Harry?'

He fumbled in the sauce rack and withdrew a couple of sachets of tartare sauce. Rhiannon was already tucking in, and by the ecstatic expression on her face, it was like nectar from the gods.

He wasn't sure he'd manage much of it, but he wanted to try, to please her if nothing else. To his surprise and relief, it tasted so good that he ate the lot and enjoyed every mouthful.

'I think that's the best meal I've had in years,' he said, meaning it.

'Wasn't it delicious? You can't beat fresh Whitby fish, and this is such a delightful café. I wish I could come here more often.'

'You should,' he told her. 'Why don't you hire more staff? Get them to take on more of the burden. You're the owner, the manager. You should delegate more. That's what managers do, after all. I don't know how you manage with just Jack and Kerry.'

'We have Aidan now,' Rhiannon told him. 'He's helping Jack with the cooking and he's incredibly good. Between you and me,

I'm hoping he edges Jack out a bit. I want him to rest more, have some fun.'

'Which is commendable, but surely that makes it even more obvious that you deserve the same?'

'I suppose so,' she said slowly. 'I seem to have got into this rut, and it's become so normal that I never considered any other way of doing things.'

'Well, I think hiring a couple of bar staff would be a start,' he said firmly.

'I do hire temporary staff in the holiday season,' she told him. 'We often have help in the kitchen and behind the bar, because of the tourists. But during the colder months I rarely bother.'

'Well, maybe it's time you started. You know what they say about all work and no play?'

'Gives Jack a stroke,' she said grimly.

He was appalled at his lack of tact. 'God, I'm sorry. I didn't think...'

'Oh, don't worry about that. Jack didn't have a stroke anyway. Not a proper one. He had a TIA — a sort of mini stroke. And he's on medication now and doing well. But I suppose you're right. I don't want to get to Jack's age and find all I've done with my life is run a pub.'

'And be a mother,' he reminded her. 'You have a son, don't you?'

'How do you know about Derry?' she asked.

'You mentioned having a son on Christmas Day, and Tally told me his name.'

'Tally?'

He realised he'd been a bit indiscreet. 'We met in the pub one night and got talking. She was a bit fed up, so she sat with me and told me about the various inhabitants of Kearton Bay, that's all. She wasn't gossiping.'

'Oh, she wouldn't be,' Rhiannon said. 'Tally's lovely. Did she tell you what happened between us?'

He raised an eyebrow. 'Happened between you?'

'About why he left.'

'Oh, no. She said he'd left Kearton Bay about three or four years ago, that's all. I didn't ask and she didn't volunteer anything else.'

'We had a falling out,' she said, sighing heavily. 'My fault entirely, I'm afraid.'

'I'm sure you can't have done anything as bad as that. It seems a bit extreme to fall out with your mother and leave home for four years.'

'I didn't tell him who his father was,' she said bluntly. 'When he found out his identity, he wasn't happy.'

'Oh.' Harry was at a loss to know what to say. What did one say to that?

'His father was Sir Paul Boden-Kean,' she told him. 'He was the thirteenth baronet, and he's Will's father. He was estranged from his wife at the time, although they still shared the Hall. They were divorced not long after. Sir Paul's dead now, of course, and Will's the fourteenth baronet.'

'Okay. Well, I don't see the problem with that,' he admitted.

'The problem is that Sir Paul was considerably older than me, and...' She hesitated, looking suddenly rather anxious and touchingly vulnerable.

Harry swallowed. 'You don't have to tell me anything else,' he said.

'The thing is, I had an affair with Will a few years ago. Before he got together with Lexi obviously. It was a short romance, something we both needed, and we've stayed friends ever since. In fact, he's one of the people I love most in the world.'

Lucky Will.

'But finding out that I'd had an affair with his own half-brother sent Derry over the edge. He — he was never happy about my dalliances. I think he wanted a normal mother who'd get married and settle down, and I was never that person. I made a lot of mistakes, Harry, I won't lie. I wasn't what you'd call well-behaved.'

'Well, not many of us are,' Harry said with feeling.

'You don't understand.' Rhiannon paused as the waitress collected their plates. 'Thank you so much, that was delicious.'

'Pleasure,' the waitress said. 'Would you like dessert?'

158

'Not for me,' Rhiannon said. 'Harry?'

He shook his head. 'I'm fine thanks.'

The waitress nodded and carried the plates away, and Harry sipped his tea while watching Rhiannon, who seemed to be choosing her next words carefully.

'I've done a lot of things I regret,' she said at last. 'I didn't understand, you see. I've never been in love with anyone, so I didn't know what it could feel like. When I got involved with married men, I genuinely couldn't see the problem. I wasn't stealing anyone's husband because I never once asked them to leave their wives. I had no interest in being with them permanently. And, you see, I thought no person could own another. No one belongs to anyone, so what right did a wife have to say I'd stolen her man anyway? I didn't get it. Not then.'

He felt a twist of dread. Was she telling him that she'd fallen in love and understood because of that? 'But now you do?'

'Oh yes. Now I do. Because I've experienced jealousy, Harry, and I'll tell you now, there's nothing like it. It's the most heart-breaking, sickening, all-consuming feeling I've ever had. I wouldn't wish it on anyone.'

Harry was silent for a moment. Her words struck a chord with him because he'd recently experienced those exact feelings. He just hadn't put a name to them before now.

'I know what you mean,' he said quietly. 'I've been there, too.'

'Really?' her head shot up and she gazed at him with obvious sympathy. 'I'm so sorry. It's horrible, isn't it?'

'Yep.' He put down his cup and stared into what remained of his tea for a moment. 'Not over a woman. Over Rufus. You see, my little boy is currently living with Melody and her boyfriend, and Chuck — that's her boyfriend's name — seems to be Rufus's hero. He doesn't want to talk to me. He has no interest in coming over here. When I've managed to get through to him on the phone — and that's not often because he's always busy doing something with Chuck — all I hear is how bloody marvellous this superhero is. Fuck, it winds me up. I want to kill him. And, to a lesser extent, I feel the same about Gabriel, because Amy calls him Dad, and she lives under his roof. It hurts like hell. But it's my own fault, I know it. If anything, that makes it worse.'

'Oh, Harry, I'm so sorry.' She reached out and placed her hand over his. 'You do understand then. With me it's Derry and my father. We've never got on, you see. My father has always hated me. I have no idea why. But he's an awful man anyway, and he never wanted anything to do with me when I got pregnant. He had no interest in Derry either. All those years and he never showed the slightest interest in his own grandson.'

'He sounds a real charmer,' Harry said.

'Oh, he is. But the thing is, Derry wrote to him after we'd had the falling out, and my father invited him to stay at our family home in Cornwall. I know he didn't care about Derry. He was just using him to hurt me. I was so sure that Derry would see through him and would come home.'

'But he didn't?'

Her eyes were wet with tears, and he put his other hand over the top of hers and squeezed it slightly.

'No he didn't. It's been almost four years now, so clearly he and my father get on well. It makes me sick to my stomach. Derry's mine, not his! He belongs to me!' She gave a strangled sob, and her hand flew to her mouth. She sank back in the chair and shook her head slightly. 'I'm so sorry. You see what I mean? Now I understand, all too well, how all those wives felt. I always said, a person belongs to no one but himself. Yet I claim Derry as my property, and I don't want my father anywhere near him. It's not a nice trait, is it? Jealousy.'

'No.' He felt sick suddenly, thinking about Eliza and how she must have felt when the news of his affair with Melody was splashed all over the papers. It was a wonder she spoke to him at all, let alone gave him access to their daughter. 'But I understand, really I do. I feel the same. It hurts, I know that.'

'I suppose we're only human,' she managed at last, giving him a wan smile.

'And we all make mistakes.'

'And we pay for them. Somewhere along the line, we always pay for them.'

'I think we probably do, yes,' he said. He certainly felt as if he had. The last few years had been hell. He was sure he must have paid in full by now.

'Thank you for not judging me,' she said. 'I don't know why I told you all this. It felt like a cork being pulled out of a bottle, and everything came pouring out like champagne bubbles.'

'I'm honoured you confided in me,' he said, meaning it.

'You're truly kind, Harry,' she said. 'Has anyone told you, you're an extremely nice person?'

He gave her a rueful smile. 'Funnily enough, no. I think my reputation is as shot as yours.'

She laughed. 'Well then, we make a good pair, don't we? We must stick together, Harry. You and me, against the world.'

It sounded good to him. He raised his cup and clinked it against hers. 'You and me.'

'You and me,' she said softly.

'Rhiannon, would you like to come to dinner one evening?' he asked her hesitantly. 'You could come to Eight Bells, and I'll cook for you. It's in a bit of a state, I won't lie, but it's better than it was, and I can cook.'

'I know you can cook,' she said, her eyes twinkling. 'You saved me, remember? My knight in shining armour.'

'Oh, yes.' He gave her a sheepish grin. 'Well then?'

'It's difficult, with work,' she said, and his heart sank. Was this her, politely giving him the brush-off?

She ran her finger around the rim of her cup, evidently giving the matter some thought. Harry waited, not daring to speak.

'I've got staff covering me next Sunday because it's Will and Lexi's baby's christening. I suppose I could come to yours after that.'

His shoulders sagged with relief, and he realised he'd been holding his breath.

'Perfect,' he said. 'I'll look forward to it.'

'But it does depend on how it goes with Derry.'

'Derry? What's he got to do with it?'

'He's coming back for the christening. He's Baby Eleanor's godfather, you see. I'm hoping things will be resolved at last. He might want to talk. I'm hoping he will. But if he does, I won't be able to come after all. But then if he doesn't...'

She looked so forlorn at the thought that Harry's heart went out to her.

'Well, you can always let me know an hour or so beforehand. I won't cook anything until I've heard from you. How about that?'

'That's so kind of you,' she said, sounding grateful. 'I don't want to mess you about, but Derry—'

'Comes first,' he said. 'I get that. It's not a problem.'

She smiled. 'Well, we'd better go and get that shopping done, just in case,' she said, getting to her feet. 'Time to brave the supermarket.'

He picked up the bill and she took it back from him. 'My treat, remember? I'll pay.'

'All right,' he agreed. 'Since I'm cooking dinner for us next Sunday. Or not, if things go well for you. But even if you can't make it on Sunday, we'll make an alternative date. Yes?'

Her smile lit up her face, and lit up something within him, too.

'Just don't try fish and chips,' she whispered to him. 'You'll never live up to this standard, and I'd hate for you to disappoint me.'

And there it was again, that nagging fear. What if he *did* disappoint her? How could he be sure he wouldn't, after everything that had happened?

For fuck's sake, Harry, he told himself angrily, *it's just dinner. Nothing else. It doesn't matter.*

Yet he knew it did matter. It mattered a lot.

IMBOLC

14

I awoke that Sunday morning with butterflies already awake and fluttering around in my stomach. Evidently, my subconscious had remembered the significance of the date before my conscious mind caught up. The christening! Derry was coming home.

I lay there in my bed, staring upwards, a hundred different scenarios playing through my mind as if the white ceiling had suddenly become a cinema screen, and my mind the projector. How would Derry react? Would there be hugs? Did I dare try to hug him?

In my heart of hearts, I was hoping there'd be a reunion scene worthy of an Oscar-winning film. Derry would be standing outside the church. He'd see me walking down the path toward him. There'd be a heart-rending cry of, "Mum!" Then he'd run down that path, arms outstretched, gather me into a hug and tell me how much he'd missed me. Oh, I must have played that scene in my mind dozens of times but interjected with not-so-pleasant ones that filled my heart with dread and fear.

I almost leapt out of my skin as the door flew open, and I clasped my hand to my chest and heaved a sigh of relief as I saw Jack standing in the doorway, carrying a tray.

'Breakfast, Rhiannon,' he said, settling himself on the edge of my bed. 'I knew you'd be awake, so here you are. Don't tell me you couldn't possibly eat a thing, because you've got a big day ahead of you and you need fuel. So sit up and eat.'

I sat up and smiled fondly at him as he placed the tray on my lap. He knew me so well, and he was such a kind man.

'I'm so glad you dressed for the occasion, Jack,' I said, nodding at him mischievously.

Jack glanced down at his stripy pyjamas and gave me a sheepish grin. 'Well, do you know what, my darling? I'm going to have a thoroughly lazy day today.'

'You are?' I was delighted to hear it.

'I am. It's my last day here, after all. I'm moving home tomorrow, so I'm going to make the most of it. While you're away at the christening, Aidan is taking care of the kitchen, with the help of the temps you hired for today. I think I'm going to take everyone's advice and have a lazy morning in bed, reading the papers and watching television. Then I think I'll go for a walk this afternoon, along the cliff tops. Might have a look at Eight Bells, see how it's coming along.'

I paused, a triangle of toast halfway to my mouth. 'Eight Bells? Why on earth would you want to check that out?' I gave him a knowing look. 'Jaaack.'

'Well, since you seem to have struck up quite a friendship with this Harry Jarvis chap, I thought I'd better see what sort of place he has. Find out a bit more about him. He's not got the best reputation, has he?'

'Neither have I,' I reminded him, taking a bite of toast, and chewing thoughtfully. 'Really, I don't understand your motives. You don't feel the need to check out any of my other friends.'

Jack sniffed. 'Yes, well, maybe that's because for one thing, your other friends aren't known philanders and liars, and for another, you seem to be moving beyond the friendship stage with this fellow, and I want to make sure he's worthy of you.'

'Worthy of me?' I spluttered with laughter. 'Jack, I don't know where you get your ideas from, but I can assure you Harry and I are just friends. Nothing more.'

'Kerry said—'

'Oh, Kerry!' I waved the half-eaten toast at him, dismissing my barmaid's gossip. 'She's got some bee in her bonnet about me needing a man. It's nothing.'

'But my darling,' he said quietly, 'it didn't look like nothing when you got home from Whitby last week. You were positively glowing. I saw it, that sparkle in your eyes. I haven't seen it for — well, I'm not sure I've *ever* seen that look on you before. Do you think there's a remote possibility that Harry means more to you than you realise?'

'Of course not!' I returned what was left of the toast to the plate and stared down at it, not really seeing it. Was there a possibility?

Harry was so different to what I'd expected. I had to admit that he'd surprised me with his kindness and generosity, and his clear understanding of my feelings. He'd made me laugh that day in Whitby, and I'd had fun. Probably the most fun I'd had in years. It had all felt so natural with him. Why else had I opened up about things that were nothing to do with him — private things that I rarely spoke about with anyone except those closest to me? And I barely knew Harry, yet for some reason, it had seemed perfectly right that I should talk to him about my innermost feelings.

I enjoyed his company. I found him highly attractive. I liked being around him. But that wasn't love. Was it?

'I can't think about all this now,' I said. 'I have more important things to worry about today.'

'I know, I know. The wanderer returns.' Jack scratched his head thoughtfully. 'Now, don't go getting your hopes up, will you? I know Derry's coming back, and I know he sent you that lovely Christmas present, and texted you after you left that voicemail and said you were welcome and he hoped you had a great Christmas, but don't go letting your imagination run riot, will you? I mean, he's a proud young man. Too proud, some might say. He's not going to beg for your forgiveness or make a big scene in front of everyone, so don't be disappointed if it's all a bit low key, will you?'

'Jack! As if I would!' Okay, so maybe I *had* got carried away earlier, but it didn't matter. I was all too aware of how proud Derry was. It was part of the reason he'd left. He felt I'd embarrassed him in front of the entire village, and he hated the sorrowful looks and comments he'd got from well-meaning people who thought it terrible that he'd found out Sir Paul was his father so late in his life.

Derry hated being pitied. He'd always been the same. I remembered Jack teaching him how to ride a bike when he was little. The number of times Derry fell off! Whenever I tried to pick him up, he would shrug me off and tell me, 'I can do it myself!'

Even though I'd begged Jack to put the stabilisers back on the bike, Derry wouldn't have it. And he'd succeeded in the end of course. Just as he and Jack had assured me he would.

'What time's the christening?'

'One o'clock,' I said. 'Heaps of time sadly. I wish it were earlier, so I didn't have time to sit here and fret.'

'Well,' Jack said, 'I don't know about you, but I'm going back to bed. I've got the papers from downstairs so I'm going to tackle the crossword and take it easy. I've even made myself a flask of tea.'

I laughed. 'Good for you.'

'And what are you going to do with yourself?'

'I think,' I said, after considering the matter, 'that I'm going to get a shower, get dressed and go for a walk myself. Clear my head.'

'Past Eight Bells by any chance?'

His eyes were twinkling, and I gave him a stern look. 'No, not past Eight Bells. Along the beach, I think. I may even have a paddle. I can't remember the last time I did that.'

'In January! Are you mad?'

'It's not that cold out there today,' I said. 'Okay, maybe it is. Maybe not a paddle then. But a walk along the sands will do me good. It's been too long.'

'You do that, my love,' he said. 'Blow away those cobwebs and get yourself ready for this afternoon. It will all go well, you know. You'll see.'

Oh, how I hoped he was right!

****

'You look lovely, Rhiannon,' Will said, before dropping a light kiss on my cheek. As he pulled away, I saw the understanding in his eyes and smiled at him.

'Thank you, Will. As do you and Lexi and Milo. Oh, and look at Ellie! How adorable.'

Lexi, her long red hair swept up for a change, was wearing a smart cream suit with matching hat. Standing outside St Hilda's church with her mother and her stepfather, holding her baby daughter, she looked every inch the Lady Boden-Kean she'd become, and a far cry from the jean and welly-clad girl she'd been when she worked on Whisperwood Farm, back in the days when Eliza's grandmother owned it.

Will, in a smart navy suit, looked a real gentleman, and two-year-old Milo in his own navy trousers and blazer, looked so cute I wanted to hug him there and then. Ellie, meanwhile, was a vision in the long, ivory christening gown that had been her brother's, her father's, and her grandfather's before her.

'You're right,' I said, stroking her head gently. 'She does have red hair! How fabulous.'

'She won't think so when she's at school,' Lexi said, with feeling. 'Hopefully as she gets older, she'll realise how lucky she is. We redheads are pretty extraordinary creatures, after all, right, Mum?'

Her mother, Zoe, smiled. 'Absolutely, Lexi.'

'You most certainly are,' Will said, putting his arm around his wife's waist then bending to softly kiss his sleeping daughter's forehead.

He straightened and gave me a knowing look as we heard Sophie's voice drowning out the general buzz of chat from everyone else.

'Any sign of the godfather yet?'

'I'm right here,' Nat drawled, ignoring Sophie's tut and pretending, as did we all, that he'd misunderstood what she meant. 'All set and reporting for duty. As is Ellie's beautiful godmother,' he added, indicating Georgia, who looked a vision in a smart pale blue suit.

It was rare that I saw her out of riding clothes, and I smiled at her in approval. 'You look so pretty, Georgia. That colour suits you.'

Georgia thanked me for the compliment, then leaned over and whispered in my ear, 'Don't worry. He'll be here soon; I know he will.'

I nodded, hoping she was right. But it was almost time for the christening to start, and there was no sign of Derry. What if he'd changed his mind?

'What if he's changed his mind?' Sophie said, echoing the thoughts in mine. 'That would be a disaster, wouldn't it?'

'Not really,' Lexi said comfortably. 'I'm sure we could arrange something. Besides, it won't come to that. Derry will be here.'

'You sound very sure,' Eliza said. 'Have you heard from him?'

'He texted me yesterday and said he'd be here, and I have no reason to believe he won't be. Just give him a minute or two.'

My legs felt almost too weak to support me. Flynn must have noticed how nervous I was feeling.

'Don't worry,' he said softly. 'Everything will be fine.'

I managed a faint smile. 'I know, I know. He'll be here.'

'This will be you soon, getting the bairn christened.'

Flynn and I glanced over at Rose, who was wearing her favourite bright pink woollen coat, and was patting the stomach of a clearly mortified Fuchsia.

'Mam, give over! Honestly, what are you like?'

'That's my grandbairn in there,' Rose said. 'He likes a pat from his nanna, don't you, pet?'

'Mam!' Fuchsia rolled her eyes. 'I can't take you anywhere.'

'Is it a boy then, Pan?' Gabriel queried. 'Your mum never said.'

'Didn't she?' Pandora sounded hurt. 'We had the scan in December, and we told her it was a boy then. I thought you'd have been telling everyone by now, Mum. You usually do.'

Sophie looked distinctly flustered. 'Be fair, Pandora, it's hardly down to me to tell people, is it? That's your job. Yours and Fuchsia's.'

'It's never stopped you before,' Fuchsia said bluntly. 'Anyone would think you didn't want anything to do with this baby.'

There was an awkward silence before Archie gave a far-too-hearty laugh and said, 'What an idea! I know for a fact she's over the moon. We both are. We can't wait to meet our little grandson, can we, Sophe?'

'No, of course not,' Sophie said.

'Tell your face that,' said Rose.

Beside me, Flynn tutted. 'I do wish she'd be a bit more tactful,' he whispered to me. 'Look at poor Sophie. She's clearly struggling.'

'What's her problem, do you think?' I whispered back.

'I don't know, but Fuchsia tells me that she's hardly mentioned the baby at all, and she's not asked any questions about the pregnancy or the birth plan. Most unlike Sophie. Rose was expecting her to fully take over, and was all set to warn her off, but there's been no need. Rose is quite upset for the girls.'

'At least Rose seems excited,' I said.

He grinned. 'She's really got involved. At first, she was horrified by the idea, but once she realised Sophie was totally against it, she went all out to prove she's nothing like her. She can't do enough for them. Even Violet's making lists of possible names for them.'

'Oh, bless her! How sweet. When does Fuchsia go on maternity leave?'

'She's insisting upon working until mid-April, as she wants more time off work after the baby's born. Which reminds me, I must ask Meggie to draft an advert for a temporary receptionist. They'll need training up for at least a month before Fuchsia goes off. I hadn't realised how little time there is left.'

Eliza sidled up to us, holding tightly to her hat. 'Nearly time to go in,' she said. 'I'll be quite glad to go indoors. I hate wearing hats, and I'm paranoid this one's going to blow away.'

'Do you think Derry has changed his mind?' I asked her anxiously.

'I'm sure he'll be here,' she said. 'He wouldn't let Lexi down. You know how much he likes her.'

'I suppose you're right. It's just, I thought maybe he'd arrive early and—'

169

'He's here!' Eliza nudged me, her eyes wide, and I turned, feeling as though my heart had leapt into my throat as I saw Derry hurrying up the path toward the church.

Words failed me. I could only stare at him in wonder, relief, fear, and joy, all rolled into one big lump of emotions that threatened to choke me. He drew near, and I saw he'd filled out, become broader. His hair was a little shorter, his cheekbones a little sharper, his face a bit more hollowed out than it had been. He was a man. My handsome young boy was a man. Of course, he'd been a man when he left, but not to me. He'd always been my little boy. But this twenty-eight-year-old standing not far from me was different. Older. Perhaps wiser?

Sophie got to him first. She hugged him and began asking him a lot of questions and telling him how people were worried he wouldn't turn up, but she'd known he wouldn't let them down. He managed to extricate himself from her and made his way over to Will and Lexi and I saw him kiss Lexi and hug Will, and then he bent to shake hands with Milo, and stroked Ellie's hair. They chatted for a few moments, clearly at ease with each other, and I saw Will nod over in my direction.

My heart thudded and my mouth went dry as I waited for what felt like forever.

Derry slowly turned his head and looked directly at me. I gave him a nervous smile, realising my hands were clenched and I was barely breathing.

Derry nodded and turned back to Will.

I gasped and Eliza and Tally put their hands on my back, so I suppose I must have staggered somewhat.

'Are you okay?' Eliza asked softly. Her eyes were full of sympathy, and I blinked away tears.

'Of course. I'm fine.'

'I'm sorry,' she said. 'I thought he'd at least come over.'

'Oh, it is what it is,' I said lightly. 'He's only just arrived. Give him chance.'

'I can't believe he did that,' Tally murmured. She sounded as shocked as I was, and I gave her a grateful smile as she put her arm around my shoulders.

170

At that moment, the vicar beckoned us all in and we filed into St Hilda's. My mind was whirling. What on earth had happened? What had I done wrong? He'd sent me that beautiful mother-and-child hair slide, and the hare and moon brooch at Christmas. He'd seemed to have forgiven me. Why had he ignored me, after all this time?

I felt sick and wretched, and if the christening had been for anyone other than Will and Lexi's child, I'd have walked out and gone home. But I couldn't do that to them, so I stayed, barely taking in a word of the service as my heart cracked a little more with every passing minute that Derry didn't look at me. Did I really deserve all this?

The service seemed to go on forever. I watched, my eyes blurry with tears, as Derry took his place at the font and repeated his promises to Baby Ellie. He looked so grown-up and mature, yet he was behaving in a most immature manner. As much as I hated to admit it, his behaviour was childish and uncalled for. I wasn't going to accept it. I'd had enough.

As we all filed out of the church and gathered outside for photographs, and to tell Will and Lexi how well it had gone, and how well-behaved their child had been, I made my way over to Derry and took hold of his arm.

He spun round and I flinched at the unwelcoming look in his eyes.

'Derry! What's wrong with you? You could at least have come over to say hello.'

He seemed at a loss to know what to say in response. I saw conflict in his expression and wondered what was going on in his mind.

'Hello, Mum.'

'What was all that about earlier? Why did you ignore me outside the church?'

He shrugged. 'I didn't. Not really. Just — well, I was talking to Will and Lexi, and then the vicar called us in, so...'

'That's a pretty poor excuse,' I said. 'You embarrassed me.'

'Yeah, well, I know how that feels.'

171

I closed my eyes in despair. 'Okay, so you're still angry with me? You still haven't forgiven me for not telling you who your father was? After all this time, you're still harbouring a grudge?'

'It's not a grudge,' he said reluctantly. 'I'm over all that. It doesn't matter.'

'Then what? I thought we were okay now. You sent me those lovely presents at Christmas. It was as if you were telling me you missed me, and that we were back on track. Why send them if you still hate me so much?'

Derry prodded the gravel with his right foot, as he seemed to be trying to think of what he could say to me. 'I did miss you, and we are. I'm over it. Who my father was, I mean.' He sighed. 'It seems like so long ago now anyway.'

'Then what is it?' I gazed up at him, silently pleading with him to be the Derry I'd once been so close to. I couldn't bear this much longer.

'Just — stuff.'

'That's not an answer,' I said. 'We need to talk. When we leave here, we'll get to the bottom of all this. Have a proper conversation and sort it out, once and for all.' I gave him a tearful smile. 'It's so good to have you back, darling. I can't wait to get you home.'

Derry glanced over his shoulder, then over at the church — anywhere, in fact, but at me.

'Derry?'

He turned back to face me, with clear reluctance.

'It's no good, Mum,' he said finally. 'I can't go back to The Hare and Moon. Not yet anyway.'

'But I thought—'

'So did I,' he said bleakly. 'But when it comes right down to it, I'm not ready for this. The truth is, I need some time away from you to think. I'm sorry.'

'Time away from me? But you've had years!'

'I know, but things haven't worked out as I thought. Coming back here — I can't explain. I thought I could, but I can't. Not yet.'

'Everyone back to Kearton Hall!' Woody, Will's much-loved housekeeper, beamed at us all as she informed us that she'd laid on an amazing spread for us.

'Great,' Derry said. 'I'm starving.'

He turned away from me, but I pulled him back.

'Derry! You can't say that and leave. What are you going to do? Are you going straight back to Cornwall?'

He shook his head. 'I'll find a room in a pub or something for now. I don't want to leave here without sorting things out, but it's going to take time. Anyway, I'm sure you'd prefer it if I wasn't around to cramp your style.'

My heart thudded. 'What do you mean by that?'

He shrugged. 'I'll book into The Kearton Arms or find a B&B in Whitby.'

'You'll do no such thing.'

I groaned inwardly as I realised Sophie had been standing right behind me and had obviously heard every word.

'Derry, my love, it's so good to have you back in the village. Now, I won't hear of you staying at a pub or a bed and breakfast. I have plenty of room at The Old Vicarage. There's my Oliver's room standing empty. You're welcome to stay as long as you like.'

'He doesn't need to stay at yours, Sophie,' I gasped. 'It's kind of you, but he has a home already, and his bedroom's ready for him.'

'Maybe so,' she said, 'but he doesn't want it, does he?'

I was dimly aware of Gabriel and Eliza moving towards us, and from somewhere I heard Archie say, 'Stay out of this, Sophie. The lad's got a home at the pub.'

'He said he's not going back there,' Sophie explained. 'What would you have me do? See him homeless?'

'Oh, Sophie, don't,' Gabriel said. 'It's between Derry and Rhiannon.'

I gazed up at Derry, silently pleading with him to come home, to give us a chance to resolve our issues. What had he meant by that sarcastic comment?

He closed his eyes for a moment, then turned to Sophie. 'Thank you, Sophie. That's kind of you. I'd love to stay at yours for a while if that's okay with Archie.'

Archie shot me a worried look. 'Well, er—'

'It's fine,' I said quietly. 'Whatever he wants.'

I stayed stock still, staring after them all as they moved away from me, heading back down the path.

Sophie turned back to me and seemed to hesitate a moment, then she hurried over and laid a hand on my arm.

'I'm sorry. It's better that he's under my roof than some pub or something isn't it?'

I stared at her in surprise. 'I—I suppose so.'

'I'll try to make him see sense; I promise.' She gave me a weak smile. 'I know what you're going through. Sons. They break your heart, don't they?'

To my amazement, she pulled me into a brief hug, then hurried after her family.

'Well, that was unexpected.'

I realised Will was standing next to me, and I let out a long breath. 'You're not kidding. She's full of surprises.'

'She means well.'

'Clearly. I've never heard Sophie speak to me like that before.'

Will gave me a sympathetic smile. 'Are you all right? That was terribly harsh of Derry.'

It all suddenly felt too much.

'I'm awfully sorry, darling,' I told him, 'but would you mind if I didn't go back to Kearton Hall? I think I should be going home instead.'

'Of course. Do you want me to come with you?'

He was so sweet, so kind. Why couldn't Derry be more like him?

'Don't be silly. This is your baby's christening. Enjoy it. I'll be fine at home with Jack and Kerry. Off you go.'

'I'm so sorry. I can't think what's got into him,' he said sadly. 'I'll try to have a word with him, I promise.'

'I think you should leave him be, Will.' I straightened, tilting my chin at him, and trying desperately to hang onto some semblance

174

of dignity. 'It's Derry's choice to make, and he's made it. I'll speak to you later.'

He kissed me on the cheek, and I turned away, only to see Tally hovering by the church door, her face pale and pinched. She looked as if she'd had a terrible shock. As I watched, she put her head down and left the church yard, but for some reason, she didn't turn in the direction of Kearton Hall, but went the opposite way. So she was ducking out of the christening party, too? Something had clearly upset her. It seemed to be the day for it.

15

I thought long and hard about going to Harry's that evening. I almost called him a couple of times to cancel, but Jack talked me out of it. He'd been a huge comfort to me that afternoon, since I'd arrived back from the christening rather distraught, to say the least.

'The little devil! What does he think he's playing at, treating you that way? I think it's time I had words with young Derry.'

'No! Don't get involved, Jack,' I'd begged. 'The last thing I want is for you two to fall out. You've always been so close, and Derry needs to have some link to his family, and his past. We can't let my father win.'

Jack smiled. 'Family, eh? Is that what I am?'

I was astonished he could even question it. 'Well, of course you are. You've been with us since before Derry even arrived, and we've seen you just about every day since. How could you think of yourself as anything but family?'

I was rather touched to see tears in his dark eyes. 'Oh, Jack! Bless you, are you all right?'

'Yes, I'm fine, my darling. It's nice to hear you say it, that's all.'

I wondered again about Jack's real family. Where were they? And why did he have no contact with them? It was all rather strange and terribly sad. He was such a lovely chap. Who could possibly fall out with him? Maybe, I mused, they were all dead. I'd never asked him much before because he always shut me down whenever the subject was raised, but with his recent illness,

I couldn't help wondering if he was having second thoughts. Surely, if there had been some sort of falling out, now was the time to put it right?

'Jack, never mind about my family troubles. What about yours?'

He looked at me, clearly taken aback by the question. 'Mine? What family troubles?'

'Well,' I said, rather hesitantly, 'you must have some. You don't talk about your family. You never have. Do you have any contact with them at all?'

Jack leaned back in the chair and stared into his cup of tea, seeming to consider how much, if anything, he should tell me.

'My parents are long gone,' he said at last. 'We hadn't spoken in years. Both they and my brother disowned me.'

'But why? What did you do?'

He gave an abrupt laugh. 'You really want to know?'

'I do. Really.'

Jack sighed. 'I became a chef. That's what I did.'

'What?' I couldn't believe it. 'You're not serious.'

'I'm absolutely serious, my darling. You see, I was expected to go the traditional way — to Cambridge, then into a *suitable* career. Politics, or the forces perhaps. When I announced I wanted to study *cooking* — well! You can imagine.'

'But to fall out with you over it? It's ridiculous!'

'Not to my family. They were sticklers for tradition. Anyway, it doesn't matter now, does it? Even my brother passed away four years ago. It's all in the past.'

'Oh, Jack. I'm so sorry. So, you have no family left at all? Did your brother have any children?'

He shook his head. 'None. Although my sister did. She's got two, a boy and a girl. They'll be a bit older than you I think. They'll have families of their own, no doubt.'

'You don't know? So your sister disowned you, too?'

He paused, eyeing me with what looked suspiciously like unease. 'Not at first.'

'She didn't mind you becoming a chef?'

He put down his cup and stared into the fire, and I realised he was remembering his past, and it wasn't easy for him to do.

'I'm sorry,' I said. 'It doesn't matter. Forget I asked.'

'I — I did something unforgivable,' he said at last. 'At least, it was unforgivable as far as she was concerned. She made it very plain to me that there was no going back from it.' He shook his head. 'She said she'd managed to overlook me embarrassing the family by going off to be a *cook*, but she couldn't overlook this, and we were finished. I haven't seen or heard from her since. As far as I know, she's alive and well. I haven't heard anything to the contrary. My brother's obituary was in the paper four years ago, but I've seen nothing about my sister, so I presume she's okay. '

I didn't know how to respond. What on earth could Jack possibly have done that would make his sister turn her back on him in such a fashion?

'We make a good pair, don't we?' he said suddenly. I realised he'd been watching me and there was a look of anxiety on his face, as if he were wondering if I would judge him. 'Both of us disowned by our families. And here we are, thoroughly splendid people!'

I knew he was trying to make a joke of it, but he didn't fool me. The pain was still there in his eyes. It didn't matter how long ago his family had severed its connection with him, it still hurt, and I could relate to that all too well.

'It's their loss,' I said, meaning it. 'And my gain. I'm so sorry you went through all that, Jack, but I'm awfully glad you found Kearton Bay and The Hare and Moon. I think the universe placed us exactly where we both needed to be, at just the right time.'

The sadness vanished and his eyes twinkled. 'The universe has a habit of doing that.'

'It does!' I agreed.

'And I think where you're supposed to be this evening is at Eight Bells with this Harry Jarvis chap. So you'd better text him and let him know you'll be going, don't you think?'

I couldn't argue with that, and quite honestly, I didn't want to. The day had been an awful strain, and my spirits were low, but I had a feeling that dinner with Harry would be just the thing to take me out of my misery.

****

Eight Bells was a rather splendid Georgian house, standing on the cliff top with fabulous views over the North Sea. It was surrounded by a rather overgrown and tangled garden, and its front door was shabby with peeling paint, but it had a charm I found thoroughly appealing.

It even had its old sign outside, left over from the days when it had been a pub, many moons before Matthew Reynolds had bought it and run it as a hotel. How charming that both Matthew and Harry had left it in place — something I pointed out immediately to Harry when he opened the front door.

'Oh, that old thing,' he said. 'I hadn't got around to taking it down yet. Why? Do you like it?'

'I think it's lovely and adds a certain something to the place. Please don't remove it.'

Harry glanced up at the shabby, wooden sign that was creaking gently in the wind, and shrugged. 'Okay, if you like it, I'll keep it.'

His eyes met mine and I realised my face had heated up again, even though the January air was terribly cold and standing up here on the top of a cliff didn't ease the situation. How could I possibly be hot? It didn't make sense. It *must* be the menopause.

'What am I thinking? You must be freezing. Come in.'

Harry stepped aside and ushered me into the hallway of his home. I was heartened to see that there were radiators in the house and heaved a silent sigh of relief as I brushed against one and felt the heat. Bliss!

'Let me take your coat.'

Harry, I have to say, looked extremely smart. He was wearing navy blue trousers and a light blue shirt, and I discreetly admired him as he moved away to hang up my coat.

He certainly hadn't let himself go, as so many men of his age had. Yet he wasn't overly groomed either. His hair was streaked with grey and kept short and neat, and the lines on his face proved he hadn't succumbed to the cosmetic surgery that seemed popular with people in his profession, and indeed in the place he'd once lived.

I could only be grateful for that. There was something terribly handsome about a lived-in face. It always seemed a shame to me that the marks of a life well-lived were erased in favour of a blank canvas. The crone had a beauty of her own, and I wished people didn't fear looking their age so much.

'I'm sorry about the state of the place,' he said, turning to me as he indicated a door on the left-hand side of the hallway. 'Do come through and make yourself as comfortable as you can.'

I could see what he meant, though it wasn't as bad as I'd feared. The room he showed me into was stripped bare of wallpaper and had bare floorboards. Apart from the rather gorgeous fireplace, there wasn't an awful lot I could say about it, except I hoped it wasn't where we would be eating, since there wasn't a stick of furniture in it.

'This is the main room,' he said. 'At least, it will be. It will mostly be for the guests.'

'Guests?' I couldn't hide my surprise. 'You're going to run it as a hotel then? Like Matthew Reynolds did? Although it wasn't exactly a grand hotel. More a glorified bed and breakfast, to be honest. Is that what you're planning to do then?'

He grinned. 'What? Run a grand hotel or a glorified bed and breakfast?'

My cheeks burned again, and I laid my hands on them to cool them down. 'I'm sorry. Did that sound dismissive? It wasn't meant to be.'

'Not at all. To be honest, I intended to live in it alone. I'd not even thought of running it as a business. But then my architect suggested it might be the sensible thing to do and, although I took a fair bit of persuading, I realised he might be onto something.'

'It is a rather large house for one person,' I agreed, following him as he led me into another room. 'Oh, this is much nicer!'

It was a decent size and had views out over the wilderness that passed for a garden. With another stunning fireplace and large windows, it was a lovely room. I suppose it helped that the walls were painted in a sort of fawn colour, and that there were rugs on the floor and a sofa and chair, as well as a TV.

'This will be completely different when it's finished,' Harry told me. 'The plan is to knock through and make one huge lounge/diner for the guests. There'll be French doors where these windows are, so they'll have access to the garden. Not that it's much of a garden now,' he added, clearly embarrassed. 'But I'll get round to sorting it eventually.'

'It sounds lovely,' I agreed. 'What about you? Will you have any private space?'

'The right-hand side rooms will be mine. There'll be a kitchen diner and a small living room, plus I'll have a master suite on the second floor. And there'll be the garden, too, of course. Providing the weather is good.'

I laughed. 'On top of a cliff in a Yorkshire coastal village? Good luck.'

He looked worried. 'Is it that bad? Even in summer?'

'No,' I assured him. 'I'm teasing. We get some glorious weather in the summer, don't worry. I'm sure it will be amazing when it's completed. Would you mind if I sat down?'

'Oh my God, I'm such an idiot! Of course, please take a seat.'

'Thank you.' I sank into the sofa and settled myself comfortably. 'This is lovely, too,' I told him. 'Very comfy.'

'It's not staying,' he said. 'At least, I'll probably put it in my upstairs suite when this room is finished.'

'It all sounds very grand,' I told him. 'A suite! How wonderful.'

'It is a bit special,' he said, sounding rather proud of the fact. 'There's a large master bedroom with en suite and sitting room, then across the hallway a couple of smaller bedrooms with a Jack and Jill bathroom. For Amy and — hopefully — for Rufus, too. One day.'

'I'm sure they'll love that,' I said gently.

'I hope so.' He bit his lip, clearly wondering if the day would ever come when both his children would be under his roof. My heart went out to him. There was nothing harder than being a parent estranged from your child, whatever the reason.

'I can smell something cooking,' I remarked, thinking it was time we changed the subject before we both got too depressed. 'And it's making me very hungry.'

'I was going to attempt fish and chips, but I thought it would doom me to failure, so I didn't.'

He grinned and I smiled back, glad that his mood had lightened again.

'So what *are* you cooking?'

'Something hale and hearty and exactly right for January,' he said. 'A chicken and red wine casserole with herby dumplings. Sound okay?'

My mouth fell open in astonishment. 'Seriously?'

'Seriously.' He looked nervous suddenly. 'You're not a vegetarian, are you? I should have asked. I know you eat fish, but some vegetarians do, don't they? What are they called? Pescatarian or something. You're not one of those are you?'

I gave him a reassuring smile. 'Don't worry. I eat meat, and I love the sound of that casserole. I'm just surprised you're cooking something so—'

'Don't get too excited,' he said. 'It's basic. I find casseroles the easiest thing in the world to cook.'

'But the dumplings! I've never even made those.'

'Dumplings aren't difficult at all,' he assured me. 'One day I'll show you how to make them, if you like?'

Jack had offered dozens of times to teach me how to make dumplings, but I'd never taken him up on his offer. I was, therefore, rather surprised to hear myself say, all too eagerly, 'That would be marvellous.' I was no cook, and didn't have much interest in learning, so where that response came from, I couldn't imagine.

He looked pleased, though, so I didn't correct myself.

'Would you like a drink?' he asked.

'After the day I've had, I'd like several,' I said.

He wrinkled his nose in sympathy. 'Like that, eh? Christening didn't go according to plan?'

'I'll tell you over dinner,' I said.

'Fair enough. I'll get you that drink. What would you like? I've got a rather delicious Portuguese red to drink with dinner, but I can get you a white wine now. Or would you prefer something even stronger? If it's that much of an emergency, I have a good whisky left over from Christmas.'

I laughed. 'Maybe tea to start with, and we'll save the whisky for afterwards.'

He nodded and hurried back into the hallway, and I leaned back in the sofa, wishing I had something to fan my face with. *Afterwards.* It sounded so… leading. Like I was trying to seduce him or something, which, obviously I wasn't. I hoped he hadn't read anything into it. Although I was quite sure he had enough on his mind, what with the renovations and his ongoing mission to win over his children.

I couldn't help but wonder what Eliza would think if she saw me sitting here right now, about to have dinner with her scoundrel of an ex. And Derry. What would he say? Probably that he'd expect nothing else from me.

Harry returned a few minutes later, bearing tea.

'Why do you use this side of the house if you're intending to make the right-hand side your living space?' I queried, taking the cup from him with a grateful smile.

He sat down on the sofa beside me. 'Because at the moment, the right-hand side is in an even worse state than this one. There's the ugliest fireplace you've ever seen, and it's a bit dark and gloomy. It will be much lighter and brighter once I have the two rooms knocked into one and I replace that fireplace.'

'I thought you'd be further on than this,' I admitted. 'The gossip in the Bay is that a builder's van has been parked up here every day for the last couple of weeks, and that there's been a lot of coming and going with other tradespeople, too. I was expecting to walk into a palace.'

He looked worried. 'Oh fuck. You weren't, were you?' He glanced around him, the crease on his forehead deepening. 'I suppose it is a bit of a shit hole now, but they've been working on the upstairs. It was truly abominable up there, and if there's

183

one thing I can't abide it's a vile bathroom. Plus, I wanted the children's rooms to be ready, just in case.'

'Has Eliza said when you can have Amy to stay over?' I asked.

He shook his head. 'Not yet. I can't blame her. There's a room and bathroom for her, but they need furnishing and decorating, and I want Amy to choose her own stuff. I thought it would make her feel more at home, you know?'

'I'm sure she'd love to do that,' I said, noting how his eyes sparkled when he talked about his children and feeling a warmth towards him for it.

'But even with a decent bedroom and bathroom, I can't blame her for saying I need to sort the kitchen out too. And then there's the garden. It needs clearing. It's a bloody mess.'

'What do you intend to do with it?' I asked. 'It's quite large, as I recall.'

'No idea,' he admitted. 'Gardening's never been my thing really.'

'But you're so lucky to have an outside space,' I said. 'One thing I do miss about living in Old Town is the lack of a garden.'

'Old Town?'

'Sorry, that's what we call the oldest part of the village – the part that goes from the top of Bay Street down to the sea. The more recent part is nicknamed Up Top. It's where the sea captains had their homes, and where the farms are, and the railway line was.'

'Right. Gotcha.'

'Obviously,' I continued, 'I have the beach on my doorstep, which is huge compensation, but even so… The gardens at our house in Polkayne were stunning. They're probably the only thing I miss about my childhood home. You ought to plant a wildflower garden,' I added enthusiastically. 'The bees and butterflies are in such danger. Anything we can do to help them… Oh, and a herb garden. Can you imagine the beautiful scents? And you'd be able to use the fresh herbs in your cooking. Jack grows some in pots on the windowsills. Perhaps we could buy some from you? And maybe vegetables. Ooh, you could plant some fruit bushes and an apple tree or two!' I blushed as I realised I'd got a bit carried away. 'Sorry.'

He smiled. 'It sounds wonderful. I need someone else's vision. Right now, all I can see is that it's an eyesore, and the fence needs repairing. I don't want my kids wandering around on a cliff top, do I?'

'Amy's lived here long enough to be smart about things like that,' I assured him. 'She knows the dangers. I'm not sure about Rufus, though.'

'He's only seven. I certainly wouldn't be happy to risk it. There's an old post and rail fence that you can just about make out through the overgrown bushes and weeds, but it's got to come down. I need something more secure for Rufus.'

'Has your ex-wife said he can stay then?'

'Melody?' He gave a snort of laughter. 'Fat chance. Honestly, I don't know if I'm kidding myself. Rufus is extremely unlikely to come over to Britain any time soon. Maybe he'll never see this house. Even so, I had to get his room ready — just in case.'

'Quite right,' I said. 'One never knows. Don't give up, Harry. Never give up.'

'I could say the same to you,' he said. 'Anyway, dinner should be ready. I'll go and serve. I'm so sorry it will be on trays on our laps. Hardly the most sophisticated meal you've ever been invited to, I should imagine.'

'Sophisticated is highly overrated,' I assured him. 'I prefer informal and friendly any time.'

'Then you're in luck,' he said, placing his cup on the floor and springing to his feet. 'Informal and friendly I can manage, no problem.'

He was right. Although it was a bit tricky, balancing a tray on my knee while enjoying Harry's red wine casserole with herby dumplings, and the rather delicious wine that accompanied it, I enjoyed the informality of the occasion, and Harry couldn't have been more entertaining. He told me lots of stories about his time in America, and some of the disasters that had befallen him during filming of his television shows, both in the States and closer to home.

'So, I'm gathering you're not a country person,' I said, in between mouthfuls of casserole which were, quite frankly, to die for.

Harry, who had just regaled me about a particularly harrowing event that had taken place when he was filming an episode of *Twice as Nice* in the Herefordshire countryside, involving a barrel of apples, an irate farmer, and an extremely hungry pig, paused, fork halfway to his mouth, as he formulated a response.

'I've never been much of a one for the rural life before,' he admitted. 'I was brought up in London and I love the buzz of a city. When Eliza first moved here, I thought she'd lost the plot. I couldn't see the appeal at all.'

'Yet here you are,' I said.

'Here I am.' He put down his fork and gazed out of the window at the tangle of undergrowth outside. I had a feeling he wasn't seeing it at all. 'I think maybe living in Malibu helped change my mind. Not that Malibu's anything like here but having the ocean on my doorstep was wonderful. Looking out at the sea every day, it does something to you. Hearing the waves when you open the window or step outside, smelling the ozone, practically tasting the salt in the air. It's so soothing. I needed it, and I knew, once I returned to England, that I couldn't deal with not being near the sea again. So where better than Kearton Bay, where my daughter was living?'

'And you don't find it too difficult? You don't miss London?'

'I love London,' he said frankly. 'But I think I need a quieter pace of life now. Things have changed. I've changed. I'm living life in the slow lane these days.'

I laughed. 'You're living life in a building site right now.'

'Well, true enough. But that won't last long. By summer it will be a home at last. I intend to make it a permanent one. I never want to move again.'

Something in his voice made any flippant remark I might have been thinking of die. There was a wistfulness in his tone that touched me. There was more to Harry's move than he was telling me, I was sure.

He blinked suddenly and picked up his fork. 'Listen to me droning on,' he said. 'You were going to tell me about the christening and what happened with Derry. I'm guessing that, since you're here, it didn't go too well?'

'You could say that,' I said. Slowly I told him the gist of what had happened at the church that morning, and he listened to me with huge patience and a sympathetic expression.

'It doesn't make sense, does it?' he said thoughtfully, when I'd finally finished pouring it all out to him. 'I could understand it if he hadn't been in touch with you since he moved away, but that hair slide and brooch... Anyone would believe they'd been forgiven if they received those gifts.'

'That's what I said!' I cried. 'I would have sworn it meant he was ready to move on and put all that unpleasant business behind us. I don't understand it.'

'You can't be blamed for thinking that. He sounds a very mixed-up young man. I'm so sorry you went through all that. It must have been horrible for you.'

'Thank you,' I said softly.

'For what?'

'For not criticising him or being mean about him. I couldn't have borne that.'

'He's still your son, Rhiannon,' he said. 'I'm sure whatever he's done, however he's behaved, you still love him as much. Besides, I'm the last person to call out anyone else's bad behaviour. I'm still living down my own.'

'You're not as bad as you make out,' I told him. 'You should be kinder to yourself.'

He gave me a rueful smile. 'Tell that to my exes. Let's face it, I've lied, I've cheated, I've broken hearts... I regret such a lot of my past. There's a part of me that thinks I deserve everything I've got.'

'You're not the only one with regrets, Harry,' I said. 'But what good does regret do? The only thing we can do is learn from our past mistakes and resolve to do better in the future. You're doing all you can to make it up to Eliza and Amy, and to build bridges with them. I'm doing the same for Derry. What more can we do?'

'You're right of course,' he agreed. 'But it's hard not to feel, deep down inside, that maybe I don't deserve a second chance.'

'If you don't, I don't.'

'Of course you do! As far as I can see you've done nothing wrong.'

'I lied to my son about his father.'

'No you didn't. You just didn't tell him who he was, and I'm sure you had good reasons for that.'

'He thinks the worst of me,' I said sadly. 'Even today, he said something sarcastic about cramping my style, as if I were seeing someone.'

Harry's eyes widened. '*Are* you seeing someone?'

'You!' That dreadful burning sensation in my face returned as I realised what I'd said, and it dawned on me that, at the grand old age of fifty, I'd finally started blushing with embarrassment. How very odd! I would have thought that the crone would have been much less prone to embarrassment than either the maiden or the mother, yet I'd never succumbed to the blushes during their years. Trust me to be contrary.

'What I mean,' I gabbled furiously, 'is that I was seeing you tonight. Not that we're *seeing* seeing each other. You know, as in *seeing* each other.'

'You mean romantically?'

'Yes, yes that way. We're not seeing each other romantically. Just tonight. As friends. Obviously.'

I stared down at my empty plate and wished I could vanish as quickly and as thoroughly as Harry's delicious herby dumplings had. Then my mouth twitched with amusement as I thought about how that sounded.

'Are you laughing?' he said, and I heard the surprise in his voice and glanced up at him apologetically, relieved to see a twinkle in his eyes.

'Sorry. I was just thinking about your herby dumplings.'

His eyebrows shot up. 'Were you indeed? How very precocious of you.'

Oh, my face was on fire!

'I'll take this into the kitchen,' I said, getting to my feet. 'It was absolutely lovely, Harry. Thank you so much.'

He put his own tray on the ground, then stood and took mine from me. Placing it on the floor next to his, he took my hand in his and kissed it gently. 'Thank *you*,' he said quietly. 'You've been wonderful company. I so enjoy being with you, Rhiannon.'

Something most peculiar was happening to me. I'd never experienced the strange, fluttery sensation in my stomach before, but right now it was like I had a caged bird in there, doing its absolute best to escape. Of course, I'd felt lust before, lots of times, but this was different, even to the gentler, more loving feelings I'd had for Will. It quite took my breath away and I wasn't sure what to do about it.

Harry's hand cupped my face as he gazed at me, and I found myself unable to look away. I saw his glance drop to my lips and my stomach lurched in anticipation. He was going to kiss me!

I felt as if I were melting into him, and an overpowering longing for his lips to crush mine seized me, making me forget all about why this was such a bad idea. Derry, Eliza, his battle for access, my son's terrible opinion of me... all forgotten as we moved closer, and I closed my eyes and waited with delicious anticipation.

There was a loud bang on the door and my eyes snapped open in alarm. Harry jumped away from me as if he'd been shot.

'What the fuck?'

'You'd better see who it is.'

I sank back onto the sofa feeling dazed with shock and, I had to admit, bitter disappointment. Whoever it was I could have cheerfully strangled them. My hormones were sloshing around all over the place with nowhere to go. How frustrating!

'I—I'd better—'

'Yes, go,' I said. 'I'll clear these away.'

He looked as dazed as I felt and hurried into the hallway. I placed Harry's plate on top of mine and stacked the two trays together, ready to carry into the kitchen. I heard a muttering of voices and then the door flew open, and Tally strode in, Harry following.

'Tally! Are you all right?'

My frustrations vanished as I saw the state she was in. She looked white-faced and rather panicky as she dropped into the armchair and ran a hand through her dark, windswept hair. I realised Harry was carrying a suitcase and gave him a puzzled look.

He stared at me, his face also suddenly pale, and a bewildered expression in his eyes.

'Tally?'

I didn't understand what on earth was happening. What was Tally doing at Harry's home, of all places?

She didn't even seem to notice me. She gazed up at Harry, her eyes shining with defiance.

'I've done it, Harry.'

He looked as baffled as I felt. 'Done what? What's going on?'

'I couldn't take any more. Today was the final straw. Of all the things to do! Anyway, I told them, that's it. You should have seen their faces when I said where I was going.'

Harry seemed to stagger a little as he stared at her in evident shock. 'Going? You mean—'

'Yes! I've done what you suggested, Harry. I'm moving in with you.'

16

Harry sipped the whisky that he so desperately needed and wondered, rather dazedly, what had happened. How had it come to this?

He nodded understandingly as Tally told him she was sorry to spring it all on him, but she'd had no choice, yet all the while he was thinking about Rhiannon, and remembering her expression as she'd hurriedly pulled on her coat and said she would leave them to it.

He'd tried to explain as he'd followed her to the door, but she seemed eager to leave.

'Don't worry about it. Another time perhaps? I think Tally needs you right now.'

Harry couldn't argue with that. There was something wrong with Tally, and what did she think she was playing at? Bad enough that she'd landed on his doorstep with a suitcase in hand, but to say that he'd been the one to suggest she move in with him! When had he ever said that? It was the last thing he needed or wanted.

Tally paused for breath, placed the mug of hot chocolate he'd made her on the floor, and took a tissue from her pocket. He realised she was crying and felt a pang of shame. Never mind his problems. She clearly needed his support.

'What exactly happened, Tally?' he asked her gently.

She sniffed.

'Are you sure you wouldn't like a whisky?'

Tally shook her head. 'Hate whisky. I'm okay with the hot chocolate, thank you.'

'Okay. So, you were going to explain...'

She dabbed at her eyes with a tissue and said, 'It's my mother. It's Derry. It's both.'

Harry frowned. What had all this to do with Rhiannon's son?

'At the christening you mean. Did he insult you? He was terribly rude to Rhiannon.'

'He's a horrible person,' she burst out. 'Selfish and thoughtless and cruel!'

Well! That was a bit harsh, especially for Tally. Whatever Derry had done he'd certainly wound her up.

'And your mother? What's she done?'

'She's asked him to stay with us! How could she?'

Harry felt thoroughly confused. He knew, of course, that Derry had refused to stay at Rhiannon's and that Sophie had asked him to stay at The Old Vicarage instead, but he wasn't sure why that affected Tally so much. Unless...

He stared at her as the fog began to clear. 'Tally, was — is Derry the man who broke your heart?'

Tally's eyes filled with tears again and she frantically wiped at them. 'How can I possibly live under the same roof as him? After everything he did!'

Harry swilled the whisky round in his glass and considered the matter. So that was why Tally was in such a state. And of course she couldn't be expected to live under the same roof as him. But surely Derry should know and understand that? What was he playing at, accepting Sophie's invitation?

'I take it then your mother doesn't know the full extent of what happened between you?'

'She doesn't know any of it,' Tally admitted. 'No one does except me and Derry. You know some of it, of course, but I was far too ashamed to admit what happened to anyone else.'

Harry sighed. 'I do think you're being too hard on yourself,' he said. 'So you had a one-night stand. It's not a big deal. Plenty of people have them and don't give it a second thought.'

'But it wasn't just a one-night stand,' she burst out tearfully. 'That's the point! And I thought — I thought—'

'Thought what?' he asked softly. 'That he loved you?'

She nodded furiously. 'Stupid or what?'

'Not stupid at all. Look, why don't you tell me the full story? I'm struggling to understand here. You told me you'd had a one-night stand with a man you'd always loved, but that he moved away a few days after you'd got together.'

'Which he did!'

'Yes, but you said he'd told you he was still in love with his ex and couldn't give you what you needed. I assumed you meant he'd gone off to be with her, which is why I never connected him with Derry. Didn't he move in with his grandfather in Cornwall? And who's his ex, anyway? What's she got to do with it?'

Tally took a shuddering breath and leaned back in the chair. 'You really want to know?'

He shrugged. 'Well, put it this way, I think it would make things an awful lot clearer if I had the full picture.'

'I suppose you're right. Okay, but it's embarrassing, so please don't look at me while I tell you, okay?'

Harry raised an eyebrow. 'Seriously?'

'Seriously. Look at the fireplace or something. This is humiliating enough.'

'Okay, if you say so.'

He turned and stared at the fireplace, thinking that it would be much better when he'd had all the wood burners fitted, and how cosy it would look once they were up and running.

'I — I've loved Derry Bone ever since I can remember.' Tally's voice, low and hesitant, dragged Harry's attention away from the fireplace and back to her. He almost forgot himself and looked round at her but remembered just in time and kept his gaze steady on the grate.

'Even when I was a little girl, he was the one I looked up to. The one I wanted to be around. I thought he was the most beautiful boy I'd ever seen, and as we grew older, he just got more handsome to me.'

193

Harry had never seen Derry, but he thought that if he were anything like his mother, he could well believe Tally's statement.

'Of course,' he never took much notice of me,' she continued. 'I was four years younger than him. Just a kid. Besides, he had his eyes on someone much more glamorous.'

Her voice had taken on a harder tone.

'His ex, by any chance?' Harry queried, still staring at the fireplace.

There was silence for a moment, then she said, 'Sorry, I forgot you can't see me nodding. Yeah, his ex. Lexi Bailey. Now Lady Boden-Kean.'

Harry was so surprised he spun round to face her, earning himself a disapproving look.

'Sorry, sorry!' He turned back to the grate, his mind whirling. 'Are you saying that Gabriel Bailey's daughter is playing away?'

There was a turn up for the books! He'd love to see the Angel Gabriel's face when he discovered that little bombshell.

'No, I'm not saying that,' Tally said heavily, and he felt a lurch of disappointment. He should have known that Bailey's family was perfect.

'Then, sorry, but I'm lost,' he admitted.

'He and Lexi had a relationship, of sorts. They were friends with benefits. He wanted more from her. He — he loved her. But she didn't want to get involved. It was just about sex, as far as she was concerned. Eventually, they broke it off entirely, and then Lexi got together with Will and that was that. True love, white wedding, two kids, the works.'

He heard the bitterness in her voice and took a swig of the whisky. This had certainly hurt her deeply, though from where he was sitting, Derry hadn't done anything wrong. You couldn't help who you fell in love with, as he knew all too well.

'I thought, once Derry and Lexi were over, he'd notice me at last. I'd tried for ages to get his attention, but I was invisible. I thought, with Lexi out of the picture, he'd see me. Really see me.'

'And did he?'

'No. He took up with some girl from one of the nearby villages. I was absolutely heartbroken.'

194

She gave a short laugh.

'I didn't know when I was well off. I should have been glad he'd not noticed me. I was happier then, even though I didn't realise it.'

'So, what happened to change things?' he asked gently, wishing she'd let him look round. It was difficult, listening to her while keeping his eyes fixed on the rather grimy fireplace. It desperately needed cleaning, he thought. He couldn't wait to get it all sorted.

'They broke up,' she said. 'Derry had discovered Sir Paul was his biological father, and he went a bit weird. That's when he fell out with Rhiannon, and the next thing I heard was that he'd finished with the girl in Moreton Cross and wanted nothing much to do with anyone. The only people he hung out with were his bandmates.'

'He was in a band?'

'Oh, yes. He's ever so good, you know. He sings and plays the guitar, and he's got a lovely voice. Really beautiful.'

He heard the wistful tone in her voice and hid a sympathetic smile. She was still carrying a torch for him, no matter what she said to the contrary.

'Anyway, Will booked him to play at the ball.'

'What ball?'

'Oh, yes. They were having a ball at Kearton Hall — a fancy dress ball. Derry's band was brilliant. Everyone said so. And Derry — Derry seemed to be different that night. Like, the magic of the evening had really got to him. He seemed to notice me. He even kissed my hand while he was on stage, and then he had a dance with me while the string quartet was playing. Oh!'

Harry risked a sneaky peek at her and saw that she was hugging herself, her eyes gazing upwards at the ceiling, her mind fixed on what had happened that magical night at Kearton Hall.

He quickly turned back to the fireplace. 'So is that when it happened? The one-night stand?'

'No. Although it almost did.' That bitter tone had crept in again he noted.

'Almost?'

'We'd gone outside, just the two of us, and we were talking, and he was flirting, and it all seemed perfect. Like, he'd finally seen me. Really seen me. And then he kissed me, and it was so beautiful and how I'd always imagined it…'

There was quiet and Harry knew she was remembering, and it was hurting her. He took another sip of whisky and waited.

'Then there was all this commotion, and Nat came running towards us yelling that Lexi had had an accident and we needed to call an ambulance, and that was that. Derry seemed to forget I even existed. It was all about Lexi. I should have known then.'

'But if she'd had an accident!' Harry thought she was being very unfair. 'How bad was it?'

Tally was silent for a moment, then she cleared her throat. 'Quite bad. She'd fallen through a trap door and knocked herself out. She had concussion and I think she broke her collar bone and some ribs.'

'Fucking hell! Well, you can't blame him for being worried then, can you?'

'No. I suppose not. But anyway, a few days later, he got in touch, and we met up on the beach, and it was all very romantic. He said he was sorry we'd been interrupted and that he thought we could have something special, and that he couldn't believe he'd never noticed how beautiful I was before.'

Harry rolled his eyes at the fireplace. Yeah, he'd used those lines himself.

'So, you know, er… one thing led to another, and I thought that was it. We were a couple. We saw each other during the following week, and it was always very romantic, although nothing much happened. I mean, we kissed and stuff, but it was mainly talking. There was never time for anything else — or any privacy. Then the next thing I heard, he'd left Kearton Bay and gone to live with his grandfather in Cornwall.'

Harry puffed out his cheeks. 'Not good.'

'Not good,' Tally said grimly. 'Not good at all.'

'Prize jerk, in fact.'

'Absolutely.'

'Total loser.'

'Complete loser.'

'And you never heard from him again until he arrived at the church?'

There was a silence. Harry waited.

'Well, not exactly.'

Harry sighed. 'Can I look at you now? I'm getting heartily sick of staring at this fireplace.'

She giggled. 'Sorry! I forgot. Yes, you can look round.'

'Thank fuck for that.' Harry leaned back in his chair and eyed her curiously. 'So you *did* hear from him?'

Tally shuffled in her chair, clearly feeling awkward. 'Well, yes. He wrote to me.'

'How very formal of him,' Harry said, surprised. 'I didn't think anyone wrote letters any more.'

Tally shrugged. 'Derry does. At least he did, at first. I got a long, rambling, apologetic letter, saying his granddad was eager to meet him. He'd prepared a room for him and had sent him a train ticket and everything. Derry didn't see the point in hanging around any longer. He thought everyone in Kearton Bay was laughing at him, or worse, feeling sorry for him. And he was so angry with his mum. So angry. He didn't want to be around her. He said he had to get away, and he was sorry for leaving me, but that it wouldn't be forever, just long enough for him to get to know his grandfather a bit, and that when he came back, we could start a proper relationship.'

'Sounds reasonable. Ish.'

'Yes, but he never came back, did he! He loved it in Cornwall. It became fairly obvious to me that he had no intention of coming back, whatever he said.'

'So he still insisted he would be coming home?'

'Oh yes. But, you see, it turned out that Rhiannon was wrong about her father. Derry said he was lovely and made him so welcome. He owns a big estate in Cornwall, and he was teaching Derry all about running it. He said, one day it would be his. So really, why would he come back here? And I knew it, deep down.'

'Then why didn't you let him go? Move on?'

'Because...' Tally shook her head impatiently. 'Oh, I'm such an idiot! Just that, to me, it felt as if we *were* in a proper relationship. Derry kept in touch, and we'd write or text or call each other regularly. I even went down to Cornwall for a week to stay at the house, about a year ago. I was nervous, but Derry said his grandfather would make me welcome, and he was right. He did. He showed me around the estate and told me how one day, Derry would be running the place. We got on really well, and he gave us lots of time to be together, and — and let me stay in Derry's room with him.'

'I'm amazed your mother let you go,' Harry admitted.

'She wouldn't have. I told her I was visiting an old friend from university, and she was delighted about that. I doubt she'd have been so thrilled if she knew I was shacked up with my so-called boyfriend.'

'Sounds like he actually *was* your boyfriend. You may have had a long-distance relationship, but he clearly hadn't forgotten about you, and wanted you to see his new home. That must say something, surely?'

'I thought so, too, but I think he was playing me all along. Keeping me dangling. It wasn't real. At least—' Tally bit her lip, thinking about it. 'At least, I don't think it was,' she finished.

'So what made you change your mind? If you believed in him all that time, what made you suddenly feel that he'd lied, used you?'

Tally's eyes filled with tears again and Harry wished he'd never asked.

'It's all so confusing. While I was in Cornwall, he asked if I'd consider staying. I mean, moving down to Cornwall permanently to live with him.'

Harry was surprised. 'Well, that sounds like he meant it then. That he was serious. How come you're still here?'

'How could I leave Mum? She was in enough misery over Oliver, who'd told her he wasn't coming back to Kearton Bay full stop and had no intention of taking over Dad's business. She'd really thought that when Dad retired, he'd come home. She was in bits, so how could I abandon her? I told Derry the time wasn't right, and he seemed to understand. But then...'

'Then?'

Tally swallowed. 'He rang me, not long after I got home from Cornwall. He sounded different, weird. He said that he wasn't coming back after all, that his future was down there, and he was sorry, but he couldn't give me what I wanted.'

She swallowed down her tears. 'I was desperate. I said I'd come back to Cornwall, move there permanently, whatever he wanted. He said — he said the truth was, spending a week with me had made him realise that he still loved Lexi and he didn't feel ready to start over with anyone else. He told me that being with me had made things clearer, and he knew what he felt for me wasn't the same and he couldn't settle for less. I've always known that — about Lexi, I mean. I know she asked him to be godfather for Milo and he refused, and even Mum said she thought it was because he couldn't bear to see Lexi married with a baby. She was the love of his life.'

She thumped the chair arm, clearly frustrated and angry at herself. 'I've been such an idiot! All that time waiting and hoping, and for what? I should have put him out of my mind the minute he left home. But what did I do? Hung on, convinced myself he'd come back one day.'

Harry didn't know what to say because, in his opinion, she was right. She'd been a fool. Derry had clearly had no intention of coming back. He was simply keeping his options open. Poor Tally deserved better.

'I'm sorry,' he said at last. 'You've had a rough deal; I can see that. No wonder you're so upset that he's back now.'

'I could deal with that,' she said bitterly. 'I'd psyched myself up for it. I thought, okay, it will be hard, but it's just a christening. A couple of hours out of my life and then that's it. Over. He'll go back to Cornwall, and we'll all move on. But then Mum had to invite him to stay at ours! I mean, why would she do that?'

Harry opened his mouth and closed it again. He didn't think it wise to express his opinion on her mother. You never knew when loyalty would kick in.

'Well, I know why she did that,' Tally continued. 'She says it's because she wanted to keep Derry in Kearton Bay and try to make him see sense, but I think it's really because she wanted to get one over on Rhiannon.'

'Why would she want to do that?' Harry felt mortally offended on Rhiannon's behalf. He knew how hurt she was about Derry, so the thought that Sophie Crook would deliberately make things worse for her rankled.

'Because she doesn't like Rhiannon,' Tally said, giving a slight shrug. 'She says she's weird, and a bit of a—'

'A bit of a what?'

'It doesn't matter. Mum's opinion is hardly the point. The point is she moved Derry Bone into my home, without even checking with me first. I couldn't take it. I really couldn't.'

'So what happened?'

Tally's face turned a rather fetching shade of pink. 'I told her it was okay, and she could move whoever she liked in, because I was leaving home.'

'And what did she say to that?'

'What do you think?' Tally rolled her eyes. 'It was like World War Three. She was screeching at me, demanding to know where I was moving to, and Dad was trying to calm her down, but she wasn't having it, so of course, the inevitable happened and he started haranguing me to tell them where I was going, to please her.'

'But you didn't.' Harry felt sick. 'You didn't tell them you were coming here, did you?'

Tally cleared her throat. 'I had to tell them something.'

'Couldn't you have said you'd found a nice cave on the beach or something?' Harry's mind whirled. Jesus, when Eliza found out that Gabriel's niece had moved into Eight Bells, she would think the worst. No doubt about it.

'The thing is…' Tally's eyes were wide and beseeching. 'The thing is, I wanted them to realise I meant it. That I was leaving home for real, and not playing at it. And I— I may have wanted to punish Derry — just a little bit. So…'

'So what?' Harry narrowed his eyes. 'So what, Tally?'

'So, I may have hinted there was something between us.'

'You did what?' Harry buried his head in his hands. 'Fuck, what a mess.' He looked up at her, suddenly suspicious. 'What do you mean, *hinted*?'

Tally squirmed. 'Well, I mean, they were convinced there was something between us. I told them there wasn't, and we were just friends, but they wouldn't have it. Mum said there was no way you could be just friends with any woman, and she wanted to know what had been going on between us. So I said, well, what do you think's been going on? And Mum went a funny shade of mauve, and Dad sort of fell on a chair and stared at me like I'd grown an extra head, and I was so glad I'd finally shut them up I left them to it.'

'You didn't? Tell me you didn't.'

'I'm so sorry, Harry. It wasn't all my fault. I did try to explain at first, but they wouldn't have it. It seemed easier in the end to let them think it. At least they finally took me seriously. I'm twenty-four, for God's sake, and there they were, trying to tell me I couldn't leave home! I needed them to know I meant it.'

'And make Derry jealous.'

'Derry wasn't there. He was still at Kearton Hall.' She sighed. 'But I knew they'd tell him — at least, Mum would. And I suppose that was the real bonus if I'm being honest.'

'Great.' Harry stood and began to pace the floor, one hand rubbing the back of his neck as he visualised all the ways in which the Angel Gabriel's family would make him pay. 'Well, this is a bit fucked up, isn't it?'

'I'm ever so sorry,' Tally burst out. 'But it's not so bad, is it? Now at least they'll accept I've left home and I'm not going back. And Derry will believe I've moved on. He can't know I've been waiting for him all this time, he just can't. It would be unbearable!'

'All right, calm down.' Harry stopped pacing as she began to cry. 'Oh hell. Look, it's okay, we'll figure something out.'

'You won't deny it then? If they ask, you'll back me up?'

'I can't do that,' he said patiently. 'I've got Amy to think of. If Eliza believes I'm playing around with Gabriel's niece they'll make my life hell. They could make it difficult for me to see her. I can't lose my daughter, Tally. Besides,' he added firmly, 'lies only lead to more problems in the end.' Christ, had he really said that? What had happened to him?

But there was no way he could let Amy's mother think the worst of him. Eliza wasn't a spiteful person, but she would have concerns, and as for that husband of hers — the Angel Gabriel would take every opportunity to deny him visits with Amy.

And what about Rhiannon? He'd have to explain it to her. God knows what she'd thought when Tally arrived, announcing she was moving in with him as he'd suggested. What if she didn't believe him? She would end their budding relationship before it had even had chance to bloom.

'What was Rhiannon doing here anyway?' Tally wiped her eyes and stared up at him, as if she'd only just remembered he'd had company when she arrived.

'What? Oh, I worked a shift for her on Christmas Day when Jack was taken ill, and she wanted to thank me.'

'By letting you cook her dinner?' Tally sounded puzzled and no wonder. He hadn't thought that answer through properly, had he?

'Er, no, she made *me* dinner. Here. She made me dinner here because, er, because the pub's too busy and she wanted to get out of there for a while.' His mind groped for a plausible reason. 'She was upset after the way Derry treated her at the christening. She wanted to get away for a while, and who can blame her?'

It worked. Tally began to ramble on about Derry's appalling behaviour again and seemed to forget all about Rhiannon being at Eight Bells. Thank God for that. But it didn't alter the fact that his reputation had just got even worse, and unkindest cut of all, Rhiannon would probably share everyone's opinion of him.

17

Harry blinked and opened one eye as the loud banging jerked him from his sleep. Not that it had been a particularly restful sleep. In fact, he felt as if he'd barely closed his eyes before he'd been forced to open them again. The sofa wasn't the most comfortable to lie on. As he turned over, he winced, his back twinging a warning that, at his age, he should be sleeping in a suitable bed.

'Oh, bugger,' he groaned. 'I can't stand another night of this.'

He jumped in alarm at the second thump on the door. Ah yes, that's what had woken him up. He'd thought he was dreaming. He yawned and sat up, taking a quick glance at the time on his phone screen. He wasn't expecting a parcel, and the builders wouldn't be here for another half hour at least. He frowned as he noted he had several missed calls, and all of them from Eliza. Great. He could guess what that was about.

He pulled on his trousers and slipped a jumper over his head.

'All right, all right, hang on!'

As he wandered into the hallway, Tally appeared at the top of the stairs, her eyes wide with alarm. 'Who is it?'

'I have no idea, but I can guess. Can't you?'

He rubbed his forehead and steeled himself for the inevitable. This was all he needed. He supposed he'd have to get used to it. He unlocked the front door and tried not to look too rattled as he was confronted with three furious faces.

'Fuck me. It's the Wyrd Sisters.'

'Good morning to you, too, Harry.' Eliza's tone was icy as she looked him up and down with disdain. He remembered that he hadn't so much as run a comb through his hair, and it would look as if he'd just tumbled out of bed. With…

'Tally!' Sophie's anguished cry nearly burst his ear drums and he winced. Brilliant. So the morning was off to a good start then.

He glanced up at the landing, where Tally was standing, wearing nothing but some sort of cotton nightdress that looked more like a long t-shirt, and bed hair.

'Shit.' He wasn't sure if he'd said it out loud or not, but he guessed he couldn't have made things worse even if he had. Sophie, Eliza, and the redheaded woman barged past him and Eliza had to forcibly restrain Sophie from galloping up the stairs, presumably to drag Tally down them.

'Well, you've really surpassed yourself this time, Harry,' Eliza hissed. 'Just when I thought you couldn't go any lower.'

'Tea anyone? Coffee?' He thought he'd better at least *try* to pacify them, though he suspected he was backing a losing horse. They'd already made up their minds. In their eyes, he'd been tried and found guilty, no question.

'Stick your kettle where the sun doesn't shine.' Sophie glared at him and Harry stepped back, alarmed by the fury in her eyes. 'How could you? I always knew you were rotten, through and through, but this — this is beneath contempt. She's just a child, you — you pervert!'

'Jesus, steady on!' Harry held up his hands. 'Don't you think you're getting a bit carried away?'

'For God's sake, Mother, I'm twenty-four! How many more times do I have to remind you?' Tally thundered down the stairs, her eyes gleaming with anger. 'You don't get it do you? Stop treating me like a child!'

'Then maybe you should stop acting like one,' Sophie snapped. 'Look at you, half naked! It's disgusting! Vile.'

'Well, I'm having tea,' Harry said, heading into the kitchen. If there was going to be a cat fight, they could leave him out of it.

'Me, too please,' Tally called, and he groaned inwardly as he realised she was following him, dragging her visitors behind her.

'How long has this been going on?' Eliza demanded, as he filled the kettle.

'Nothing's *going on*, as you charmingly put it,' he said. 'Tally's just a friend.'

Sophie gave a shriek of laughter. 'As if! That's not what she told me last night. See? He's a liar! As if we didn't already know.'

'I didn't say we were together,' Tally mumbled, so feebly even Harry wasn't convinced. They all ignored her protest — such as it was.

Eliza gave him a reproachful look. 'God, I'm such a fool. All this time you've been laughing at me behind my back.'

'I haven't been laughing at you. Why would I?'

'Then why keep it a secret?'

Harry glanced across at Tally, but she was staring out of the window, and he could see her trembling from where he stood.

'Why don't you get dressed?' he asked her, thinking she looked ready to burst into tears at any moment. 'I'll make you a cup of tea.'

'Listen to him! The doting husband!' Sophie said, her lip curled in scorn.

'Hardly,' Eliza said bitterly. 'He wouldn't have a clue.'

Harry was getting a bit fed up. 'Look, I don't see what any of this has got to do with you. I've already told you, there's nothing going on between us, but Tally's a grown woman. What she does and where she lives is entirely up to her. What's your problem?'

Sophie looked ready to explode. 'What's my problem? You're an old man. She's a child! You're a known philanderer and a serial cheat, plus a professional liar.'

'I don't get paid for it you know,' Harry said calmly. 'I wish I did, but such is life.'

'Do you ever take anything seriously?' the redhead asked him, her voice like flint.

'I try not to,' he said. 'I make it a point of principle to treat everything in life as one big joke.'

'Like my daughter,' Sophie said.

'Not at all,' he replied, wondering how the hell he was going to get out of this without Tally backing him up.

'Like *my* daughter,' Eliza said.

'Amy's not a joke to me,' Harry retorted. 'Don't ever say that!'

'Fine example you are to her,' Eliza said. 'I thought you were here to build bridges with her, not chase the next bit of skirt you could get your hands on.'

'It's all he knows.' Sophie gave him a filthy look. 'He's not capable of anything else.'

Harry looked over at Tally, silently pleading with her to come clean and get him out of this mess. It wasn't fair. He'd done nothing to deserve it. Tally nibbled her thumb nail, watching him with an answering plea in her eyes. She wasn't going to bail him out, that was obvious.

He gave an exasperated sigh. 'For God's sake, how many times do I have to say it? There is *nothing* going on! Look, it's Monday morning. The builders will be here at any moment. Don't you lot have jobs to go to? Children to feed? Husbands to shag?'

'See?' Sophie turned to Tally. 'This is what you're shacked up with. Are you proud of yourself?'

'Mother, will you go home and leave me alone. I'm not moving back so you're wasting your time.'

'Tally, listen to me.' Eliza's voice was urgent. 'You don't know what you're dealing with. He'll hurt you, break your heart.'

'I can assure you I won't,' Harry said, dropping teabags in two mugs. 'I presume you're not staying for tea?'

'Just have some decency!' Eliza said. 'It's not right, Harry. She's too young for your games.'

'You really are as low as I thought you were,' the redhead said. 'Call yourself a man. You're a snake.'

'Sorry, who the hell are you, anyway?' Harry questioned.

'I'm Lexi, Tally's cousin,' she said.

Harry's eyes widened. So this was the famous Lexi!

'I've heard a lot about you,' he said.

'Not half as much as I've heard about you,' she snapped. She peered round him, a plea in her eyes. 'Tally, think what you're doing. You deserve so much better.'

Tally's head jerked up and she stared at Lexi. Harry swallowed. Uh oh. Lexi was probably the last person in the world Tally wanted advice from.

'So much better? You think so?'

Lexi and Tally stared at each other. Tally's eyes were burning with anger. Lexi looked rather taken aback, and Harry wasn't surprised. There'd been real venom in Tally's words. Who was the snake now?

'Yes, I do think so,' Lexi said at last. 'Why on earth would you shackle yourself to — to *this*?'

'Charming,' Harry said, pouring milk in Tally's tea. 'Don't mind me.'

'What should I do then, Lexi?' Tally demanded. 'Hang around and wait for Prince Charming? Like you did? Except it's a bit pointless, isn't it? We all know you've bagged the prince in this story.'

'I don't think there's any call for that tone,' Sophie said.

'Just what do you mean by that?' Lexi retorted.

'We can't all have your perfect life,' Tally snapped. 'I mean, what do you know anyway? What gives you the right to tell me how to live my life? It all fell in your lap, didn't it?'

Lexi blinked. 'What are you talking about?'

'Men! Drooling over you in that pathetic way. You never had to do a thing did you? Just clicked your fingers and they came running. Derry, Robbie, Nat... Oh, you had a great time, didn't you? No commitment, no effort. And all that time, poor Will was having his heart quietly broken by you. You slept your way through half of Kearton Bay, so don't tell me that I should avoid men like Harry! What makes you any better than him?'

'No offence taken,' Harry said quietly. 'I think.'

'Are you serious?' Lexi had gone quiet suddenly, which should have been a relief, but Harry had an awful feeling it wasn't a good sign.

Eliza seemed to sense the same thing. 'Right, we're wasting our time here,' she said briskly, steering Lexi back into the hallway. 'Sophie, come on. Leave them to it.'

'Tally, please,' Sophie begged. 'You're breaking your father's heart.'

'Don't bring Dad into this,' Tally said. 'He's not the one constantly telling me how to live my life.'

'What do you mean by that?' Sophie demanded.

Harry thought they were heading into dangerous territory.

'Right, that's enough. Sorry but I'll have to ask you to leave. You're clearly not listening to a word I say, and we can't hang around here all day. Tally has a job to go to and I have builders coming.'

Sophie glanced around the kitchen in evident disdain. 'You should call a demolition crew if you ask me. What a dump. And you seriously prefer living here to The Old Vicarage?'

'Yes,' Tally said. 'I do.'

'This is what you've done to her,' Sophie said to Harry. 'I hope you're proud of yourself. You've ruined her life. I'll never forgive you for this. Never.'

'I'll carry the shame to my grave,' Harry assured her. 'Good day to you, Sophie.'

'It's Mrs Crook to you,' she replied. She gave Tally one last, pleading look, then swept out of the house after Eliza and Lexi, slamming the door after her.

'Well, that was fun.' Harry sipped his tea and motioned to Tally to sit down. He worried she was about to fall if she didn't.

She slipped into the chair beside him and cupped her mug of tea, eyeing him with some shame.

'I'm so sorry, Harry. You shouldn't have had to deal with all that.'

'No,' he said. 'I shouldn't. You need to tell them the truth, Tally.'

'I did! They wouldn't listen.'

He sighed. 'Maybe if you'd said it loud enough for anyone to actually hear they might have done. Although,' he acknowledged, 'I did try, and they clearly weren't having any of it. Look, Tally, if this impacts on my access to Amy, I'm sorry, but we'll have to *make* them listen. Both of us. I can't let anything come between me and Amy. You're welcome to stay here for now, but if this causes problems, well, I must put Amy first. You understand?'

Tally sighed. 'I guess so. Of course. Of course you have to.'

'Good. Right, do you want breakfast before you get ready for work?'

Tally's eyes widened in alarm.

'What is it? What's wrong?'

'Work! I've just realised I'm going to be working with Lexi today. Oh boy, that's going to be fun, isn't it?'

Harry said nothing. He had a feeling that the *fun* was only just beginning.

****

'Are you going to tell me what happened?'

I glanced across the table to where Jack was sitting, cradling a mug of tea, watching me with a worried look in his eyes. Did he know something had gone on at Eight Bells last night? I'd said nothing, but I couldn't deny my confusion might well have given it away. Hopefully, he'd assume it was all about Derry. Goodness knows, that was bad enough.

'I told you what happened,' I said. 'That's why I didn't go to the christening tea. Derry happened.'

'I know all about that,' he said. 'But are you sure there's nothing else? Only, you set off for Eight Bells looking a lot more optimistic, and you came home with a face like a wet weekend. You've been ever so quiet today. I'm worried about you. Did Harry Jarvis—'

'Harry did nothing,' I said quickly. 'We had a very pleasant dinner, and easy conversation. It was fine.'

'So it *is* about Derry,' he said, sounding cross. 'You know, much as I love him, I'd like to throttle that boy. You should have let me go to The Old Vicarage when I wanted to so I could give him a piece of my mind.'

'You'd only have made things worse, and in your state of health I'm certainly not allowing you to confront anyone. Besides, Derry's not a boy any longer. He's a man, Jack. He's all grown up.'

'Shame he still acts like a moody teenager then,' he grumbled. 'Those gifts he sent you seemed like a real gesture of reconciliation. Why send them to you, only to snub you again? It's downright cruel, and I'm bitterly disappointed in him. I thought better of Derry than that.' He sighed. 'I'll admit, I'm running out of patience with him.'

'I know,' I said softly. 'Just give him time.'

I suspected that I wasn't the only one hurt by Derry's apparent indifference. Jack missed my son badly. They'd always been close, and the fact that Derry hadn't bothered to contact Jack since coming home would be affecting him.

I knew they'd argued before Derry left for Cornwall, because Jack had done all he could to persuade him to think again. In the end they'd had to agree to disagree and had parted as friends. Jack hadn't wanted to lose Derry, and he'd told me he thought it best that Derry had a point of contact who could act as a go-between for us if necessary. I could only hope Derry wouldn't throw all that back in his face. Surely, Derry missed Jack as much as Jack missed him?

'Another cup of tea, I think,' Jack said, hauling himself out of the chair.

'Leave it. I'll make it,' I said. 'Finish your breakfast.'

He wrinkled his nose. 'Wholemeal toast? I need a bucket full of tea to wash that down with.'

'Well, I did offer to make you porridge,' I said, smiling.

'Are you sure there are no bacon sandwiches on that diet sheet?' he asked hopefully, heading to the sink, kettle in hand. 'Maybe one a week?'

'Nice try,' I said. 'I'm afraid the answer's no.'

'Thought as much.' He shook his head. 'Big mug of tea it is then.'

'Sit down, Jack. I'll make that.'

I jumped in shock, and Jack almost dropped the kettle at the sound of Derry's voice behind him. I could hardly believe my son was standing there in our kitchen.

Jack found his voice before I did. 'What are you doing here?'

'Visiting you. Why didn't you tell me?' Derry nodded at me. 'Morning, Mum.'

'Good morning, Derry.' I didn't know what else to say. My voice had come out as a croak anyway.

Jack carefully filled the kettle with water and switched it on, then he sat back in his chair and eyed Derry suspiciously. I sat, trembling, wondering what this unexpected visit was about.

Derry sat opposite Jack and propped his chin on his hand. 'Well?'

'Well what?' Jack nibbled at his toast, and I thought how sad it was that, after all this time, their reconciliation wasn't more joyful. They'd not exchanged so much as a hug, or even a smile.

'Why didn't you tell me you'd been ill?' Derry sat back in the chair and folded his arms. 'Christmas Day Sophie said. You've had all this time and you couldn't even pick up a phone?'

'You can talk,' Jack mumbled.

Derry scowled. 'So that's it? You're punishing me. You didn't think I deserved to know?' He gave me an accusing stare. 'Either of you?'

'It wasn't like that—' I began, but Jack cut in.

'No, Derry, that's not it at all. Your mum wanted to call you, but I didn't want to worry you.' His expression softened. 'It can sound so much worse than it is is when you hear it over the phone, and I thought, well, I was doing all right. Improving every day. Why give you all that anxiety when there was no need? And I said to your mum, I'd tell you when you got back home, and I always meant to. Just, Sophie got in first.'

Derry shook his head. 'Mum, you could have told me yesterday, at the christening. You didn't say a word.'

Jack gave him a knowing look. 'And did she have the chance? From what I've heard you gave her plenty of other things to think about yesterday.'

Derry looked uncomfortable. 'Yes, well, about that...'

'Disgusting behaviour,' Jack said.

'All right, Jack,' I said. 'Leave it.'

'No, I won't leave it,' he said. He turned to Derry, wagging an accusing finger at him. 'Your mum begged me not to say

211

anything to you, but I can't pretend it never happened. What were you thinking? Showing her up like that in front of all those people, hurting her. How could you ignore her when you'd got her hopes up at Christmas with those gifts? Now, that's cruelty. I would never have thought you could stoop so low.'

Hearing the kettle click, he got up to make the tea, and I braced myself, fully expecting Derry to launch into a defensive rant. When none was forthcoming, Jack turned around, clearly as surprised as me to see Derry sitting with his head hung low.

'Still got a conscience then. I'm glad to see it. I wondered if the Derry I once knew and loved had vanished forever.' When Derry didn't respond, he asked, in a gentler tone, 'Tea?'

Derry shook his head.

Jack raised an eyebrow at me, and I shook my head, too. I couldn't manage to swallow a mouthful of tea. My throat felt like sandpaper and my stomach was churning with nerves.

Jack made his tea then sat back at the table.

'So is that why you're here?' he asked at last since Derry didn't seem inclined to speak. 'Because you heard I'd been ill?'

'Yes. At least, sort of.'

Derry's eyes held a pleading expression as he turned to me.

'The thing is,' he said, 'I never intended to upset you like that, Mum. When I got on that train to come home, I was looking forward to seeing you, to working things out with you.'

'Then what changed?' Jack demanded. 'Because you don't work things out with people by humiliating them in public, I can tell you that much.'

Derry sighed. 'I know. And I'm sorry for that, I really am. But you see, I got the wrong end of the stick.'

Jack raised an eyebrow. 'About what?'

Derry hesitated, and I saw a faint pink tinge to his skin. He was embarrassed about something and was clearly dreading telling us what it was. I reached out and laid a reassuring hand on his arm.

'You can tell us anything. You should know that by now. I've missed you. We've both missed you. Nothing you can say will spoil the fact that you're home again.'

Derry didn't look too sure about that.

'When I got back to Kearton Bay, I thought I'd visit you first, before I went to the christening. I thought, maybe we could have a talk, then go to the church together. I thought it would make things much easier for everyone, not least you.'

'That would have been lovely,' I agreed.

'So why didn't you visit her?' asked Jack.

Derry groaned. 'I did! That's the trouble. I screwed up, Jack. I really did, and I'm so sorry.'

'Sorry for what?' Jack glanced at me and I realised that, like me, he couldn't get his head around it. Derry was making no sense.

'I came upstairs to surprise her, and she wasn't around, so I—I—'

'You what?'

'I went into her bedroom to see if she was in there and...'

Derry's eyes were like saucers, and I could see the anxiety in them.

'So you went into her bedroom and what?' Light clearly dawned as he stared at Derry in horror. 'You saw me! You saw me in her bed?'

Derry nodded miserably. 'You were asleep. I saw the papers scattered around, and the mug on the bedside table, and I just — I just flipped. I thought — I thought, you and she—'

I felt sick. He'd thought that of me!

I realised Jack was shaking, and that he looked angrier than I'd ever seen him.

'You thought me and Rhiannon were...' He took a deep breath. 'How the hell could you? How could you think that about me and her? What sort of people do you think we are? For God's sake!'

'Oh, Derry,' I murmured, 'that's—'

'Disgusting!' Jack ground the word out, the rage within him palpable. 'No other word for it. Shows what you think of us, doesn't it?'

'I'm sorry!' Derry sounded genuine in his apology, but it didn't ease the anger in Jack, nor the hurt within me.

'But how could you imagine that Jack and I...' I gulped down the tears, unable to say any more.

Jack thumped the table. 'Now you've made your mother cry,' he said. 'Happy, are you?'

'It's not all my fault,' Derry protested. 'Jack's about the same age as Sir Paul isn't he? Or not much younger at any rate. If you'd sleep with him then why not Jack?'

Jack stood up, clearly unable to listen to any more. 'I'm going for a walk.'

I caught his hand. 'No, don't go out, Jack. Not when you're feeling like this.'

'I need some fresh air,' he told me, his tone uneven. 'I won't go far, I promise. I just — I just need to get away from this.' He took a deep breath. 'Clearly it's a good job I'm moving back home today. We wouldn't want anyone else to jump to such terrible conclusions.'

'Jack!' Derry called.

Jack paused in the doorway.

'I'm sorry,' Derry said quietly. 'Really I am.'

Jack gave an abrupt nod and left the room. As the sound of his footsteps on the stairs faded away, I exhaled slowly and leaned back in my chair.

'I don't think I've ever seen him look so angry,' Derry admitted, his voice small.

I had to agree. Jack didn't get angry. Not really angry. He was an easy going, relaxed sort of man. It worried me that he'd taken such offence at Derry's assumption, although I could understand it.

'He shouldn't be getting stressed like that,' I murmured. 'I've been trying to protect him, make things easier for him. This is the last thing he needed.'

'I shouldn't have said anything,' Derry said miserably. 'But when Sophie told me about his stroke this morning, I had to come and see him. I had to apologise to him for what I'd been thinking. To both of you really. I was wrong.'

'Yes,' I said. 'You were.' But how could I blame him for jumping to conclusions, given my past behaviour? This was my fault, not his. I couldn't let him carry that guilt. 'I understand why you thought it, though. I've hardly led an unblemished life, have I?

No wonder you thought the worst of me. Even so, Jack's not like that. You should know that by now. He's not that sort of man, is he? He and I have never seen each other in that way.' I shivered. 'Actually, it makes me feel queasy thinking about it.'

Derry eyed me, clearly curious. 'Never?' he asked. 'I know he's been more like a father to you, and to me, come to that. But in the early days when he first arrived here? Even then? There's never been anything between you?'

I shook my head in vehement denial. 'Never! There was no spark of attraction between us. We were always friends. Nothing more than that.'

'He's a rare man,' Derry said. 'Not many who fail to fall for you.'

I stood up. 'So we're back to that again are we? Already?'

'No, No!' Derry held up his hands. 'I wasn't having a dig at you, Mum. Just stating facts, that's all. Men like you. If Jack didn't see you in that way, even at the beginning — well, it shows what a rare man he is.'

'I think you overestimate my powers of attraction,' I told him wryly. 'You make it sound as if I bewitch all unsuspecting men who arrive in this village, like some sort of mythological creature. Not every man thinks of me in that way, you know.'

'I know. I'm sorry. Again.'

I managed a smile. 'It's okay.' I sat down again. 'How are you? How are things at The Old Vicarage?'

Derry hesitated, then shrugged. 'Fine and fine.'

There was silence for a moment, then he said, 'This is bloody awkward, isn't it?'

'It is,' I agreed. 'But then, I suppose it was always going to be. And it's better that we talk here in private than have another public argument, don't you think?'

'I'm sorry about that, too,' he admitted. 'I guess thinking about you and Jack together brought it all back — about you and Sir Paul, I mean. I felt as if I'd been made a fool of all over again, and all I could think was, how long has this been going on? Was it something you'd always done, and I'd just never known about it? I should have known better, but the red mist descended, and I couldn't seem to think straight.'

'I expect you were already emotional and full of adrenaline at the thought of meeting me again,' I said. 'I know I was — about meeting you, I mean. When you're in such a heightened state, the smallest thing can tip you over. I wish you'd told me what you'd seen and given me the chance to explain before the christening.'

'So do I,' he confessed. 'Why didn't you tell me? About Jack's illness?'

'Like he said, he didn't want me to. He didn't want you worrying about him while you were stuck in Cornwall. And you would have worried, wouldn't you?'

'Yes,' he said. 'I would.'

'Well then.'

We sat in silence as I struggled to think what else I could say. 'Are you staying in Kearton Bay for long?' I asked eventually.

Derry shrugged. 'I thought I'd hang around for a while,' he said. 'I'd like to get to know Milo and Eleanor, for a start.' He smiled, and for a moment he looked like the old Derry again, and my spirits lifted. 'I still can't believe Will and Lexi have kids. It's amazing. They're so happy, aren't they?'

'They are. They were made for each other. I always thought so.'

'Yeah, I guess.'

He sighed and I felt a fluttering of compassion for him, along with some concern.

'You're over her, though? Lexi. You're not still—'

'Oh, God, no! No!' Derry sounded appalled at the very idea, to my relief. 'Me and Lexi, it was never going to work. No, I'm well over her. She's a good friend, though, and I'm glad to see her so happy. Especially with Will. He's a great bloke.'

'He is,' I said, with some caution, knowing how Derry had reacted to my own relationship with Will. I didn't want to give him yet more ammunition to hurl at me.

'Nat surprised me,' Derry said. 'I didn't think he'd still be with Georgia, but they seem happy. Weird, isn't it? How love changes people I mean.'

There was something wistful in his tone, and I wondered if there had been someone special to him in Cornwall. He had that look in his eye that I'd seen in so many people before. Someone had hurt him. I wished he'd tell me, but we were nowhere near that stage yet. Would we ever be?

'So, you're staying a while then?'

'Yeah, maybe. It's all up in the air now.'

I swallowed. 'But you *are* going back? To Cornwall?' I couldn't say *to your grandfather.* The words would stick in my throat and choke me.

Derry sat up straight. 'It's great there. I love Cornwall. It's beautiful.'

I wanted to ask how my father was treating him, what life was like for him at the estate, but I couldn't bring myself to do so. Too afraid of what his answer would be. I didn't want to know how welcome his grandfather had made him, or how happy he was in his company. I didn't want to hear how close they'd become. I felt a twist in my guts, and an unexpected stab of jealousy. This was so hard. When had I become this person?

'Right.'

'I need to catch up with everyone. I want to see the lads from the band,' he said. 'I left them in the lurch, and I want to know we're okay. I've missed them.'

'I'm sure they missed you, too,' I reassured him. 'And you're all right at Sophie's?'

'Yes, I'm fine there.' He shrugged. 'You know Sophie.'

'How *is* Sophie? Word has it that Tally left home last night.'

Derry let out a short burst of laughter. 'God, I'd forgotten what this place is like. The way the gossip goes around like wildfire. Yeah, she left home.'

'Do you know why?'

'How would I know? I've only been back five minutes.'

There was a defensive note in his tone, and I sighed inwardly, sensing I'd somehow managed to annoy him again.

'Sorry. Didn't mean to snap. Things are a bit tense at their place right now. I felt in the way, to be honest. I offered to leave but Sophie wouldn't hear of it.'

'You can always come back here. I know things aren't great, but we can work on it, can't we? And your room's just as you left it. You'd always be welcome, and—'

'I don't think so, Mum.' Derry shook his head, but his tone was regretful. At least, I thought I detected a hint of regret in his voice. Maybe I was imagining it. Wishful thinking.

'No, of course not. Stupid of me.'

'No.' To my surprise, he reached out and took hold of my hand. 'You're not being stupid. I've messed up, I know I have. I've done some things, ridiculous things. Behaved like a kid. I've hurt people. You. I'm so sorry.'

I didn't know what to say. It was so unexpected.

'I haven't been honest with you,' he burst out. 'I was too embarrassed, too ashamed, but you deserve to know. I'm not going back to — him. You were right about him. He's not a nice man, not at all.'

I could hardly believe it. 'What happened? Oh, darling, what did he do to you?'

Derry shook his head. 'Nothing, nothing. I'm okay. He's just not what I thought he'd be. He's exactly what you said he was, and worse. I should have listened to you. I wish I had and I'm sorry I doubted you. I'm sorry I put you through all that.'

'Oh, Derry, none of that matters,' I said urgently. 'I'm sorry it didn't work out for you. I never wanted you to be hurt. I'd hoped he'd mellowed but…'

'But you didn't really believe he had?' He gave a bitter laugh. 'Well, you were right. He's horrible. I feel sorry for you, being brought up by him. Still, you live and learn, don't you?'

'So…' I hesitated, not sure where that left us.

'So?'

'Are you — I mean, will you be staying in Kearton Bay?'

He was quiet and I held my breath, longing to hear the words I'd waited for. Had Derry finally come home for good?

Eventually he shrugged. 'I don't know, Mum. I'm still working out what I want to do. I've had a lot of time to think, and I know something has to change. I need to figure out what I'm doing with my life, because nothing's as I thought it would be and I have to adapt, make new plans.'

'You can come back here,' I said eagerly. 'That would be a start.'

He gave me a rueful smile. 'I'd like us to work on our relationship, I really would. But look at how I reacted to seeing Jack yesterday. Thing is, we have a long way to go, and we can't rush into it. I don't want to screw it all up again, and if I'm living here… Right now, I need to get my head together, and I can't do that under your roof. I'm sorry.'

'It's okay. I understand.'

He gave me a faint smile. 'You don't. Not really. But anyway, if I stay at Sophie's, I think we've got a better chance of working through this. It won't be forever. I need the space. Okay?'

'Of course. Whatever you want. I'm only glad we're speaking.'

'You won't — you won't tell anyone what I've just told you, will you? It's humiliating enough to admit I got it all wrong to you, but if everyone else finds out that I made a fool of myself…'

'You haven't made a fool of yourself,' I said fiercely. 'It's that man who's to blame, not you.'

'It was easily as much my fault,' he said. 'I can't say I wasn't warned, but I chose to ignore it. I brought it all on myself. But for now, I can't bear others to realise that. Would you please keep it to yourself?'

'Of course,' I said. 'I won't tell a soul. Even Jack.'

Derry blinked. 'Oh, Jack doesn't count. I expected you to tell Jack and that's okay. I know we can trust him. He's family.'

I smiled through my tears. He hadn't changed that much. Not really.

'I do love you, Derry, so much.'

'I know, Mum,' he murmured. 'I know.'

He let go of my hand and looked away, and I knew I couldn't push him any further. It was as far as he could go today, but that was all right. He was staying in Kearton Bay, at least for now, and so long as he was here, we had a chance to fix things properly. I wasn't going to risk losing him again.

'Cup of tea?' I asked, my tone deliberately light.

He looked back at me, and his face broke into a smile. 'Love one,' he said.

I hurried over to the cupboard and took out another cup. As I gazed out of the window, I saw a forlorn figure strolling along the beach, hands in pockets, head down. Jack! That was my next task — fixing things between Derry and Jack. But for now, I just wanted the chance to sit at the table, drinking tea and making small talk with my son. Nothing else in the world mattered.

18

February started out bitterly cold, but mostly dry. The builders made huge progress with Eight Bells, which was something to be grateful for. There wasn't much else, Harry thought glumly, as he trudged down a flight of wide, shallow steps, clutching a posy of white flowers to his chest. He suspected he was on a hiding to nothing, but he had little to lose.

Amy had clearly picked up on the gossip about him and Tally. Eliza hadn't stopped their daughter's twice-weekly visits to his house, so nothing had changed on the surface, but Amy wasn't stupid. She'd obviously noticed the icy atmosphere between her parents, which didn't surprise Harry. He'd have been a bit worried about her if she hadn't, as Eliza made it strikingly obvious that she thoroughly disapproved of Harry's behaviour and thought him disgusting.

'So, is Tally your girlfriend then?' Amy had asked him one evening, as they sat by the fire, playing Monopoly.

'No, she's not,' he said firmly.

'Then what is she?' Amy persisted. 'Why does she live here now, and not at Sophie's?'

'Er, because she feels she's a bit old to be living with her mum and dad,' Harry said, throwing the dice and sighing inwardly as he landed on Mayfair. Amy owned it, and she had a hotel on there, too. He'd be bankrupt at this rate.

'Sophie doesn't want her to live with you. She came to our house. She was crying in the kitchen. Joe put brandy in her hot chocolate and Charlie tried to tell her some jokes, but she didn't laugh. That's two thousand pounds you owe me,' Amy said, not missing a beat.

Harry flicked through his paper money, wishing they'd played Cluedo instead. 'Well, I'm sorry she was upset,' he said carefully. 'It's hard for parents when their children leave home.'

'It's hard for children when their parents leave home, too,' Amy pointed out. 'We just have to deal with it.'

'That's it, Amy,' Harry said. 'Go for the jugular.'

'What's a jugular?'

'Never mind. It's always sad when parents and children part company, whoever leaves. But that doesn't mean they stop being family, does it? They still love each other. They still see each other.'

'You didn't see me when you lived in America,' Amy said, holding out her hand for the money. 'And Oliver never sees Sophie. Do you know, he's married now? And he didn't even invite Sophie and Archie to the wedding.'

'That's a shame,' Harry said, thinking he wasn't surprised. Sophie was so judgmental she'd have given the bride marks out of ten no doubt. He didn't blame Oliver for keeping his new wife far away from her.

'Why isn't Tally here?' Amy asked, taking the dice from him, and rattling them around in her hand.

'She's gone to see her friend from work,' Harry explained. 'He invited her for tea, and she thought it would be nice for us to spend some time alone together.'

'In case I asked her any awkward questions,' Amy said wryly.

She threw the dice and Harry gaped as he saw them both land, six up. How did she *do* that?

'I wouldn't have done,' Amy continued. 'I don't care if she's your girlfriend. I like Tally anyway. And I don't care if you *are* twice her age.'

'I'm not twice her age!' Harry winced as he remembered that, actually, he was. 'And she's not my girlfriend.'

'Isn't she?' Amy sounded doubtful. 'Are you sure? Everyone says she is.'

'Well, everyone's wrong then,' he assured her. 'Tally's a girl, and she's my friend, but she's not my girlfriend.'

'I don't see the difference,' Amy said.

Harry frowned. 'Are you moving your playing piece or not?' He nodded at the little metal dog.

Amy duly obliged, then threw the dice for a second time. 'Except for sex, of course.'

'Amy!' Harry gaped at her, horrified. 'What do you know about that?'

Amy rolled her eyes. '*Hello*! Dad, I'm nearly eleven.'

'Exactly! Who told you about sex?' Bloody hell, it had better not have been Bailey. Just because he was a doctor didn't give him the right to fill Amy's head with all that stuff. She was far too young.

Amy tutted, then moved her metal dog another four places, landing on the Chance square. She turned over the top card and pulled a face.

'Go to jail. Crap.'

'Who told you about sex?' Harry repeated, feeling a fleeting triumph as she grumpily slammed the playing piece on the jail square.

'Me and my friends figured it out ages ago,' Amy said airily. 'Then Mum told me loads, which was a bit gross. They'll be teaching us all about it at school when I go up to St Hilda's and that's going to be embarrassing. I think it's going to shock some of the boys. You know how stupid they are, and I don't think they know half as much as they make out.'

Harry's mouth twitched in amusement as she rolled her eyes again. Affectionately, he reached out and ruffled her hair. 'Yes, boys are definitely stupid. Do keep that in mind, Amy, and avoid them at all costs.'

'So are you and Tally having sex?'

'No! And you shouldn't ask such questions. There are some things no child should discuss with their parent. Especially when you're only ten.'

'Nearly eleven.'

'So still ten. Not that eleven makes any difference. We're not having this conversation, no way.'

'So you are then. Interesting.'

Harry felt a flutter of panic. How to deal with this? 'May I remind you that you're currently languishing in jail?' he said, desperate to return the conversation to safer ground.

'Oh, I'll soon get out of there,' she said confidently.

'I doubt it. I'm going to win now.' He threw the dice and moved his piece the appropriate number of squares, groaning as he landed on the Community Chest. 'Now what?'

Amy squealed with delight as he read out, 'Go to Jail. Bloody marvellous.'

'We can be cell mates!' She giggled. 'I'll let you have the top bunk.'

'Those cells are terribly small,' he said. 'I like room to breathe.'

'Don't worry,' she told him confidently. 'I'll be out of here in a minute.'

'That's what you think,' he said smirking. 'You'll — bloody hell!'

'Told you!' Amy grinned as she scooped up the dog and headed out of jail.

'How do you keep throwing doubles?' he said suspiciously. 'Are you sure this game isn't fixed?'

'Of course not. How would you fix Monopoly? You're just a rubbish player and a sore loser.'

She was right. Twenty minutes later, Amy declared him bankrupt and herself the winner, and he wasn't best pleased about it.

'Next time,' he said, 'we'll play Cluedo. Or Scrabble. Anything but this.'

'Will Tally be here?' Amy enquired, giving him an innocent look that didn't fool him for a second. 'I'd like to ask her advice about something.'

'About what?' Harry had a sudden horrific vision of Amy asking Tally personal and embarrassing questions.

'My bedroom. You said it's ready to decorate, and I want her to help me choose the design.'

'The design? You have big plans then?'

'Of course. These things can't be rushed. I have to think about a theme.'

'Of course you do.'

'So will Tally be here?'

'I expect so.' She certainly showed no signs of going anywhere, much to his dismay.

'Great. She can't avoid me forever, you know. It's been one excuse after another, but she'll have to face me sooner or later. Tell her I don't mind about her being your girlfriend, so she needn't worry.'

'I'm sure she'll be delighted but, like I said, she's not my girlfriend.'

All he got from Amy in response was a knowing look and a 'Hmm.'

The problem was, he thought, as he made his way down the steps of Jim Rumm's Yard, heading towards Bay Street, that Tally was becoming an accepted fact in his life. Eliza was convinced she was his girlfriend, and now Amy seemed to believe it, no matter what he said to the contrary. He didn't want her to think that. And he certainly didn't want to give them all ammunition against him.

If this wasn't sorted out soon it could only get worse. They'd expect him to put a damn ring on Tally's finger soon, or, more likely, to break her heart.

He wouldn't mind, but none of this was for his benefit. It was a nightmare. He could feel his blood pressure rising every time he thought about it. How had he ever got involved in all this?

Just last night he'd had another chat with Tally about the situation, reminding her, yet again, that this was only supposed to be temporary.

'It's not my fault,' she'd said, looking worried. 'I thought Derry would have gone back to Cornwall by now. I don't know why he's still hanging around, but he can't be here for much longer. Please, Harry, keep it going until he goes home. For my sake. I know it's a lot to ask but...'

It *was* a lot to ask, and he'd been on the point of telling her that he couldn't go on with this charade any longer, but her eyes had filled with tears and she'd looked so upset he couldn't bring himself to do it.

'Okay,' he heard himself say. 'But just a couple of weeks, Tally. If he hasn't gone back to Cornwall by then — well, it's tough. You have to make it clear we're not together. They're not listening to me. In fact, the more I deny it, the more convinced they seem to be.' Perhaps, he thought, he ought to tell them they were madly in love. Maybe then they'd believe it was purely platonic.

'I understand. That's all right. Thank you, Harry.'

Harry, old chap, he thought to himself as he left the passageway where it came out halfway down Bay Street, and began the short walk down to the seafront, *you're too old for all this malarkey now. You can't have this sort of stress in your life. You're going to have to be firm with her. You've gone soft in your old age, that's your trouble.*

He remembered how angry Melody had got with him whenever he mentioned his age. Well, she would. She was quite a few years older than him, so it probably hit a nerve. Even so, she'd accused him of turning him into an old man before his time and, retracing his thoughts, he realised she might have a point. It was hard not to feel old these days though. He wasn't the same man, and he knew it.

He glanced down at the flowers and felt a fleeting panic. Was he wasting his time? Being a fool? Wasn't love a young man's game when all was said and done?

Love?

Oh, God, what the fuck was he doing? Making a total idiot of himself no doubt. And yet, his legs still carried him down the hill, and before he knew it, he found himself climbing the steps to the front door of The Hare and Moon.

Sadly, Kerry was in the bar, restocking the coolers with bottled drinks. There was no sign of Rhiannon. Resigned to his fate, he lowered the flowers and walked towards the bar, bracing himself for her displeasure.

'Won't be a minute!'

Kerry closed the cooler door, stood, and turned round, the welcoming smile on her face vanishing as she realised who'd entered the pub.

'You! You've got a nerve.'

'Nice to see you, too, Kerry.'

'Don't you try that old flannel with me. I can't believe you're shacked up with Tally! And there I was, pushing you towards Rhiannon. You made a right fool of me, didn't you? I felt proper stupid when I found out.'

'And clearly, it's all about you,' Harry said.

'You're not even sorry,' she gasped. 'The cheek of you!'

'I'm here to see Rhiannon,' he said, deciding it best not to get into a slanging match. 'Is she in?'

'She's upstairs,' Kerry said. 'But she won't want to see you, I can tell you that much. Why would she? Played fast and loose with her, didn't you?'

Harry frowned. 'Hardly. We weren't exactly engaged.'

'Oh my God! You're unbelievable.' Kerry waved a hand at him as if flicking away a particularly annoying bluebottle. 'Go away. I'm not serving you.'

'I don't want serving,' he reminded her. 'I want to see Rhiannon.'

'Yeah, well, what's it like to want?'

'Kerry, I don't see how it's your decision to make. Maybe Rhiannon won't want to see me, who knows? But she at least deserves to be asked. I'm not budging from here until she tells me to go, so you may as well get it over with and tell her I'm here right now.'

Kerry glared at him, but to his relief she pushed open the door behind the bar and vanished into Rhiannon's private quarters. He waited, biting his lip as he wondered what he'd do if she said she didn't want to see him. He didn't suppose there was much he could do. He'd never get past Kerry in full Rottweiler mode, even if he wanted to.

'You can go up.' Kerry's tone was sullen as she lifted the hinged part of the bar top to let him through. She clearly didn't approve of Rhiannon's decision.

As he passed her and headed towards the door she muttered, 'Mess her about and I'll kill you. And you'd best not be leading Tally a merry dance either, or I'll do worse than kill you.' She looked him up and down. 'A lot worse.'

Harry didn't want to think what could be worse than being killed by Kerry. He ran up the stairs, thinking he must be mad to get embroiled in all this craziness, and wondering how on earth his peaceful life in Kearton Bay had already got so messy.

Rhiannon called to him from the living room.

'Harry, how lovely to see you. How are you?'

He entered the room, wondering why he put himself through such ordeals. She'd clearly been avoiding him. It was days since their disastrous dinner date, when Tally's arrival had scuppered what could have been a truly memorable moment. She hadn't made any attempt to contact him since. Then again, he hadn't tried to contact her either. But how could he? He could imagine that being a pub landlady she had first dabs at local gossip, and though she didn't strike him as being one to listen to idle chatter, she couldn't have failed to notice that Tally was now living with him, and no doubt deemed by everyone to be his girlfriend.

Maybe he shouldn't have come. She didn't look particularly pleased to see him, although she was making a valiant effort to be polite.

He didn't want polite. Not from Rhiannon. He wanted honesty and passion — whatever form that took. He'd rather she raged at him than sat there with that fixed smile on her face. This wasn't her. He knew that instinctively. Whatever she was, fake wasn't it. And for some reason, the one thing he didn't want to be was fake around her. She made him want to tell the truth and screw the consequences.

'I've missed you,' he said. 'I've brought you these.'

She blinked, clearly astonished, as he thrust the simple bunch of snowdrops at her.

He watched, heart thudding, as she lowered her head and inhaled the delicate scent of the flowers.

'They're lovely,' she said at last, her eyes meeting his finally, a wary look in them. 'But Harry—'

'I know they're not expensive roses or anything,' he said desperately. 'Maybe they should have been, I don't know. But I found them growing in the wilderness that passes for my garden. Something drew me to them, and I knew I had to pick some for you. Like they were what I was supposed to give you.'

She would think he'd gone mad. Perhaps he had. He'd certainly never put himself in such a position before. Harry had always been the predator, never the prey. But he felt helpless to fight this, whatever it was. Why else would he be putting himself through this humiliation?

Rhiannon watched him closely, seeming to be scanning his mind.

'Do you know what day it is today, Harry?'

He shrugged. 'I'm not sure to be honest. I'm losing track. Is it the first of February? The second?'

'It's Imbolc.'

Harry had no idea what she was talking about. 'It's what?'

'Look around you.'

He glanced around the room. It was just a room, like any other. A rather lovely painting of The Hare and Moon hung on the chimney breast. A fire blazed in the hearth, but there was nothing unusual about that. It was necessary. It was a freezing cold day, and the warmth from the flames was most welcome.

Then he noticed that there were orange and white candles burning on the mantelpiece, and a strangely shaped cross made from reeds was hanging down between them above the fire.

'What is this?' he asked, suddenly nervous. Was she carrying out one of her witchy spells? Was she cursing him? He supposed he couldn't blame her if she were.

'Imbolc is a sabbat,' she told him. 'It represents the coming of spring. It means *in the belly*, or *ewe's milk*. Because of lambing, and new life, you see? The goddess has awakened from her sleep and will bring light and love to us all.'

Harry shrugged. 'Okay.'

'It's the time of the maiden, who will awaken the lust of the newly-risen Oak King.'

'That sounds promising,' he said.

She laughed. 'It's one of my favourite sabbats,' she admitted. 'I've been burning my intentions in the fire.'

'Your what?'

'New beginnings,' she said quietly, gazing into the flames. 'A chance to start again.' She looked back at him. 'For all of us, perhaps?'

'I'd like that,' he admitted.

'So would I. Snowdrops are Imbolc flowers. You couldn't have given me anything more perfect, today of all days. It's as if it were meant to be.'

She laid the flowers on her lap and held out her hand. Harry clasped it hopefully.

'Thank you. They mean the world to me. But what about Tally? Where does she fit into all this?'

His hand tightened on hers in case she decided to pull it away. 'She doesn't. It's not what you think, what it seems. You have to let me explain.'

'I won't hurt Tally,' she said calmly. 'I don't know what this thing is between us—'

'So you accept that there *is* something?' It was more than he'd hoped for and he couldn't give up now. 'I'd like you to listen to me and believe me.'

'I *am* listening,' she said calmly. 'Whether I believe it or not is a different matter. I want to, of course, because yes, there is something between us. I don't know what it is, or why it is, but it's there, and it's powerful. But I'm not that woman any more. I've learned my lesson the hard way, and I won't betray Tally. She doesn't deserve this, Harry. Did you give her flowers this morning?'

'Of course I didn't!' Harry tutted impatiently. 'There's nothing between Tally and me. Nothing at all. She wanted to leave home, and she knew her parents would never let her go. She let them think we were in a relationship because that way they'd take her seriously.'

Rhiannon looked unconvinced. 'Why would she go to all that trouble? Why not just say she wanted to leave home? She's twenty-four, for goodness' sake.'

He wanted to tell her. He wanted to tell her so desperately about Derry's behaviour, about his awful treatment of Tally. But he didn't think she'd believe anything so bad about her son. And hadn't she thanked him for not saying negative things about him?

'She has a complicated relationship with her mother,' he said feebly. 'I think Sophie walks all over Tally's feelings, and Tally seems unable to fend her off. I think she's using me as some sort of shield.'

As he said the words, he realised they were probably true. Tally resented her mother's control but seemed powerless to stand up for herself. Pretending to be involved with Harry was indeed a shield against Sophie. She could hide behind their so-called relationship. In a weird sort of way, it made perfect sense. Poor Tally. But she needed to be stronger, to learn to fight off her mother without needing any shield at all. He wondered if that day would ever come.

Rhiannon was clearly considering his words.

'I understand that,' she said at last. 'But why you? Why choose you, of all people, to pretend to be in a relationship with? And what did she mean when she said you'd suggested she move in with you? I wasn't even aware that you knew Tally very well. There has to be more to this than you're telling me.'

Harry sighed. 'Have you got ten minutes? I can tell you all about it if you have.'

She eyed him dubiously, clearly not sure whether to give him a chance or not. Then, to his relief, she nodded. 'Follow me.'

She led him into the kitchen, and motioned to him to sit at the table, while she hunted for a vase for the snowdrops.

'Well,' she said. 'You have one chance to explain yourself, so you'd better make it good.'

Harry had never longed for a strong coffee more than he had at that moment, but since she showed no signs of offering one, and since he was drinking mostly tea and decaffeinated instant coffee these days anyway, he knew he'd have to do his best to manage without it.

Carefully he explained to Rhiannon about the evening at the pub, when he and Tally had got talking, and had decided, rather foolishly, to have a night of passion at Eight Bells.

He saw her hands falter and gulped as he saw the glass vase halt in mid-air. Maybe he should have waited to tell her that bit until she'd finished with the flowers.

'So what happened?' she said quietly.

'Nothing! I couldn't go through with it. It was a stupid mistake, made because we were both drunk and at a low ebb. But I knew it was the wrong thing to do, and Tally did, too, once she'd sobered up.'

'So you're saying you've never had an intimate relationship with Tally?'

He pulled a face. 'God no! I mean yes, that's what I'm saying. Not because she's not lovely, because she is. But she's just a kid. Half my age. And besides—'

'Besides what?'

'Besides, she doesn't affect me in that way. I don't think of her like that. She's just a friend.'

'Really?'

'Yes, really. She's been great company for me. I won't lie to you, Rhiannon, she's been coming round to Eight Bells regularly, but there's nothing in it. She needed someone to talk to, and I needed companionship. It's lonely up there. I don't know anyone around here except you and Eliza and Amy. Tally was fun and she was kind. She was someone who didn't see me as some sort of lecherous monster. She just—'

'Just what?'

'Just saw me.' He shrugged. 'That's all.'

'It sounds to me,' she said, standing back to admire the pretty snowdrops in the dainty glass vase, 'that you really like Tally.'

He wanted to deny it. To reassure her that she was nothing to him. But he couldn't.

'I do like her,' he admitted. 'A lot. She's a lovely girl.'

'And very pretty.'

Harry nodded. 'Yes. She is very pretty. But she's not for me, and I'm not for her. Believe me, Rhiannon, there's nothing romantic between us. It's not like this thing—'

'Between you and me?' Rhiannon turned round to smile at him, and he was relieved to see the sparkle in her eyes. She pulled out a chair and sat down beside him. 'No. I see that.'

'So you believe me?'

'If you'd told me you didn't find her attractive, or that she meant nothing to you, I'd have thrown you out of the house. As it is, I believe you're telling me the truth.'

'Really?' He wrinkled his nose. Women were a mystery to him, even after all these years, and all his so-called experience.

'Tally's a pretty young woman, and she's kind, generous, and funny when she gets the chance. I'd have been suspicious if you'd denied liking her, not to mention offended on her behalf.'

'Oh. Right.'

'But that doesn't explain why she said you'd asked her to move in with you.'

Harry sighed. 'No, I know it doesn't. I'm still not sure about that myself. I certainly didn't ask her to move in to Eight Bells. I didn't want her to, so where she got that idea, I can't imagine. I can only assume it's because I told her that if she wasn't happy at home she should leave, and at some point, I told her she was always welcome at my house. But I didn't mean to live there! I think she muddled up those two statements and came to the wrong conclusion.'

'I see.' Rhiannon leaned forward, elbows resting on the table. 'Does Tally know you're here?'

'No, she doesn't.'

'Why not?'

'Because I don't know what this is,' he admitted. 'I don't know what you want from me, what you're hoping for, if anything, and I certainly don't know if you want other people to know about...'

He'd almost said, about *us*. Luckily, he'd stopped himself in time. He didn't want her to think he was making assumptions, and he didn't want her to say, 'There is no us.' Even if she were thinking it.

Rhiannon twirled a strand of her hair between her fingers as she considered the matter.

'None of this seems fair on you. It must have put a strain on your relationship with Eliza.'

'It has. I keep telling her there's nothing going on, but she seems determined to believe the worst of me.'

'It would help if Tally's denials were a bit more vocal.'

'I know.' He sighed. 'I think it suits her to have everyone believe it's true, because of—'

He broke off, horrified, as he realised he'd almost said Derry. Tally would never forgive him if she revealed what had been between her and Rhiannon's son.

'Because of Sophie,' she said, jumping to conclusions. 'It's all rather a mess, isn't it?'

'You can say that again. So what happens now?' he asked, half dreading the answer.

'I think, for now, we say nothing to anyone. Tally's clearly under a lot of strain. I feel partly responsible. I saw the way this was going and did nothing to help her. Until she realises she doesn't need an excuse to leave home, or indeed, to do whatever she likes, it's best we don't add to her stress.'

'And my reputation's bad enough,' he admitted gloomily. 'I don't want you getting dragged into some imaginary love triangle. You know what people are like.'

'Oh, I do. My reputation's as bad, so even if they knew you were seeing me it wouldn't convince them you weren't involved with Tally. I *am* the scarlet woman of Kearton Bay, after all. I must say, Harry, I think it's terribly generous of you to carry the can for her like this. You do know that many people around here are deeply unimpressed with you because of it?'

He gave an abrupt laugh. 'Well, what's new? No one likes me much anyway, because of what I did to Eliza. And of course, Gabriel Bailey's a local hero, the charming village doctor. How can I compete with that?'

'You can't,' she said. 'But then again, why would you want to? You're not Gabriel. You're Harry. You have your own particular gifts and charms.'

'Do I? You must tell me all about them one day,' he said glumly.
She beamed at him and took hold of his hand. 'Now, Harry. No wallowing, and no fishing for compliments. Besides, I don't know what all your gifts and charms are yet. I'm looking forward to discovering them for myself.'

His fingers entwined with hers as he looked hopefully at her. 'Are you saying…? I mean, do you think…? Are we—?'

'Harry,' Rhiannon said.

'Yes?'

'Do shut up waffling and kiss me.'

Harry smiled. 'With pleasure.'

'Imbolc blessings, Harry.'

OSTARA
19

'You're whistling again!'

Harry spun round, giving Tally an anxious smile as she stared at him, hands on hips. 'Am I? Well, it's not a crime, is it?'

'You're awfully cheerful these days,' she said, eyeing him quizzically. 'What's put you in such a good mood?'

She'd be horrified if she knew, he reflected. It was funny. He'd only met up with Rhiannon two or three times since Imbolc, and then not for long, yet his life had completely changed. He felt lighter, happier, even though their relationship so far consisted of quick drinks in the kitchen of The Hare and Moon, brief conversations, kisses that had made them both hot under the collar but went nowhere…

'Well, look at it,' he said, feeling hot and bothered again at the thought, and waving a hand around the living room to distract both himself and Tally. 'Things are looking so much better already. Don't you love the new fireplace? How can I not be cheerful when the house is coming on so well at last? We'll be up and running as a guest house before you know it.'

'Harry, about that…' Tally threw the paint brochure she'd been browsing onto the coffee table and folded her arms, as if protecting herself.

Harry frowned as she eyed him, clearly nervous. What now?

'Go on,' he said. 'What about it?'

'I was thinking,' she said slowly. 'About the guest house. There's going to be a lot more to it than cooking a decent breakfast every morning you know.'

'Meaning?'

'Well, think about it! There's going to be bedding to change and laundry to do and cleaning the bedrooms and the bathrooms, and lots of messy stuff I'm sure you'd hate. Then there's washing the dishes—'

'I'm getting a dishwasher installed. Remember?'

'And shopping! You'll need to do plenty of food shopping, and you know you hate that.'

He did, he couldn't deny it. 'Tally, what's your point?'

'Well,' she said, 'I was thinking, what if I quit my job at Kearton Hall and work for you full-time? I could do all those jobs you won't enjoy, leaving you to do the breakfasts. Then you'll have all day to yourself, every day.'

For a fleeting moment he considered the matter. It would give him more spare time to see Rhiannon, after all. Her work hours made fitting in any meetings with her tricky, particularly as they had to be conducted in secret — something which she seemed to find surprisingly exciting. But reality soon kicked in.

He shook his head. 'I'm sorry, Tally. For one thing, I don't intend to take guests in all year so where would that leave you during the winter? And I don't think there's that much work to be honest. Certainly not enough for me to justify another wage.'

'But I could work for board and lodgings,' she said eagerly. 'You wouldn't have to give me any money at all.'

'Don't be ridiculous!' Harry half-laughed, then realised she was serious. 'What are you talking about? I can't not give you any wages! What's this about, Tally? Why are you so desperate to get away from Kearton Hall?'

Tally shrugged. 'I'm not. Just bored.'

His eyes narrowed. 'There's more to it than that. Come on, tell me the truth. Hell, Derry hasn't started working up there, has he?'

'No, thank God. He's got his own estate to think about now, remember?'

'It's not as big as Kearton Hall though, surely?'

'It's bigger! Didn't I mention that bit? Rhiannon's father is absolutely loaded. Apparently, her mother belonged to some aristocratic family, and her father was a hugely successful businessman. Put them together and money dripped from them. When the old man goes, Derry will inherit everything.'

'It should be Rhiannon's,' Harry grumbled. 'Nothing against Derry, but she's his next of kin.'

'He hates Rhiannon. He's not going to leave her anything is he? Besides, I told you, Derry's granddad was teaching him what needed to be done. Training him up. Left him in no doubt he was inheriting the lot.'

Harry thought Rhiannon's father a monster, although he was reasonably sure she wouldn't want anything from him anyway. She wasn't that kind of person. He wondered why he was so confident about what Rhiannon would and wouldn't do. It wasn't as if he'd known her long, and yet it felt as if he'd known her forever.

'So if Derry's going back to Cornwall to learn more about that estate,' Tally continued, 'he's not going to work for Will is he? At least that's one thing to be grateful for.'

'Then why do you want to leave Kearton Hall? You still haven't explained.'

Tally sank down onto the sofa, looking pensive. 'I can't help it. I don't like being there.'

'But there must be a reason! Is this all because of Lexi?'

'No!' Tally spat the word out immediately, but a second later she dropped her shoulders and he noticed she was twisting her hands in her lap, so clearly, she wasn't telling the whole truth.

'I think it does have something to do with Lexi,' he said. 'And I think that's a terrible shame. You can't let something like that come between you, and you certainly can't let Derry Bone, of all people, ruin your career.'

'Career!' Tally laughed. 'That's just it. It's not a career, is it? It's just a job I accepted because Lexi offered it to me, my mother thought it would be a wonderful idea, and I didn't know what else to do with myself.'

'Oh, okay.' Harry joined her on the sofa, not sure what to say. 'But you like your job?'

'I told you before, it pays the bills.'

His lips twitched. 'Did you have many bills, living with your parents?'

She gave him a sheepish look. 'Okay, you've got me there. I mean it paid my board and gave me money to buy clothes or makeup or anything else I needed, and it enabled me to save, too.'

'You're talking about it in the past tense,' he pointed out. 'It's as if you've already left the job.'

'In my head, I have. Many times. You have no idea how often I picture walking into Will's office and handing him my resignation.'

'It's that bad?'

'It really is. All I can see when I go in there is how I've been manipulated into a life I don't want.'

He didn't want to defend anyone connected with Gabriel Bailey, but he felt she was being unfair.

'They were trying to help. It seems to me that, since you had no better plans, they thought they were doing a kind thing for you. I think you're being a bit harsh on them to be honest.'

'Oh, well thanks a lot.'

'You said yourself you're good at it. You've been there ages, so you must have enjoyed it once. Did all this sudden hatred for the job begin when Derry told you he was still in love with Lexi, by any chance?'

'Fancy saying that to me!'

He saw by the colour in her cheeks that he was right, but she clearly wasn't going to admit it.

'Let's not argue about it. I'm sorry, Tally, but I don't see how I can justify taking you on. At least not yet. Let's see how it goes, eh?'

It hadn't escaped his notice that she was angling to stay at Eight Bells. Work for board and lodgings indeed! In other words, *please don't make me leave, Harry.* But she couldn't stay here forever. It just wasn't possible. He noticed the glum look on her face and felt bad.

'Tell you what, why don't we go into Helmston, to that DIY place you keep telling me about? We can pick up some paint samples and look at the wallpaper. What do you say?'

She smiled. 'Sounds great. I'll get my coat.'

The DIY store and garden centre just outside Helmston wasn't huge by the standards of similar nationwide establishments, but it was adequate. It had, Harry thought, that rather lost and confused feel that DIY stores seemed to take on when Christmas had passed, and the shelves and display areas had been cleared of decorations and Christmas trees, but it was too soon to promote spring decorating, or garden furniture and barbecues for the summer.

The good thing, from his point of view, was that it wasn't too busy. Not only because it would mean a shorter queueing time at the checkout, but because he was less likely to be stopped by any fans of *Twice as Nice*, or any other of his programmes. It was the bane of his life that anyone spotting him in shops like these would think it obligatory to ask him about his own decorating projects, and worse, ask his advice on their prospective purchases. The latest cruelty from fans was enquiring if it was true that Melody Bird had dumped him and had gone off with some young American hunk. Harry had quite run out of jokes to make at his own expense. Just let him buy a tin of paint, for Christ's sake!

'What are we actually looking for?' Tally asked, frowning as she surveyed shelf upon shelf of paint tins.

'Paint,' Harry said helpfully.

'Very funny. I mean, what room are you concentrating on first?'

Good question! Harry considered the matter. 'I can't do Amy's room because she wants to choose everything herself.'

'I know that,' Tally said, grinning. 'And I've got to help her. I got the memo.'

Harry laughed. 'Yes, well, you know Amy.'

'So what then? The bathrooms don't need paint since they're fully tiled.'

Harry raised an eyebrow. 'You've never done this before, have you?'

'Why do you say that?'

'Because, my dear Tally, there's a little matter of ceilings to emulsion, and skirting boards and door frames to paint. Or would you prefer the bare plaster and wood look?'

'Fair point.' Tally wrinkled her nose. 'Bit boring though. I don't want to look for white. I want to look for something interesting.' She held up a can that could best be described as bottle green. 'That's different.'

'For which room?' Harry queried.

Tally shrugged. 'Just pointing it out. Ooh, that's nice.' She reached for a large tin of chalky blue emulsion. I love that.'

'For…?'

She put the tin back and shrugged. 'Well, er, I have to sleep somewhere. Maybe, my room?'

'Your room?' Harry could hardly hide his shock. Tally had moved into one of the recently finished guest bedrooms on the first floor, and he'd even gone so far as to buy a bed for her to sleep in, figuring it would come in useful for guests after she left. But that didn't mean she could claim it as her room. This was supposed to be temporary. What part of that wasn't she getting?

'I could pay rent,' she gabbled. 'I don't mind what you charge.'

'How are you going to pay rent?' he queried. 'Since you seem to have made up your mind to quit your job.'

'I haven't actually done that yet, though, have I? And even if I did, it would be to take on another job. So I could afford rent. And like I said, I have savings. So, you know.'

'Tally—'

'Aw, look at this. What a touching scene.'

Harry spun round at the sound of a rather sarcastic male voice. He didn't need to see Tally's face to guess who the sudden arrival was.

'What are you doing here, Derry?' Her voice was strained, and Harry felt a pang of sympathy for her.

'Your mother asked me to get her some fence paint. She's decided to do up the garden to take her mind off — things.'

Harry could easily guess what *things* Sophie needed distracting from. Despite the clear hostility radiating from Derry, he held out a hand and gave the young man a warm smile. He was, after all, Rhiannon's son, and she loved him. Even if he was a complete arse.

'Derry Bone? Pleased to meet you. Harry Jarvis.'

Derry gave him a withering look. 'Yes, I can guess who you are, thanks. Who else would be in here buying paint with Tally for the love nest?'

Harry surveyed him, pushing down a rather sharp stab of annoyance as the young man refused to shake his hand, but held his gaze steadily, no trace of embarrassment. He really was as rude as Tally had said. How had someone like Rhiannon raised such a little shit?

He was definitely her son, though. No question about it. That dark hair and those dark, dark eyes... He was Rhiannon through and through, and Harry had to admit he was an exceptionally good-looking man. He could understand why Tally had fallen for him, despite his charmless personality.

'You could at least shake his hand,' Tally said coldly. 'Stop being so rude.'

Derry's attention snapped back to her. 'Why would I shake his hand? He's making a complete fool of you. Using you. It's a shame you can't see that.'

'Oh, shut up, Derry,' she said. 'You know nothing about him.'

'Using her?' Harry glared at the arrogant young man as he watched Tally, lip curled in disgust. 'Who says I'm using her?'

Derry didn't even do him the courtesy of looking at him but addressed his remarks to Tally. 'Everyone knows he is. We all know what sort of man he is, so he needn't think he's fooling us, not for a minute. If you weren't so innocent, Tally—'

'For God's sake!' Tally sounded as if she were about to stamp her foot in exasperation. 'You're as bad as all the others! Treating me like a stupid kid.'

'You're not a stupid kid, and I certainly don't think of you like that,' Derry said angrily. 'But you don't have much experience with men, and you clearly don't see what's obvious to the rest of us. This man's a predator, Tally. A womaniser, a cheat, a liar. Look what he did to Eliza, for God's sake! Is that really who you want to be shacked up with?'

'I don't see,' Tally said, with sudden deathly calm, 'what makes him so much worse than you in that respect.'

Derry looked stunned, which gave Harry a fleeting sense of satisfaction.

'How can you even say that? You can't compare me to — to him!'

'Cheers.' Harry leaned against the shelves and folded his arms, recognising that his presence was no longer relevant, or probably even noticed. This was between the two of them.

'I can, though,' Tally snapped. 'And we all know why.'

'Tally…' Derry's voice trailed off and he stared at her, a stricken expression in his eyes.

Harry tilted his head, watching in curiosity. Something in Derry's face, his posture, told him that there was a lot more to this scene than he was revealing.

Hadn't Tally said that it was Derry who broke it off? Yet, judging by the look in his eyes, it was clear that, if he had, he regretted it. Whatever Tally thought, whatever Derry had said, he obviously still had deep feelings for her. So why hurt her so badly?

'If you've nothing else to say, I'll bid you good day,' Tally said haughtily.

Harry couldn't help but smile. She sounded like a heroine from one of those period dramas that Eliza used to love watching. He felt a sudden pang of sadness as nostalgia overwhelmed him. He used to mock Eliza for her romantic nature when they were married, he recalled. It used to get on his nerves when she swooned over Regency heroes on the television. He'd never understood it, and Melody's preference for stunt-heavy action films had seemed to confirm that she was a much better match for him. Funny how things changed. He had a feeling he'd look at those soppy films Eliza loved so much with different eyes now.

He blinked, startled and a little irritated as Tally linked her arm through his. 'Come on, Harry. We've got paint to find. For the bedroom.'

Her voice grew louder on that last remark and Harry winced inside. Great. That would add fuel to the flames all right. He was beginning to feel like a sacrificial lamb — his entire life given away on the altar of Tally's pride.

'When are you going back to Cornwall?' he asked Derry, mentally crossing his fingers that the answer would be, tomorrow, or even sooner.

'That's my business,' came the cold, non-committal answer. 'I have things to attend to here first. When they're sorted, I'll go back.'

'Well, good luck with — er — everything.'

Derry gave him a look so cold it would have frozen lava and walked away.

'Pillock,' Tally muttered, and Harry shot her a sympathetic look, realising she was far more shaken by Derry's appearance than she was letting on.

'Come on,' he said. 'Let's choose this paint and get out of here.'

As they made their choice, however, he realised something was niggling away at him, and he found it hard to concentrate, eventually letting Tally make the final decision on the colour. Something was bugging him, and he wished he could figure out what it was, as it was making him feel extremely uneasy.

It was only as they were driving home, and Harry was mentally reliving the conversation with Derry that it came to him. Derry had said he would be leaving for Cornwall when he'd sorted out some things in Kearton Bay, and his words had left Harry in the unenviable position of feeling torn in two by his response.

It should have been a no-brainer. The minute Derry left for Cornwall, Harry could force Tally to come clean and finally be free of this charade, so why wasn't he delighted to hear Derry would be gone soon?

Because when Derry did leave Kearton Bay, Rhiannon would be hurt all over again. And it finally dawned on Harry that he wanted Rhiannon's happiness more than he wanted his own. Which led him to one startling conclusion…

But it couldn't be love! Harry didn't do love. Not any longer. After everything he'd been through, and everything he'd put Eliza and his children through, he'd long since concluded that love was for other people. So, if not love, what was he feeling? And crucially, what on earth did he do about it?

20

Mrs MacLean hurried up to me just as I rang the bell at Ivy House.

'Here for the baby shower, pet?' she asked me. 'Should be a laugh, and it's free grub if nothing else.' She beamed as Flynn opened the door. 'Eeh, here he is! The man himself.'

Flynn didn't make a sound, but I could sense the horrified groan that he was emitting within as his mother-in-law stepped cheerily into the hallway ahead of me.

'Come here, you gorgeous man, you.'

I couldn't help but laugh as he was dragged to Mrs MacLean, who planted a big kiss on his cheek while, beside him, Violet pulled disgusted faces.

Rose hurried into the hallway and gave me a resigned look. 'She always does this. Mother, put him down. You know it embarrasses him.'

'Aw, Rose, don't spoil me fun.' Mrs MacLean smoothed down her hair, pulled a lipstick from her coat pocket, and reapplied it most expertly without so much as a glance in the hallway mirror. 'Are you off out, pet?' she asked Flynn, a gleam of mischief in her eyes. 'Anywhere good? I might come with you if it sounds more fun than a baby shower.'

'We're going snail collecting,' Violet informed her grandmother.

Mrs MacLean visibly shuddered. 'Sod that for a game of soldiers. You're welcome to it. Off you go then, and have a good time, though how you'll manage that I don't know.'

'Good luck,' Flynn whispered, winking at me as he took Violet's hand.

Rose kissed her husband and daughter then closed the door behind them as they escaped Ivy House and headed off to Whisperwood.

'Here we are then,' Mrs MacLean said. 'Are we the first, pet?'

Rose shook her head. 'You're the last, I think. Come in, let's get you a drink.'

She ushered us into the living room, which was decked out with blue balloons and strings of bunting and packed with females. No wonder Flynn had been so eager to escape with so many women around.

Everyone chorused a greeting to us, and we waved back and said our hellos.

'By hell,' Mrs MacLean said, shrugging off her coat and throwing it on the back of a chair, where it was immediately scooped up by Rose, 'you've got enough people here, haven't you? Hope you've made enough grub to go around. I haven't had me dinner.'

'Don't worry, Mother, there's plenty.' Rose held out her hands for my coat then draped them both over her arm and called over to Cerise, who was scrolling down her mobile phone, looking completely uninterested in her sister's baby shower. 'Cerise! Hang these up for me will you, pet? I'm just getting these two a drink.'

Cerise, to her credit, didn't complain, but put down her phone and reached for the coats. 'You can have my chair, Gran, if you like,' she told Mrs MacLean.

'What stuck over there in that corner? I don't think so.' Mrs MacLean scanned the room and her eyes fell on Fuchsia and Pandora, sitting together on the sofa. 'Pandora, you'll give up your seat for an old lady, won't you?'

Pandora looked a bit put out. 'Er...'

'Thanks, pet. I knew you wouldn't mind. I need to sit next to me granddaughter on her special day, don't I?'

'It's *our* special day, Gran,' Fuchsia reminded her, giving Pan an apologetic look. 'Not just mine.'

'Oh, aye. Whatever.' Mrs MacLean patted her on the head as Pandora stood. Before Fuchsia had time to object, she'd swooped down to sit beside her granddaughter.

'Typical Mam,' Rose murmured. She shook her head slightly at me. 'Do you want to come into the kitchen for a minute while I fix those drinks? There's a few of us in there.'

I thought that sounded like a good idea, so I followed her into the kitchen and smiled upon seeing Eliza, Lexi and Sophie huddled around a wine bottle and several glasses.

'I'm on the apple juice,' Lexi said immediately. 'Don't judge me.'

'Why on earth would I judge you?' I asked, perplexed.

'Because of the breastfeeding. Bloody hell, I miss wine. Almost as much as I miss sleep, but not quite.'

'Bless you.' I remembered the early days with Derry, and how Jack had helped me out when I was ready to drop with sheer exhaustion. He used to look after Derry between feeds, allowing me to sleep as much as I could. What on earth would I have done without him?

'It will pass,' Eliza assured her stepdaughter. 'When we had the twins, your dad and I were on our knees with exhaustion, but we got through it eventually.'

Lexi nodded. 'I know. We've done it once and we can do it again. Ooh, Eliza, Will asked me to tell you he's managed to source that, er, item that you wanted.'

Eliza squealed with delight. 'Really? Oh my God! Do you have pictures?'

She shook her head. 'Not yet, but this man's reliable, apparently. Will knows him of old, and he says there won't be a problem. You can drive down there next week if you want. Pick which one you want.'

I wondered if everyone else was as bemused by this conversation as I was. Judging by the blank expressions I thought it was safe to assume they were. Of course, Sophie was the first to voice her confusion.

'What's this about? What am I missing?' she demanded.

Eliza looked round at us all. 'It's a surprise for Amy,' she explained. 'She's always wanted a puppy, and Will's found us a litter.'

'They'll be ready in time for Amy's birthday next month,' Lexi added. 'Perfect timing really.'

I thought of Harry and wondered how he'd react to this bit of news. He'd laughingly relayed a conversation he'd had with Amy to me, concerning her assertion that the only thing she'd ever wanted was an iPhone, puppy, pony, and goodness knows what else. He'd got a lot of grief for buying the iPhone. How would he react to Amy finally getting her dog from Eliza and Gabriel?

'What sort of dog is it?' Sophie sounded less than enthusiastic. 'Not one of those huge, hairy things, is it? You'll have dog hair all over the place, and muddy paw prints.' She shuddered. 'Rather you than me, Eliza.'

'It's a cocker spaniel,' Eliza said. 'They're fairly small, but very bouncy.'

'You're not kidding,' Lexi told her. 'It's going to need a lot of exercise. I hope Amy understands that.'

'Well, she seems to,' Eliza mused. 'I'm still not a hundred per cent convinced, I must admit, but Gabriel insisted so…'

She sighed and Lexi shook her head.

'I think Dad's being daft, giving in like that. If he's not certain that Amy will take care of this dog—'

'Why now?' Sophie asked, her eyes narrowing as she sensed something more to the story. 'You've both said no to a dog for years. Suddenly you think it's a good idea?'

'Well, isn't it obvious?' Lexi asked.

'I knew it!' Sophie gave a triumphant cry. 'This is all about sodding Harry Jarvis, isn't it?'

I straightened, and my heart gave an involuntary thud at the mention of Harry. I braced myself for the inevitable character assassination.

'It's Gabriel really,' Eliza said. 'You can't blame Harry for this. It's just, with the bedroom he's promised Amy, and then the iPhone he bought her, I think Gabriel's feeling a bit…' She shrugged. 'I don't know. Insecure, I guess.'

'It's ridiculous,' Lexi said. 'As if Harry could ever replace Dad in her life.'

'But he *is* her father,' I said, compelled to defend Harry. 'Amy loves him, I'm sure.'

'Of course she does,' Eliza said. 'I'm not saying she doesn't.'

'Then you can't blame Harry for Gabriel's insecurities,' I said.

'I'm not,' she said, sounding rather indignant. 'I just said that didn't I?'

'*I* blame him.' Sophie poured herself more wine. 'That man is poison. He comes back here after all this time and expects everyone to fit in around his wants and needs. Where was he when Amy started school, eh? When she had chicken pox? With his fancy piece in America, that's where. It was Gabriel who was there for her. Some people should remember that.'

'I know, Sophie. I know,' Eliza said. She sounded defeated, and I felt terribly sorry for her. It must be hard for her, wanting to do what was best for her daughter, while keeping the peace between the two men who loved Amy most in the world, yet couldn't see eye to eye about anything to do with her.

'And now he's broken my family apart, too,' Sophie continued, after taking a large gulp of wine. 'Seduced my innocent daughter, like some ageing Casanova. It's heart-breaking that she can't see him for what he is.'

'There's nothing between Harry and Tally,' I said firmly. 'Tally's already told you that.'

'Well of course she did,' Sophie said. 'Because she's protecting him, that's why. She knows Archie would thump him one if she admitted it. But she doesn't fool us, not for an instant.'

'Well,' I said, gripping my glass tightly, 'I believe them.'

Rose let out a peal of laughter. 'Oh, come on, Rhiannon! You're not serious? Why else would she be shacked up at Eight Bells?'

'Perhaps,' I said carefully, 'she needed a roof over her head, while she worked things out in her mind.' I gave Sophie a pointed look. 'Much like you gave Derry a place to stay when he needed it.'

'But that's different,' Sophie said. 'I've known Derry all his life, and I'm happy to help out. You can't tell me that Harry Jarvis would do anything that wasn't for his own benefit. If he's taken Tally in, there's a reason. And, much as I hate to say it, it's pretty obvious what that reason is.'

'I think you should have more faith in your daughter,' I said. 'And maybe give Harry the benefit of the doubt.'

'Do you believe that?' Eliza asked.

'Of course,' I said. 'They've both told me it's just friendship, so why shouldn't I?'

'Because Harry's a liar and Tally's been corrupted,' said Sophie dramatically.

'I have to say, I wish it weren't true,' Lexi said thoughtfully, 'but I can't help feeling that there is something between them.'

'Why do you say that?' I asked, stung.

'It's just a feeling,' she admitted. 'There's something about Tally. She's behaving very much like a girl in love, although I can't say it's making her happy.'

'How could he make any woman happy?' Sophie said scornfully. 'Oh, my poor Tally. If only she'd stop being so stubborn and come home.'

I sipped my wine. Had Tally fallen for Harry? It wasn't like Lexi to read something into things that weren't there. But Tally would get hurt if she *had* developed feelings for him. They would never be reciprocated.

'You'd have thought Tally would be here at her own sister's baby shower,' Rose said sadly. 'The old Tally wouldn't have missed it for the world. Poor Pan must be so hurt.'

At that very moment, Pandora popped her head around the door. 'Are you lot planning on staying in here all afternoon? Rude, I call it. Fuchsia's gran's managing to offend just about everyone, so we could do with some help managing her if it's not too much trouble.'

Rose groaned. 'Should have known. All right, we're coming now, pet.'

Feeling some relief that the subject of Harry was closed, I followed the others into the living room, where Meggie and Chrissie were smothering their laughter as Mrs MacLean tried to coax Fuchsia into giving details of exactly how she'd managed to get pregnant. She seemed particularly fascinated by the process of choosing a donor.

'What, a catalogue?' she asked, as we all squeezed into any vacant seat we could find. 'You mean, like picking a new frock?'

'Well, not quite the same thing, Gran,' Fuchsia said, squirming with embarrassment.

'So, do you see photos, like? Do you do that thing like they do on the dating apps?'

Pandora and Fuchsia exchanged puzzled glances. 'Huh?'

'I think what my mam is trying to say,' Rose said with a sigh, 'is do you swipe right, or left, or whatever it is they do on Tinder and other sites.'

'You don't actually see him,' Fuchsia explained. 'You get some general information, like eye colour and hair colour and occupation, and stuff like that.'

'Ooh, and what did you pick?' Mrs MacLean asked.

'He has dark hair, since we both have dark hair,' Fuchsia said, 'and he has blue eyes, but as I've got grey eyes and Pan has brown eyes it doesn't matter what colour the baby's eyes end up being. None of it matters. We'll love him anyway.'

'Oh aye, you say that now!' Mrs MacLean pulled a face and let out a whoop of laughter. 'You wait until he's here. You'll be wishing you'd put that money on a deposit for a house instead.'

'Charming,' Pandora muttered.

'Have you decided what sort of birth you're having?' Cerise sounded fascinated by the subject, and Fuchsia smiled at her.

'Not really. No point in making much of a plan is there? You never know how it's going to turn out.'

Mrs MacLean patted her leg. 'Too right you don't, pet. Very wise. I don't understand all this, *I'm having the baby in a swimming pool with candles and mood music*. Mood music! You won't hear a thing for the screams. Take the drugs, pet, that's my advice. Whatever they offer you, grab it with both hands.'

Fuchsia looked distinctly alarmed by now and Rose obviously thought it was time to step in.

'Don't worry, it's not as bad as she's making out. It's a lovely experience. One you'll always treasure.'

'Well, you'll never forget it, that's for sure,' her mother agreed. 'By God, I suffered having our Rose. And you're never the same again you know. Your body's had it after that. It makes a difference, once a baby's been through that road, if you know what I mean.'

'Someone shut her up,' muttered Sophie.

'Then again,' Mrs MacLean said thoughtfully, 'I don't suppose it matters as much with you being a lesbian, does it?'

'Cup of tea anyone?' called Meggie. 'I'll put the kettle on, shall I?'

'There's lots of food in the kitchen,' Rose said. 'I'll start bringing it through, shall I? Anyone want to help me?'

'I'll help,' I said.

'Me, too,' called about five different voices.

Mrs MacLean was never particularly good at taking a hint. 'Mind you, I doubt you'll have as much to worry about as your poor mam,' she said, grimacing. 'How much did our Violet weigh, Rose?'

Rose's face went a fetching shade of her beloved pink. 'Er, ten pounds two,' she muttered.

'Ten pounds two! And she went out the door, not through the sunroof,' Mrs MacLean announced to those brave souls who were still actively listening. 'God knows what that's done to her. Poor Flynn is all I can say. Must be like chucking a chip up Bay Street.'

Around four people got jammed in the doorway in their haste to get out of the room. I bit my lip as Fuchsia groaned.

'One of these days I'll bloody throttle you, Mother,' Rose snapped.

Luckily, Mrs MacLean was soon distracted by the plates of food that arrived. Before long, she was happily tucking into sandwiches while Fuchsia looked like she was going to need therapy.

Lexi edged her way over to me. 'Derry's been coming round to the Hall a bit,' she said hesitantly.

If she worried I wouldn't be happy about that, she was wrong. I was delighted. She and Will could only be a good influence on him, and he needed his friends.

'How is he?' I asked. 'Did he mention his old band mates? He was going to look for them, see if they were still speaking to him after the way he left.'

She grinned. 'Oh, he found them. They gave him a really hard time. He was mortified. Then they burst out laughing and several hugs were exchanged.'

'Oh, that's wonderful,' I said. 'I'm so glad they understood.'

'I think they were pleased to see him, after all this time,' she said. 'They've moved on anyway. A couple of them are married. Derry needn't have worried.'

'That's one less thing for him to be anxious about anyway,' I said, staring unseeingly at my plate.

'He told us,' she murmured. 'About your dad and how horrible he was to him. Isn't it awful?'

My head shot up in surprise. 'He told you? He asked me to keep it a secret.'

'I know, he asked us to do the same. I think he's trying to build on his relationship with Will, you know. Derry apologised to him for how he spoke to him before he left. He wants them to be real brothers. You can imagine how Will reacted to that.'

I couldn't wipe the smile from my face. I knew how much that would mean to Will, and a closer relationship between the two of them could only benefit Derry.

'Do you know any details?' she asked curiously. 'About what went wrong between Derry and his granddad I mean?'

I shook my head. 'Not a clue. He said he was exactly what I'd told him he was, if not worse. I shudder to think.'

She tilted her head, considering. 'Weird, isn't it? Will says he's gained a lot of knowledge about running an estate. He's been having chats with Will and Bernie about the house and grounds, and Will said it's clear your father has been training him. Derry didn't have a clue about any of that before, did he? Well, he knows now. Seems he hasn't been wasting time down there.'

She eyed me steadily and I knew all too well what she was thinking.

'My father was grooming him to take over the estate,' I murmured. 'He's planning on leaving it all to Derry, isn't he?'

'I honestly don't know,' she said. 'But Will seems to think it's a strong possibility. Which makes it even stranger that he walked away. Will offered to find him a job at Kearton Hall, if he wanted it, but Derry said no. He said it's not his sort of thing, even though he's quite knowledgeable now. Do you think that's why they fell out? Maybe Derry realised he didn't want the estate and your father was upset about that?'

'Perhaps.' I thought about it. 'I think there's more to it than that, though. Then again, one never knows with my father. If he doesn't get his own way he can be appalling.'

'Well,' Lexi said with a sigh, 'I guess whatever went on, he'll tell us when he's good and ready.' She winked at me. 'At least it means he's more likely to stay on in Kearton Bay, right? Especially now he's so close to Will, and he wants to build a relationship with our kids, and be a proper godfather to Ellie, and he's friends with all his old mates again. It can only be a good thing.'

'Let's hope so,' I agreed.

'There's something else. He's been asking Will about his father. Just little bits, but it's a start, isn't it? And Will was showing him the photograph albums the other day, and Derry didn't freak out when he saw pictures of Sir Paul, so…'

I wondered what that meant. Was Derry finally beginning to accept that he was Sir Paul's son? After all if he was accepting Will as his brother…

At that moment, Rose announced that it was time to give the mums-to-be their baby gifts, so Lexi and I pushed all thoughts of Derry aside and concentrated on the moment, delighted for Pan and Fuchsia as they exclaimed in surprise and pleasure at the amount of presents they were given.

'He's going to be the best-dressed baby in Yorkshire,' Cerise said, holding up a cute little sleepsuit with Peter Rabbit on the front.

'He won't be in them five minutes,' Rose remarked.

'He won't be in most of them at all if he comes out as fat as our Violet,' said her mother, with her usual tact and diplomacy. 'Mind you, I think that was down to your diet while you were pregnant, our Rose. Too many marshmallows, no doubt.'

'I never ate the marshmallows!' Rose protested.

'I told you, you should have followed the Lightweights maternity plan,' Sophie said, sounding smug. 'But you wouldn't have it. If you'd done that you wouldn't have had to lose all that extra weight afterwards.'

'*And* you wouldn't have had a baby the size of a sumo wrestler,' Mrs MacLean added.

'That, too,' Sophie agreed.

'How are the wedding vows plans coming on, Mum?' Pandora asked hastily, before the conversation could deteriorate any further.

Thankfully, her tactics worked. Sophie's entire demeanour changed, as she settled back, sandwich in hand, and began to tell us all about her forthcoming ceremony, capturing the attention of even Mrs MacLean. It was to be held at Kearton Hall, naturally, and Will was performing the ceremony.

'Will?' Meggie asked. 'Why Will? No offence, love,' she added, nodding at Lexi. 'Just seems a bit strange.'

'Because, well, because he's part of the family,' Sophie said uncomfortably. 'And because it's his home we're getting married in, after all. And because he has such a lovely speaking voice.'

I grinned to myself as I heard Rose mutter to an amused Eliza, 'And because he's a baronet, and she can tell everyone she was married by Sir William Boden-Kean.'

'And Joe's going to be Archie's best man,' Sophie continued.

'Of course he is,' Rose said, barely able to keep a straight face.

'And Charlie's giving me away,' Sophie finished proudly.

There was no doubt in my mind — and probably anyone else's — that they wouldn't have been asked at all if they hadn't both been celebrities. Sophie was nothing if not predictable.

'It all sounds lovely, Sophie,' Lexi said. 'I've been looking at the plans and—'

'Don't tell them!' Sophie squealed. 'It's a surprise. This is going to be a day to remember, and you're all invited.' She glanced nervously at Mrs MacLean, clearly regretting her rash invitation already.

'I wouldn't miss it for the world,' Rose's mother said. 'Can I bring a plus one? Only I think Maurice would love a day out.'

'Oh yes,' Sophie said immediately, sounding relieved. 'Maurice is lovely. You can bring him.'

'Are you having bridesmaids, Mum?' Pandora asked.

'Don't look at me,' Fuchsia said immediately. 'I'll be about ready to pop by then. Peach satin won't do me any favours.'

'Peach satin doesn't do anyone any favours,' Rose said fervently, clearly remembering her own mother's wedding day, when Mrs MacLean had insisted that she be maid of honour and had chosen peach as the colour scheme.

'I was thinking I'd maybe have Amy and Hannah as flower girls,' Sophie said. 'And Michael as a page boy. What do you think, Eliza?'

'I'm sure they'd love it,' Eliza said.

'Oh, that's smashing. I've found some lovely patterns for the dresses. Meggie's offered to make them.' Sophie sighed. 'They're going to look adorable.'

I couldn't help but feel sad. Something else Harry would miss out on. Seeing his daughter dressed as a flower girl would make his day, but there was no chance at all that Sophie would invite him to her vows renewal ceremony.

'Have you organised the flowers and cake?' I asked.

'Eliza's making the cake,' Sophie told me. 'I'm sure she'll do a good job, won't you, love?'

Rose grinned. I saw her nudge Eliza and was almost sure I heard her whisper the words, *dose it with laxatives*. I fervently hoped I'd been mistaken.

'And Tally's organised the flowers, in consultation with the Kearton Hall gardener. She's been very efficient. I've hardly had to interfere at all.'

'Well, I hope you're not counting on her being at the actual ceremony, Mum,' Pandora said grumpily. 'She obviously can't drag herself away from that man for five minutes to even come to her own sister's baby shower.'

I groaned inwardly. I'd hoped the subject of Harry and Tally was closed, but I suppose I should have known better.

'I don't know what a lovely young girl like Tally sees in him,' Meggie said. 'I mean, all right he's good looking-ish if you like that sort of thing, but he's past his best, isn't he?'

'Money.' Chrissie hurriedly swallowed the last of her sausage roll and added, 'Well, that's what it is, isn't it? What else could it be? He must be loaded after working in America for that long. And why else would Tally throw herself at him, with his reputation?'

'She never threw herself at him!' Sophie snapped. 'He seduced her, that's what happened there.'

'And you were there were you?' Mrs MacLean smirked. 'I find it more surprising that someone of his age and experience would want a daft young lass on their arm. It's all an ego boost you know. It won't last five minutes. Men like him, they never stick around for long anyway. My advice would be to let it go on for as long as it needs to. She'll see sense, and he'll get bored and that will be that. It's a different shag, that's all. Mark my words, he'll be onto the next lass before you can say Casanova.'

I couldn't bear to listen to any more. 'I think Harry's nowhere near as bad as people think,' I said defiantly. 'He's a decent man who's made some mistakes, but he's trying to make up for those now. I think we should all give him the benefit of a doubt.'

Sophie glared at me. 'Well, you would say that, wouldn't you? Cut from the same cloth!'

'What do you mean by that?' I asked, as if I didn't know. I hadn't wanted to get embroiled in this discussion, but I couldn't stand by and let them all trash Harry's name, especially when I knew the truth about him and his relationship with Tally. It seemed desperately unfair that he was taking so much abuse for seducing Sophie's daughter, when in fact he was protecting her, and behaving extremely honourably.

'If the cap fits,' Sophie said.

'Let's not get into a row,' Lexi said. 'It's Fuchsia's and Pandora's baby shower. Now's not the time or place to discuss Harry Jarvis.'

'You're right, pet,' Rose said firmly. 'Can we drop the subject now please?'

'Far be it from me to spoil the girls' big day,' Sophie said stonily. 'Nevertheless, I want it here on record that Harry Jarvis is a cruel, lying, cheating, philandering swine, and the sooner Tally sees sense the better.'

'He's not all bad,' said Eliza reluctantly. 'He has his good points.'

'Like dumping you for Melody Bird?' Sophie blurted. 'Abandoning Amy? Causing all sorts of trouble for you and Gabriel now he's back? Forcing you to get a *dog*, for heaven's sake!'

'Mum, leave it,' Pandora snapped. 'It's like Lexi said. Now's not the time or place.'

I turned away, unable to look at Sophie for a moment longer. It wasn't like me. Usually, anything Sophie said was like water off a duck's back. I never got involved in skirmishes like this, and always tried to stay neutral. Yet Sophie's words had angered me, and I found myself in the usual position of wanting to yell out the truth and defend Harry's honour to the end.

I thought wistfully that all I wanted to do was go to Eight Bells to comfort Harry, to put my arms around him and tell him I was on his side. He deserved more than he was getting in Kearton Bay.

Just when had he come to mean so much to me?

21

Harry wondered when it was that he'd turned into such a wimp.

'Get on with it, for God's sake,' he muttered, staring at his mobile phone as if it possessed the power to destroy his life, when in fact, it wasn't the phone itself that would make or break the day, but the person who'd be on the other end of the line.

It was his day to telephone Rufus, and as much as he wanted to speak to his son he dreaded making the call.

The last time he'd tried to contact him, Melody had insisted he was at a friend's house and couldn't be reached. Harry had got quite irate, as this was becoming a regular occurrence, and had insisted on pinning Melody down to a specific date and time when he could call his son and know he would be in.

He therefore couldn't back out of it, but on top of everything else, it felt more like an ordeal to endure than something to look forward to, as it meant he'd have to speak to his ex-wife first, something that was becoming increasingly unbearable.

He could only hope she'd put Rufus on the phone straightaway, and he wouldn't have to speak to her. Fat chance. Tormenting him seemed to be the highlight of her life.

Just do it! He glared at the phone as if it were mocking him, then he grabbed it and made the call, his heart thumping, his eyes closed as he sent a fervent prayer that it would be Rufus who picked up, as unlikely as that was.

'Oh, you remembered him then.'

Harry opened his eyes as Melody's voice snarled into his ear.

'Of course I remembered him. He's important to me. May I speak with him please?' *Just get off the phone, Melody, and let me talk to my son.*

'Sorry, I can't.'

Harry glared at the screen as if she could see him. 'What do you mean, you can't? We had an agreement. You promised!'

'I know I did, but I can't help it if he's not well, can I?'

Harry's eyes narrowed in suspicion. 'You're saying he's not well?'

'I'm not just saying it. He's *not* well. Believe it or don't believe it, I don't care. The point is, he can't come to the phone because he's in bed sleeping.'

'What's wrong with him?' Harry pictured Rufus tucked up in his bed, his dark hair falling over one eye, his little face flushed with fever. 'Does he have a temperature? What is it? Have you called a doctor?'

'It's just a cold,' Melody said. 'A few of his friends have had it. It's nothing to worry about.'

'If it's nothing to worry about,' Harry said, 'why can't I talk to him?'

'Because he's asleep, I've just told you. It may only be a cold, but he still feels ill with it. Have a little compassion.'

'I have plenty of compassion for some people,' Harry snapped. 'It seems an amazing coincidence that he gets ill today of all days, when we've arranged this phone call.'

'I know,' Melody drawled. 'It's almost like fate's against you, isn't it?'

'Melody if you're playing games—'

'You'll what?' She laughed. 'Oh, relax, Harry. I'm not playing games. It's tough luck, that's all. Bad timing, like so much of your life.'

He wanted to argue but didn't have the energy. He had nothing to fire back at her, no ammunition left.

'Are you still there?' she said sharply.

'Yes. I'm still here. Though I may as well not be since I don't get to speak to my son.'

'Call again in a few days. I'm sure he'll be better by then.'

'Yes. Sure.' Harry doubted it. Melody would probably tell him the cold had turned out to be Bubonic Plague knowing her. He might never talk to Rufus again at this rate.

'How are things going with Amy?'

Harry frowned. Why would she care? 'Okay,' he said cautiously. 'We're getting there.'

'Oh great. That's something then. How are you settling in at Kearton Bay?'

'Why would you want to know?' he demanded. 'Since when have you been interested in what's going on in my life?'

'Jeez, Harry, don't have a cow,' she said. 'I thought, since you couldn't talk to Rufus, I could tell him what's going on with you, that's all. When he wakes up, I mean. He may ask.'

'Do you think so?'

'Not really, no,' she said, and he wondered why he'd fallen for it again. God, she was a total bitch. What had he ever seen in her?

'I'll be off then,' he said.

'Oh don't be like that.' Melody's tone was suddenly conciliatory, and Harry was immediately on guard. He didn't trust her when she was being nice. Not for a moment.

'I'm not being like anything,' he replied. 'I rang to speak to Rufus and since that's impossible, *again*, I may as well hang up.'

'How's the house renovation going?' she asked, as if he hadn't spoken. 'You must be nearly done by now, surely?'

'It's coming along,' he said.

'So you're still working on it? Good grief, how bad was it?'

'Not that bad,' he said, stung. 'It needs a bit of knocking into shape for the customers.'

'Customers? What customers?'

Harry took a deep breath. Him and his big mouth. 'I'm opening it up as a bed and breakfast. It used to be a hotel, and it seems silly to waste all that room and—'

'A B&B!' Melody let out a shriek of laughter. 'You're not serious? An old-fashioned seaside boarding house! Oh, I never thought I'd see the day. The great Harry Jarvis, reduced to that!'

Harry bristled with anger. 'The house is too big for one person,' he said. 'Gordon thought I may as well make some money out of it, and it seemed sensible. There's no shame in it.'

'But you're a television presenter,' she pointed out. 'At least you were. I guess that's all over now, huh? Oh dear. I don't know how Rufus is going to explain this to his friends. I guess it's a good thing he has Chuck to brag about.'

Harry was wounded, but there was no way he was letting her get the last word.

'For your information,' he said furiously, 'I'm not done quite yet. I've had talks with Martin.' *Which was true.* 'There's a possibility I might be getting my old job back.' Which, he had to concede, was certainly *not* true.

There was a pause, then Melody said, 'Your old job? You mean, *Twice as Nice?*'

'That's right. *Twice as Nice.*'

'Are you sure?' she said, sounding doubtful. 'I wouldn't have thought you'd have been welcomed there, given how we left. Are they even looking for a new presenter?'

'Yes they are.' At least he wasn't lying about that.

'Right. Well, who'd have thought it? And you're definitely in the running?'

'More than in the running,' he said. 'It's practically a done deal.'

'Well,' she said, 'good luck to you. I'm sure you'll enjoy yourself. A lot of happy memories on that show for you, no doubt.'

'You must be joking,' he said. 'This time around I'll be keeping away from the other presenter.'

'Why?' Melody asked, clearly stung. 'Isn't she sexy enough for you? Not in my league?'

'From what I've heard,' Harry said bravely, 'she's a decent woman who doesn't play games and, unlike my last co-star, actually knows something about property. It will be lovely to work with a true professional for once.'

He hung up before she could say anything else. What on earth had he told her that rubbish for? Now he'd have to come up with some excuse as to why the producer didn't want him after all, and she would no doubt think that hilarious and make fun of him because of it.

The old Harry wouldn't have let Melody get to him, he thought ruefully. Nothing much used to bother him, yet so much seemed to be getting him down lately.

'You don't have time for this,' he said angrily, catching sight of himself in the mirror in his bedroom and wondering, with some horror, when he'd got so old. 'For fuck's sake, pull yourself together.'

He had no choice. He was taking Amy to Pleasure Planet, a theme park and zoo on the North York Moors, and he had a long day of being happy and entertaining ahead of him. Melody may be ruining his relationship with his son, but there was no way he was going to let her spoil the precious time he had with his daughter.

****

Harry had to hand it to Amy. The girl knew how to eat. She'd gone through three courses and was now eyeing his dessert with hungry eyes.

'Aren't you going to finish that?' she asked, as he'd expected she would.

Harry pushed the plate towards her. 'I'm not hungry,' he admitted. 'Can you manage that, on top of everything else?'

'I'm a growing girl,' she pointed out. 'I'm going through a growth spurt now, so I need all the food I can get.'

Harry grinned. 'Sure you do. But you've managed mushroom soup, fishcake and chips and a bowl of ice cream, and now you're going to tackle cheesecake?'

'Dad, if you want it, you only have to say.'

Harry shook his head. 'I don't want it. But if you're sick when you get home your mother's going to throttle me, and let's face it I don't need to give her any more ammunition,'

'I won't tell if you don't,' Amy said. 'So,' she added, digging a spoon into the strawberry cheesecake, 'how are things?'

Harry's lips twitched with amusement. 'Things are fine, thank you. How are things with you?'

'Same old, same old. But we're not talking about me. I want to know what's up with you.'

'Nothing's up with me,' Harry assured her. 'We've had a good day at Pleasure Planet, haven't we? You went on plenty of rides, and loved seeing all the animals, didn't you?'

'I did,' Amy said thoughtfully, 'but I'm not sure you had such a great time.'

He thought he'd hidden his low mood from her, but he should have known better. Amy was a smart kid and picked up on everything.

'Dad?'

'Sorry, darling. What were you saying?'

'I was saying you look miserable. You've looked miserable all day. You smiled but I can tell you're faking it.' She prodded the cheesecake but made no attempt to eat it.

'What's wrong, Amy?' he asked, seeing a sudden wariness in her eyes.

'I was wondering,' she said slowly, 'if you're getting fed up here. You know, of Kearton Bay.'

'Of course I'm not,' he said immediately. 'Why would you think that?'

'I dunno. It's not America, is it?' she pointed out. 'And you've been doing boring things every day like painting and wallpapering, and you've had all those workmen in bothering you, and then I've been a bit...'

'A bit what?' he asked, surprised.

'A bit greedy,' she admitted.

He laughed. 'I don't mind you having the cheesecake, Amy. I told you—'

'I don't mean about that,' she said. 'I mean, about the bedroom. You know, asking for that special wallpaper, and the bedding, and the new furniture. Mum says I should stop nagging you, and Da— I mean, Gabriel thinks I'm getting spoilt.' She put down her spoon and met his gaze. 'Do you think I'm getting spoilt?'

'If I did,' Harry said, 'I wouldn't have let you choose whatever you want for your bedroom, would I?'

'I suppose.' She didn't sound too convinced.

'Look, Amy, I've not seen you in a long time, and I missed out on being with you. The least I can do now is give you a decent bedroom, so you'll enjoy staying with me, don't you think?'

'So you're not getting fed up with me?'

Her lip wobbled a little and Harry reached over and squeezed her hand. 'Darling, I'll never get fed up with you. I love you. Please tell me you believe that.'

Amy shrugged. 'I suppose so. But if it's not me, what is it? Are you missing Rufus?'

'Yes,' he agreed. 'That's it exactly. I'm missing Rufus.'

'So will you be going back to America then?'

'No, Amy. I've told you. My home's in Kearton Bay now. I'm staying put, I promise you.'

She spooned some cheesecake into her mouth and chewed thoughtfully. Harry took a sip of tea and waited.

'That's good then,' she said. 'Because I really like having you around.'

'You do?'

She had no idea, but she'd made his day. He found he was smiling for the first time in what felt like ages and meaning it.

'Yeah. I love you too.'

Tears? Bloody hell, what was going on with him? Harry blinked them away furiously. To his alarm, he realised that he wanted to put his head in his arms and sob, whether from happiness or sadness he wasn't sure. His emotions were swirling around inside him, mixed up and confused.

'Dad?'

'Yes, Amy?' he managed in a voice gruffer than he'd intended it to be.

'You're not poorly, are you?'

'Of course not. Why do you say that?'

'Because…' Amy paused, as if deciding whether she ought to say anything.

'Go on,' he said.

'Well, Mum said to Gabriel that you'd lost a lot of weight, and you were looking tired. She said she was worried about you.'

Harry stared at her. 'Did she?'

'Yes, she did. And now that I'm looking at you, she's right. And you don't eat much, do you?'

'I eat enough,' he assured her. He hesitated, then asked, 'What did Gabriel say?'

'He said you ought to register at the surgery,' she told him.

Hell would freeze over first. Imagine that man having access to all his medical records! There was no chance that was ever going to happen.

'Don't worry about it. I registered at another practice a few miles away.'

'But you ought to be with our surgery,' she said. 'You don't want to get poorly and have no doctor close by, do you?'

'No. I suppose not.'

'And Gabriel's a good doctor. Everyone says so.'

'Hmm.'

'And if you don't want to see him, you can always see Uncle Flynn.' Amy beamed at him. 'He's lovely.'

Who the hell was Uncle Flynn?

'He's married to Auntie Rose,' Amy explained, when he voiced the question. 'She works with Mum at the marshmallow shop, and Uncle Flynn works with Dad at the surgery.'

'He's not your dad,' Harry said automatically.

'I mean Gabriel. Sorry.'

He pushed away his annoyance and smiled at her. 'It's okay. So, Uncle Flynn isn't really your uncle?'

'Not really, but that's what we call him. He's ever so nice. You could go and see him. I'm sure he wouldn't mind.'

'Honestly, my doctor's close enough,' he said. 'And anyway, I'm absolutely fine. Right now, I have other things to think about.'

'What other things?'

He couldn't begin to tell her. Feeling washed up, disliked, blamed for something which, for once, he hadn't done. Lonely. Very lonely. Only Amy and Rhiannon filled the empty space within him, and he spent most of his time worrying that he'd lose one, or both, of them. It didn't make for a relaxing life.

'Dad? What other things?'

Harry blinked. 'Oh, er, I don't know. I was thinking about your birthday,' he said as inspiration struck. 'That's coming up next month, and I haven't got a clue what to get you. You'll be eleven, won't you?'

'It's my last birthday at this school,' she said glumly. 'I'll be going up to high school in September.'

'You'll love it,' he promised her.

'What if I don't? What if I hate it? It's a lot bigger than my school, and I won't know many people.'

'But neither will the rest of your classmates, and they'll be going up with you,' he pointed out. 'Everyone feels the same when they start high school, Amy. But most people end up loving it, and I'm sure you will, too. You're bright, and I think you'll do well there.'

'That's what Mum says,' she told him. 'She said I can be anything I want to be. She'd quite like me to be a doctor like Gabriel.'

'And is that what you want to be?' he asked, fighting the jealousy that twisted inside him.

'Maybe. I'd rather be a farmer like Uncle Joe and Uncle Charlie.' She considered the matter. 'What I really want to do is run a riding school like Georgia. We'll have to see what happens, won't we?'

'I guess we will.'

'Dad?'

'Yes, Amy?'

'If I tell you a secret, do you promise not to tell anyone?'

Harry's eyes widened. 'Of course I promise. What sort of secret?'

'A good one.' She gave him a wide grin. 'I'm not supposed to know about it, but I heard Mum and Uncle Charlie talking about it at Whisperwood. They thought I was outside with Uncle Joe, feeding the chickens, but I'd come in 'cos I needed the toilet, and they were in the kitchen and—'

'Is this something I should know?' Harry asked. 'Is it private? Because if it is—'

'It's about me,' Amy said. 'I should think you'd want to know if it's about me.'

'Well, yes.' He couldn't deny that. 'So what is it?'

'Cross your heart, hope to die.'

'Really?' Reluctantly, he made the gesture across his chest and repeated her words.

Amy leaned towards him, her nose wrinkling with excitement. 'They're getting me a dog!'

'What? Are you sure?'

'Yep. I heard it clear as day. Mum's going to hide her at Whisperwood and then they're bringing her round to me on the morning of my birthday. She's only a baby, and can't leave her mum yet, but she'll be ready for my birthday. Isn't it exciting? I hope she's a spaniel. I've told them loads of times that I want a spaniel. Do you think you could find out for me?'

'And how can I find out when I'm not supposed to know anything about it?'

'I guess so,' she said. 'I can't wait to meet her. I've been dying to tell you all day, but I was a bit worried you'd tell Mum. She'd be upset if she knew I'd found out, but I can't help hearing things, can I?'

'No,' Harry said. 'You can't. Although it must be said, Amy, you do hear an awful lot of things. It seems you have a real gift for it.'

'I know.' Amy beamed at him. 'Isn't it great?'

Harry managed a smile, but he felt increasingly miserable. He was pleased that Amy was getting her dog, of course he was. Yet again, he'd been left out of something so important in her life. He could have gone halves with Eliza if he'd known about it. It could have been from both of them. Now she'd always know that the dog was from her mother and that man. Why had they changed their minds anyway? They'd refused her a dog all this time, and suddenly it was okay?

'And,' Amy added, 'I'm to have a party, too. Mum's inviting all my friends. Everyone's coming. Isn't it ace?'

Harry's stomach churned with anger. This was to do with the bloody bedroom, wasn't it? Gabriel was jealous of him, that's what it was. Harry had given Amy the bedroom of her dreams, and bloody Angel Gabriel couldn't stand it, so he had to go one better. Two better really. A dog and a party. He'd bet a pound to a penny that he wasn't invited.

'Fabulous,' he said.

'But that's a secret, too, so don't say anything. I sort of overheard it. It was an accident.' Amy pushed away the cheesecake. 'I think I'm full now,' she announced.

'Thank goodness for that,' he said, determined that she wouldn't know how upset he was feeling. 'I was beginning to wonder if you'd grown a second pudding tummy.'

Amy laughed and he experienced a sudden surge of love for her that quite took his breath away.

'Would you like a drink before we go?' he asked, glancing at his watch. 'We'll need to set off soon though. I promised your mother you'd be back by seven.'

Amy shook her head. 'I'm good thanks,' she told him.

'Right, well I'll go and pay the bill. You wait here.'

She nodded, and Harry headed over to the counter to pay for their meal. As he took his receipt and put his credit card back in his wallet, he felt a tap on the shoulder and spun round to see a middle-aged woman beaming at him.

'It *is* you, isn't it? I said to my friend Alison, that's that Harry Jarvis from *Twice as Nice* over there, and she insisted I was wrong, but I knew it.' The woman beamed at him. 'Fancy bumping into you here of all places. I thought you were living in America now.'

'No, no back in England,' Harry said. Of all the times to bump into a fan! Although, he supposed he should be grateful he still had a fan.

'I haven't seen you on the telly for ages,' she said. 'Have you given it up?'

'It's, er, a work in progress,' he told her. 'Nice to meet you.'

Heaving a sigh of relief that she didn't try to stop him, he went to collect Amy.

'Get your coat on, darling,' he said, reaching for his jacket as soon as he got back to the table.

She did as she was told and he put his arm on her back, guiding her carefully through the pub to the exit. As they passed one of the tables, he noticed the *fan* was sitting with another woman and groaned inwardly as she nudged her and nodded towards him .

'See? Harry Jarvis. Told you he was back in England.'

'You were right, Jenny,' her friend agreed. 'I knew he wouldn't make it in America. They all get too big for their boots, that's their trouble.'

'Should have stayed where he was.' Jenny sniffed disapprovingly. 'If he had, he'd still be somebody.'

Whereas now, thought Harry bleakly, he was clearly nobody. As if he'd needed reminding.

****

'Are you mad?' Tally handed Harry the wallpaper scissors, her eyes wide with shock.

Harry, busy keeping an errant roll of wallpaper as flat as he could manage, took the scissors, and tried to ignore her tone. 'Just hold that bit down, will you? There, put your hand there,' he instructed, before slicing through the paper with a little less finesse than usual.

'Harry, are you listening to me?' Tally said. 'It's a crazy idea. You can't go ahead with it.'

Harry picked up the sheet of wallpaper and carried it over to the pre-pasted wall. He climbed up the stepladder, holding the paper gingerly by the corners.

'You can ignore me all you like,' Tally said, 'but it won't change anything. It's a stupid idea, and I can't imagine what you're thinking.'

Harry remained silent for a few minutes, easing the paper into place, removing it, putting it back again more carefully. He picked up the brush from the top step of the ladder and deftly smoothed the paper down, relieved to see it aligned with the strip next to it perfectly.

'Gosh, you are good at that,' Tally said admiringly, her disapproval of him apparently on pause.

'I've had a lot of experience,' he said briefly. He turned to face her at last, job done for the moment. 'Now, what were you saying?'

Tally assumed her lecturing position once again. 'I was saying it's madness,' she said firmly. 'I can't go along with this. Have you any idea what a huge commitment a pony is?'

'Not really,' he admitted. 'I expect it's somewhere on the scale between a cat and an elephant.'

'That's not funny,' she told him sternly. 'Ponies are expensive.'

'Not that expensive,' he said. 'I've been looking them up online. You can get them quite cheaply, in fact. I was surprised.'

'You can get anything cheaply if you're not fussy,' Tally said. 'It doesn't mean it's the smart thing to do, does it? And if you want Amy to be safe, you have to be choosy.'

'Of course I want Amy to be safe! What a ridiculous thing to say.' Harry stretched and rubbed the small of his back. 'God, I'm done in. Thank fuck that's all finished.' He glanced around the living room and smiled to himself. 'Looks good, doesn't it?'

'It does,' she admitted, rather grudgingly he thought. 'But, Harry, we have more important things to talk about. You seriously can't be going to buy Amy a pony.'

'It's her eleventh birthday,' he said. 'What else am I going to get her?'

Tally rolled her eyes in exasperation. 'I don't know! Roller blades, a trampoline, a bloody gold watch if you like—'

'Don't be silly,' Harry said.

'It's no sillier than buying her a pony. You do know how long she's been asking for one, don't you?'

'Years apparently,' he said. 'Which just goes to prove how much she wants one.'

'And has it ever occurred to you why Eliza and Gabriel have consistently said no?'

Harry shrugged. 'Because Gabriel's a tight git?'

Tally let out an exasperated cry. 'For God's sake! It's because they're expensive to keep. There's grazing, and feed, and shoeing, and vet bills, and insurance, and that's not all. Where exactly are you planning to put this pony? Even if you chop all the weeds down and clear the garden out there, there's no chance you can graze it at Eight Bells if that's what you're thinking.'

'Good Lord,' Harry said, rather indignantly, 'you must think I'm stupid. Of course I'm not planning on putting it in the garden. Look, there's hardly a shortage of places to choose from is there? That brother-in-law of hers owns an entire estate, and already has horses. I can't see one more making any difference. And if he says no, Joe and Charlie have stables at Whisperwood which would be even better, come to think of it, since Amy could walk there every day. There's even a riding school in the village, and I'm sure they'd take a pony in if it were necessary. Not that it will be. Once it's a fait accompli they'll all be falling over themselves to offer it a home.'

'And what if they tell you to take it back?' Tally asked.

'They're hardly likely to do that,' Harry said smugly. 'I shall present it to Amy before any of them know about it, and once she's seen it, there'll be no way on earth that any of them will prise it away from her. Not if they value their lives.'

'Harry, that's disgraceful!' Tally shook her head. 'I'm appalled at you. You're going to buy a pony without any idea where it's going to end up living?'

Harry yawned and dropped onto the sofa. He linked his hands behind his head and gazed up at her. 'Don't you think it's the best plan? Amy will love it. It beats a cocker spaniel hands down.'

Tally frowned. 'What cocker spaniel?'

'Didn't I tell you? Eliza and your uncle have bought her a puppy for her birthday. Now don't you think that's an extraordinary coincidence, given all the years they've said no? I'm back on the scene and suddenly it's, *let's get her a dog*. Nothing to do with the iPhone I bought her, or the fact that her bedroom here far outshines anything she might have at Wychwood of course. This is all down to jealousy and one-upmanship. Well, two can play at that game.'

'Oh, Harry.' Tally sat beside him and folded her arms as she turned to face him. 'This isn't right. Animals aren't chess pieces, and this isn't a game. They're living, breathing creatures, and they have needs.'

'I'm aware of that, Tally,' Harry said. 'I intend to make sure the pony is well looked after. But think of it! Amy will love it. She'll be so happy. How can you deny her that happiness?'

'Her mum and Gabriel say no,' she said. 'You can't go against that.'

Harry scowled. 'I'm her father. I have rights, too, you know. I shall present Amy with her birthday present at her party.'

'She's having a party?'

Something in Tally's voice alerted Harry to the fact that his announcement hadn't come as a total surprise to her. 'You knew!'

Tally squirmed. 'Mum might have mentioned it,' she admitted. 'But she was mortified once she'd slipped up. She made me promise I wouldn't tell you.'

'Well, that's charming. And you went along with it?' he said, hurt. 'After all I've done for you?'

'Oh, Harry, don't say it like that,' she pleaded. 'I'm sorry, honestly, but what could I do? I didn't want to drop Mum in it with Eliza, did I?'

'And you didn't trust me to keep my mouth shut.'

'With good reason, clearly,' she pointed out. 'You're planning on gate-crashing the thing with a pony!'

Harry pursed his mouth. 'Serve them right. They should have invited me.'

'How did you find out anyway?' Tally asked.

'Amy told me.'

'Amy! But she's not supposed to know!' Tally eyed him knowingly. 'She's been eavesdropping again, hasn't she?'

'Naturally.' Harry's lips twitched with amusement, despite his annoyance. 'She's bloody good at it, you know. She'd make an excellent spy.'

'You're not going to change your mind, are you?' Tally asked, a note of resignation in her voice.

Harry shook his head. 'Nope. Not a chance in hell. But I would appreciate your help.'

'My help? What do you want from me?'

'Well, what do I know about ponies? You're the expert. I want you to help me buy one — a good one. Please, Tally, I know it's a lot to ask, but don't you see? I've been excluded from Amy's party, and they've gone over me to get her the puppy they insisted she couldn't have. I could have got her a dog if I'd known! They could at least have asked me to go halves for it, so it was from both of us. But no, I'm out in the cold, yet again. Have you any idea how hurtful, how frustrating that is?'

Tally sighed. 'I suppose so. I can see why it upsets you. But Harry, if we go ahead with this, you must promise me that you'll make sure the pony is well cared for. You do understand that you'll be responsible for its upkeep? You can't expect Eliza and Gabriel to pay for it. And believe me, it doesn't come cheap. My dad used to tear his hair out over the cost of our ponies. And I don't want to find, a year down the line, that you've decided it's too much trouble and you're selling it.'

'I wouldn't do that to Amy,' he said indignantly. 'I'm aware of the implications. I know what a responsibility it is, and I'm prepared for that. It will be worth it.'

He'd worry about the expenses later, he thought. Surely, it couldn't be that much? And there was no way the lord of the manor, or Joe and Charlie come to that, would let any pony go hungry anyway. They had plenty of room, plenty of cash. It would be okay.

'So you'll do it?' he asked hopefully. 'You'll help me?'

'She ought to try the pony before you buy it. It has to be the right one for her.'

'That can't happen,' he insisted. 'It's a surprise. What sort of surprise will it be if she gets to see it before her birthday? Besides, if Eliza and Gabriel get the slightest whiff of this, they'll put a stop to it. You know it as well as I do.'

Tally groaned. 'I suppose I have no choice. At least if I help, you won't buy a dud, or a rearer or something.'

She got to her feet.

'Where are you going?' he asked. 'I don't suppose you're putting the kettle on, are you?'

'No I'm not,' she said. 'I'm fetching my phone. I have some calls to make if you want this pony in time for Amy's birthday.'

Harry stared at the bucket of paste, the brushes, the step ladder, the paste board, the unused roll of wallpaper and sighed. He supposed he'd better get it all cleaned up. It wasn't his favourite part of the job, but it had been worth it. The room looked amazing, with freshly painted woodwork and ceiling and the new paper. The floor had been sanded and varnished, and he had new rugs on order, as well as new furniture and blinds for the windows. It would all be in place within the next couple of days, and he couldn't wait. This sofa could go in his suite upstairs. That had already been completed. Things were moving fast now. He'd be open for business before he knew it and then, just maybe, he could start to see some money flowing into his bank account, instead of out of it for a change.

He glanced up as Tally walked back into the room, eyes fixed on her phone screen.

'Are you all right?' he asked. 'You look as if you've seen a ghost.'

'Harry, have you seen this?' she asked, in a voice that said he really ought to have done.

'Seen what?'

'This. I went on Facebook to speak to an old pony club pal who might know of any ponies for sale in the area, and Pan had sent me a link to this.' Tally held up the phone and he stared in horror at the video she was watching on YouTube, which showed him having a rather heated argument with the infamous farmer from Herefordshire that he'd told Rhiannon about, while peals of laughter punctuated the row.

'What the hell?' he snatched the phone and stared it, feverishly scrolling through the comments, and seeing that it had been watched thousands of times already. As the scene faded, another began, showing him in a location he didn't recall. He was talking to camera about the joys of country living, and bent down to pat a fat Labrador, who snapped at him. Harry's hand jerked back, and he gave the camera a wry grin, before continuing with his speech. But when someone called cut, he glared at the dog and launched into a foul-mouthed tirade about fucking animals, and why he hated working with them, and why anyone would want to live in the sodding country anyway was beyond him. Another outtake began but Harry couldn't watch. He turned off the phone and handed it back to Tally.

'Don't watch it,' he told her.

'But it's you,' she said, quite unnecessarily. 'What were you doing? Was that your television show?'

'No,' he said. 'At least, it's not the bits that were shown on the television.'

No, they were the bits that had been filmed for fun, and should have remained totally private, but they'd now been plastered all over YouTube for the whole world to laugh at. As if he wasn't a laughing stock already.

And he knew who'd filmed them all too well. Melody Bird, with her phone. It was just a laugh, she'd promised. And when he'd told her to delete them, she'd given him all that rubbish about wanting to see him when he went back home to Eliza, and how it made her feel close to him. When they'd moved in together, she told him she'd deleted them. She'd even showed him her phone to prove it. He should have known better. She'd obviously saved them elsewhere, and now she'd decided to humiliate him even more than she already had.

But why now?

He checked the date the video had been posted and groaned inwardly as he realised she'd put it up on YouTube the same day they'd had their conversation about him being in the running for *Twice as Nice*.

Had she done this to scupper his chances? Did she think that by embarrassing him like this, she would make sure that the producers never wanted to hire him again? Well, she'd wasted her time there, because they didn't want him anyway.

But now he had something else to deal with. Something else to be ashamed of. Harry wasn't sure how much more he could take.

22

'I still can't believe you managed to get a table at The Fox and Hounds.' Rhiannon beamed at Harry as they took their seats at a table in the corner of the elegant restaurant at the Helmston pub, which was renowned for its fine dining. 'I feel quite spoiled, being invited here. Of course, award-winning, or not, I'm quite sure Jack is up to the standard of any chef working here, but even so.'

'I was a bit worried,' Harry admitted. 'With you working in a pub it feels a bit like a busman's holiday, but it has such a good reputation, and we never get the chance to eat together, or sit and talk.'

Or anything else, come to that. There was no peace to be had at Eight Bells, even though the workmen had finally left, as Tally was often hanging around. And since Rhiannon worked long hours at The Hare and Moon, it was proving tricky trying to have any sort of relationship with her, even if they'd been able to get any privacy above the pub, which wasn't likely. He relished the thought of a few hours with no distractions and the opportunity to find out more about her.

After some debate, Harry ordered chicken liver pâté and Rhiannon chose dressed white crab meat with carrot and coriander salad.

'So,' said Harry, raising his glass of wine and clinking it with hers, 'here's to us, and our first proper date.'

Rhiannon laughed. 'Is that what this is?'

'Well...' Harry raised an eyebrow. 'Isn't it?'

'I suppose it is, yes. How terrible that it's taken us this long to manage it.'

'I know. Things haven't gone according to plan, have they?'

She took a small sip of wine. 'I don't know. Did you have a plan?'

'Not really,' he admitted.

'What? No schedule of seduction? The great Harry Jarvis had no great scheme in mind? You astonish me.'

'I astonish myself,' he told her. 'I must be getting old.'

Rhiannon waved a hand at him, dismissing his remark. 'Getting old indeed! In my opinion, you're like fine wine, getting better as you mature. So, Harry Jarvis, tell me. Who are you? What makes you tick?'

Harry wasn't too sure. 'I'm not sure I am still ticking,' he joked. 'I seem to be treading water at the moment. I've never felt so unsure of everything.'

He hadn't meant to admit that and wondered why he had. 'It's not that bad,' he added hastily. 'I suppose it's with me not being gainfully employed right now. It all feels a bit strange. I'll get over it. Something will turn up.'

'Have you been actively job hunting?' Rhiannon queried, as she forked up some crab meat which looked, Harry had to admit, far more appealing than his chicken liver pâté.

'Not really,' he confessed. 'I've been busy, what with the house and everything.'

'Don't you have an agent?' she asked, surprised.

'Not over here. Well, not anywhere, not any more. I parted company with my UK agent, and found another in the States, but we agreed to terminate the contract before I left to come home.'

'Oh,' she said. 'I see.'

He had an uncomfortable feeling she did see and couldn't stand the deception any longer.

'I had a row with my UK agent. Thought I was bigger and better than her company, and that I could do well without them. I doubt they'd want anything to do with me, now I'm back, and

I'm not about to go begging for them to represent me again. As for the one in the States — we didn't agree to terminate the contract. They dropped me, months ago. Well, over a year ago actually. Bet you're glad you asked now.'

Rhiannon swallowed the crab meat and dabbed delicately at the corner of her mouth with a napkin.

'Goodness,' she said. 'You have little faith in me. Why should I care whether you have an agent or not? This isn't a job interview, Harry. It's not a test you can pass or fail.'

'Bloody good job,' he said cheerfully. 'I'd fail dismally.'

'Have you investigated the possibility of a television role since you got back?'

He wondered why he couldn't bring himself to lie to her.

'I contacted someone I knew back in the days of presenting *Twice as Nice*. Martin. He's the producer and I thought if anyone could give me a hand it would be him.'

'And?'

Harry cringed at the memory of that excruciating meeting. 'I took him to lunch. We met up in a little restaurant we used to meet in back in the day. It was all very pleasant at first, and he seemed genuinely pleased to see me again. Then I mentioned that I'd heard rumours about the current presenter of the programme leaving at the end of the next series. I stupidly thought he'd offer me my old job back.'

'But he didn't?'

'Did he fuck! Far from it. Apparently there are difficulties with my public image. I'm perceived as a bit of a cad. Who'd have thought it? The British public apparently isn't too forgiving of my affair with Melody.'

Rhiannon sighed. 'That seems terribly unfair.'

'I know! How many of those viewers have been at it with the neighbours, I wonder? Anyway,' he admitted, 'that's not the worst of it. I did something stupid. Melody goaded me on the phone, so I lied and told her Martin had practically guaranteed my job back.'

'Not your wisest move.'

'No, it bloody wasn't, because then of course she decided to take revenge on me and posted some of my less-than-glorious moments from *Twice as Nice* on sodding YouTube, so now I'm a laughing stock with absolutely everyone.'

'Hardly everyone, Harry. There are, believe it or not, people like me in the world. I never go near YouTube or any other social media, and I can't be the only one. And anyway, don't they say that in show business, all publicity is good publicity?'

'Only the successful twats say that.' He sighed. 'The only consolation in this whole mess is that Melody's popularity is even lower than mine, not that she'd care. She's done with Britain. She's a superstar in the States with her sporting hero boyfriend and her celebrity pals.' He tutted, finding it impossible to keep the bitterness from his voice. 'So while she's having a whale of a time out there in my home, with my son, I'm back here feeling totally redundant.'

Rhiannon pushed away her plate and took another sip of wine. 'I see.'

Harry pushed his own plate away, suddenly realising chicken liver pâté wasn't his thing after all. 'Christ, I'm a miserable bugger,' he said.

'You're just going through a hard time; that's all.'

'No harder than you. You'd better not ask me any more leading questions. For some reason I find it impossible to lie to you. It's terribly annoying.'

'I'm glad to hear it.' She smiled. 'That you can't lie to me, I mean, not that it's annoying.'

The waiter appeared at their side and scooped up their plates. He looked rather worried that Harry had barely touched his pâté.

'Was everything to your satisfaction, sir?' he enquired, in a tone that begged Harry to answer in the affirmative.

Harry was barely listening, but Rhiannon gave the waiter a beaming smile and assured him everything had been perfect.

'Saving himself for the main course,' she told him, and he nodded and hurried off, looking relieved.

Harry raised an eyebrow. 'How do you do that?'

'Do what?'

'I don't know. That thing you do. Making everyone feel safe.'

It was Rhiannon's turn to look surprised. 'I wasn't aware I did.'

'Well, you do,' he said. 'It's quite a gift.'

'Thank you. So, you were saying, about—'

'Oh, don't worry about all that,' he said. 'Anyway, if I can't get television work it doesn't matter. I've got my bed and breakfast business to look forward to. I'm sure I won't starve.'

'You're a fortunate man,' she told him. 'You have a lovely home, or it will be when it's finished, you have two healthy children, and you're living in a beautiful village full of friendly and utterly delightful people.'

He burst out laughing. 'Friendly and delightful? I must have met the wrong people.'

'Oh, you need to give them a chance. Once you're settled, they'll accept you into the community and you'll never look back.'

'You think so?'

'Absolutely. I was a stranger here once, you know, and look at me now.'

He nodded. 'I guess so. Sorry, remind me again, whereabouts in Cornwall are you from?'

'Polkayne on the south coast. Not totally dissimilar to Kearton Bay, but without the hill.'

'Is it true,' he asked hesitantly, 'that your family is part of the aristocracy or something?'

She rolled her eyes. 'The gossips have been filling you in?'

'No, not at all. I just heard it somewhere.'

'Mm. Well, my mother came from an aristocratic family, but my father doesn't. That was part of the problem I think.'

'What do you mean?'

'In their relationship. It was unbalanced. He had a huge chip on his shoulder, despite—'

She broke off as a waitress arrived carrying their main courses. 'Spring lamb?'

Harry nodded. 'That's for me, thanks.'

'And the monkfish is mine,' Rhiannon said, smiling her gratitude as the waitress placed the dish in front of her. 'That looks delicious. Thank you so much.'

After being reassured they needed nothing else, the waitress hurried off and Harry said, 'Carry on. What were you saying about your father having a chip on his shoulder?'

She shrugged. 'Oh that. Does it matter?'

'Well,' he said, 'it might shed some light on you, and the person you are now, and I'm extremely interested in that person. So yes, it does matter. Unless you really don't want to discuss him. I know things aren't great between you.'

Rhiannon prodded her food, clearly thinking things through. 'That's an understatement,' she said eventually. 'But if you want to know... Father came from new money, and that made a difference to the way he viewed himself, and, I must admit, to how Mother's family viewed him. He was far wealthier than they were, but he was never quite accepted, you know? It's all about lineage, and the family name in that world. Inherited wealth, homes, titles — they matter. My father's father found success on his own merit, through aptitude, hard work and sheer guts, rising from an ordinary lower middle-class background to extraordinary achievements in manufacturing. In my opinion, his meteoric climb should have been celebrated, applauded, not hidden away like a shameful secret.'

She sighed. 'I did love my mother so much, but she was rather a snob, and her family was even worse. I have no love for my father, but I do have sympathy for him over that. It can't have been easy for him.'

'Well, your mother can't have minded that much, or she'd never have married him.'

'I know. I never understood why she did to be honest,' Rhiannon mused. 'They had so little in common, it confused me why they'd ever married. Sometimes I'd hear Father shouting, and Mother would cry. He never apologised or tried to comfort her. That's when I started to hate him, I think. And as I grew older, it became clear that the feeling was mutual.'

'No wonder you were at your wit's end when he invited Derry over. Why would you want him around someone so toxic?'

'Quite.' Rhiannon shook her head slightly, thinking about it.

'Maybe he's mellowed a bit over the years? Derry would never put up with him so long if he still behaved the way he did around you. Maybe age, and time, have softened him?'

She gave him a wistful smile. 'I sincerely doubt it.'

'Too late for your mother, even if he has.'

'Yes,' she said, spearing fish with her fork. 'Far too late.'

Harry cut into his lamb and thought how sad she sounded. Families were nothing but a bubbling cauldron of misunderstandings, sadness, anger, and grudges. And that was just his own.

'What about you?' she said suddenly, and he blinked as he realised she was watching him with that intense expression she sometimes wore — like she was trying to x-ray his soul.

'What about me?'

'Your family, your background. Are your parents still alive?'

My mother is,' he said. 'My father died years ago.'

'I'm sorry.'

'Oh, it is what it is.'

'Didn't you get on with him?'

Harry paused, thinking about it. 'Yes,' he said eventually. 'I did really. We weren't too close when I was a kid because he was always working; he had his own estate agency and letting business, and he worked long hours. But when I grew up and joined him in the firm — well, yeah, we sort of developed a mutual respect, you know? And, I suppose, we got quite friendly, too. We used to have long, cheerful lunches in the pub, far away from Mother's incessant nagging. Bound to bond really.'

'So you and your mother…'

'Don't get on. At least,' he amended, 'I don't get on with her. She gets on fine with me and pretends not to notice that our relationship is mostly one-sided. She has an opinion on everything and everyone, and insists I get to hear it. She hated Eliza you know. Couldn't bear her.'

Rhiannon looked astonished. 'How could she not love Eliza? There's nothing to dislike about her!'

Harry shifted, on dangerous ground. 'Yes, well…'

'This isn't an attack on you, Harry,' she assured him. 'I'm just puzzled by your mother's attitude.'

'Join the club,' he said. 'Funny thing is, she adored Melody, right from the off. She totally encouraged my relationship with her, even though I was married to Eliza at the time. What sort of woman would do that?'

'Why do you think that was?' Rhiannon asked, smoothing down her napkin.

Harry felt rather ashamed. 'I think, partly it was because of prejudice.'

'Prejudice? Against what?'

He tugged at his collar, feeling hot suddenly. 'It was — it was about Joe really. He'd brought Eliza up, and my mother didn't approve of his *lifestyle choices*. Her phrase, not mine.'

'You mean, she didn't like Eliza because Joe was *gay*?'

She sounded so appalled that Harry felt his face burn with shame. 'Yeah. I wish I could deny it, but it's true.'

'But you never — I mean, it never bothered you, did it?'

Harry took a gulp of wine as she watched him closely. Too closely.

'I'd love to say that were true, but it did bother me at one point.' Seeing the look of horror on her face he held up his hands. 'Look, I can't defend it and I'm not going to try. I was stupid, okay? I mean, I liked Joe — at least, I did until things went pear-shaped with Eliza and he started to act like some evil guardian. But I will admit that, for a short time, I was uncomfortable with him. I suppose growing up, knowing how my mother felt about gay people had more of an effect on me than I realised.' He sighed. 'I've screwed this up, haven't I? You despise me now.'

'I don't despise you, Harry,' she said slowly. 'How do you feel about Joe now?'

He didn't answer, as he examined his conscience for the truth. 'I suppose it's a mixture of emotions,' he said eventually. 'I feel guilty that I was so blinkered about him back then. I don't even recognise the egotistical idiot I was in my late twenties and thirties, convincing myself that all gay men would automatically be attracted to me, and that I'd have to be horrible to them to make it perfectly clear I wasn't interested. I mean, really?'

He shook his head, remembering how stupid he'd been and feeling embarrassed by his lack of understanding and empathy.

'But,' he admitted hesitantly, 'I also feel angry that he's not willing to forgive and forget what happened between me and Eliza. And I feel sad that I blew it so spectacularly and ended up at loggerheads with someone who I think, in the right circumstances, would have been a good friend. Joe was always incredibly good to Eliza. He sacrificed a lot to bring her up after her mum died, even though he'd lost his own parents and his sister at a young age. He took on a lot of responsibility, and he made a good job of raising her. She's a lovely woman. And he was always brilliant with Amy. It was me. I was stubborn and — and I suppose, if I'm honest, a bit jealous.'

'Jealous?' Rhiannon sounded genuinely interested. 'Jealous of what?'

'Jealous that they had such a close relationship. All three of them. It all seemed so effortless for him. He was closer to Amy than I was, and Eliza adored him. He was always there, and it got on my nerves. I suppose I wanted him to leave us alone, and that coloured my judgment of him. And it's been easy to loathe him from afar ever since Eliza and I separated. Easy to blame him for his reactions to me, for holding a grudge. Really, I can't blame him. I'd be the same if some jerk of a man ever treated Amy the way I treated her mother.'

He realised he had no appetite for the lamb either and thought what a waste of money it had been, booking a table at a Michelin-starred restaurant.

'The truth is, I admire Joe for the way he's always put Eliza first. And I owe him, big time. He took care of her, and of Amy, after I messed up so spectacularly.'

'Have you ever told him that?'

'You must be joking!'

'But why not?' Rhiannon asked, sounding surprised. 'It could be exactly what he needs to hear. If you want to start building bridges, you need to lay a foundation first. An apology, and a thank you, an acknowledgment of what he did for your family at the time, could be exactly what's needed to start bringing him round.'

'Here's a better idea; let's leave it as it is.'

She eyed him sternly. 'Harry, if you want to stay in this village, and you want to play happy families with Amy for the rest of your life, then you need to put things right. Joe's a wonderful man. All he needs to hear is that you know you behaved badly, and you're sorry for it. A thank you for taking care of your mess would probably go a long way towards healing the wounds, too.'

He nodded, knowing she was right. 'I guess,' he said at last. 'It's going to be hard, though. I've never been good at eating humble pie.'

'You're not that good at eating spring lamb either,' she pointed out, nodding meaningfully at his plate. 'Nor pâté, come to that. Aren't you hungry?'

'Not particularly,' he admitted. He smiled suddenly. 'You clearly enjoyed your meal, though.'

She glanced down at her empty plate and grinned. 'I did. It was delicious.' She leaned forward and whispered, 'Between you and me, though, I still think Jack's the better chef.'

'You're a very loyal woman, Rhiannon,' he told her.

'No. Just an honest one,' she said.

'I think maybe you are a bit of a witch after all,' he said.

Her lips twitched. 'A *bit* of a witch? Oh, I'm more than that, surely?'

'I'm serious,' he said. 'You have a funny effect on me. Like you've cast a spell. You make me tell the truth to you, even when I know perfectly well that the truth won't cast me in the best light.'

'There's nothing wrong with being imperfect, Harry,' she said quietly. 'Lies, however — they ruin everything. I don't need a perfect man, but I do need an honest one.'

'I understand that,' he said, taking her hands. 'And that's what I want to be, always. I don't think I could lie to you if I tried.'

'It's not just to me,' she said. 'If you're serious about making amends with everyone, you need to be honest with them all.'

'Are we talking about Tally here?' he asked.

'I think it's unfair, what you're both doing,' she admitted.

'I know, but I've tried to make them believe me,' he reminded her. 'It's hardly my fault they won't listen.'

'They might listen if you tried harder,' she said. 'And Tally needs to make things clear, too.'

'You've changed your tune,' he said, offended. 'Not long ago, you said it was best for Tally if we let them believe what they wanted to.'

'Yes, well, things have changed. I think Sophie has enough on her plate,' she said. 'And it can't be much fun for Eliza either, thinking you're having some sort of relationship with Gabriel's niece. And…'

'And what?' he asked, dreading to hear whatever was next on her list.

'And — and I don't like it,' she said in a rush.

'But you believe there's nothing between us?'

'Of course. It's not that. I mean, I don't like people thinking badly of you. I don't like them blaming you for something you haven't done.'

'I can live with it,' he said.

'Well, I can't,' she murmured. 'It hurts me. It hurts me deeply.'

He stared into her eyes and saw something within their velvet brown depths that made his heart thud.

'It hurts you that people blame me?' he said quietly, hardly daring to hope what that could mean.

'Of course it does,' she said fiercely. 'You don't deserve it. You're not the person they think you are, and I want to tell them all the truth. I want to shout it from the cliff tops that you're a good person, and—'

'And what?' he breathed, his hands tightening on hers.

'You know, Harry,' she said, shaking her head a little so her brown curls danced, 'this is all new to me, and it's most awfully confusing. The thing is — and I assure you I've never said this to another living soul — I think I may be falling in love with you.'

He knew instinctively that this was a huge deal for her, He had no doubt that she was telling the truth, and he was the first man she'd ever said those words to, and it made him feel like a giant — invincible and magnificent. Yet at the same time, it made him feel small, and incredibly humble.

How had they got to this point so quickly? And yet, didn't he already know that he felt the same? Hadn't he realised that ages ago?

'Have I scared you, Harry?' she asked softly.

'No, Rhiannon. You haven't scared me at all. You've changed my life. Suddenly, everything seems possible.'

'Oh it is,' she assured him, smiling. 'You just watch us.'

He knew she wasn't a needy person, but even so, he thought he she probably hoped he would say the same to her. So why, he wondered, didn't he?

You know why, Harry, he groaned inwardly. *This can never work. You can never make a woman like this happy.*

And yet, somehow, he couldn't dismiss the thought that, more than ever before in his life, he really wanted to try.

23

March flew by, and before I knew it Ostara — the spring equinox — was upon me. I'd got some of the younger children involved in an egg-painting competition as part of the Ostara celebrations. We'd sat on the benches outside the pub, and I'd handed them all hard-boiled eggs, paintbrushes, and paints, and they'd set to work creating the most adorable little faces and patterns on the shells.

Fuchsia and Cerise had very kindly agreed to help me supervise the children. As she was nearly eight months pregnant I thought that extremely noble of Fuchsia, but she said it was fun and she'd enjoyed it.

Eddie had arrived just in time to judge the entries, and the winner got a large Easter egg, and all the children got a free ride on Eddie's donkeys, so everyone went away happy.

I was quite tired by the time we'd finished. I'd had rather an early start to the day, having decided Harry and I deserved some time alone for once. I'd therefore arranged to meet him on the beach at sunrise.

'Remind me again why we're here,' Harry said, as we strolled, hand in hand along the shore.

I nudged him. 'Aren't you happy to be here with me?'

'Of course! That's not what I meant,' he said. 'It's just…'

'Just not what you had in mind when you asked me out on a date?' I smiled. 'It's okay, Harry, you can say it. You're right, of course. It's hardly conventional. But then, we don't seem to be a conventional couple, do we?'

'Not really,' he admitted. 'No one even knows about us, and we've barely managed to see each other over the last few weeks, what with one thing and another. Still,' he smiled suddenly and squeezed my hand, 'we're here now. Alone at last.'

'Indeed we are.'

'I've never been asked out so early in the morning,' he told me. 'That's what I meant. The sun's only just rising.'

'Exactly. And look over there,' I said, gazing into the distance. He followed my gaze. 'The moon.'

'The moon is setting as the sun is rising. Sun and moon, god and goddess, male and female, sharing the sky, complete harmony and balance.' I sighed. 'I do love Ostara. Do you know, it's the time when the maiden goddess meets her consort? He's been reborn in the form of the Horned God.'

Harry looked perplexed. 'This is all complicated stuff,' he said. 'How do you know all this?'

'How do you know the story of Easter? How do you know the significance of Christmas?'

He shrugged. 'Point taken, I guess. Sorry. It's just all very new to me.'

'And you think I'm weird,' I said wryly.

To his credit, Harry didn't issue an instant, and unconvincing denial. He considered the matter as we walked, our bare feet sinking into the wet sand as waves lapped over them.

'Not weird,' he said at last. 'Unusual. But that's what makes you so fascinating. All this god and goddess stuff — you really believe it, don't you?'

'Of course,' I said. 'What do you believe in? Really? And don't give me all that stuff about champagne again. I know there's more to you than that.'

'I honestly don't know that there is,' he said. 'I kind of hope there's nothing to believe in. I've led such an awful life, hurting so many people, I'll be punished for all eternity if there is an afterlife or a higher power. It's comforting to think that when we die that's it. The end of our existence. No penance.'

'Oh, Harry.' I linked my arm through his. 'You're so hard on yourself.'

'Not really. Just being honest. I was a shit, there's no denying it. I behaved appallingly.'

'But that was then, and this is now,' I insisted. 'And you can change at any point in time. Every moment is a chance to start again, Harry. Remember that. Every single second, you can create a new reality for yourself, just by choosing to. And you've done so much good, too, remember?'

'Like what?' he said, laughing. 'Found a few house buyers somewhere to live? Yep, that's made a huge difference in the cosmic balance sheet.'

'You've made me happy,' I said. 'Doesn't that count?'

He stopped and took both my hands in his. 'I hope so,' he said. 'You deserve to be happy, and there's nothing I want more than to be partly responsible for your happiness.'

Harry, I decided, needed cheering up. I gave him a mighty shove and squealed with laughter as he staggered into the sea and sat down in the waves with a splash.

'What the—? What the hell did you do that for?' He tried, and failed, to get up as a wave tumbled over him, knocking him off balance before he could find his feet. 'Fuck! It's freezing in here!'

'You wanted to balance the cosmic books,' I said, giggling. 'I think making me laugh just earned you a few bonus points.'

'Well, of all the bloody cheek.' Harry stared up at me, clearly stunned. 'And I can't even do the same to you. I call that unfair.'

'Why can't you do the same to me?' I queried.

He looked indignant. 'Because you're a woman,' he said. 'It's not very gentlemanly, is it?'

'Oh don't be such a sexist—' I began, then shrieked as I landed in the water. 'You said you couldn't do that!'

'And you said that was sexist, so I took full advantage of the fact.' Harry burst out laughing and splashed water at me.

'Don't you think I'm wet enough?' I said, pushing back my soaking hair.

'Nope.' He splashed me again, and I decided he was being a little bit too cocky. I sloshed loads of water at him and howled with laughter as he spluttered and shouted.

'You know, these were my best jeans,' he said at last. 'I hope the sea water doesn't ruin them.'

'Never mind your jeans,' I said. 'My hair will be a nightmare to comb now. The salt will make it unmanageable. I'll have to wash it again, and I only washed it last night.'

'It's even curlier now,' he said. 'It looks terribly sexy, and rather gothic.'

He staggered to his feet and pulled me up.

We laughed at the state we were in; our clothes were soaking wet, and we looked half-drowned.

'You're quite mad,' he said.

'I know,' I agreed. 'But life's more fun when you stop trying to pretend you're sane.'

I kissed him lightly on the lips and felt the slight sting of salt. I licked it away and Harry reached out and pushed my wet hair over my shoulder. I saw a flicker of desire in his eyes and my veins began to tingle as I realised how sexy he looked in his clinging wet shirt and jeans.

'Come on,' I said. 'I'll show you one of my favourite places.'

'What? On a beach?'

'Yes.' I laughed as I ran out of the sea and away from him. 'It's a secret. Come on!'

He looked baffled, but he followed me, as I'd known he would. I rounded the bay and entered a small cave.

Harry stumbled in after me and stared around. 'What is this?'

'This is Hob's Cave,' I said. 'It's where Kearton Bay's very own hob is reputed to live.'

Harry frowned. 'What the hell is a hob? I thought it was what you cooked on.'

'Don't insult the hob, Harry,' I warned him, only half joking. 'They're sort of little goblin creatures. They can be extremely helpful if needed, but they can take offence quite easily. If the mood takes them, they can sour milk and be terribly troublesome, and you must never give them a name because then there's no reasoning with them.'

Harry looked as if he wasn't sure whether I was having him on, or if I really believed such things existed.

'It's true,' I told him. 'Just up the coast at Runswick Bay, there's a famous hob. He lives in Hob Hole and he can cure whooping cough. The locals used to take their sick children to him to cure them. Like I said, they can be kind and helpful, but you have to be careful in your dealings with them or they get rather naughty.'

Harry glanced around, as if expecting to see a fierce goblin rushing at him with a stick.

'Right,' he said at last. 'So why have you brought me in here? Aren't we risking it a bit? I mean if this is his home…'

'You see?' I hooked my arm through his and beamed at him. 'Your belief is growing already. I knew you weren't a lost cause.'

Harry blew out his cheeks. 'It's when I'm with you,' he said slowly. 'It's crazy. It feels as if anything's possible when you're around. Like if a winged unicorn flew by I wouldn't bat an eyelid. I don't know.'

He gently stroked my face. 'I don't know what happens to me when I'm with you, but you make me believe in anything. Even myself. As if maybe I'm not so useless after all.'

'You're far from that, Harry,' I said, meaning it. 'You're a special man, and there's so much good in you. I can see it. I can feel it.'

I kissed him and hoped that, by doing so, I could convey all I was trying to tell him. Harry put his arms around me, and I found myself with my back pressed against the wall of the cave, as he kissed me with a delicious passion that stirred my blood and made my pulse race.

His hand slipped inside my blouse as I pulled him closer to me, and I could feel the thud of my heart as my body strained to be part of his.

But Harry let me go and stepped back. He stroked my hair and smiled at me, and I could see the yearning in his eyes, but something else, too and wished I could decipher what it was.

'We don't want to annoy the hob,' he murmured.

'Don't you want this, Harry?' I whispered.

294

'Here? Now?'

'Is there a more perfect place or time?' I gazed out of the entrance to the cave, seeing the orange-streaked skies reflecting on the sea. 'The maiden has slumbered a long time.'

'She's not the only one.' Harry gave me a rueful grin. 'There's no rush, is there?'

I tilted my head, watching him. I can't deny I was surprised. I hadn't expected him to be so reluctant. I'd thought we were ready, but clearly he wasn't.

'Rhiannon, don't be offended,' he said urgently, his thumb stroking my cheekbone. 'I want you, never doubt that. You're the most beautiful woman I've ever met, and any man would want you. But there's more to it than that, isn't there? More to us. This — this is what we always do. You and me. It's how we communicate. We have sex and think that's enough, but it isn't, is it?'

He moved closer, feathering my lips with tender kisses.

My back arched in pleasure as he murmured, 'And we deserve more, don't we?'

More gentle kisses up and down my neck.

I gasped.

'And I want there to be more. I want *us* to be more.'

I moaned, thinking how jolly unfair he was being.

'To be better.'

He whispered into my ear and, unable to bear it any longer, I took his face in my hands and kissed him, long and hard. I felt him melting into me as our kiss went deeper and deeper. I wanted him so badly it hurt.

But — he was right. This had been my path all my adult life. Keeping men at an emotional distance but drawing them close physically. Giving my body to them as a sort of compensation for withholding any real feeling.

Not this time. Not with Harry.

I let him go.

He took a deep breath and gazed at me, a plea in his eyes. 'You understand?'

'Yes, Harry, I understand,' I murmured. 'And you're absolutely right. We *are* more than this. But one day…'

'Oh yes,' he breathed. 'One day.'

I took his hand and we emerged from the darkness of the cave into the light of a world daubed in brilliant streaks of orange, gold, pink and blue. The air was rich with the smell of salt and seaweed. A breeze blew my hair, caressed my face, and cooled the heat of passion. The waves lapped on the shore, reminding me that were other ways to play, to have fun, to connect. I bit my lip, remembering how we'd laughed together in the sea just minutes before. My lips tasted of salt and of Harry.

Ostara. A time to rid ourselves of that which no longer serves us; to awaken our spirits, bloom with the spring flowers and blossom, and be reborn as our most enlightened selves. When everything begins…

I glanced at Harry, and he squeezed my hand and smiled. Something amazing had just happened between us. Something new and fresh and wonderful had begun.

And we both knew it.

24

'Well, someone's full of the joys of spring.' Jack's eyes twinkled as he nudged me gently, almost making me spill my orange juice.

I laughed. 'Oh, don't be silly. Eat your breakfast. I didn't slave away in the kitchen for nothing, you know.'

He prodded his bran flakes with a spoon. 'Must have taken you hours. I appreciate it, although I don't know why you felt the need to make breakfast for me. I told you, I could have had something to eat at home if I'd been hungry.'

'You've got to take care of yourself,' I scolded him gently. 'No skipping meals, no bacon sandwiches. A nice, healthy cereal and a banana for afters. Never say I can't cook again.'

He burst out laughing. 'Move over, Nigella Lawson. She must be quaking in her boots.' He placed his hand over mine and smiled. 'It's good to see you looking so happy. It's been a long time. What's brought about the change? As if I didn't know.'

I shrugged. 'Oh, just spring and sunshine and daffodils. How can anyone not be happy seeing all that?'

'Mm. If you say so. Nothing to do with a certain gentleman taking you out for dinner the other night then?'

I put my glass on the table and narrowed my eyes. 'Well, someone's been gossiping.'

'Kerry,' he admitted. 'Did you think she wouldn't tell me?'

'I suppose not.' I sighed. 'I just hope she keeps it within these walls. It's all very delicate, what with the Tally situation and then there's Eliza's feelings to consider. I only told her because she wouldn't cover for me unless I told her the truth about where I was going. She can read me like a book. It took me ages to convince her that Harry wasn't cheating on Tally, and that his intentions towards me are honourable.'

'I'm glad to hear it. Kerry won't say anything to anyone else. Even Aidan's in the dark about it. We both know the score.' He hesitated. 'You are sure though? About Tally, I mean. You don't think—'

'I'm sure,' I said firmly. 'He's telling the truth. It's not his fault that people won't believe him.'

'Maybe it *is* his fault a bit,' he said carefully. 'It's all because of his reputation, after all. If he hadn't been such a swine in the past, people would trust his word now.'

'That's the past,' I said. 'He's not like that now. He's kind, gentlemanly.'

'Not at all what we thought then?' He sounded concerned and I squeezed his arm.

'Nothing like it. People can and do change all the time,' I reminded him. 'Harry's a different man now.'

'I hope you're right,' he said. 'I'd hate to see you getting hurt when this is the first time you've — well, I've never seen you like this about any man before.'

'I've never felt like this about any man before,' I admitted. 'Maybe it's my age.'

'Does it scare you, sweetheart?'

I didn't even need to think about it. 'No. It's exciting, but not scary. The truth is, I can't wait to see where this adventure takes us. We need to sort things out with Tally and Eliza and then — well, I'm not rushing in, but I think it's going to be amazing. I don't want to fall out with Eliza. It worries me, how she'll take it. And then there's Amy to consider. But if we can find a way through…' I couldn't wipe the smile from my face. 'It will be worth it.'

He smiled. 'I'm glad for you, I really am. Well, this won't get the baby his bonnet.' He pushed the half-eaten bowl of bran flakes away. 'Time for work.'

'Oh no you don't,' I said, giving him a knowing look. 'You're not due to start work until this afternoon. Don't try to fool me. I know the rota. Aidan can manage perfectly well, and you're taking it easy until your shift starts. Plus,' I added sternly, 'you need to finish your breakfast. No arguments.'

I got up and placed my empty cup in the sink. 'I, on the other hand, do have to start work. You stay up here and relax, and I'll see you later.'

'You're a hard woman, Rhiannon Bone,' he called after me as I headed out onto the landing.

I laughed and ran downstairs, a smile on my face. Life felt good. It was going to be an amazing day.

It was almost lunchtime when Sophie entered the pub, her face tight and pinched. I knew immediately that she hadn't come in for a drink, although one look at her expression and I considered pouring her a large brandy.

Sophie, however, refused the option of anything alcoholic.

'What I want,' she said quietly, as she leaned on the counter, 'is a quiet word with you, if you don't mind.'

'Of course.'

I struggled to hide my surprise. It was unusual for Sophie to seek me out, though I guessed it was probably something to do with Tally.

'Would you like to follow me upstairs?' I asked. Jack would tactfully make himself scarce. He could go and watch some television in the living room for a while. He wouldn't mind.

Sophie nodded, and I led her upstairs to the kitchen. In the event, Jack wasn't there. I popped my head around the living room door, and smiled to myself, seeing he'd dozed off on the sofa. I quietly closed the door and crept back to the kitchen, where I proceeded to put the kettle on. Sophie looked as if she were in dire need of a strong cup of tea.

'How can I help you, Sophie?'

'It's a bit awkward.' Sophie nodded her thanks as I handed her a mug of tea.

I sat next to her and gave her a sympathetic smile. 'I can see that. So, how can I help you?'

'I wanted to apologise,' she said. 'What I said to you at the baby shower — it was awful. I'm ever so sorry.'

Well, there was a surprise. Sophie apologising. Whatever next?

'Emotions were heightened,' I said slowly. 'I could see you were upset about Tally. I'm sorry I pushed you.'

'Kids.' Sophie sighed and cupped the mug of tea. 'If it's not one of them giving me grief it's the other. It makes you wonder why you bother doesn't it?'

'Has Derry said anything to you about looking for a job?' I asked hopefully. If he found something to do in or around the Bay, there was far more likelihood of him staying.

'No.' She looked at me, surprised. 'He'll be going back to Cornwall soon, won't he? Why would he want a job here?'

Realising my mistake, I could have bitten off my tongue. 'Well, er, I mean that while he's here he must be getting a bit bored. I thought maybe a temporary job would give him something to do.'

She shrugged. 'I can't understand what's keeping him here, to be honest. It all seems very odd to me, but he's very vague about his plans and I don't like to push him. He doesn't say much about Cornwall, except it's a beautiful county and some of the fishing villages remind him of here. He's either at the Hall with Will, or round at one of his old band mate's houses, so I don't think he's bored.'

'I hope he's pulling his weight at yours though,' I said. 'He's not taking advantage?'

'Oh no. No, he's very polite, and very tidy, and always offers to do things for me. He's a nice boy.' She managed a genuine smile. 'He turned out well. I wish Oliver was as thoughtful. You know he's married I suppose?'

'I did hear something about it,' I confessed. 'I'm sorry he never told you, Sophie. It must have been a shock.'

'Broke my heart,' she said. She took a sip of tea. 'I don't understand why he'd do something so cruel. What did Archie and I ever do to deserve such thoughtlessness?'

'I expect he doesn't realise how much it meant to you,' I comforted her. 'I'm sure if he had, he'd have made sure you were invited. Children don't always realise how much their actions can wound us mothers.'

'No. Well, that's true enough.' She dabbed at her eyes with a tissue. 'And now I've got Pandora to worry about, and all this with Fuchsia's baby.'

'He's Pandora's baby, too,' I pointed out, struck by the way she'd phrased her remark. 'I should have thought having your first grandchild could only be a good thing. Am I wrong?'

'But that's just it, isn't it?' Sophie gave me a beseeching look, and I realised for the first time how troubled she was about the pregnancy. 'He's not my grandchild. Not really. He's Rose's grandchild. Rose's and some other woman we'll never know. The donor's mum. I'm nothing to do with him.'

'But you're his grandma, Sophie,' I said. 'Whether you're genetically connected or not, it's you he'll think of as his grandmother, and you he'll want to see. You he'll grow up loving.'

'But what if he doesn't love me?' she asked. 'What if there's no bond? What if — what if I can't love him, Rhiannon?'

My heart went out to her. She looked so thoroughly wretched it hurt to see her.

'Is that why you haven't made much of a fuss about this baby?' I asked. 'You're worried you won't love him?'

'I've tried to get excited,' she admitted, 'but all I can think is, what if he's born and there's nothing there? What if I look at him and feel nothing? How will Pandora ever forgive me? And then there's Rose. You know what she's like. She's going to be all over him, and he'll probably idolise her from the start, and she'll have every right to hog him, because after all, he is her grandbaby, not mine. Not really. Is there any point me getting interested in his arrival when it's going to be another rejection, another heartbreak?'

'Oh, Sophie,' I said, taking her hand, 'you have nothing to fear. I know you. You're fierce about your family. Nothing means more to you. When this baby arrives, you'll take one look at him and you'll forget all about genetics. You'll love him. You couldn't do anything else. It's not in you. And I know that you'll be a doting granny from the start, and you'll wonder what on earth you were worried about.'

She sniffed. 'I can't imagine it,' she admitted.

'Well, I can. Whenever I think of you, I think family. It's the word I connect with you, Sophie. That little boy is lucky to be part of yours.'

She laughed. 'You think so? When my eldest son gets married and doesn't even tell me he's courting, my eldest daughter's wife gets pregnant and they don't even tell me they've been having treatment, and as for Tally...'

Another tissue appeared from her pocket. 'The cruellest blow,' she said dramatically. 'Tally was the reliable one. I could always count on her to be sensible and thoughtful. I can't believe she's done something so utterly stupid.'

'She's just moved out,' I said quietly. 'She's twenty-four. Plenty of women her age have left home, Sophie.'

'To have an affair with a known lech?'

'He's not a lech,' I managed, with some difficulty. 'And besides, they're *not* having an affair.'

'Do you genuinely believe there's nothing going on?' she asked wistfully.

I could at least give her an honest answer to that question.

'I absolutely do believe it,' I said. 'Harry's assured me they're just friends, nothing more. He was simply helping her out when she wanted somewhere to go.'

'Oh, Harry!' Sophie's lip curled as she said his name, as if even the sound of it was disgusting to her. 'How can anyone believe a word he says? Let's face it, he's got his hooks into her and there's only one way to get her free.' She pushed the mug away and sat up straight. 'And for that,' she said, rather nervously, 'I need your help.'

I tried to keep my tone neutral. 'My help? What can I do about it?' I asked, wondering if Sophie had heard something that would connect me with Harry. Surely we hadn't been spotted in Helmston? We'd been incredibly careful...

Sophie twisted the tissue in her hands. 'Tally's not — she's not Tally any more. She's not being very enthusiastic about this wedding vows ceremony. She's the co-ordinator, but it's clear she can't be bothered.' She blinked away tears. 'Don't get me wrong, she's very professional, but there's no enthusiasm. Nothing over and beyond what she'd do for any couple. Sometimes, I feel that she doesn't even like me any more. She's not interested in our vows, I'll tell you that much.'

'I'm sure that's not true,' I comforted her. 'She's going through some stuff now, that's all. She'll come through the other side.'

'We've always been there for her,' Sophie said bitterly. 'If this had been her wedding, I'd have done everything I could to make it special. I'd have been involved in every single decision.'

And maybe that's the problem.

'She doesn't mean to be cruel,' I said. 'She's just processing things, growing up.'

'Growing up!' Sophie snorted. 'She's twenty-four.'

Eureka! I eyed her steadily. 'Yes, Sophie. She is.'

'Oh, I can see where this is going,' Sophie said. 'You're blaming me, aren't you? Think I kept her tied to my apron strings for too long. I'm sick of it, sick of being blamed when this is all down to that — that gigolo.'

I rubbed my forehead. 'Harry?' I said wearily. 'Sophie, how many more times? There's nothing going on with Harry and Tally. They're friends, and he kindly let her stay at Eight Bells, that's all.'

'As if! No one in their right mind believes that. I saw them that day, that first day after she moved in. Barely dressed they were. It made me feel ill. I know what I know, and Tally's mooning around after him like an idiot. That's what's going on, you know. She's lovestruck. Can't concentrate on her work. Lexi told me so herself. Well, I'm not having it. I'm going to break them up, and that's where you come in.'

I was so busy thinking about what she'd said about Tally being lovestruck that I didn't register the final part of her statement at first. When I did, I eyed her nervously.

'Me? Where do I fit in?'

'Rhiannon, I know I can trust you,' Sophie said, her eyes wide as she leaned towards me, an earnest expression on her face.

'You've had your problems with Derry, so you understand how it feels. I know you're a good person, deep down, so I'm asking you this, woman to woman, mother to mother.'

I experienced more than a flutter of apprehension. Just what was Sophie about to ask of me?

'I'm begging you,' Sophie continued. 'Wouldn't you do everything you could to fix things with Derry?'

Did she really have to ask?

'Of course I would. But I still don't see—'

'Then please, please help me to fix things with Tally.'

'But how? What do you want me to do?'

Sophie took a deep breath. 'I want you to seduce Harry Jarvis.'

I covered my mouth with my hand to stop myself from laughing out loud. 'Seduce him? Are you serious?'

'Deadly serious.' Sophie certainly wasn't laughing, and I felt my own laughter evaporating under her hard stare.

'I don't know how to respond to that,' I admitted at last.

'Oh, come on. It's not like you've never seduced a bloke before,' Sophie said. 'You know how to do it. It's what you're known for round here. You can charm any bloke into bed, that's what they say about you.'

'Do they?' I asked bleakly. 'Well, I think *they* may be exaggerating.'

'Please! Don't fob me off. It's too important. Harry Jarvis is a player. If he sees you're interested he won't be able to resist you, and then we can show Tally what he's really like.'

'Sophie, you're basically asking me to prostitute myself. You do realise that?'

Sophie tutted in annoyance. 'Am I heck! You don't have to go the whole way if you don't want to, but it would be better if you did, I'll admit that. And let's face it, you're not exactly shy about that stuff, are you? Would one more make all that much difference?'

I gripped the handle of my mug tightly. So this was what she thought of me? Was it what all my so-called friends believed, too? I'd made a lot of mistakes and I was all too aware of that, but I'd thought people like Sophie saw beyond that.

I tried so hard not to judge other people but to take them as they were, whatever dark deeds they may have done in their past. Why was I not afforded the same kindness? Were my mistakes truly so unforgivable? Did I not deserve a fresh start? I didn't believe it. Maybe I had once, but the advice I'd given to Harry must surely apply to me, too? How could I tell him everyone could have a clean slate and a new beginning, yet deny it was possible for me?

Whatever Sophie thought, whatever *anyone* thought, I was worth more than this.

'I know you're worried about Tally, Sophie,' I said, trying to keep calm, 'but what you just said is downright offensive. What on earth do you take me for?'

'So you won't do it?' Sophie said, clearly not caring that she'd upset me and made me feel like dirt.

'No,' I said coldly. 'I won't.'

'Well, thanks very much,' Sophie snapped. 'First time in your life you turn down the chance to have sex with a man who's attached, and it has to be the one time it really matters.'

'Sophie, you have to see it from my point of view,' I said, feeling bewildered. 'It's an appalling idea, not to mention insulting.'

'Well don't blame me for that,' Sophie said, pushing the tea away and getting to her feet. 'It wasn't my idea. It was Derry's.'

Her voice echoed around the kitchen, and I stared at her, barely able to take in what she'd said.

'Wh—what did you say?'

'It was Derry's idea. Your son came up with it. I said we needed to break Tally and Harry up, and he said the best solution would be if Harry showed Tally his true colours. He said we needed a woman who could seduce him without making him suspicious, and he said you'd be perfect for the job, because you'd had enough practice.'

She peered at me and her mouth fell open in shock. 'Are you crying?'

I brushed a tear away. 'I think you should go, Sophie.'

Sophie looked horrified. 'I've — I've never seen you cry before. I'm sorry. I didn't mean—'

'Could you leave now please?' I begged. 'I don't want to talk about this any more.'

Grabbing her handbag from the floor, Sophie hurried to the kitchen door.

'I really am sorry. I never — well, I'll be going.'

It should have been some consolation that Sophie, my old frenemy as I sometimes affectionately referred to her, obviously felt ashamed of what she'd said, but it wasn't. As I listened to her footsteps hurrying down the stairs, I sat back in my chair and gazed unseeingly out of the window.

So that's what Derry really thought of me. That I could be hired out to seduce someone else's partner on demand. What did that make me? What did it say about our relationship?

Sophie's scorn I could stand. Maybe I could even cope if my friends and neighbours refused to give me a second chance. But Derry? I couldn't bear that. If we couldn't get beyond the things I'd done in the past there was no hope for us, no hope for our future, and what would be the point of it all?

I wondered what he would say when he knew Harry and I were involved. He wouldn't believe it was genuine. He'd think it was as tawdry and shabby as he and Sophie had tried to make it. He'd believe I'd betrayed Tally because he'd want to believe it, and he'd never accept that Harry and I could care about each other. That it wasn't some grubby little affair that meant nothing. Any relationship I had would always be tainted by his opinion of me. How could I ever repair my relationship with my son with all that mistrust and contempt going on in the background?

I couldn't. If other men were involved, he would always see the worst in me, always despise me. And I needed to have Derry back in my life. Every time I saw Sophie, the pain wrenched through me, like a knife twisting in my gut. He should never be with her at The Old Vicarage. He belonged here, at The Hare and Moon. I had no idea if he even planned to remain in Kearton Bay, and how could we repair our relationship if he didn't even live under the same roof as me?

But if he knew about Harry…

I wiped away more tears, astonished to realise how many had fallen.

If it came to a choice between Harry and my son, I could only choose Derry. I would have to tell Harry it was over, despite my feelings for him. There was no other way through this mess.

****

Kerry's tone was quite aggressive as she leaned over the bar counter, arms folded, and fixed Harry with a forbidding stare.

'I've just told you, she's not in. She went out earlier. What do you want, CCTV evidence?'

Harry shrugged helplessly. 'I need to see her. Do you have any idea where she is?'

'No I don't,' Kerry said, 'and if I did I wouldn't tell you. Everyone's entitled to privacy, you know.'

He had no idea what to say to that, no idea what was going on. One phone call from Rhiannon, and everything had changed. He didn't understand it. They'd been getting on so well, and he'd thought they'd made huge strides in their relationship. Had he got it so wrong?

He thought back to their date at The Fox and Hounds. He'd been a bit miserable at first, he couldn't deny it, but then, after she'd told him how she felt, and after what had happened on Ostara…

Things had changed, there was an excitement between them. They'd both known they were on the verge of something completely unexpected and potentially wonderful. At least, he'd thought they had. Had she thought about it in the cold light of day and changed her mind?

'Do you want a drink or are you going?' Kerry asked him.

Harry didn't think he could stomach a drink, but the thought of going back to Eight Bells, none-the-wiser made him feel sick. Why had she telephoned him? Why hadn't she told him in person that it was over? He could have reasoned with her, or at least got her to explain why she'd changed her mind. This way he was totally in the dark, and she'd given him no opportunity to beg for answers, as she'd delivered her message coldly and calmly and hung up on him.

He'd tried to ring her back repeatedly, frantically pressing redial, but it went to answer machine every time. She'd said it was over, and clearly she'd meant it. But he needed to know what he'd done wrong. Surely, he deserved that if nothing else.

He shook his head, defeated. 'No thanks. I'll get off. Will you tell her I called? Ask her to come round to my house? Please?'

'I'll ask,' was Kerry's noncommittal response.

Harry slumped and turned away, knowing he'd get no more help from her. Whether she knew where Rhiannon was he had no idea, but she clearly knew, or suspected, the reasons why he was suddenly unwelcome here. He wished she would let him in on the big secret.

He was about to leave when he noticed the door behind Kerry open a little, and Jack popped his head round. He motioned to Harry to meet him outside, then shut the door again quickly.

Harry frowned, but in the hope that Jack could enlighten him, he hurried outside and waited at the side of the pub. Leaning on the railings he gazed down on the beach. One solitary dog walker strolled along the sands, and Harry wasn't surprised there were no other people. It was freezing out here, and the wind was whipping the waves up into a frenzy. It certainly wasn't the weather for paddling. Or for splashing around in the waves with the woman you loved…

'Thanks for waiting.'

Harry swung round and nodded as Jack hurried towards him. 'It's okay. I'm hoping you can help. Rhiannon tells you everything, doesn't she?'

'Well…' Jack looked awkward. 'Not everything, but enough.'

'I'm not asking you to break any confidences,' Harry pleaded, 'but she called me earlier this afternoon, and I don't understand. She and I — we—'

'Yes, I know,' Jack said. 'Look, Harry, I feel for you, I really do. But it's over, and you've got to accept that. Whatever it was between you, it's done. Okay?'

'No,' Harry said, anger beginning to break through the fog of confusion, 'It's bloody well not okay. If I've done something wrong, don't I at least deserve to know what it is? Can't I have the chance to put it right, whatever it is?'

Jack eyed him suspiciously. '*Did* you do something wrong?'

'No I didn't!' Harry thought about it then shook his head. 'No, honestly. I can't think of anything. We were getting on so well. It felt as if we were moving forward, taking things to the next level.' He paused then said, 'Is that the problem? Did I push her too fast?'

He couldn't imagine it. She'd been the one who'd said she was falling for him. He hadn't said it. Or was that the cause of all this? The fact that he hadn't said those three little words. Surely, Rhiannon wasn't the sort of person to drop him because of that? She didn't seem the type. None of this made sense.

'I don't understand,' he said miserably.

Jack sighed. 'It's nothing to do with you, or anything you've done,' he admitted. 'But look, I shouldn't be telling you this. She'd throttle me if she knew I was, but I think you have a right to know. It's not fair otherwise.'

As Harry's expression lightened, he warned, 'Don't get your hopes up. Nothing I'm about to tell you will change things. You can't put this right, I'm afraid. The truth is, it's not about you.'

'Then — what?'

He listened incredulously as Jack relayed the conversation Rhiannon had shared that morning with Sophie.

'So you see, it's put her in an impossible position. She wants Derry back in her life, and so long as there are other men involved, he's never going to see her as anything but the woman who can be persuaded to seduce any man. She wants him to realise she's not that person. She's terrified of losing him for good, Harry. You see?'

Harry did see, but he was livid with both Derry and Sophie.

'Calm down,' Jack advised. 'I can see you're furious, but this isn't about you.'

'I'm not furious for myself,' he said. 'I'm furious for Rhiannon. How can they think so little of her?'

Jack hesitated. 'It's complicated,' he said at last. 'She's not had the most conventional past.'

'I know all about her past,' Harry spluttered. 'She's told me it all, but so what? How could they judge her like that? How can Derry treat her in this way when he's lived with her all these years? He must know what a good person she is, what a kind heart she has. What's wrong with the man?'

Jack smiled. 'I agree. Something's gone terribly wrong with Derry these past few years. I don't know how to get through to him. He's only been to see me once, you know. Me! I've been with him since he was born, and now I don't even merit a five-minute visit.' He shook his head sadly. 'I'm glad you can see past all that stuff, Harry. Glad you see her for the woman she truly is.'

'Of course I do!' Frustrated, Harry kicked at the railings. 'Well, that spoilt brat isn't going to ruin this for us. I won't let him break us up and that's final.'

Jack laid a hand on his arm. 'Now listen to me, I've just told you, she can't lose Derry. Whatever he's done, however he's behaved, he's her son, and she loves him more than anyone or anything in this world. She won't risk driving him further away, and if you care about her the way you claim to, you won't do anything to put their relationship in jeopardy. You understand?'

'But—'

Jack held up his hand. 'I don't want to hear it. You think it was easy for Rhiannon to pick up the phone and call you about this?'

'She could have told me in person,' Harry said, anguished. 'Didn't I at least deserve that?'

Jack hesitated, then his shoulders dropped. 'Yes, you did. But see it from her point of view. She cares about you a lot, Harry. If she'd gone to your house to end things, she might not have been able to go through with it. And even if she had, how painful do you think it would have been for her to look into your eyes while she hurt you so badly? She was happy this morning, and I was happy for her. Sophie's visit changed everything. She had a choice to make, and she made it. Now tell me this, if you had to choose between Rhiannon, or your little girl, which would you choose?'

Harry stared at him. His mind ran through multiple possibilities — stupid, impossible schemes that could ensure he and Rhiannon could be together without damaging or risking her relationship with her son. He thought about Amy. Everything he'd done to make a home here in Kearton Bay, putting himself in the path of the Bailey family and facing scorn and disbelief and insults, all because he needed his daughter back in his life. He knew that if Eliza had made him choose between Tally and Amy, he'd have thrown Tally under the bus, however much she begged him. But if Eliza asked him to choose between Rhiannon and Amy…?

He slumped. 'You're right of course. Her son must come first.'

He couldn't lose Amy again. How could he ever ask Rhiannon to risk losing Derry?

'I'm glad you understand.'

'I understand,' Harry said dully. 'I hate it, but I understand. Will you do something for me?'

'Of course,' Jack said. 'Name it.'

'Tell Rhiannon, tell her I get it, and there are no hard feelings. Tell her I hope she and Derry make it up. I won't get in the way, promise.'

Jack held out his hand and Harry shook it.

'It seems you're far more decent than your reputation suggests,' Jack said. 'You and Rhiannon have a lot in common. Thank you, Harry. You're a good man.'

Harry didn't feel like a good man. He felt quite murderous as he made his way back to Eight Bells. If he'd bumped into Derry, he'd have been tempted to punch the little shit in the nose. But then, that wouldn't do him any favours with Rhiannon either.

He found himself hoping that she and her son would make it up and live happily ever after. There had to be some reason for his noble sacrifice, after all. He couldn't bear the thought of being this unhappy for nothing.

25

Even though I knew it was for the best that he stayed away, over the course of the following week or two, I found myself glancing at the door every time I heard it being pushed open, and the disappointment in the pit of my stomach gnawed at me when anyone but Harry stepped into the bar.

Kerry tutted impatiently upon seeing my crestfallen expression when a young couple entered the room.

'For God's sake, get a grip. If you miss him that much, make it up with him. What did he do that was so bad anyway?'

'He didn't do anything,' I told her for what felt like the hundredth time. 'I told you, I just decided I don't want a relationship, that's all. I've got enough going on in my life.'

Except I hadn't, and the lack of a distraction was making everything so much harder. It was bad enough that I was missing Harry and feeling guilty about letting him down so badly, but with nothing to focus on except work, I was struggling, and growing increasingly tired of a life revolving around these few small rooms.

'You need to do something with your life,' Jack had told me, as I'd poured out my frustrations to him during a tea break in the kitchen. 'Take up a hobby or something. Join a club. Anything.'

'What sort of club?' I asked. 'The only club round here for me is Lightweights, and I won't be going there, thank you very much. Even if Sophie wasn't the leader.'

'Not Lightweights,' Jack said. 'Why would you need to join a slimming club? Something that interests you.'

'There are no clubs round here that interest me,' I'd said gloomily.

'Then start one up,' he suggested. 'Why don't you teach tarot card reading, like that chap from the shop in Whitby suggested? You'd be good at that, and it sounds as if he's got a waiting list of eager customers all set up and ready to go.'

'And how can I do that?' I wondered. 'It takes time and effort. I'm too busy working in the pub to give it the attention it needs.'

'So take on more staff,' he said slowly, as if I were about six. 'It's not difficult to find bar staff, is it? Especially round here. There aren't that many jobs and people are queueing up to find local work.'

'I know but—'

'But what? Sounds to me like you're looking for excuses,' Jack said. 'If you don't like your life, change it. How many times have you told people that, eh? Time to practise what you preach.'

I couldn't deny he had a point, and the more I thought about it, the better it sounded. I needed something to take my mind off Derry, who seemed as far away from me as ever, and Harry, who was occupying my thoughts far more than was healthy. It was most unnerving. I was in danger of becoming thoroughly depressed and turning into one of those women who faded away, pining for lost love. I absolutely mustn't let that happen to me.

'Well, if it was your decision,' Kerry said, 'cheer up.' She put her arm around me. 'Not like you, this. I rely on you to keep me going. You're supposed to be the optimistic one, remember?'

I laughed. 'You're right. Sorry.'

'That's better. Now serve this customer and work your old charm.'

A few minutes later, I dropped some loose change into the customer's hand and smiled. 'There you go.'

'Cheers, love.' The man shoved it into his pocket and picked up his pint of beer.

As he moved away from the bar I slumped, and the smile slid from my face.

'Well done,' Kerry said, sidling up to me, a sympathetic look in her eyes. 'You managed to hold that smile for a whole three minutes. Impressive.'

'I'm not that bad,' I protested. 'Am I?'

'Honestly? Yeah, you are. It's not the same with you down in the dumps, Rhiannon. What's going on? Really.'

I shook my head. 'Nothing. Honestly, I'm fine.'

'Sure you are.' Kerry sighed. 'I can see you're not going to tell me, but I hope you're talking to someone. Everyone needs someone to confide in, don't they?'

I was rather touched by her concern. 'Please don't worry, Kerry. It's just one of those days. Nothing to fuss about.'

Except it wasn't one of those days, and I knew I wasn't fooling her. Worse, I wasn't fooling myself. I'd never felt this low in years, and I was even beginning to worry myself. I was struggling to concentrate on anything, and even my tarot readings were becoming darker. What on earth was I going to do about it? I'd always been able to lift myself out of my sadness before, but this — this low mood seemed to be stubbornly refusing to go anywhere.

Jack was adamant that I should tackle Derry if I were to have any hope of sorting myself out.

'You must have a word with him. He's ruining your life. Don't you think he's spoiled things for you enough already?' he'd demanded, just the previous night. 'First he throws a tantrum like a toddler over who his father is—'

'You can hardly blame him for that,' I'd protested. 'It must have come as a terrible shock to him. And besides, it wasn't just that was it? All the things I've done — all the stupid, selfish things…'

'In the past,' he said. 'Everyone does things they shouldn't. But for him to go off like that, with that man, of all people, and stay away for years. That was cruel. And now he's back he's still calling the shots, even though he's admitted he was wrong about his grandfather. Despite everything, he's still punishing you.'

'He's not punishing me,' I said wearily.

'No? So you're not bothered that his appalling attitude stopped you from seeing Harry then? You're not missing him at all? And you don't mind Derry practically pimping you out?'

I turned away, not wanting to hear it, but he wasn't going to let it go.

'I mean it, Rhiannon, this has to stop. It's disgusting. It seems to me that your — that man — has had a shocking influence on Derry. He's not the same man he was when he went away. He needs someone to put him straight, and if you won't, I will.'

'Just leave it,' I said. 'Things will work out in the end. I'm sure of it.'

Except, the truth was, I was no longer sure they would. I couldn't see a way forward, and even the cards weren't giving me clear directions any more. I'd never been this uncertain about myself, about the future. I was scared, and it was an unfamiliar feeling.

'Rhiannon.' I blinked back into awareness as Kerry nudged me and saw her nodding over at the door.

My heart jumped into my throat as Derry approached the bar, looking even more downcast than I felt.

'Derry! How lovely to see you,' I said, trying to sound bright and welcoming. 'Would you like a drink?'

He shook his head, and I saw sadness in those dark eyes of his and wanted nothing more than to reach over and hug him. What had we come to that I no longer felt able to do so?

'Can we talk, Mum?' he asked quietly. 'Upstairs?'

'Of course.' Nervously, I glanced at Kerry. 'Are you okay to hold the fort?'

'Sure, no worries. Take your time,' she said, squeezing my arm.

Giving her an appreciative smile, I motioned to Derry to follow me, and led him upstairs into the living room.

'What's this about?' I asked him, half dreading his answer. I couldn't imagine that I'd done anything else to annoy him, but these days I could never be sure.

'I'm — I'm here to apologise,' he said. 'And to explain. It's not what you think, it really isn't.'

'What isn't?' I asked, baffled. 'And what are you apologising for?'

'Jack came to see me this morning,' he said, shuffling nervously from one foot to the other.

My heart sank. I'd told him not to go near Derry! How could he?

'Sit down,' I said, seeing how awkward he looked, standing there as if he'd never been in the room before.

He sat in an armchair, and I sat in the other, and we faced each other, like two soldiers from opposing armies, about to negotiate a truce. Oh, I hoped it *would* be a truce!

'Jack told me what Sophie said,' he burst out at last. 'It's not true. I never said that to her, really I didn't. Well,' he added, sounding suddenly uncomfortable, 'not in so many words.'

'You never told her that I'd be the ideal person to seduce Harry?'

'Not exactly, no. It's not what I meant anyway. We were talking about Tally, and she was in such a state about her and Harry. She's really worried about her. She doesn't trust him, and she's scared he'll break her heart. She said, if only Tally would meet someone else, and I said it would be better if *Harry* met someone else — now, before she gets in too deep. I thought it would be good if he revealed his true colours to her, and she'd realise what sort of man she was dealing with.'

'Did you indeed?' I murmured, thinking, *poor Harry*. His reputation might just be worse than mine.

'Sophie said there was fat chance of that, because why would he look elsewhere yet? Tally was young and pretty, and it would be ages before Harry got bored, and by the time he did she'd be so much in love with him that it would devastate her. And I said, it would have to be a special woman. One who could compete with Tally. One who had experience in seduction, and could match Harry, and challenge him, like that Melody Bird did. I was thinking, Tally is very much like Eliza — or at least, how Eliza used to be. You know, putting up with stuff, too meek and mild for her own good. Harry got bored with that after a few years, and Melody sparked something in him. She couldn't be more

316

different, could she? Older, confident, with a bit of a history with men…'

His voice trailed off and he stared at me, looking miserable. 'And we sort of looked at each other and we both said, *like you*, at the same time. But I wasn't thinking she should go to you and ask you to sleep with Harry Jarvis to rescue Tally. Honestly, I never said any such thing, and I certainly didn't think it. I had no idea Sophie took that seriously and went to see you. I was mortified when Jack told me, and that's why I'm here, because I don't want you thinking that I would do that. That I'd put you forward like that. That I think so little of you.'

I was quiet for a moment, watching him, and I saw the plea in his eyes and my heart ached for him.

'Don't you think that little of me?' I asked gently. 'Everything you've said and done over the last few years has given me reason to believe that you have an extremely low opinion of me.'

He shook his head. 'I don't, Mum. That's the thing. I know I was stupid when I left here. The things I said, the way I spoke to you. But I've had a lot of time to think. I know what you did, keeping my father's identity a secret, was done to protect me. And not just me. There was Will, too. I still wish you'd told me, and I still think it's — well, horrible. He was so old and— well, anyway, let's not go over all that again. The point is, no matter what you've done or not done, I still love you, and I don't want you to believe I'd offer you up to Harry Jarvis or anyone else. I think far too much of you for that. Honestly, the thought never crossed my mind. I've had words with Sophie this morning, and she's mortified, too. She's sorry for what she said. She didn't think it would upset you, but that's Sophie, isn't it? She can be a bit…'

'Yes,' I said ruefully. 'She can.'

'I've messed up, Mum,' he said, his voice wobbling a little. 'You have no idea how much. Sometimes, I hate myself. I don't know what to do.'

As he buried his head in his hands, I hurried over to him and put my arms around him. 'Derry, darling, please don't upset yourself. It's all right. I understand.'

He shook his head and looked up at me, his eyes wet with tears. 'You really don't.'

'Then tell me,' I said, puzzled. 'What's going on, Derry? You're not yourself any more. What's happened?'

'I'm an idiot,' he said bitterly.

'What's this about?' I asked, tentatively. 'Why won't you tell me what went on between you and your grandfather?'

There, I'd mentioned him. He was between us now as if he were standing in the room, glaring at me with that hateful expression he always wore.

Derry wiped his eyes and leaned back in the chair. 'It's nothing, Mum. Honestly.'

'Please, you can tell me anything,' I said. 'Anything at all. I won't judge, you know that. I'm the last person to judge.'

He opened his mouth, as if he were about to speak, but no words came out. I waited, hoping that finally I'd get to the bottom of why Derry had behaved so oddly since arriving home.

'Honestly, it's nothing important.' He gave a short laugh. 'Girl trouble if you must know.'

'A girl? In Cornwall?'

Derry shrugged. 'Pathetic, isn't it? You'd think I'd have learned after Lexi.'

So some girl had decided they could only ever be friends, just like Lexi had? Poor Derry.

'The thing is,' he hesitated, then ploughed on, 'she wasn't in Cornwall. She was here, in Kearton Bay. I can't get over her. It's a bloody mess.'

My heart thudded. 'Not — not Lexi?'

He frowned. 'No, of course not. I told you, that's over and done with. It ended ages ago.'

'Then who…?' Suddenly, a thought occurred to me, and I stared at him. 'Derry, is it — is it Tally?'

His flushed face told me all I needed to know.

'But when did this happen?' I asked, confused. 'I didn't realise you'd seen much of her since you came back.'

'I haven't,' he said bitterly. 'Harry Jarvis saw to that.'

'Harry— So this happened before you left for Cornwall?'

I could barely take it in. How had I not known? 'What happened?'

Derry pulled a face. 'You want to know?'

'I want to know,' I said firmly. 'If you want to tell me.'

He hesitated, then said, 'You know what? I think I'd like to.'

I tried to keep my voice steady, even though I was an emotional wreck at this sudden change in his attitude towards me. This wasn't about me. This was about Derry. And Tally. Tally, of all people!

'I'm listening,' I said.

'We sort of got together at the Kearton Hall Grand Ball,' he admitted sheepishly. 'At least, we were moving towards it, but then Lexi had her accident and it all got pushed aside, remember?'

I remembered all too well. What an eventful night that had been! 'Go on,' I encouraged him.

'Well, anyway, a few days later we met up again, and it sort of went on from there,' he said. 'I really liked Tally, and it turns out she'd had a thing for me for years. I had no idea. She'd never said a word, but then why would she? She's Lexi's cousin, and she knew how I felt about Lexi back then. Anyway, I — I did something I'm not proud of. I sort of led her on. I knew, you see. Knew that I was leaving for Cornwall, but I let her believe we were going somewhere. That it was the start of a real relationship.'

'Oh, Derry,' I said sadly.

'I know! You don't have to tell me. I was bloody awful. But the thing is, I wasn't being entirely untruthful. I did want us to build on what we had. I liked her, and I wanted it to go somewhere. But my head was in bits. I was so angry. I had to go away.'

'What did you tell her?' I asked. 'Did you say it was permanent, or temporary, or...'

Derry hung his head.

'You didn't tell her, did you? You didn't say goodbye.'

He shook his head. 'I couldn't. I couldn't bring myself to do it.'

'So,' I said, trying to hide my disappointment in his behaviour, 'was that the end of it?'

'No. I wrote to her, explained the situation.' He gave a slight smile. 'She was lovely about it. So understanding. I must have hurt her, but she never had a go at me. I told her I'd be back, and I just had to work some stuff out, and I meant it. At the time.'

'But then you changed your mind,' I said flatly. 'You decided to stay.'

'I settled there,' he admitted. 'It wasn't about you, Mum. It was me. I was enjoying myself. Cornwall is stunning. Polkayne was beautiful. Grandfather was — welcoming. He started to teach me about the estate, show me what he said I'd need to know after…'

'I know,' I said quietly. 'Lexi told me you'd clearly been shown how to run an estate. It's obvious my father plans to leave the whole place to you.' I saw an anguished look in his eyes and held up my hands. 'It's all right, Derry. I don't mind. I never expected him to leave anything to me, and I wouldn't want it anyway. I'm glad for you. Really I am.'

Derry shook his head. 'I don't want it,' he said fiercely. 'I want no part of any of it.'

'Is that why you fell out?' I asked gently. 'Because my father wanted you to take over the estate and you refused?'

He hesitated. 'Something like that,' he said at last. 'But at first it was all great. I felt at home there. After a while, I told Tally how I felt. By then we were in a weird sort of half-relationship. We texted each other a lot and did video calls and stuff. It was as close to the real thing as we could get, and I fell for her.'

'You did? And she felt the same?'

'Yes,' he said miserably. 'She did.'

How had Tally kept that a secret from me? From us all? She'd shown incredible loyalty to Derry, that was for sure. And more patience than anyone could reasonably be expected to display.

'About a year ago, Grandfather invited her to stay with us for a week,' he said slowly. 'We had an amazing time. She said she loved me and I — I told her I loved her too. I asked her if she'd consider moving down to Cornwall permanently to make a new life with me.'

'You didn't!' I was stunned, not least that Tally had managed to escape to Cornwall without any of us, even Sophie, knowing. 'And she said no?'

'How did you guess? She said she'd think about it, but a couple of days after she got home, she told me she couldn't upset her mum like that. Oliver had made it clear that he wasn't moving back to Kearton Bay, and she said she couldn't do that to Sophie. I told her she was being an idiot, but that didn't help.'

'No,' I said. 'It wouldn't.'

'Anyway, I said I understood and that was that. But then…'

'Then what?'

Derry looked anxious. 'I — I realised I didn't want to run the estate, and Grandfather and I had a row and I left. So everything changed in an instant. I had nothing to offer Tally, so I ended it with her.'

'But that was a year ago!' I stared at him, horrified. 'You left your grandfather's home a year ago?'

He nodded. 'Yeah. I couldn't stay. It was toxic between us by then, so I walked out.'

'But where did you go? Why didn't you come home?'

'I felt stupid, admitting I'd been wrong about him. I drifted around Cornwall, taking bar work where I could get it. I got by, but I couldn't expect Tally to live like that, could I? Not when I'd basically promised her a life of luxury in Polkayne.'

I could hardly believe what I was hearing. I wanted to know more, to wring out every detail about his argument with my father, and what he'd been doing for a whole year, and how he'd managed, and why he felt he couldn't come home and face me all that time. But I didn't, because I sensed his focus was on Tally and their relationship, and it was about that he wanted to unburden himself to me.

'Poor Tally,' I said. 'How did she take it?'

'Badly. She called me, crying. Told me she'd leave Kearton Bay and would move to Cornwall after all, but it was too late by then.' He swallowed. 'I said our week together in Cornwall had made me realise I still loved Lexi, and there was no future for us.'

'Derry!' I gasped. 'Why on earth would you say that?'

321

'It was all I could think of to make her believe we were over,' he protested. 'She would never have accepted it otherwise. I had to convince her I didn't love her, and it seemed the easiest way. One that would make her hate me enough to get over me.'

'You must have broken her heart,' I said. 'And she had to work with Lexi every day, knowing that.'

'I did it for her own good,' he said dully. 'I was acting in her best interests, whether you believe it or not.'

'I do believe it,' I said. 'It's just terribly sad, that's all.'

'Yeah,' he said. 'It is.'

'And how do you feel about her now?' I asked gently.

'How I've felt about her for years,' he said. 'I'm crazy about her. I was so stupid. I thought, I actually thought, that when I got back here I could make it up to her, tell her the truth, and we could pick up where we left off. It never occurred to me that she'd meet someone else. Certainly not someone like Harry Jarvis, of all people. But even though no one approves, Tally's sticking by him. She must love him. Really love him. I've blown it, and it's my own fault.'

'Derry,' I said. 'There's something you should know about Tally and Harry, and I want you to listen to me and believe it.'

Quietly I told him the truth about why Tally had moved in to Eight Bells, and why Harry had let her. I didn't mention my own failed relationship with Harry, though. Things were messy enough as it was.

Derry looked stunned. 'So, so they really *are* telling the truth?' he asked. 'There's nothing going on?'

'Nothing,' I said. 'Tally has her own room. Harry's not interested in her, and she's not interested in him. I think…' I hesitated, wondering if it would be wise to say anything or not.

'You think what?' he asked, a note of hopefulness in his tone that hadn't been there before.

'Lexi tells me Tally is lovestruck. They're all assuming it's down to Harry, but I think she's still in love with *you*, Derry. Why else do you think she found it impossible to stay under the same roof as you when Sophie offered you a room?'

'I thought it was because she despised me,' he admitted. 'I offered to move out, but Sophie was adamant that it wasn't down to me. She blamed Harry completely. I feel terrible now. I should have believed her.'

'But don't you see?' I asked. 'It's not too late to tell her how you feel. You have a chance now that you know the truth. Don't let it slip through your fingers, Derry. Tell her how much she means to you. See if you can both find a way forward.'

'I haven't even got a job,' he pointed out. 'She thought I was going to be lord of the manor in Cornwall. Now I'm a drifter, with no future. Why would she want me?'

'Do you honestly think Tally cares about things like that?' I asked him. 'Give her some credit, Derry. She loves you, I'm sure of it. You must give this relationship a shot. You have to be brave.'

He bit his lip, thinking. 'I'd never live with myself if I didn't try, would I?'

'Exactly.' I beamed at him, so excited and happy for him. For them both.

His eyes fixed on mine, and I saw the old Derry looking back at me and felt a fluttering of hope that maybe there was a way forward for us, too.

'Mum, can I ask you a favour?' he said, almost reluctantly.

'Of course. What is it?'

Whatever it was, he could have it. If I could do something, anything to make him happy again, I'd do it.

'Can I have my old room back?'

My heart thudded. 'Seriously? You want to move home?'

'Not because I'm angry at Sophie or anything like that,' he said hastily. 'I just — it feels like the right time now. Is that okay?'

'Oh, Derry! Of course it's okay. You're welcome to stay here for as long as you like.'

'Thank you,' he said, then suddenly he reached out and I was pulled into a hug. After all those long years, it seemed I finally had my son back. I didn't know where the future would take him, but if I held his heart, I could cope with the uncertainty. After all, it wasn't so much the physical distance that had hurt me so badly, but the emotional distance. It seemed the lonely days were over at last.

26

Tally picked up the Easter egg from the mantelpiece and held it out to Harry.

'There must be something wrong with you. You've had this for days and you haven't even opened it. If that were mine, I'd have scoffed it within half an hour of getting it.'

'You *did* scoff yours within half an hour of getting it,' he pointed out. 'I was quite impressed, given the size of it. You'd have made the Guinness Book of Records if they knew about it.'

Tally put the egg back on the mantelpiece and tucked her shirt into her skirt. 'Are you sure you didn't buy it for me?' she asked suspiciously. 'Massive Easter eggs don't just appear on the doorstep overnight, do they?'

'I told you,' he said. 'Must have been the Easter bunny.'

'Hmm. Well anyway, you know who got *your* egg. Amy. I'd have thought you'd be delighted that she bothered.'

'I am,' he said softly. 'I was touched, especially when Eliza told me she insisted on paying for it herself, out of her pocket money.'

'So eat it,' Tally said. 'You should have eaten this on Easter Sunday and it's Tuesday now. I mean, it's not normal. Anyway having chocolate around the house makes me twitchy, especially when it's not mine and I can't touch it.'

He laughed. 'Have some if you want it that badly.'

'No way! Amy bought you that. I wouldn't have any of it. Are you okay, Harry?'

'Of course. Why shouldn't I be?'

'You're not yourself. You're ever so low, and you're not eating an Easter egg. That means something's seriously wrong.'

'Not for me. I don't eat much chocolate,' he said. 'Got to be careful what I eat at my age.'

'There's nothing on you!' Tally shook her head. 'Honestly, you've got the appetite of a sparrow lately. I think you should see a doctor.'

'A doctor? What for? There's nothing wrong with me.'

'Have you ever thought you might be depressed?' she asked quietly. 'Nothing seems to make you happy — really happy, I mean. Your appetite's low. Your energy levels are low—'

Depressed? Try heartbroken. Devastated. Inconsolable.

'Oh don't be ridiculous. I'm only tired, what with working on this place night and day, and having you going on at me all the time. Enough to make anyone go off their food.'

'Are you sure?'

'Of course I'm sure. Look, if you don't set off in a minute you're going to be late for work, and I'll probably get the blame for that, too.'

'I know, I know. I'm going. Where's my phone?'

'You left it in the kitchen on charge, remember?'

'Oh, God, yeah! What would I do without you?'

He was beginning to think neither of them would ever get the chance to find out and sighed as she rushed into the kitchen to collect her mobile, wondering how he could broach the subject of her finding her own place without hurting her feelings.

As she walked back into the living room, though, all thoughts of that fled his mind. He could see in her face as she stared at her phone that something had upset her.

'What is it?' *Please God, not another video of me on YouTube!*

Tally's eyes were wide, and her voice held a definite tremble as she replied. 'It's a text message from Derry. He wants to meet up. He wants to talk. What do you think that means?'

'I don't know.' Harry gave her an encouraging smile, which came easier due to the relief that this wasn't about him. 'But it's progress, isn't it? Maybe he's seen the error of his ways.'

'Do you think so?'

She couldn't keep the hope out of her voice, and he felt a momentary pang of anxiety for her. What if Derry hurt her all over again?

'What exactly does he say?' he asked gently.

'He says — he says he hopes I enjoyed the Easter egg he left for me.'

Harry whistled. 'So it was Derry who left it for you! Well, that's that mystery solved.'

'I know! To be honest, I suspected it was from Mum and Dad. I never imagined it would be Derry.'

'What else does he say?' Harry asked, noting the flush on her cheeks.

'He's been doing a lot of thinking, and he wants us to talk and sort things out. He's asking me to meet him at The Copper Kettle in my lunch hour today. What do you think I should do?'

'I think you already know what you're going to do,' Harry said. 'Just make sure you let him know that if he upsets you, I'll punch him on the nose.'

'I will,' Tally said, her eyes shining. 'Promise.'

Bloody hell, he hoped she wouldn't! He'd been joking. Harry had, after all, never been much of a fighter.

****

The Wednesday after Easter, I was outside, wiping down the tables and sneaking admiring glances at the view over the beach as I worked. Eddie was back on the sands with his donkeys again. The year was rolling on.

The day before Good Friday, I'd been into Whitby to chat to Robert about the tarot classes. I was trying not to get too worked up about the prospect of holding them, but as Robert and I talked, I felt the excitement bubbling up inside me. He told me there was a lot of potential there if I was interested. He got queries all the time about how to read the cards, about crystal therapies, about meditation. That was on top of people who wanted their tarot cards read for them.

Rashly, I'd told him I would try to work out a rota at the pub so that people could visit me for lessons and readings. At the time it had seemed perfectly possible. Easy, even. I'd wondered what had taken me so long to come round to the idea, as I was carried along by an enthusiasm I hadn't felt for a long time. I realised this was my path back to the old me — the Rhiannon I used to be. She'd been away far too long.

Easter Sunday had been a bright, sunny day, perfect for the annual Easter egg hunt. Several of the business owners in Bay Street and King's Row had contributed chocolate eggs and agreed to hide them in or around their premises, and the village children had a wonderful time running up and down the hills looking for them, while their parents sat at tables enjoying drinks outside The Hare and Moon, The Mermaid Inn, The Kearton Arms, The Copper Kettle, and various other places.

Easter marked the beginning of the tourist season, and the village was already buzzing with life. I could feel the difference in the air, and I certainly saw the difference in the pub, as the bar was overflowing, and I was kept busy serving with barely a minute for a break.

Before too long, the beach would be full of locals and tourists, sunbathing, playing rounders or football, swimming, or paddling, building sandcastles, crabbing in the rock pools, strolling hand in hand, and gazing at the sea between kisses…

I sighed. No use thinking about that sort of thing. Harry was avoiding The Hare and Moon, there was no doubt about it, and with every day that passed with no sign of him my energy and optimism ebbed further away, as did my enthusiasm for fitting in the lessons and readings.

It seemed the brief candle that had been our love affair had flickered and died. All I had to look forward to now was a lot of hard work. Day trippers and holidaymakers would be flooding in before the month was out, and life would revolve entirely around the pub. Where, I wondered, was I going to fit in my tarot classes, my readings, my meditations, my crystal therapies? Why had I ever imagined this would be easy? It was out of the question. It would have to wait until summer was over.

Jack had told me to get help in the pub, to hire staff, but I didn't have the energy that would entail. Placing an advert, sifting through CVs, interviewing them, training the new employee up... it all seemed like too much effort, which was most unlike me. If I didn't know better I'd have said I was depressed.

I needed to take control of my life. I needed to stop moping about Harry. I'd made my choice and Harry had accepted it. Surprisingly easily, admittedly, which had upset me far more than it should have. I didn't want Harry to be unhappy. If he'd taken our break up well then I should be glad, or what sort of unselfish monster did that make me? Even so, it would have been nice if he'd protested, at least tried to change my mind.

I flicked the cloth half-heartedly over the table, tired of running the same sad thoughts through my poor, weary mind. I never used to be this person. I didn't play games, and Harry wouldn't have been able to persuade me so why did I want him to fight for me? Was I really that insecure and needy? Time to get a grip. If I wanted things to change, I had to be the one to change them. No one else would do it for me.

'Need a hand?'

I looked up and smiled, delighted to see Derry holding out his hand to take the cloth from me. He was wearing jeans and an open-necked shirt, and had sunglasses perched on his head. I lifted a hand to shade my eyes, and my heart leapt as I saw the sparkle in his own eyes.

'You look happy,' I said, passing the cloth to him.

'I am, Mum,' he admitted. 'I was going to tell you yesterday, but I thought, well, better to show than tell.'

'Show me what?'

I followed his gaze and clapped in excitement. 'Tally!'

Tally hurried forward, and Derry grasped her hand.

'Oh, my goodness!' I could barely contain my delight. 'You worked things out?'

'We did,' Derry confirmed. 'We've both been a bit daft. Well, I've been a real idiot, let's be honest. But we had a long chat yesterday at The Copper Kettle, and got things sorted.'

'Not just The Copper Kettle,' Tally said, nudging him. She grinned at me. 'I met him in my lunch hour, but he ended up walking me back to the Hall, and since we were still talking, he spent over an hour sitting in my office while I was supposed to be working.'

'Shameful,' I said. 'But it seems to have done the trick, so I take it you think it was worth it.'

Tally nodded. 'One hundred per cent.'

'I'm so glad you've worked things out,' I said, dropping onto a bench. 'I wish you'd told me what was going on, Tally. I could have been a shoulder to cry on if nothing else.'

Tally sat beside me. 'I wanted to, Rhiannon, I really did. There were times when I almost told you, but I didn't want to upset you any more than you already had been. I knew how you felt about Derry, how much you missed him. I didn't want to burden you with my problems.'

'You could never burden me,' I assured her. 'I'm your friend, and I'd have been here for you.'

'Well anyway,' Derry said, 'it doesn't matter now. It's a fresh start, right? For all of us.'

'And maybe for Harry, too,' I said hopefully.

'Harry?'

'He's taken a lot of abuse because of Tally living at Eight Bells,' I said gently. 'It hasn't been fair on him. I know you tried to convince everyone there was nothing in it, Tally, but you didn't try awfully hard, did you? And it didn't do much to stop the gossip. Even your own family didn't believe you.'

'Neither did I,' Derry said, sounding ashamed. 'I should have done. I'm sorry.'

'We already discussed this yesterday,' Tally reminded him. 'You don't have to worry about Harry, Rhiannon. I told Mum and Dad this morning about me and Derry. She was absolutely beside herself but mortified when I told her about Harry. I pointed out that I've been trying to tell her ever since I left home, and it was her own fault if she jumped to conclusions. She feels terrible. Dad's even worse. He couldn't apologise enough, and they're going to tell Eliza and Gabriel the truth, so that should ease things for Harry. I hope so anyway. I feel bad about him. He's shown me nothing but kindness.'

'I can't believe it really,' Derry admitted. 'Who'd have thought it of him? I guess I owe him an apology too. I was pretty foul to him at the DIY shop.'

'When was this?' I asked, surprised.

'Oh, ages ago, when I first arrived home,' he said with a shrug. 'He and Tally were buying paint and he tried to introduce himself to me, but I was—'

'An arse,' Tally finished for him.

'Yeah.' Derry sighed. 'I was.'

Harry hadn't breathed a word to me. I felt a wave of sadness. I missed him so much. Maybe now that people knew the truth about him and Tally, things would be easier for us? Maybe Derry would accept me and Harry? Maybe Eliza would too? But it was all ifs, buts and maybes. There was no way of knowing until we revealed the truth, and since we weren't even together any more there wasn't much chance of that.

I should go to him, ask him to forgive me for the way I ended things. Ask him if there was any hope for us…

I didn't seem to have the strength. Like everything else in my life, it was on hold until I recovered my energy.

But there was one thing I could do to improve things.

'Derry,' I said cautiously. 'How would you like to work here again?'

His face broke into that wide, dimpled smile I knew and loved, and had missed so much.

'Thought you'd never ask, Mum,' he said.

＊＊＊＊

His name was Lewis Palmer, and he came highly recommended by Tally, as he worked as a gardener at Kearton Hall.

Harry and Tally watched, impressed, as he made short work of the tangled weeds and long grass in what passed for a garden at Eight Bells.

'He used to be freelance,' she explained, 'but it was too risky, with it being mostly seasonal, so he took a permanent job at the Hall. But he does the odd job as a favour, and when I told him about this place, he said he'd be happy to help out.'

'That's good of him,' Harry said. 'How much does he charge?'

'Oh, absolutely nothing. He said there'll be no charge.'

Harry's eyes narrowed. 'Don't be ridiculous, Tally. No one's going to come here and clear this wilderness for nothing, and I wouldn't expect him to. Why should he give up his weekend for someone he doesn't even know?'

'He's my friend,' Tally said, somewhat evasively.

She didn't fool Harry. There was something she wasn't telling him.

'I won't allow him off my property until either you or he tells me the truth,' he said, 'so you may as well spill the beans right now.'

Tally sighed, twisting a lock of her dark hair between her fingers as she gazed up at him, the very picture of innocence.

'If you must know,' she said, 'he's sending the bill to me. I insisted. And you can argue all you like, but that's what's happening, so tough.'

Harry dropped into a chair and shook his head. 'No way! I'm not letting you pay. Why on earth would you want to?'

Tally let the lock of hair slip from her fingers and leaned forward, suddenly tearful. 'Because it's the very least I can do, Harry. After everything you did for me, after all you put up with…' She took his hand and squeezed his fingers. 'I'll never be able to thank you enough. It's been the most interesting experience of my life.'

'Good grief.' Harry couldn't help but smile. 'You must have led a very dull life, that's all I can say.'

'I have,' she said, smiling back. 'But it's all about to change, and that's thanks to you.'

'Not thanks to me at all,' he insisted. 'You and Derry sorted this out between yourselves. I had nothing to do with it.'

'But you gave me the space I needed,' she explained. 'You let me break away, think things over, live my own life at last. I'm so grateful, Harry. And I'm so sorry for all the stick you got for our imaginary affair. I know it must have been hard for you. I did try to tell them all the truth, you know. I wouldn't have let Eliza take Amy away from you.'

'I know, I know.' He shrugged. 'I'll miss you, you know. Are you sure about moving back to your mother's?'

'I think she and Dad will be different now. We had a long talk the other night, and she understands that she'd made it difficult for me, and why I had to spread my wings. She's over the moon I'm with Derry. She really likes him, even if he is Rhiannon's son.'

'That's big of her,' Harry muttered.

'Well, think about it. He's also Sir Paul's son. Even though he doesn't talk about it much, all my mum sees is that Derry is the son of a baronet, and his brother is a baronet, and they have an ancestral home and all that jazz.'

'And there's the estate in Cornwall don't forget,' Harry pointed out. 'She must be thrilled about that. Derry will one day inherit it, although I suppose it will hit her hard when you move down there.'

Tally glanced away. 'Oh, that's all off.'

'Off? What do you mean off?'

Tally blushed. 'Derry — er — he doesn't want it. He's decided running an estate isn't for him.'

'So he's staying in Kearton Bay for good?' Harry asked eagerly, knowing how thrilled Rhiannon would be by the news.

'I don't know yet,' she admitted. 'He's working at The Hare and Moon for now, but he wants more from life than being a barman. He's got a lot of thinking to do. I don't know what will happen in the future.'

'Whatever he does, I hope he plays fair by you next time,' Harry said. 'Not to mention playing fair with his mother.'

'Oh, don't worry about all that,' Tally said vaguely. 'Anyway, the point is, Mum's delighted, and like I said, she really likes Derry, so it's all good as far as she's concerned. I did point out to her and Dad, though, that they've been appalling to you, and that they accused me of being a liar, and that they've blackened your reputation—'

'My reputation!' Harry burst out laughing. 'They could hardly have made it much worse than it already was.'

'You're too hard on yourself,' she said sternly. 'They know they were in the wrong — Mum especially. She's feeling very ashamed of herself, and quite guilty, which I suspect is a new experience for her. Anyway, I'm warning you now that she's coming round today to pick me up, and she may feel the need to apologise in person.'

'Oh fuck no.' Harry groaned. 'Can't she send me flowers? Much easier and far less embarrassing.'

Tally laughed. 'No, she can't. Anyway, talking of flowers, what do you think?'

She nodded out of the French doors towards the garden, and Harry turned to look at where Lewis was happily strimming the edges of what now appeared to be a lawn.

'I can't believe he's done so much already,' he admitted. 'He's almost filled that skip.'

'Told you he was good. Your lawn's going to need some attention, but he'll take care of it all. It will take some time to give you the garden of your dreams, but he's up for it.'

'I can't let you pay though, Tally,' Harry said firmly. 'I won't hear of it.'

'It's fine. I've saved loads of money,' she told him. 'Nothing to spend it on, have I? And…'

She shifted uncomfortably and Harry watched her suspiciously. 'And what?' he asked.

'Well, it's just, you still haven't found any work. And you've done nothing about starting this bed and breakfast place up.' She tilted her head, thinking. 'Why haven't you done that, Harry? I've been saying for ages you ought to start advertising, but you've made no move whatsoever. You need to get on to it you know. You need some income.'

'I know,' he said huffily. 'You don't have to remind me.'

'I wasn't being mean, just concerned.'

His expression softened. 'I know that. I just—' He shrugged helplessly. 'I don't have the energy to do anything about it. The truth is, I'm having second thoughts. Me and a load of strangers, rattling around this place. Doesn't feel like something to look forward to.'

'But you need—'

'I know, I know. I need the money. You're quite right.'

'And you seemed really happy getting the place ready,' she pointed out. 'I thought you were looking forward to it.'

He blew out his cheeks. 'Not really. It wasn't opening the house up I was looking forward to. I enjoyed the renovating. That's the part I always loved, even years ago, before I started the television work. I used to run a property company, and it was the transformations I liked best. Taking a run down, ramshackle house and making it beautiful again.'

'Well,' Tally said, looking round in pleasure, 'you've certainly achieved that here. It's unrecognisable. Typical that it finally looks like a dream home, just as I'm moving out.' She hesitated. 'Maybe you should do something with the annexe now? It would give you something to do, and you'd clearly enjoy it.'

'Turn it into a holiday let, you mean?' Harry nodded. 'I'd love to. I think it could be beautiful. I can see it in my mind's eye. I reckon we could fit two decent-sized bedrooms in there, not to mention an open plan kitchen/diner/living room. I can see it now.'

He thought wistfully that it would be another fabulous project to get his teeth into, but he couldn't see it happening for a while. He had some money left, but daren't spend it. He needed to hang onto that, because right now there was nothing else feeding into his bank account. The annexe would be too expensive to renovate, and Tally was right. He needed to get some guests into this place, get some income coming in. He wished he could feel some enthusiasm for it.

'Tally! Tally, darling, are you there?'

Harry and Tally exchanged glances.

'Brace yourself,' Tally advised. 'At least it won't be as bad as the last time she came here.'

Harry wasn't so sure, but as Sophie walked into the living room, he could see there was a huge difference in her attitude. She gazed around her in evident amazement, then hurried over to

Tally to hug her, before turning to Harry, a rather sheepish expression on her face.

'Well, this looks lovely. Haven't you done an amazing job? Who'd have believed it could look so good?' she said. 'Of course, I always knew you'd do it, what with all your experience in houses. You have good taste, Harry. Incredibly good taste. Did I tell you that Archie and I — that's Tally's father — we renovated The Old Vicarage? It was a terrible mess when we bought it, but now it's like something you'd see on the telly. You must come and look at it one evening. We'd love you to see it.'

Harry raised an eyebrow. *Really?*

Sophie cleared her throat. 'Anyway, what I wanted to say was, I'm sorry for that little misunderstanding we had.'

Little misunderstanding?

'I know I was a bit rude to you last time I was here,' she continued, with breath-taking understatement, 'but I'm sure you, as a parent, can understand how I felt.' She hesitated, then said, 'And after all, Harry, I'm sure you'll be the first to admit your reputation does precede you. And I'm not saying you've always acted well. I mean, you turned up here and caused all that bother for poor Gabriel and Eliza, and it was all very awkward, so what was I supposed to think?'

'What Mum means,' said Tally firmly, 'is that she's sorry for accusing you of something you didn't do, sorry for not believing either of us, and sorry she was so rude to you. Isn't that right, Mum?'

Sophie had the grace to blush. 'Er, yes. That's exactly right.' She held out a hand to Harry. 'I am sorry, I really am. I know you were just looking out for her, and I'm grateful you took her in and treated her so well. Truce?'

Harry knew better than to argue. He shook her hand. 'Truce.'

She beamed at him. 'Now, you must come to our wedding vows renewal. Did Tally tell you Archie and I are having a ceremony at Kearton Hall? Will himself is performing the ceremony. He's the baronet, you know. He's Derry's half-brother. Did you know that?'

Harry grinned. 'I think Tally mentioned it.' And hell would freeze over before he went anywhere near a place owned by Bailey's family, for a ceremony that celebrated Bailey's family, officiated over by Bailey's family, and with a guest list no doubt packed with Bailey's family. Hell, it would be torture. He'd be the most hated man in the room.

'Most of the village will be there, so you must come. Amy's going to be flower girl, and I'm sure you'd love to see that.'

Harry felt a rush of pleasure. 'She is?'

Hell, he hated to admit it but that changed things. He couldn't miss out on yet another important moment in his daughter's life. He'd have to lump it.

'Yes, I'd love to see that. Thank you.'

'Wonderful. I'll send you a formal invitation,' she told him. 'Now, Tally, are you ready to go? All packed?'

'My suitcases are upstairs, Mum. You go on up. My bedroom door's open. You can't miss it.'

Sophie nodded and hurried out of the room, and Tally and Harry faced each other.

'Well,' Harry said, feeling surprisingly choked, 'I guess this is it.'

'I guess it is,' Tally agreed. Her eyes shone with tears. 'You know, now it comes to it, I'll miss you. Thank you, Harry. You were the best friend I could have hoped for at a time I really needed one. I don't know what I'd have done without you, I really don't.'

'It works both ways,' he said gruffly. 'I needed you, too. And I'd have been lost without your company, really. It would have been a lonely few months if not for you.'

'If there's ever anything I can do to repay you—' she began.

Harry held up his hand. 'Don't be silly. There's only one thing I want from you, Tally. Go off and live your life, love Derry, and be happy.'

She threw her arms around him and pulled him into a tight hug. 'Take care, Harry. Love you.'

'Love you too, mate.' He dropped a kiss on the top of her head, and she let him go and hurried after her mother.

As she reached the door, she paused and turned back to him. 'Still totally paying for Lewis, though.'

'Oh, go on. Get out of here,' he said, laughing.

But as she grinned and hurried upstairs after Sophie, his laughter died, and he stared around him at the big, empty room. It felt different already. He could fill it with guests, of course he could, but that wouldn't take away the loneliness. With Tally leaving, it brought home to him even more that there was only one other person who could fill the emptiness in this place, and in his heart. But despite Derry's rekindled relationship with Tally, there'd been no word from The Hare and Moon.

Rhiannon, who at Ostara had seemed to be almost a part of him, now appeared to be completely out of reach.

BELTANE
27

Eliza leaned against the door frame and gave an admiring whistle. Harry couldn't help but feel impressed.

'I didn't know you could whistle like that!'

'There's a lot of things you don't know about me,' she said. 'I've got to say, Harry, you've done a great job. No wonder Amy's so pleased with it.'

Harry followed her gaze around the bedroom, which looked like something from a glossy magazine. Decorated in pale blue and white, pride of place went to a double bed with a beautiful white wrought iron headboard. On a soft, thick grey carpet stood a sturdy desk, chest of drawers and wardrobe, and a bookcase packed with brightly coloured books. Various paintings — mostly on a horsey theme — and a flatscreen television mounted on the wall ensured it was a bedroom any child would be delighted with.

'I can't take any credit for it,' he admitted, as much as he'd have liked to. 'It was Amy's design. She knew exactly what she wanted.'

'And you paid for it,' Eliza reminded him.

'Tally had some input,' he said hastily. 'I mean, she took her shopping, and they found the paintings and the ornaments together.'

Eliza nodded. 'About Tally.' She took a deep breath. 'I'm sorry. I should have believed you, but I was too ready to think the worst of you. It seemed so unlikely that you'd have someone as pretty as her under your roof without there being something going on. But you told me there wasn't. So did Tally. I chose not to listen. I'm sorry, Harry.'

'Forget it.' He could have milked the subject, but he wasn't interested in doing so. As far as he was concerned, the only thing that mattered was that Tally was okay and back in the bosom of her family, and happy with Derry. It wasn't as if it had cost him his relationship with Amy, and besides, he'd gained a lot from having Tally under his roof. He couldn't complain.

'Have you explained to Amy?' he asked.

'We didn't need to. She's been telling us for ages that we'd got it wrong, and Tally was just your friend.'

'Has she?' Harry hadn't thought she'd bought it. 'She kept telling *me* I was fibbing, and that she knew Tally and I were dating. She was quite rude about it on occasion.'

Eliza grinned. 'She was playing you. No doubt she got something from it, even if it was just a sense of satisfaction at seeing you trying to convince her. She's a little madam.'

'She is,' he admitted. 'But she's our little madam.'

'I guess so.' Eliza sighed. 'I should have taken it at face value, but I thought you were an expert at covering your lies.'

'Yes, well.' Harry shrugged. 'I can't blame you for that. I do have form, after all.'

'In the past, yes.' She picked up a snow globe on Amy's chest of drawers and shook it gently. The flakes drifted down over the little model village below, and after watching the scene for a moment, she replaced the ornament and turned to face him. 'I can't deny, I was dreading you seeing Amy. I thought you'd hurt her all over again. But you seem to be proving me wrong. She loves coming to see you, and you've done all this for her, so I guess it's not a temporary thing on your part.'

'Did you think it was?' he asked.

'Yes, I did. I couldn't imagine you staying in Kearton Bay. I thought you'd get bored, that you'd be offered a job somewhere and off you'd go. It seems I was wrong.' She hesitated. 'Sophie tells me she's invited you to the wedding vows renewal.'

'She has,' Harry confirmed. 'I wasn't going to go, but when she said Amy was going to be a flower girl I couldn't resist. I've missed out on so many landmark moments in her life, I don't want to miss another. You don't mind, do you?'

'Of course not.'

'And Gabriel?'

'Gabriel's fine about it. Amy's excited that you're going to see her in all her finery, so why would he object? You know, Harry, at the end of the day, he wants the same thing you do — Amy's happiness.'

'I suppose so.'

'We're having a birthday party for her next week. It's a surprise, so please don't mention it to her. We were wondering, would you like to be there?'

Harry stared at her in shock. 'Are you serious?'

'Absolutely. It's just close family and some of Amy's school friends. Rose and Flynn will be there, but they're our best friends, and besides, their little girl will be coming. But other than that, it's just the children and Joe and Charlie.'

'Joe?' Harry frowned. 'Do you think he'll want me there?'

'Joe's all right,' she said. 'I do wish you'd try to be nicer about him.'

'It's not that,' he said, 'but he's hardly been welcoming to me, has he? Threatened to set the bloody dog on me when I arrived. How was I to know it was a sodding Yorkshire terrier?'

Eliza let out a peal of laughter. 'Sorry, but the thought of Honoria Glossop attacking anyone, let alone you, is too funny. You've got to admit, it was hilarious.'

'Oh yes,' he said. 'I still laugh about it even now.'

'Harry.' She nudged him, and he saw the twinkle in her eyes and laughed, despite himself.

'Okay, he got me,' he admitted. 'I suppose I can't blame him for the way he is with me, but I don't want any arguments. Not at Amy's party.'

'There won't be any,' she said. 'Er, Mrs Travers is coming, too. She's staying at Joe's for a few days. Just warning you.'

Mrs Travers! She'd been the cleaner at their house in Chiswick and she'd never been Harry's biggest fan.

'That should be fun,' he said, pulling a face. 'Maybe I should hire a food taster.'

Eliza laughed. 'I'll protect you. It's at Wychwood at one o'clock.'

'Wychwood? Wow! You're letting me into your hallowed home?'

'Yes I am. Seeing as you've let me into yours, I can hardly refuse can I? Besides, I think I'm over all that now. A new start, right?'

Harry smiled. 'Fine by me.'

'Great.' She turned to leave, having clearly satisfied herself that Amy's bedroom was as brilliant and amazing as their daughter insisted.

Harry followed her down the stairs, feeling lighter than he'd felt for ages. It seemed he and Eliza had turned a corner at last. Maybe things were heading in the right direction after all.

'I'll see you next Saturday then,' Eliza said, smiling at him as he opened the front door for her. 'It will be nice for you to see her on her actual birthday, rather than the day after. Ooh, you can give Amy her birthday present, along with the rest of us. I'm sure you'd prefer that — being part of everything. Right?'

'Right.' Harry's stomach plummeted and he tried to keep the dismay out of his voice. Bloody hell! He'd forgotten all about that!

'Wait until she sees what we've got her!' Eliza leaned towards him and murmured, as if Amy were hiding around the corner, 'We've got her a puppy. She's going to be so excited. It's what she's always wanted.'

'Great! That's — great.'

Just when things were going well, and he and Eliza finally seemed to be putting the past behind them, he was going to turn up to Amy's birthday party with a pony, of all things. That was going to put the cat among the pigeons all right. Harry wished, with all his heart, that he'd taken Tally's advice. If he'd bought his daughter a solid gold iPhone it would have caused less trouble.

****

I had, as my days went, had an eventful one. Having realised Amy's birthday was just around the corner, I'd taken the opportunity to grab a couple of hours away from the pub, and had left Jack, Kerry, Aidan, and Derry to it.

Derry seemed to be settling in well, and it was like he'd never been away. He'd certainly not lost his touch with bar work, and our regular customers were clearly delighted to see him back again. I only wished it was a permanent thing but knew I couldn't push it. I suspected that Sophie would be worrying as much as I was, which gave me no pleasure.

Sophie and I were back on track, since she'd issued a heartfelt apology to me for what she'd suggested.

'I don't know what I was thinking,' she said tearfully. 'How can you ever forgive me?'

'It's okay, Sophie,' I said. 'I know you were upset about Tally. Grief and worry make us do the most extraordinary things.'

'Even so,' she said, 'there's no excuse. I'm ever so sorry, Rhiannon, really I am.'

'Let's forget it, shall we?' I suggested. 'There's no harm done, and it's all cleared up now. Derry and Tally are together, and we should be celebrating that, not dwelling on the past and our misunderstandings.'

Sophie wiped her eyes. 'You are lovely,' she said. 'I don't care what other people say about you. You're all right really. Let me buy you a drink.'

I bit my lip, amused at her backhanded compliments. 'That's quite all right. Have one on the house, just to show there are no hard feelings.'

So with that sorted out and Derry back at work and he and Tally clearly smitten with each other, I had a lot to be grateful for and a lot to be happy about. Only one thing clouded that happiness, and I still wasn't sure what to do about it.

Keeping away from Harry hadn't dimmed my feelings for him. If anything, they were stronger than ever. But after I'd pushed him away so cruelly, how could he trust me again? Besides, I still wasn't sure how Derry would react. Yes, he was happy with Tally now, and knew Harry had been good to her, but that didn't alter the fact that he knew Harry's reputation, and mine. We were getting on so well. I didn't want anything to jeopardise that, and me announcing I was in love with Harry Jarvis, of all people, might do that.

Then there was Eliza to consider. She had loved Harry deeply and had been badly hurt by his behaviour. I knew, of course, that she was extremely happy with Gabriel, and had built a new life for herself here in Kearton Bay, but that didn't change the past. It didn't wipe out her marriage to Harry. I was her friend. A close friend. How would she feel if I began seeing her ex-husband? How would Amy feel about me seeing her father, especially when she'd only just learned that Tally wasn't his girlfriend? It was all terribly messy, and I couldn't even begin to work out how to fix things.

The truth was it was all new to me. I hated to admit it, but I'd honestly never loved any man before. I wasn't quite sure how to handle my feelings for Harry. And all my previous relationships had been clandestine — secret out of necessity or for the thrill of it. I'd never had a relationship that was normal, whatever normal was. I wasn't sure I knew how to.

I was determined that, today, I was going to put all that out of my head and enjoy my freedom for a change. I'd nipped into Henderson's Store and purchased a birthday card for Amy, exchanging pleasantries with Milly Henderson, who told me how nice it was to see Derry back behind the bar, and how glad she was that we seemed to have resolved our differences.

I felt nothing but shame and guilt as I left the store. Milly was married to Marty, another of my previous lovers. I'd known he was married when we began our affair. I'd also known he was unhappy and thinking of leaving her. At the time, it seemed straightforward in my mind. I'd give him what he was missing at home, and he'd be happier, which would help their marriage.

Looking back, it seemed incredibly naïve. I could have wrecked their marriage. Yes, I'd made it clear to Marty from the beginning that it was just for fun and we'd never be together, and the last thing I wanted was for him to leave his wife, but it could have backfired. The fact that it hadn't, that the two of them had patched up their marriage and were happier than ever, was more luck than anything to do with my haphazard scheme.

Why had I done it? All those affairs with married men. They filled me with shame when I looked back at them, but at the time they seemed to make perfect sense. I honestly believed that I was doing it to help them.

Eliza had seen right through that, of course. She was suffering back then, knowing Harry was having an affair with Melody Bird. She was heartbroken over her husband's deception, and when she'd accidentally discovered I was seeing Marty, she'd told me in no uncertain terms what she thought of me. I hadn't understood. I'd never had a jealous thought in my life.

It was only when Derry left to live with my father, of all people, that I saw the light. I suppose it was then that I understood what I'd done, how much I'd risked hurting other people. I never wanted to hurt anyone again — least of all Eliza.

Maybe, I thought, as I made my way down Clover Lane to Wychwood, this was my punishment. Losing Harry was the price I must pay for the hurt I'd inflicted on other women, even if they didn't know about it. I could hardly argue that I deserved it. No wonder Derry had been so ashamed of me.

Eliza had welcomed me in, which made me feel worse, and I didn't stay long, even though she kept nagging me to make the most of my time out of the pub and have a glass of wine or two with her.

I couldn't face her. She told me all about Amy's bedroom, and how she'd made peace with Harry, and how she and Gabriel had agreed that he should be invited to Amy's birthday party. It seemed he'd also been invited to Sophie's and Archie's wedding vows renewal. He'd clearly been forgiven, and I was happy for him. He deserved this second chance.

I left Wychwood after around forty minutes and headed back down Bay Street, smiling at various locals who seemed astonished to see me out of The Hare and Moon. I'd just rounded a bend in the steep hill when I stopped short, and my heart thudded. Coming out of The Mermaid was Harry, and he looked as if he had the weight of the world on his shoulders.

As I waited, knowing the moment would come, I thought of all the things I should say to him, but when he finally looked up and saw me, my mind went blank.

'Rhiannon,' he said slowly.

'Hello, Harry.'

Was that all I could manage? It seemed so. We both stared at each other. He looked as awkward as I felt.

'You've been to The Mermaid then?' I said at last. Goodness, that was an example of witty and intelligent conversation, wasn't it? Talk about stating the obvious.

Harry glanced behind him, as if he hadn't realised where he'd been. 'Oh yes. Yes. Well, I thought it best to avoid The Hare and Moon.'

My heart sank. 'Oh, Harry! Why? You know you're always welcome. Don't avoid me. I'd love to see you.'

He gave me a rueful smile. 'It's not for your benefit, Rhiannon.' He sounded as sad as I felt.

'This is awful, isn't it?'

'Yep. But I guess you reap what you sow,' he said. 'Karma's bitten me on the arse, just as Joe hoped it would.'

'Oh, but I've just seen Eliza,' I said. 'She's told me you're invited to the wedding vows, and to Amy's birthday party. It seems you're forgiven. That's wonderful.'

He ran a hand through his hair, looking thoroughly distracted. I was quite distracted, too. He really was the most handsome man. Keeping a distance from him was much more difficult than I'd ever have expected.

'I've screwed that up already,' he confessed. 'You have no idea.'

'Well, tell me then,' I said.

'You don't want to know.'

'I do, Harry. Really I do.' I took hold of his hand. 'Come back to the pub,' I said. 'Come upstairs and tell me what's wrong.'

'And what would Derry say about that?' he said, raising an eyebrow.

'I—I'll tell him I'm giving you a tarot reading,' I said, as inspiration struck. 'In fact, why not? Why don't I do that?'

'Are you serious?'

'Absolutely. I'll tell you what the cards reveal, and maybe it will help you figure out a way to solve whatever it is that's making you so anxious.'

'I doubt that very much,' he said, 'but yes. Okay. Why not?'

I smiled at him, and he shook his head.

'Don't do that.'

'Don't do what?'

'Don't smile at me. When you smile at me like that, I just want to kiss you, and since we're standing in the street and God knows who is spying on us, that wouldn't be the brightest idea I've ever had, would it?'

'No,' I said sadly. 'But I'd rather like it if you did.'

'Has anything changed?' he asked wistfully. 'Have you spoken to Derry?'

'No.' I sighed. 'Have you said anything to Eliza?'

'God no. I'm going to be in enough trouble there,' he admitted.

'Well then,' I said.

'Well then.'

There was silence for a moment, then he said, 'But friends?'

'Of course. Always. And the tarot reading?'

Harry thought for a minute. I saw the battle going on in his mind. The anguish was clear in his expression, and I understood and sympathised. I felt much the same.

'Oh, fuck it,' he groaned. 'I need all the help I can get. Why not tarot?'

'Come on then,' I said. 'Let's see what the fates have in store for you.'

'Just tell me the good bits,' Harry warned, as we set off down Bay Street towards the sea front. 'I don't think I can cope with any bad. And if there *are* no good bits — well — fucking lie.'

****

Harry wondered if he'd taken leave of his senses. If anyone had told him, a few months ago, that he'd be sitting at a kitchen table in a seaside pub, having his tarot cards read by a self-confessed witch, he'd have assumed the person telling him was on drugs. Serious drugs.

Rhiannon, though, seemed to find nothing strange in the situation at all. In fact, he thought, watching her as she carefully unfolded a black silk square, she looked positively radiant. God, she was beautiful. He didn't just mean physically either. Yes, she was stunning to look at, with those dark curls and big brown eyes, but she was even more beautiful within. Goodness radiated from her. Why she couldn't see that in herself was beyond him. She was trapped in a delusion that she was a bad person when nothing could be further from the truth. There was nothing bad about Rhiannon Bone. She made him want to be good too, to be kinder, wiser, a better man. If only he were capable of it.

Rhiannon lay the silk cloth carefully in position in front of her and touched the pack of tarot cards with what looked like reverence.

Harry knew that if she'd been anyone else, he'd have dismissed the whole thing as hocus pocus, but he realised he was fascinated watching her. She was clearly taking this very seriously, and it made him want to, too. Maybe there was something in it? Who was he to judge? Anyway, any guidance she could offer him would be welcome. He needed to know what to do about Amy's pony and how he was going to put it right with Eliza.

'Now, Harry,' Rhiannon said, 'I want you to shuffle this pack, and as you do so I want you to focus on what it is you want to know. When you've finished shuffling them, cut the pack in half with your left hand, put the top pile to the left and then place the bottom pile on top for me. Okay?'

Harry nodded and she handed him the cards, which he shuffled with due care. He tried hard to focus on his question: *What do I do about Eliza and Amy and the pony?* But his mind kept wandering. Why should Eliza forgive him for yet another blunder after the way he'd treated her? She'd adored him at the beginning of their

348

relationship and had done her absolute best to build a loving home for him, and for Amy when she arrived.

Harry had been too busy chasing television work and building up his career to take much notice of all the little things she did for him every day. He'd found her attention cloying. All Eliza wanted from life was to be his wife, and Amy's mum. He'd found it stifling and had resented it. When Melody came along, she'd seemed so different. He couldn't help himself and had left Eliza and Amy behind with few regrets.

But he'd paid the price for that. Yes, Melody was independent and challenging, which he'd loved, but he'd soon discovered she was also cold and selfish. She'd loved him at the beginning, but that had worn off quickly. She'd grown as bored with him as he'd been with Eliza and hadn't bothered to hide her change in feelings. When he'd needed her — when he'd really needed her — she'd been nowhere in sight. He guessed he'd got what he deserved, but it was tough to take.

And now look at him. Middle-aged, with no career, rapidly running out of money, and about to mess up with his ex-wife yet again. And hopelessly in love with a woman who seemed to be so far out of his league it was laughable. No wonder God, or the universe, or the goddess, or whatever it was Rhiannon believed in, had decided to keep them apart. It would be sacrilege to place someone as pathetic as him with someone as wondrous as her.

She was the sun, moon, and stars. He could never make her happy. He didn't have it in him.

He realised he was still shuffling the cards, and that she was watching him patiently, and hastily cut them as she'd directed.

'There you go,' he said. 'Now what?'

'Now I want you to take three cards and lay them face down in a row,' she said.

'Only three?'

'I'm going to do you a simple spread. Past, present and future.'

'Dear Lord,' he said. 'This should be fun. Not.'

He did as she'd requested, and she moved the rest of the pack out of the way and stared down at the three cards in front of her.

Harry stared at them too, willing them to be something good. He didn't know much about the tarot cards, but he knew there was a Lovers card and a Death card. He hoped fervently for one and prayed he wouldn't get the other.

Slowly, Rhiannon turned over the first card.

'The past,' she said, and studied the card carefully.

Harry stared at it, too.

'That doesn't look too bad,' he said at last. 'He looks like Prince Charming from a fairy tale. I rather like that.'

'This is the Knight of Swords,' Rhiannon told him. 'He's full of action, life and energy. He has ambition, determination, and drive.'

Harry nodded, quite pleased. 'Those were the days,' he said. 'Typical that he's the past. I don't suppose there are two of those in a pack, are there?'

Rhiannon shook her head. 'The knight is so driven by his passion to succeed that he doesn't notice the consequences of his actions,' she explained. 'This drive and energy should be balanced with compassion, with a sense of responsibility, but the knight lacks that. His ambition could lead him into danger.'

Harry couldn't argue with that, and had a sinking feeling this tarot reading wasn't going to cheer him up or offer him any comfort at all.

'So, what does that mean for me?' he asked, rather dreading her answer. 'It's not important, is it? I mean, this is the past, right?'

'This *is* the past, but it's important to take note of it,' she said. 'After all, it's who you were in the past that colours who you are now, and just as importantly, what you'll become. We're all the products of our past, Harry. This card reveals that you found it hard to commit to relationships. You grew bored very easily, you struggled to connect with anyone emotionally. You had a clear idea of what you wanted and went after it with almost ruthless efficiency.' She sighed. 'If people were hurt or scared along the way, it wasn't something you gave much thought to. Money meant a lot to you. Status. But in the process, it wasn't only others you hurt but yourself.'

Harry swallowed. 'Okay. So not really a Prince Charming at all.'

'What you can learn from him, though, is to balance your ambition with compassion. And think things through more carefully. You may be impulsive. Your enthusiasm for what you want to achieve can lead you to act rashly, and you may find that what you thought you wanted wasn't what you wanted at all or wasn't what you thought it would be. This card is warning you to take note of what's going on around you as you move forward, to be certain you're heading in the right direction, and to think of others as well as yourself.'

Harry nodded. 'Well, I can't argue with that.'

Rhiannon smiled. 'The present?'

Harry put his head in his hands. 'May as well,' he said glumly. 'I already know it's a pile of shit, so there shouldn't be any surprises there.'

Rhiannon turned over the card and Harry's eyes widened, then he groaned. 'Fuck me. Me and my big mouth.'

'It's not what you think,' Rhiannon said. 'Judgment is a positive card in so many ways, Harry.'

He peered up at her. 'It is?'

'Yes. This card is telling you that this is your moment of reflection. It's time to re-evaluate yourself, where you are, and what steps you must take to improve and grow.'

'I should think that would be an exceptionally long list,' Harry said. 'I doubt I have that much time to spare.'

'You need to be kinder to yourself,' Rhiannon said gently. 'This card is telling you that you need to be true to yourself and your own needs.'

She hesitated and Harry looked at her suspiciously. 'What?'

'Things you did in the past, a moment perhaps that changed the course of your life — now is when the consequences of the actions you took then will catch up, and you'll face up to them.'

'Great,' Harry muttered. 'I feel better already.'

'You're already in the process,' she said. 'This is about taking responsibility for your actions and your part in anything that has caused pain. It's basically saying that what you needed to learn in the past is being learned right now. It's an awakening. Any mistakes you made before — well, you can use the lessons you learned from them to make changes for the future. If — if you have issues in your love life that perhaps you haven't dealt with, then it's time to stop ignoring them. You'll start to see them clearly and know how to deal with them.'

Harry felt hot suddenly, He ran a finger around the collar of his shirt, thinking it felt rather tight, which was ridiculous, given the top two buttons were open.

'I think maybe you're being urged to look at a new career,' she said thoughtfully. 'Something is nagging away at you, refusing to let go.' She looked up at him suddenly. 'Are you having doubts about this bed and breakfast?'

Harry squirmed. 'Maybe.'

'Really?' She looked back at the card. 'Well, if you have something else you feel called to explore, now is the time to go for it. But you need to be careful with finances. This card is telling you to look at your spending habits and change your relationship with money.'

Harry had no words. He wasn't sure if having his tarot cards read had been a good decision or a bad one. Either way, it had certainly given him plenty to think about.

'So, I suppose now I have to know the future?' His voice sounded croaky, and he cleared his throat. 'Got to be an improvement, right?'

'Just remember,' Rhiannon said, 'the future isn't set in stone. This card is based on the vibrations you're emitting at present, and it may only represent what you want. Changes in the present can and do affect the future, so don't be too afraid, okay?'

Harry stared at the card, willing it to be the Lovers. If it were to represent what he wanted, it couldn't be anything else, could it?

He gasped and slumped in his chair as he saw the final card. The Devil! Well, if that didn't put the lid on the tin of biscuits.

'Fuck me,' he said. 'That says it all, doesn't it? So that's my future? I'm going to hell?'

Rhiannon burst out laughing. 'It doesn't mean that at all! And look, it's reversed, see? This is good, Harry.'

'I fail to see how even you can make the Devil good.'

'This card, reversed, means you're breaking free,' she explained patiently. 'All the negative ways of thinking that have prevented you from living your best life, from being your best self, are being left behind. You'll feel more in control, more independent. This card's about restoring control in your life. In your love affairs, in your career, in your finances. It's about becoming self-aware, breaking the chains that bound you through bad habits. I feel, very strongly, that you're taking actions which will leave you more fulfilled. You're weary right now, Harry, I can see that. You need to change. It's not easy, and breaking those chains can and will be painful, but you'll be rewarded, trust me. You're on your way to finding who you really are, what you really want. You're going to make yourself so proud one day, I promise you.'

Harry kept his eyes fixed on the card, which had suddenly become very blurry. Make himself proud? He honestly couldn't imagine that day would ever come.

'And I'm going to be so proud of you, too,' she said quietly. 'I already am.'

He glanced up at her. 'How can you be proud of me?' he asked. 'I'm nothing, Rhiannon. Nothing. And you're — you're everything.'

She was, too. She overwhelmed him. At that moment, she was the only thing that mattered, and whatever emotions he was feeling she seemed to share them in that moment, because somehow they were standing together. As Harry kissed her, he felt as if the stars themselves were exploding inside him. He felt almost drunk with desire and passion. If there was a devil in his future, he could defeat it with Rhiannon by his side. She made him feel everything was possible.

'Harry,' she said at last, and he pulled her close, not wanting to let her go.

'I know,' he murmured. 'Wrong time. Wrong place. Wrong man.'

'No.' She pulled back and shook her head. 'Not the wrong man at all. The perfect man, the man for me.'

He realised she was crying, and it broke his heart. She'd always seemed to be the stronger of the two of them, but now she looked fragile, broken.

'Don't,' he whispered, wiping away her tears. 'It will be all right, Rhiannon. You'll see.'

'Will it?'

'I promise.'

'I'm so sorry,' she said, dabbing at her eyes with a handkerchief. 'It all seemed too much suddenly.'

'Don't apologise to me,' he told her. 'Don't ever apologise to me. There's no need.'

'Do you think, Harry, that this is my fault?'

He stared at her, unable to comprehend why she would blame herself for their situation.

'Of course I don't! Why would you think that?'

She shrugged. 'We've both made mistakes,' she said, 'but you've done all you can to put yours right. Maybe it's me. Maybe it's my bad karma we're both paying for now. All the people I wronged in the past — all those wives, Derry…'

'You're a good person,' he said fiercely. 'I refuse to believe this is a punishment, certainly not for you. It's just —' He cast around for something that would reassure her, something she would understand. 'It's just that the universe has decided it's not time yet,' he said, as a flash of inspiration hit him. 'But you know what you always say about it unfolding just as it should, and it will. Please don't give up on us.'

'I'll never give up on you,' she said, smiling at last. 'So, when you said we could always be friends…?'

'I was talking bollocks,' he said roughly. 'You and I will never just be friends. There's more to us than that, isn't there? I love you. You know I love you. I only wish I'd had the guts to tell you sooner.'

'And I love you,' she said simply.

'I just can't hurt Eliza.'

'And I can't hurt Derry. I have to know that he won't hate me for being with you. I can't risk losing him, any more than you can risk your relationship with Eliza, for Amy's sake, if nothing else.

I don't want this to be like my other relationships — if you can call them that. They were based on deceit, on hurting people. I won't do that again, Harry. I won't taint myself; I won't taint you, and I won't taint what we have by reverting to that sort of behaviour. This is out in the open, or it's nothing.'

'Yes,' he said. 'I agree.' He kissed her lightly on the forehead. 'We need to be patient,' he told her.

'And we need to be brave,' she added. 'Things are improving with Eliza and Derry. A little more time, and perhaps they'll be ready to hear it from us, and they'll understand.'

He felt sick as he realised he'd messed up with Eliza already. The pony was paid for and was due to arrive in a horse box on Amy's birthday. The paperwork had been signed. He couldn't back out now. And part of him didn't want to. It wasn't about getting one over on Eliza and Gabriel any longer. It was for Amy. He owed her. But what price would he pay for that?

And as he gazed into Rhiannon's eyes, so dark, so intense, so full of love and passion and desire, he felt suddenly lost. Because the truth was, there was another obstacle in their path, one he hadn't dared put into words, even to himself. The devil was on his shoulder all right, and he was having a splendid time making Harry's life hell.

'Remember what the cards said, Harry,' she said urgently, as if sensing his sudden doubt. 'This is your time to put into practice all the lessons you've learned. It's going to be okay, isn't it?'

He detected the anxiety in her tone and pushed his own fears away, wrapping his arms around her as if to protect her.

'Of course it is. How could it not be?'

'Mum, we need more cheese and onion crisps!'

Derry stepped into the kitchen just as Harry and Rhiannon sprang apart.

Harry picked up a tarot card. 'Well, thanks for that, Rhiannon. It was most interesting. I'll have a think about what you said.'

'You do that,' she said, taking the card from him and wrapping the pack carefully in its black silk cloth. 'I'm so glad you found it useful.'

355

Derry leaned against the fridge freezer, watching them, making Harry feel deeply uncomfortable.

'I never would have thought you'd be the type for this,' he said at last. 'It just shows you. People are never what you think, are they?'

'I expect that's true,' Harry agreed.

'What were you saying about the crisps, Derry?' Rhiannon said.

'I'd better be going,' Harry mumbled, pushing past Derry, head down. He stopped at the door and turned to face her. 'Goodbye, Rhiannon. Thank you for your time.'

She nodded in response, and he hurried out of the room and down the stairs, not stopping for breath until he was at the bottom of Bay Street, and facing the long, steep climb up to Jim Rumm's Yard, the short cut to Eight Bells.

28

Eliza opened the door and greeted Harry with surprising enthusiasm.

'Come in, come in. It's all a bit chaotic right now, I'm afraid,' she gabbled, ushering him inside. 'Amy's in a state of high excitement because of the puppy. She's beside herself. We've put the puppy crate in her bedroom for now, because the last thing a pup needs is a lot of excited children prodding it, and all her friends will be here soon, so we thought we'd keep her out of the way until the party's over, but of course, that means we can't prise Amy out of her bedroom just yet. I'll call her down in a minute. Gabriel won't be long. He's at Whisperwood, fixing the paddock gate. We wouldn't want any escaped donkeys, would we?'

She finally paused for breath. 'Would you like a drink? I'll show you round.'

She sounded nervous, as if she were expecting Harry to give her home marks out of ten. In fact, Wychwood was everything Harry had expected; a spacious, contemporary interior, lovingly furnished by Eliza in the way that she had of making a house look a home. She'd done the same at their old place in Chiswick he remembered, feeling a pang of sadness at the memory. It had been an ordinary three-bedroomed semi when they bought it, but her love and care had transformed it into a place he was glad to get home to. How much he'd taken for granted in those days!

Gabriel, apparently, was some sort of woodworking wizard, which astonished Harry. He hadn't expected him to be so handy, but then he vaguely remembered that Gabriel had once worked on Whisperwood Farm, and he'd had some sort of workshop. He couldn't remember the details, but it didn't matter. The point was, it seemed Gabriel had built the kitchen at Wychwood himself, and Eliza was bursting with pride as she showed him round.

They were the perfect couple, Harry thought suddenly. Gabriel, clearly a whizz at carpentry, Eliza a born homemaker. No wonder the house was so beautiful, and so welcoming. He had to admit, it was a lovely place. Beautifully decorated and tidy, with enough children's toys and books, family photographs and mementos to turn it from a show house into a warm, family home. He couldn't help but admire it, while also feeling a pang of envy.

Eight Bells was completed, in the sense that all building work, electrics and plumbing were done, and he'd decorated every room and furnished most of them. But it didn't feel like this. There was something missing. Family. Yes, he could fill those empty rooms with people — paying guests who'd finally start putting some money into his bank account — but it wouldn't feel like this. It wouldn't be the same.

He fantasised for a moment about some dream day in his vision of the future. The living room at Eight Bells was no longer empty. Amy and Rufus were sitting next to each other on the sofa, chatting about school, and their favourite programmes, and telling each other about their friends. Harry was in the kitchen, pouring wine, not even minding that Amy's cocker spaniel was getting under his feet. And out in the garden, picking flowers to fill their home with colour and fragrance, was Rhiannon.

He gave a loud sigh and Eliza looked at him sharply.

'Am I boring you?'

'God no! I was thinking how stunning it is, and how lucky you are,' he admitted.

Her eyes widened. 'Really?'

'Yes, really. It's amazing, Eliza. You've done a great job. You both have.'

A smile lit up her face, and he remembered when she used to smile like that at him all the time and wondered how long it would be before the smile was replaced by a scowl. What had the cards said? *Time to face up to the consequences of your actions.*

Through the patio doors he could see bunting strung across the garden, a Happy Birthday banner tacked to the summer house, and dozens of brightly coloured balloons tied to the fence posts. There was a large table set up in the garden, ready for the party. Eliza had said that if it were a warm, sunny day, they'd eat outside, and the gods had smiled on her. It was a beautiful day. At least for now...

He risked a brief glance at his watch and his heart thumped. Less than an hour to go and that bloody horse box would be pulling up outside the gates. God help him.

He heaved a sigh of relief as he noticed, out of the corner of his eye, Tally arriving.

'I didn't know you were invited,' he said, hurrying to her side like a nervous child after his first day at nursery, catching sight of his mummy at last.

'I'm not,' she admitted. 'I'm not staying, but Mum asked me to drop Amy's present and card off.'

'Isn't Sophie coming?' Eliza asked. 'She didn't take offence at not being invited, did she? It wasn't me being rude. It's a kid's party, that's all, and I didn't think she'd find it interesting.'

'Oh, she's not upset,' Tally assured her. 'She's wedding dress shopping in Moreton Cross, so she's perfectly happy.'

'And you've not gone with her?'

Tally pulled a face. 'No thanks. She's taken poor Dad with her. I was amazed because I thought she'd want it to be a surprise. But she says it's for his benefit, so she wants his opinion and, besides, she's determined to get him a new suit.'

'She's left it a bit late,' Eliza mused. 'It's the ceremony next week. She sorted out the flower girl dresses ages ago.'

'I know, but it's not like she's buying a proper wedding dress. She wants a nice, smart outfit. If she can't get it in Moreton

Cross, she'll drag Dad to Helmston, or even York if she must. You know Mum.'

'How are you getting on, Tally?' Harry asked. 'Living back at The Old Vicarage, I mean. Everything okay?'

She smiled. 'Yes, it's fine thanks. We're getting on a lot better. Mum's doing her absolute best not to boss me around or tell me what to do. Thank God for this ceremony. She's so preoccupied with it that she hasn't got time to worry about me. Besides, as far as she's concerned, I'm sorted. I'm with Derry, so all's right with Mum's world. Ah!' she held out her arms as Amy entered the kitchen. 'The birthday girl herself. Happy birthday, Amy. Some presents and cards here from your Auntie Sophie and Uncle Archie and the rest of us.'

'Thank you, Tally.' Amy gave her a hug, then turned to Harry. 'Dad! You came!'

'Of course I did,' he said, feeling ridiculously pleased that she was clearly so thrilled to see him. 'I wouldn't miss it for the world.'

Amy threw her arms around him and hugged him. 'I got a puppy from Mum and Gabriel,' she told him, giving him a knowing look. 'I couldn't believe it. It was *such* a surprise.'

He ruffled her hair, shaking his head slightly. She was hardly subtle.

Luckily, Eliza didn't seem to pick up on it.

'Are you going to stay?' Eliza asked Tally. 'You'd be very welcome.'

'No, honestly, I can't.' Tally beamed at her. 'I'm meeting Derry. We're off to his mate's house to meet his wife and baby. They live over in Whitby, so I need to go really.' She turned to Amy. 'Have a lovely day. Enjoy your party.'

Harry took her arm. 'I'll see you out.'

He went with her to the front door.

'Have you told her?' Tally whispered. 'About the pony, I mean. Have you warned Eliza?'

Harry swallowed. 'No. I keep meaning to, but then my courage fails me.'

'Oh, Harry.' Tally shook her head. 'Good luck.'

'I wish you were staying,' he said. 'I could do with some support.'

'I'm sorry. I would if I hadn't arranged this, but I can't let Derry down. It will be okay. They might be a bit cross to start with, but when they see Amy's face... And you must make it clear that you're going to pay for the pony's upkeep. That should help.'

God, yes. That was another thing. How much was this going to set him back? He wished he'd thought it through. Why had it ever seemed like a good idea?

'I feel sick,' he admitted. 'I'm dreading this.'

Tally gave his hand a sympathetic squeeze. 'Just take a deep breath and go for it,' she said. 'Give them some warning. You don't want—'

'What is it?' But Harry could already see — and hear — what it was. A horse box was trundling slowly down Daisyfield Walk. Horrified, Harry could only stare at it as it slowly pulled up outside Wychwood.

'Oh dear,' Tally said.

'They're early!' Harry's stomach was doing most peculiar things, making him feel nauseated. 'They're bloody early! Oh my God, what do I do?'

'Stay calm,' she advised. 'Act like you think you've done a kind thing, a good thing.'

'What do you mean, act?' he demanded, somewhat indignant. 'I *have* done a kind thing. Amy will love it.'

'You know what I mean,' she said. 'I have to go, Harry,' she added, glancing at her watch.

He felt the blood drain from his face as Gabriel hurried up the lane with Joe, Charlie and Mrs Travers at his side. They were all eyeing the horse box with dismay. Gabriel turned and caught sight of Harry standing at the door, and it was clear from his thunderous expression that he'd joined the dots immediately.

Harry cringed as Mrs Travers said loudly, 'See? What did I tell you? I warned you he'd be trouble.'

'Please give it ten minutes,' Harry pleaded to Tally. 'I can't face this on my own.'

'Don't be silly. Everything will be fine, you'll see.'

Eliza's bellow almost shattered their eardrums.

'Harry! What the hell have you done?'

Tally pulled a face. 'Hmm. Or maybe not.'

****

A vanilla ice cream with a chocolate flake! I couldn't remember the last time I'd eaten one of those, and I can't think what possessed me to pop into Ted and Dawn's ice cream shop at the top of Bay Street, but I couldn't resist. Five minutes later, I was sitting on the bench not far from The Kearton Arms, looking out over the bay, stuffing my face, and wondering why, exactly, I'd waited so long to enjoy such delights.

I thought about Harry, knowing he'd be at Amy's birthday party now. I hoped it went well. His cards had certainly given him a jolt.

I'd so enjoyed doing the reading for him. Robert, I realised, had been quite right when he'd told me how much my gifts would be valued.

'You could do this full time,' he'd told me. 'Honestly, people need this, and you're just the person for the job. You're wasted, running a pub.'

I disagreed with him about that, but even so, there was no more denying that I'd love to spend my time teaching people the things I loved doing myself. And it felt that I'd be doing good with my tarot readings, too. So many people required a helping hand, a little guidance. Look at Harry. His reading had been quite telling, although I had the feeling it hadn't made much sense to him. Or maybe he just didn't want to reveal too much to me.

He'd been brooding about something, and there had been real anxiety in his eyes. I wondered what he'd done that was causing him so much worry and hoped the cards had given him some reassurance at least.

I leaned back on the bench and closed my eyes. The sun was warm and soothing on my skin, and I found I was smiling. I had some big decisions to make, but I felt surprisingly calm about it

362

all. The universe, after all, always unfolds as it should. Why worry?

I opened my eyes and stared at the water. It had been a while since I'd been so accepting of fate. In fact, I realised I'd been fighting against fate for years — probably since Derry had left for Cornwall. I'd been so broken, so devastated, so angry...

It felt as if I hadn't been the real me for ages, and now, suddenly I felt she was coming home. Things were happening. Fate was moving the chess pieces of my life into position. I could almost hear them sliding into place, and I smiled again, soothed by the memory of Harry reassuring me that everything would be all right.

I remembered the ice cream and hastily licked the drops from the cornet. It was melting. I'd better focus.

'That looks good.'

'Harry! What are you doing here?' I couldn't hide the delight in my tone, even if I'd wanted to. 'I'm so glad to see you. I have such a lot to tell you! Oh, but I thought you were at Amy's birthday party?'

'I was.'

I raised an eyebrow, hearing the gloom in his response. 'Oh. I'm guessing it didn't go too well.'

'It was terrible. Awful. Worse than I'd expected. And it's all my own fault.'

'I'm sure it's not as bad as you think,' I said. 'These things seldom are.'

'Well, I'm the exception to the rule then,' he replied. 'Mind if I join you?'

'Of course. Sit down.'

I felt suddenly pensive as I noticed the tension in his shoulders as he sat, staring out over the sea, a frown on his face. Whatever had happened at Wychwood, it wasn't good.

'What happened?' I asked him, after dropping what was left of my ice cream in the bin. Suddenly, it had lost its appeal.

'I fucked it all up again, that's what. Everybody hates me, and who can blame them? You're probably the only person in the entire village who doesn't want to kill me and give it time and I'm sure you'll come to your senses and join them.'

'As if that would ever happen,' I said. 'And anyway, I'm sure it's not as bad as that. What could you possibly have done that was so bad?'

'I bought Amy a pony for her birthday,' he said.

I blinked, not quite sure that was a reasonable explanation for his misery.

'Well, that's good, isn't it? We all know she's pony mad. Didn't she like him?'

Harry sighed. 'Oh, she loved him. You'd have thought I'd given her the world.'

'Then I don't see?'

'Eliza and Gabriel got her a puppy,' he explained. 'So of course, it looks as if I was trying to outdo them.'

'But you didn't know,' I protested. 'No can think—'

'I did know, to be fair,' he said. 'Amy knew, although Eliza has no idea she'd found out. You know, Amy's got a real gift for eavesdropping. She overheard her mother and Joe talking and told me all about it.'

'So, you got the pony because they got the puppy?'

Harry rubbed his forehead. 'Yes, I did. I was annoyed that Eliza hadn't let me go halves with her. I acted like a spoilt child. I was worried Amy would prefer Gabriel's gift to mine, and I couldn't deal with it. How pathetic is that?'

I thought about it for a few moments, remembering the conversation at Fuchsia's baby shower about the puppy.

'It seems to me,' I said slowly, 'that Gabriel was just as worried. He's said for ages that Amy can't have a dog. It's rather a coincidence that you arrive in Kearton Bay and suddenly it's okay for her to have one. I think, after the Christmas iPhone saga, he didn't want to be outshone again. I think you two are caught up in a bidding war for Amy's affections.'

'He doesn't have to bid for her affections,' Harry said bitterly. 'She loves him already. She's with him all day, every day, and as everyone keeps reminding me, he's brought her up since she was three years old, whereas I didn't see her for years. Who's the real father figure in her life?'

'You are,' I said gently. 'But he is too. He's a kind-hearted man, Harry, and he loves her like his own. Isn't that what you want for her? How lucky is she, to have two men who adore her and want nothing but the best for her? I wish I'd been so blessed.'

Harry took my hand. 'Sorry. I must sound so full of self-pity. You're right, of course. Far better that Gabriel loves her and takes care of her, than some awful stepfather who doesn't want her around.'

'So, what happened at the party?' I asked. 'Did you take the pony with you?'

'It arrived in a horse box,' he explained. 'And it was early. Bad timing really, because Gabriel had just arrived back at Wychwood with Joe and Charlie and our old cleaner, Mrs Travers, in tow, so they all witnessed the full shock of this bloody big vehicle pulling up, and the driver getting out and announcing he was delivering the pony. I had to explain and, oh God, you should have seen their faces when I confessed.'

'They didn't take it well?'

'Nope.' He shook his head, clearly remembering with horror. 'Gabriel was absolutely furious, although he couldn't say much because Amy was ecstatic. Eliza grabbed me and pulled me into the kitchen, and it wasn't pleasant. Accused me of one upmanship, and of trying to buy Amy. Then Gabriel came through and started ranting about how irresponsible I was, and didn't I realise how much ponies cost to keep, and did I even know if it was safe, blah, blah, blah. Thank God for Tally.'

'Tally was there?' I frowned. 'I thought she was meeting Derry?'

'She wasn't supposed to be there. She'd dropped Amy's card and presents in from Sophie, and was rushing off to meet Derry, as you say, but when the pony arrived early and they all started ranting, she stayed and stuck up for me. Explained she'd helped choose the pony and it was perfectly safe, and—'

'Tally helped choose the pony?'

'Who else would I ask? I certainly wasn't going to buy Amy a pony on my own. I don't have a clue, and I needed to know it was safe, and suitable for her. Tally tried to talk me out of it,' he admitted. 'Something which I pointed out very forcefully to Eliza and Gabriel, who started having a go at her for being in on it. I promised them I'd be paying for all the bills and feed and grazing and everything else, but Gabriel said Amy can't ride the wretched thing until Georgia or Will have looked it over and given it their approval. Which is fair enough, I suppose.'

'Well, yes, I can't blame him for that,' I said. 'He's just protecting her. I'm sure if it had been the other way around, you'd have done the same.'

'I don't see why,' Harry grumbled. 'They didn't let me check the puppy, did they? It could bite.'

I laughed. 'True,' I said. 'I hope you didn't point that out to them though.'

Harry shrugged. 'I didn't say anything. I just let them rant.'

'But you must have said something?'

'What's the point? We went back outside, and Amy was over the moon, and I had to sign the papers, and I could feel their eyes boring into the back of my head. I knew I'd blown it, just when we'd been getting on so well. Joe looked at me in disgust, although there's nothing new in that. I didn't have the energy to go over it all. They spent the next fifteen minutes, after the horse box had gone, arguing about where the horse was going to live. Obviously, I'd not thought about transporting it from Wychwood to its new home, and the horse box owner said he couldn't take it because of insurance or something, so that left it stranded on the front drive, along with a lot of tack.'

I could picture the scene quite clearly, and wished I'd been there to help. Poor Harry.

'In the end, Joe said he'd take it back to Whisperwood as a temporary measure and put it in the paddock with the donkeys. Eliza rang Will and he said he'd bring over a trailer and take the pony back to Kearton Hall. There's not enough grazing at Whisperwood apparently, and the stables aren't in good condition, so it's going to live at the Hall. I'm to ring Will later and sort out livery terms.'

'Will won't charge you much,' I said confidently. 'He's not like that.'

'I thought it would be easier than it was,' he admitted. 'I thought it would stay at Joe's, and that's only a short walk from home for Amy. I never thought about whether there was room, or anything really. That's me all over. I don't think.' He gave me a rueful smile. 'The Knight of Swords, remember? I never consider the consequences of my actions.'

'You were trying to do something nice for Amy,' I said. 'I'm sure Eliza understands that, deep down.'

'I wouldn't bet on it. She was furious. After Joe took the pony to Whisperwood, Amy wasn't interested in her party. She wanted to take all her friends, as soon as they'd all arrived, to see her pony instead, but Eliza wouldn't let her, so she got into a bit of a sulk about it. Gabriel clearly wanted to punch me in the face. We all had tea, but you could have cut the atmosphere with a knife. Mrs Travers kept muttering about leopards and spots, and quite frankly, I couldn't wait to get out of there.'

'I'm sorry,' I said. 'It sounds awful.'

'It was. I tried to make it up to them. Amy showed me the puppy, and I couldn't have been more enthusiastic about the bloody thing if I'd tried. To be fair, it was awfully sweet, and I rather took to her. But even though I praised her, and told Amy what a lucky girl she was, and how this spaniel was the best thing ever, and reminded her how long she'd wanted a puppy, Gabriel and Eliza could barely crack a smile. As I was leaving — before anyone else left, I might add — Eliza told me I was a pain in the arse and said she couldn't imagine why she'd ever thought I could change. Made me feel like shit if you must know. Mainly because she's right. I'm a total waste of space, let's face it.'

'Of course you're not. Oh, Harry, you're not!' I wanted desperately to cheer him up, and I thought I had the perfect way to do so. 'I have something to tell you. You know yesterday, when we were doing the tarot reading, and Derry walked in?'

He nodded. 'Yes, of course. And gave me a suspicious look as if I were doing something unspeakable with you in the kitchen.'

I giggled. 'Yes, well, the thing is, he'd been outside for a while, and he'd heard us talking.'

Harry looked furious. 'So he was eavesdropping on us? That's a bit bloody rude, isn't it?'

'But he heard us talking about *us* — about our love for each other.'

Harry groaned. 'Fuck me, this day gets better and better. Let me guess, you're grounded?'

'He gave us his blessing,' I said, smiling.

Harry's mouth dropped open.

I took his hand. 'Did you hear me?'

'I heard you,' he said. 'But why would he do that?'

'Because,' I said, 'he sees what I see. That you're a changed man, and this relationship is different. He asked me if we were having a sexual relationship and—'

'Bloody hell!' Harry gasped. 'Fancy asking your mother that! He's not backwards in coming forwards, is he?'

'Oh, I don't mind that,' I assured him. 'The point is, he understood immediately that this is different. All my other relationships have been about sex, except for Will. But that was about other things, something we both needed at the time. And we did have sex, of course. Quite—'

'Yes, all right.' Harry held up his hand. 'I don't need the details.'

'I'm sorry. What I mean,' I said, 'is that this is special. Unique. We've never had a physical relationship, Harry, and yet we love each other. It's based on who we are, what we mean to each other, not some chemical urges that dictate our feelings. You see? And Derry understood the difference.'

He didn't answer but studied the path at his feet in silence.

'Anyway,' I said, suddenly uncertain at his lack of enthusiasm, 'it turns out he wasn't convinced when I took you upstairs to do the reading, and he'd questioned Jack about you. Jack told him about us breaking up after Sophie's remarks, and about how you'd backed off when I asked you to, for the sake of my relationship with Derry. He was touched by that. He's happy for us, Harry. We don't have to hide from the world any more. You see?'

'That's not quite true,' he mumbled.

'Sorry?'

'That's not quite true,' he repeated, louder that time. He looked up, and I saw a bleakness in his eyes that alarmed me. 'Eliza doesn't know yet, does she? And quite frankly, the way she spoke to me today, I can't imagine her cutting me any slack any time soon. It will be another weapon to attack me with.'

'I'm sure she'll understand,' I said. 'We'll give it a little time for her to calm down, and then—'

'It's no use.' His shoulders dropped and he slumped, defeated.

'What — what do you mean?'

'Eliza told me what a waste of space I was, or words to that effect, and she's absolutely right. I can't have a relationship with anyone, let alone someone like you. Trust me, you're better off without me.'

'Harry! That's not true.'

'It is true. I've got to sort myself out, grow up. I don't even know what I want to do with my life, and I'm pushing fifty for God's sake.'

'Well, you're not the only one figuring that out,' I said. 'As a matter of fact—'

'And I have to think about Amy,' he continued, clearly set on his mission to shake me off. 'She's got to come first. I've already messed up big time, and I can't risk any more catastrophes. I'm going to spend the next few months grovelling to Eliza and Gabriel as it is. There's no point…'

'What are you saying?' I asked, determined to hear it from his own lips, stated in clear English.

'I'm saying — I'm saying forget me,' he said. 'I'm not good enough. I'm a walking disaster. I have absolutely nothing to offer you. You're everything, Rhiannon. You're bright and beautiful and funny and warm and clever and — and good. You're everything I'm not. Please, stop wasting your time on me. I'm truly not worth it.'

'Of course you're worth it,' I said, stunned at how low his self-esteem had sunk. 'What about the things you said to me

369

yesterday? You said it would be okay, that it would work out. You said—'

'I know what I said,' he admitted, not able to look at me. 'I was grasping at straws. I'm sorry.'

'This is a bad day, that's all. You'll see things differently when you've had chance to think about it.'

'I won't.' He got to his feet. 'I'm so sorry, I really am. One day, you'll realise you had a lucky escape. Trust me.'

He walked away, and I watched him as he headed down Bay Street, his head down, hands in pockets, looking as if he'd just learned that the apocalypse was happening tomorrow.

'You're wrong, Harry,' I called. 'It will all be okay. You'll see.'

Because Harry and I were meant for each other. I knew it, and deep down, he knew it, too. I just had to wait for him to admit it to himself.

29

The banging on the front door woke him up.

Blinking, Harry lay for a moment or two, hoping he'd imagined it. Then it came again, and he groaned, knowing it was all too real. What time was it anyway?

He peered at the clock and was shocked to discover it was gone eleven. How had he slept in so late? It seemed to be a pattern that he was developing. He'd sleep fitfully through the night, wake up early, groan to himself about the arrival of yet another day, and promptly fall into a deeper sleep than he'd had all night. Sometimes, he didn't wake up until early afternoon. He'd never done that in his life before, but he seemed to be permanently exhausted, and after all, there wasn't an awful lot to get up for was there? He'd finished the house, and it wasn't as if he had a job to go to.

The banging noise came again.

What the fuck was wrong with people? Why couldn't they leave him alone? He had nowhere to be, so— Oh shit! Despondently, Harry remembered that today was the day of Sophie's and Archie's wedding vows renewal ceremony. He would have to get up, get dressed, face the world. He didn't think he could do it. He *couldn't* do it. Fuck it.

He pulled the duvet over his head and tried to block out the hammering on the door as it came for a third time. Whoever it was they were clearly rubbish at taking a hint.

'Go away,' he mumbled, as if they could hear him.

What time was the ceremony anyway? Around two he thought, and remembered that Amy was flower girl, and he'd promised he'd be there to see her. He had no choice. He had to go. He couldn't let her down again.

Groaning, he climbed out of bed, pulled on his dressing gown, and staggered downstairs. Cursing, he fumbled with the keys and opened the door. Peering round, he almost leapt back in fright as Eliza loomed up before him.

'So you *are* in!' She looked him up and down, clearly astonished. 'Have you just got up?'

'Yeah, sorry. What's up? What have I done now?'

'Harry, you look a fright. Let me make you coffee.'

She pushed past him and headed into the kitchen. Bemused, Harry stared after her for a moment, and ran a hand through his hair as he tried to figure out what was going on. Why was Eliza here? And why was she offering to make him, of all people, a coffee?

He closed the door and followed her into the kitchen.

'Have I missed something?' he asked. 'Shouldn't you be getting Amy ready for her big day?'

'So you have remembered then?' She handed him a glass of orange juice. 'Get that down you. Vitamin C. I'll put the kettle on.'

He took a sip of the juice and sat down at the kitchen table. 'Well?'

'I just dropped Amy and the twins at The Old Vicarage. Sophie's got lots of help, she doesn't need me getting in the way. And I had more important things on my mind.'

She spooned decaf into two mugs and flicked the kettle on, then sat down opposite him.

Harry studied her face, looking for signs of anger, and wondered what he'd done that would bring her here unnecessarily. Must have been something bad. She wouldn't choose to be in his company, he was sure of that.

'Why didn't you tell me, Harry?'

Her voice was soft, kind even. Harry wondered if he were still in bed, dreaming the whole thing.

'Tell you what?'

Eliza rummaged in her handbag and pulled out a rolled-up magazine. 'I take it you don't know.'

Harry stared at it in dread. 'Know what?' He had an awful feeling she was about to tell him.

Eliza's eyes were full of sympathy, which unnerved him. She unrolled the magazine and lay it on the table in front of him.

He stared down and his heart sank as he saw the pouting face of Melody, of all people, staring back up at him. Splashed across the top of the cover was the headline:

LoveBird: Why Ending My Marriage Was the Best Thing I Ever Did.
Melody sings like a Bird about leaving Harry Jarvis behind, her new Californian lover, and why, in her fifties, she's never been happier.

'Oh, no. No. No.' Harry buried his head in his hands. 'Tell me I'm still in bed, dreaming.'

'I'll make the coffee,' Eliza said. 'You read it.'

So not dreaming then.

With dread in his heart, Harry flicked through the magazine and found the double page spread. Well, it was a triple page spread actually. Melody had certainly made a splash, and she had plenty to say. He read every word, wincing at some of the more cutting lines. Melody had never been one for holding back, and she clearly wasn't about to start now.

Blinking away tears as he read the final paragraph, which hammered home to him that Rufus looked upon Chuck as a surrogate father — a young, virile, fit father, who could do fun things with him and play sports and teach him baseball — Harry pushed the magazine away.

Melody's admission that their sex life had fizzled away to nothing stung. Her bitchy boasting about how her toy boy had rejuvenated her and taught her things she'd never dreamed of humiliated him. Her revelation that Harry's career had died a death in America hurt and angered him. But it was the other thing she said that devastated him. How could she? She'd promised. She knew the situation; knew how he'd fought to keep it quiet…

The mug of tea landed on the table in front of him. He heard Eliza take a seat again and knew she was watching him. His heart thudded, he felt sick. So this was it. No getting away from it now.

'I'm so sorry, Harry,' Eliza said. 'I didn't want to tell you, but then I knew you'd want to be made aware it was out there. I suspect people are going to be asking about it, and you needed to be prepared for that. Not just locals. I mean journalists. There'll probably be interest in this.'

'She swore to me,' he murmured, finally looking up and meeting her gaze. 'All this time I've tried so hard to keep it quiet. Why would she do this to me?'

Eliza, he noticed, was in tears. It touched him that she could still feel sad for him, after all he'd done. But it was hard to take, too. He didn't want pity.

'Harry,' she said, 'why didn't you tell me? It's nothing to be ashamed of. Why hide it?'

'Why hide it?' Harry gave a bitter laugh. 'Do you know what it's like in television? What it's like out there, in La La Land? You can't show weakness. You can't show signs of ageing. You can't show signs of anything that might mean a hike in insurance premiums. The last thing I needed them all to know was that I'd had a heart attack.'

Eliza wiped her eyes. 'Melody says it was a serious one. Was it?'

'Bad enough,' he said briefly. He closed his eyes, not wanting to remember.

'Worse than Joe's?' she asked tentatively.

Harry took a sip of tea. 'You really want to know?'

'Yes, of course I do.' She sounded incredulous, as if she couldn't believe he was even asking the question.

'It was bad enough. I had a stent fitted, and I'm on a ridiculous amount of medication.'

Eliza shook her head. 'You were always so health-conscious. It seems so unfair.'

'I know. I didn't smoke, hardly drank, kept fit, ate healthily. There you go. Now I'm reduced to drinking bloody decaffeinated coffee. Life doesn't get much worse.'

'But you're here, Harry,' she said gently. 'That's the main thing. You're still here.'

'Am I?' he heard the catch in his voice and was appalled. He cleared his throat, determined not to come across as weak or self-pitying. 'I ought to get ready to go to this wretched ceremony. If I wasn't looking forward to it before, I'm dreading it even more now.'

'You don't have to go,' Eliza said. 'If you'd rather not—'

'And let Amy down again?' he said. 'Bet Gabriel would love that. I expect he's enjoying all this, isn't he?'

'How can you say that?' she asked. 'He's a doctor, for a start. He knows what you've been through. He was sorry to learn what happened. You never registered at the practice. You have got a GP?'

'I registered at the Castle Street practice in Helmston as soon as I moved here. I wasn't sure I'd be allowed to. I thought they'd insist I registered here in the village, but apparently the Kearton Bay Surgery is part of the same group, so it was fine. With all the different tablets I take I could hardly put it off, could I?'

'I'm relieved to hear it,' Eliza said. 'And how are you? Really?'

'Really?' Harry shrugged. 'I'm okay. It took a while to feel anywhere like normal again, but I managed it. Somehow, we kept it out of the papers over there. Not that it would have been big news because of me, but Melody's newsworthy. People would have wanted to know if her husband was a crock. Luckily for me, she was ashamed, so it wasn't difficult to persuade her to say nothing.'

'Ashamed?' Eliza sounded annoyed. 'Why should she be ashamed, for God's sake?'

'She said it reflected badly on her.'

Eliza's eyes widened. 'She actually said that?'

'She did.' That and a lot of other stuff, none of it complimentary. 'Said it made me look old and useless, and she didn't want her *brand* contaminated by that. I was bad for her image. Luckily for her, she'd already met Chuck. They were at it before my heart attack, as I later discovered, and my being in hospital came in extremely handy.'

'Oh, Harry. How awful.'

'No more than I deserve, as I'm sure you're thinking,' he said lightly. Deep down, though, he knew he was being unfair. He could see by her expression, hear in her voice, that she was far from gloating. She was devastated for him. Why had he ever left her for Melody? He must have been mad. Eliza might be kind and generous enough to forgive him, but he wasn't sure he'd ever forgive himself.

'I'm thinking no such thing,' she said. She glared at the photo of Melody in the magazine. 'Oh, that bloody woman!'

She shut the magazine, turned it over so that the only thing visible was an advert for vitamin tablets, and slammed it down on the table, as if hoping Melody would feel the bang in her face for real.

'So, while you were seriously ill in hospital, and while you were going through rehabilitation, she was, she was...'

'Yeah,' he said grimly. 'She was. They were. And six months later, she told me in no uncertain terms that I'd outlived my usefulness and it was time to go. Chuck had moved in before I'd even packed my suitcase.'

'But surely you had rights? Wasn't it as much your house as hers?'

Harry shook his head. 'You're going to make me say it, aren't you? You want the truth, Eliza? My American television career was a big fat flop.'

'But, but the stately home programme?'

'One series. It was a fluke. After that, ratings tanked, and the network couldn't drop it fast enough. Work dried up. You're only as good as your last show, so I had no chance. Meanwhile, Melody soared. She got a job on that afternoon show with some other female celebs, chatting about yet more celebs, and she got more and more popular. The work offers started flooding in. She was never at home.' He sighed, remembering. 'The only good thing about it was that I was at home with Rufus more, and I got to know him, to bond with him. That all changed when Chuck came along. After the heart attack, I wasn't so good. I think I scared him. Chuck was full of life and energy. Obviously, Rufus responded to that. I felt like an old man. And in answer to your earlier question, no, the house wasn't mine. I just lived there. Melody bought it. She earned the big bucks, a fact she reminded me of at least once a day. I walked away with a pittance in comparison'

'But surely, there was a divorce settlement?'

Harry held up his hands. 'No way. I didn't want any handouts from her, of all people. I couldn't bear it. I'd saved enough when I was working, and from selling my old house in Chiswick. I walked away with that, and that's how I financed Eight Bells.'

'But surely, there can't be that much left, can there?'

'No,' he said. 'Not really.'

'So that's why you lived here while all the work was going on,' she said. 'To save money. And that's why you're opening it up as a bed and breakfast.'

'Embarrassing, isn't it?'

Eliza narrowed her eyes. 'So why buy a pony? You do know how much they cost, right?'

'Tally did try to warn me,' he admitted.

'Then why?'

'Do you have to ask? Amy told me it was what she wanted more than anything, and I owe her. I missed out on so much with her, Eliza. The least I could do was make this dream come true for her, whatever the cost.'

'Oh, Harry.'

'Yes, I know. I'm an idiot.'

She smiled. 'Yes, but you're a good-hearted idiot. I'm so sorry all this has happened to you. I do wish you'd told me from the start. I'd have been a lot nicer to you.'

He laughed at that. 'Thanks. I think.'

'You could have told me,' she said sadly. 'I'd have listened. You can tell me anything, you do know that don't you?'

Harry stared at his cup of coffee. 'Anything?' he asked eventually.

'Of course.'

'Then maybe there's something else you should know,' he admitted, cringing inside at the thought of confessing all.

'Go on.' She leaned forward, propping her head in her hands, all attention.

Harry took a deep breath. 'It's about Rhiannon.'

'Rhiannon?' She raised an eyebrow. 'What about her? Oh!' She reared back, clearly understanding what he meant. 'You and Rhiannon? You've been having an affair?'

'Yes,' he admitted. 'That is, no.'

'Well, make up your mind. It's either yes or no.'

'No. Not really. Not if, by affair, you mean a sexual relationship?'

Eliza looked dumbfounded. 'Hang on, are you saying you and Rhiannon have been seeing each other, but you haven't had sex yet?'

'You needn't sound so surprised. People do have platonic relationships all the time, you know.'

'Not you. And not Rhiannon, for that matter. How long have you been seeing her?' she demanded.

'Properly? Since Imbolc.'

Eliza laughed. 'Imbolc? Oh, my word. You have got it bad.'

'I mean, the first of February. Imbolc is what she—'

'I know,' Eliza said wearily. 'I know.'

She considered the matter for a few moments, and Harry waited, his stomach churning, for her verdict.

'So, you and Rhiannon have been seeing each other for nearly three months, and you haven't had sex?' She tutted. 'Well, that's got to mean something. I mean, you and Rhiannon — you're all about the sex usually. A match made in heaven.'

'Don't,' he said.

'Don't what?'

'Don't say anything mean about her. I couldn't bear it.'

Eliza took a sip of her tea. 'Well,' she said at last, 'this is serious, isn't it? For your information, Harry, I wouldn't say anything bad about Rhiannon. I love her. She's one of my dearest friends, and I know what a good person she is.'

He couldn't deny he was relieved to hear it. It was important to him that people saw the best in Rhiannon — especially people who mattered to him, like Eliza.

'I'm a bit hurt she kept this from me though,' she continued. 'I'd have thought she'd have mentioned it.'

'We didn't want to upset you. And it's been tricky, because of Derry. She didn't want to do anything to jeopardise her relationship with him, although he knows about it now, and he's okay with it, thank God.'

'And you had all that stuff with Tally going on, too,' Eliza said thoughtfully. 'I take it that, unlike me and Sophie and most of Kearton Bay, Rhiannon believed you when you said there was nothing going on there.'

'Yes, she did.'

'Immediately?'

He nodded. 'Yes. She did.'

Eliza gave a short laugh. 'Well, well. And you like her? I mean, really like her?'

'I really do. We—' he hesitated, not wanting to hurt her.

'You what?'

'We love each other,' he admitted.

She tilted her head to one side, smiling. 'You can say it, Harry. I won't burst into tears. If you and Rhiannon are in love, I couldn't be happier for you. I think you're the perfect match, and no, I don't mean that in a bad way. She'll always have your back; I can guarantee you that. She's not dull and boring like I was.'

'You weren't dull and boring,' he protested. 'I was an idiot.'

'Well, whatever. But she's not me. She's different enough to intrigue you, and to keep you intrigued. But she's not Melody either. She may be exciting and a bit wild, but she's kind, and loyal and generous. She won't let you down.'

'I know that,' he said. 'I've always known that.'

'And she actually told you she loved you?'

'She did.'

Eliza whistled. 'I never thought I'd see the day. Do you know how long we've been waiting for Rhiannon to fall in love? We'd given up. You must be pretty special.'

379

'Hardly.'

'You're all right you know, Harry, despite your mistakes. It just took you a bit longer to grow up than most of us. But if Rhiannon sees something in you, it's there. Trust me.'

'Thank you.'

Eliza folded her arms. 'There's something else, isn't there? Something you're not telling me.'

Startled, he fended off the suggestion. Eliza wasn't fooled for an instant.

'Oh come on, Harry. This is me you're talking to. You're being shifty. What is it?' She looked worried suddenly. 'You are telling me the truth about your health? You're on the mend, right? There's nothing—'

'I'm fine,' he assured her. 'Taking it one day at a time. Well, physically.'

He heard that croak in his voice again and ran a hand through his hair, wondering how much he could tell her and retain any dignity whatsoever.

'Harry, please. I'd like to help. Let me.'

He knew she was genuine, and he also knew he could trust her. She wouldn't tell anyone, except maybe her husband.

'If I tell you, you promise not to tell Gabriel?'

'Of course I won't! Not if you don't want me to. What is it? You're worrying me now.'

'It's nothing. Honestly. Just me being stupid.'

'Stupid, in what way?'

Harry wished he'd never started the conversation. 'I'm struggling a bit,' he admitted at last. 'I don't seem to have any energy. Look at me! Have you ever known me sleep in this late? But it seems to be what I do these days. I can't see any point in getting up, so I don't. Tally helped when she lived here. She was company, at least. And she kept me going. Since she left, I feel sad all the time. And worried. Not that there was anything between us, you understand. But she was my friend — is my friend. And I was so alone when I moved here, and now it's just me and my thoughts, and they're never good ones. I hate this!'

he burst out suddenly. 'I don't feel like me any more, and I have no idea what to do about it.'

'You know,' Eliza said thoughtfully, 'you ought to speak to Joe. He'd understand.'

'Understand what?' he questioned. 'That I'm a complete idiot? I think he understands that all right. He hates me.'

Eliza rolled her eyes. 'Don't be so dramatic. Joe doesn't hate anyone.'

'I'd hate me if I were him.'

'Why?'

'You know why. What I did to you! Joe loves you. He's never going to welcome me into the bosom of his family, is he?'

'It was a long time ago, Harry.'

'Not that long.'

'I wish you'd give him a bit of credit. He's not the demon you think he is.'

Harry frowned. 'I don't think he's a demon at all. I think he's a good man. I owe him a lot.'

'You — did you really just say that?'

'Yes, I did. I was telling Rhiannon the same thing, not that long ago. Joe took care of you when I let you down. He was there for you, for Amy. Where would you have been without him? And when you think how he stepped up for you when you had no one else. He was pretty young himself, but he looked after you. Brought you up. It must have been bloody tough. He's a way better father than I'll ever be.'

Eliza said nothing, but her expression was full of amazement.

'I've never heard you speak like that about him before,' she said at last.

'Like I said, I told Rhiannon not long ago.'

'What did she say?'

'She said I ought to tell him.'

'She's right,' Eliza said. 'It would make a huge difference if he knew how you felt. It would show him that you really have changed.'

He shrugged. 'I shouldn't think he's that fussed one way or the other,' he said dully.

Eliza sighed. 'Look, Harry, it's normal, okay?'

'What is?'

'Feeling like this after having a serious heart attack. This depression. This feeling of hopelessness. Surely the doctors told you this?'

They had, he recalled, but he'd shrugged it off. He didn't do depression. It only applied to other people. That's what he'd honestly thought.

'You're bound to be anxious,' she continued. 'It was a big, scary event, and of course it's shaken you. You've always been so fit and healthy, and so in control of your own life, doing what you want to do, when you want to do it. This was out of your control. You did all the right things, but it still happened. That would scare anyone. Even Joe went through this, you know. He wasn't himself at first. Oh, he put on a great show of being all smiles and jokes. You know what he's like. But eventually he cracked, and I saw the fear and sadness underneath. So don't ever think you're alone in this. You're not.'

'How did Joe pull himself out of it?' he asked.

'He decided to change his life, move to Kearton Bay, give up the television work. He got excited and focused on something new, and it gave him a new lease of life. And then he met Charlie, of course, which changed everything.'

Harry bit his thumb nail, wondering whether he dare ask the next question.

'What is it?' Eliza asked gently. 'What are you thinking?'

'Joe and Charlie,' he said hesitantly. 'Do they — I mean, is it a normal relationship?'

Eliza stared at him. 'Pardon?'

'You know. I mean, do they have — do they sleep together?'

'Are you asking me if they have sex?' Eliza looked puzzled.

'Well, er—'

'It's just, it's just, I'm not sure I can!' he blurted out.

There was a stunned silence as Eliza clearly wondered what she could say to that, and Harry wished he'd never opened his mouth.

Eliza prodded at the magazine. 'So what she said in the interview,' she said, her lip curling at the mention of Melody, 'about your sex life…'

'I couldn't,' he admitted. 'After the heart attack, I was too scared that something would happen. The doctors gave me the go-ahead after six weeks, but I was afraid. I thought, what if it brings another one on?'

'What did Melody say to that?' Eliza asked grimly, as if she already suspected the answer.

Harry closed his eyes against the memory. 'She wasn't impressed,' he murmured. 'Luckily, she had Chuck to take away the pain.'

'Oh my God.' Eliza slumped in her chair, seemingly finding it hard to believe anyone could behave in such a fashion. Then she sat up straight and gave Harry a sharp look. 'Is this why you and Rhiannon haven't done anything?'

He shrugged. 'There were other reasons, but it's probably the reason I haven't tried to move it on.'

'Rhiannon's a passionate woman,' Eliza said. 'Have you told her all this?'

He gave a bitter laugh. 'Yes, because that's exactly the sort of thing I should tell a woman like her, isn't it?'

'Yes, Harry,' she said. 'I think it is.'

'Eliza, for god's sake! Think about it. She's had so much experience, and she's, as you say, a passionate woman. What use am I going to be to her? What if I can't manage it? What if I let her down? What if—'

'What if it's wonderful?' Eliza said. 'Harry, Rhiannon *is* passionate. But she's not just passionate about sex, you know. She's passionate about life, about her friends, about people! She's the most understanding person I've ever met. She seems to instinctively know what's wrong with someone and how to help them. She listens, she cares, she empathises. You shouldn't judge Rhiannon by Melody's standards.'

'I'm not!' he said indignantly.

'Aren't you? Then why aren't you giving her the chance to show you what she's made of? Why keep this anxiety from her? Does she even know about the heart attack?'

He shook his head, a bleakness descending on him once again.

'I couldn't bring myself to tell her. I don't want to see that look in her eyes.'

'What look?'

'That sympathetic look. I don't want her to see me like that — an object of pity. I'm more than just a fucking heart attack!'

'Exactly,' Eliza said triumphantly. 'You're so much more than that. And that's what Rhiannon will see, too. You're safe with her, Harry. Trust her.'

'Safe with her? I don't need to be safe with anyone!'

'Yes, you do,' Eliza assured him. 'We all do. And I think you haven't felt safe with Melody for a long time, and it's made you wary.'

There was a small part of Harry that acknowledged that Melody's behaviour had coloured his own behaviour, particularly with Rhiannon. He'd wanted nothing more than to be honest and open with her from the start, and he had been. Except about the biggest thing in his life. Why was that? Because he was afraid he would see the same scorn in her eyes that he'd seen in Melody's. Was Eliza right?

'I don't know how to trust her,' he admitted at last. 'I mean, I know she's honest and open and has a good heart. I know all that. But there's this tiny little nagging voice in my head, telling me I'll lose her if she knows the truth.'

'Do you think I don't understand that?' she asked. 'After you and I broke up, do you know how hard it was for me to believe that someone would treat me differently? How I struggled to believe the best in Gabriel?'

'I'm sorry,' he muttered. 'Again.'

'Oh, Harry, I'm not saying this to attack you! That's not what I meant at all. I'm just trying to explain how it was, and that I get it, I really do.'

'So how did you trust him in the end?' he asked.

384

'I don't know. He just won me over,' she admitted. 'He wasn't one for words, but everything he did, every action he took, showed me he cared. And then I heard someone say something bad about him, and I knew with absolute certainty that they were wrong. And I guess that's when I knew for sure that I trusted him completely, and I could trust him with something as precious as my heart.'

'My heart's hardly precious,' Harry said. 'It's pretty much fucked.'

They looked at each other, and both started laughing.

'You have to tell her, Harry,' Eliza said. 'I won't be the only person in the village to read this magazine. Rhiannon won't, but someone's bound to mention it in front of her at some point, and how unfair would that be? She needs to hear it from you.'

'I know,' he admitted. 'You're right. What if someone mentions it at the ceremony?'

Eliza considered. 'I think the person most likely to read it is Sophie, ironically. She buys this sort of thing. I think she'll be far too distracted today to think about magazines though, and I can't think, offhand, of anyone else who would read it. But you never know — especially with Melody on the cover. Which is why it's even more important you tell Rhiannon.'

'I don't have time now,' Harry said, panicked. 'After the ceremony perhaps? I'll walk her home. Tell her then.'

Eliza nodded. 'Good plan. Just make sure you do. Now, drink that coffee before it's only fit for throwing away.'

As Harry picked up the mug, he thought how strange it was that his ex-wife, of all people, should be the one to offer him comfort and advice. How far they'd come. He was so glad to have her back in his life again. He'd not realised how much he missed her.

'So,' he said tentatively. 'Tell me honestly. Me and Rhiannon. Do we have your blessing?'

'Do you need my blessing?' she asked, surprised.

'Very much so,' he confirmed. 'I don't want to hurt you ever again.'

He was astonished, and deeply moved, when she walked over to him and put her arms around him. 'Then you have my blessing, Harry. I hope you'll be incredibly happy together.'

He wiped his eyes as she kissed him lightly on the forehead.

'Now,' she said, sounding suspiciously emotional herself, 'go and get dressed. We've got a ceremony to get to, and our daughter is about to outshine the bride. You wouldn't want to miss that, would you?'

'Not for the world,' he said, and smiled as he realised he meant it.

30

The marquee in the grounds of Kearton Hall looked amazing. 'Oh, this takes me back,' I said, gazing at it from the drive. 'The night of the Grand Ball, remember? Four years ago now, can you believe it?' I smiled as I caught sight of Bernie standing by the entrance, patiently waiting as Darcey adjusted his tie for him. 'The night Bernie declared his love for Darcey,' I remembered. 'What a night that was.'

'Wasn't it just.' Will put his arm around me. 'My overriding memory is of Lexi's accident. I was terrified. I thought she'd been killed.'

'I know,' I said softly. 'It was awful. Horrible. But look what came of it,' I added, nodding over to where Lexi and Georgia were fussing over Milo and Eleanor. 'Bernie and Darcey got together, you and Lexi, Nat and Georgia... Do you know, that's when Tally's and Derry's relationship started, too?'

'Really?' Will laughed. 'I never knew that. It just shows you. I wonder what today's event will bring. I hardly dare think.'

Tally and Derry appeared, arm in arm. Tally had a clip board in her other hand and a wide smile on her face.

'Don't you both look smart?' I said, noting Derry's new suit and Tally's print dress. 'How's your mother, Tally? A nervous wreck no doubt.'

'She's in her element,' Tally assured me. 'Oliver and Stephanie turned up last night. We weren't sure they'd come, so Mum was over the moon.'

'And how did she get on with Stephanie?' Will asked. 'Must have been pretty awkward.'

'You must be joking!' Tally burst out laughing. 'Stephanie presented her with a bouquet of flowers and a photo of their wedding in a posh frame, and Mum melted. All it took was a few well-chosen compliments and a bit of gushing about how beautiful The Old Vicarage is, and how much Oliver's told her about home, and how she's been dying to visit, and Mum was putty in her hands. Oliver stood there, looking smug. He knew what would work. Honestly, he gets away with murder every time.'

I noticed she didn't seem to mind any more and smiled to myself. Tally was finally standing on her own two feet, and focusing on her own happiness, rather than worrying about everyone else's. And about time, too.

'It's a bit chaotic at The Old Vicarage,' she admitted. 'What with Mum and Dad getting ready, and Stephanie and Oliver there, and Amy, Hannah and Michael.' She nudged Derry. 'Didn't they look cute?' She turned to me, eyes shining. 'Amy and Hannah are flower girls and Michael's a page boy, and you should see their outfits. That's why I'm a bit late, sorry,' she added, addressing Will. 'I was helping them get ready. Eliza dropped them off and then vanished.'

'Did she? Not like Eliza,' I said.

'She had somewhere to be. She said she's coming back to get them to the Hall, but Mum was a bit put out. Luckily, the lovely Stephanie stepped in to help.' She giggled. 'Well, I'd better get off and make a final check on everything.'

'Is the ceremony actually going to be in the marquee?' I asked. 'Is that allowed, with it being a temporary structure?'

'The ceremony's not a legally binding one,' Will explained. 'It's a token thing really. That's why I can perform it.'

'Are you nervous?'

He grinned. 'What gave it away? I've been dreading it for weeks. Still, I'll do my best.'

'You'd better,' Tally said. 'This is Mum's big day. She's been dreaming about it forever. Don't be the one to spoil it, for your own sake.'

'Isn't it funny how no one mentions Archie's big day in all this?' Derry said, grinning. 'Almost like he's surplus to requirements.'

'We all know whose day this is,' Tally said. 'And none of us had better forget it.'

She hurried away, clip board in hand, and Derry's smile faded.

'Mum, when this is over, would it be all right if I had a talk with you? There's something I need to tell you.'

I felt the joy within me ebb away, to be replaced by cold, stark fear. 'Of course,' I managed. 'We'll walk home together, shall we?'

He nodded. 'Think I'll go and find Nat and Georgia,' he said. 'See you later.'

Will and I exchanged glances as Derry moved off.

'What was all that about?' Will murmured.

'Isn't it obvious?' I felt sick, knowing my time with Derry was almost over. 'He's moving on, isn't he?'

'You don't know that,' Will said.

'I knew he was looking for a new direction,' I reasoned. 'He made it clear he wanted more from life than to be a barman, so I can't blame him.'

'Derry loves working at The Hare and Moon,' Will argued. 'He told me so himself.'

'Yes, but it's not much of a future, is it? He's nearly thirty. He wants his own business, a home of his own. He's not going to find that around here. I can't stop him. He wouldn't stay even if I asked him to. And if he's made the decision, he must have found something he wants to do, somewhere to go, so it's probably too late to change his mind anyway.'

'Do you think Tally will move with him?'

'I think she might follow him on,' I mused. 'Not yet obviously. She hasn't given in her notice, I take it?'

Will shook his head. 'She's not said a word about leaving, no.'

'Then it seems Derry will move on alone, and Tally will follow later. I shouldn't think Sophie will take that very well.'

'And what about you?' he asked gently. 'How are you going to take it?'

'At least,' I said heavily, 'Derry and I are mother and son once more. That's the main thing.'

'You're right,' Will assured me. 'It's pretty obvious Derry's much happier now you're friends.'

'I don't know,' I said, feeling a sudden uncertainty. 'There's something he's not telling me. He's holding something back, I know that. There's a look in his eyes sometimes, like he has something to say but doesn't know how to. Oh, I don't know. It is what it is.' I tried to feel positive. 'The universe unfolds just as it should.'

But it certainly kept us guessing while it did so, I thought, my mind flickering from Derry to Harry. He would be here soon, I realised. How was I supposed to face him, after the last time we'd met and all the things he'd said? Was I about to lose both the men in my life?

Will smiled. 'Hold that thought, Rhiannon,' he said. 'It's all going to be work out fine. I know it.'

****

Sophie looked radiant and was clearly loving all the attention as she stepped out of the car to the cheers of her friends and neighbours.

Dressed in a pearl pink chiffon dress, with a lace bodice and knee-length A-line skirt, she was every inch the star of the show. Beside her, Archie looked a bit sheepish as he adjusted his tie and smoothed his silver hair, clearly feeling the weight of such an important occasion.

We got our first glimpse of the newest member of their family, too, as Oliver and his wife stepped out of the car behind his parents. Clearly, they were considered important enough to merit a ride in the bridal car.

'Good to see you again, Oliver,' Will said, shaking his hand. 'You must be Stephanie,' he added, turning to the pretty brunette at Oliver's side. 'Pleased to meet you.'

Lexi squealed and pulled Oliver into a hug. 'Fancy getting married and not telling us! And you didn't even come to our wedding. You owe us big time!'

Oliver grinned. 'Nice to see you, too, Lexi. Look at you, lady of the manor! Who'd have thought the scruffy farm girl would scrub up so well?'

'Cheek!' Lexi laughed and hugged Stephanie. 'I hope you know what you're doing, tying yourself to this one. Nothing but trouble.'

Stephanie seemed totally unfazed by all the attention. 'Oh, I've already figured that out,' she said. 'Great to meet you all.'

It seemed Archie's brother and sister-in-law had been forgiven for whatever part they'd played in Oliver's wedding, as they were also at the Hall, along with Sophie's and Gabriel's mother and father, Wendy and Raphael.

As various members of the wider family and community gathered round to welcome the wedding party, I noticed Eliza's car pulling up outside the Hall. I smiled as Gabriel hurried over and opened the back door, and two pretty flower girls and a cute page boy stepped onto the drive. Surprised, I watched as Harry climbed out of the passenger seat. I saw him and Gabriel exchange a few words, with seemingly no animosity at all. Well, that was progress. Eliza hurried round to his side, slipped her arm through Harry's, and gave him a squeeze.

What on earth was all that about?

It seemed that a breakthrough had occurred. To my amazement, Joe and Charlie then joined them, and there was another discussion then…

No! I watched, stunned, as Joe held out his hand and Harry shook it.

What on earth?

Sophie squealed in excitement. 'There they are! There are my beautiful attendants. Don't they look lovely, everyone?'

The crowd moved towards the Baileys, and I stepped back, feeling confused.

'Has anyone seen Pandora?' Sophie called.

'They're not here yet,' Rose told her.

She and Flynn looked wonderful. Rose with her dark, pink-streaked hair and pink lipstick, was wearing a dusky pink dress and coat, and looked incredibly elegant. Flynn meanwhile wore a navy-blue suit, with a tie that exactly matched the colour of Rose's outfit and suited his dark hair and blue eyes perfectly. They were accompanied by little Violet, looking adorable in a cotton print dress, Rose's mother and her friend, Maurice, and Cerise who, dressed in a regal shade of purple, held a mobile phone to her ear with one hand, and clutched Violet's hand with the other.

'Have you got through yet?' Rose asked.

Cerise shook her head. 'Fuchsia's goes straight to voice mail, and Pan's phone is engaged. They're probably on their way.'

'They'd better be,' Sophie wailed. 'We can't get married without them.'

'I should think it takes Fuchsia quite a while to walk here,' Lexi said sympathetically. 'She's only got a few weeks to go. It's hard work up that hill when you're pregnant, you know.'

'Aye, it'd probably be quicker to roll her here,' said Mrs Maclean, oozing sympathy as always.

'They were getting a taxi,' Flynn said. 'I offered to pick them up, but they said they'd already booked one.'

'They won't be long,' Meggie said comfortably. 'Now, are we all going inside, or what? My feet are killing me.'

'Mum, Charlie, attendants, you come with me,' Tally called suddenly. 'The rest of you, into the marquee please. Dad, Joe, Will, take your places. We won't be long.'

Sophie was bursting with excitement. She squeezed Archie's arm, and waved to everyone as they passed by, heading down the path to the marquee on the lawn.

'This is the best day of my life,' she kept telling him. 'I can't believe it's here at last. Ooh, Archie. It's going to be perfect. Look after him, Joe. Don't let him jilt me!' she called, as she and Charlie gathered Amy, Hannah and Michael to them and followed Tally into the Hall.

Joe and Archie headed into the marquee, and we slowly followed them in.

It was stunning inside. The marquee Will had hired for the ball had been decorated in elegant black and white, but today's theme was pale pink and cream, and Rose was in her element.

'Remember the day you gave me a pink rose?' she asked Flynn. He beamed at her. 'I do. And I asked you to marry me,' he said. 'So you did. And I bet you've never regretted it for a second.' He kissed her gently. 'Not a single moment,' he confirmed.

I spotted Harry sitting quite near the front with Eliza and her family. It seemed he'd well and truly been welcomed into the fold, and I couldn't help but wonder what had happened to bring about this sudden thaw in their frosty relationship. Whatever it was, I was glad for him. He needed to be part of Amy's life, and I knew it would be a lot easier for him to do that with Eliza and Gabriel on side.

'Rhiannon, come and sit with us, love.'

I was happy to oblige Bernie. He was sitting on the same row as his wife, Darcey, his son Robbie, Robbie's wife Chrissie, Chrissie's parents, Meggie and Ben, and Bernie's best friend, Eddie. Chrissie budged everyone up, and I took the newly vacated seat between her and Meggie.

'Pan and Fuchsia are cutting it a bit fine, aren't they?' Chrissie murmured. 'Sophie will never forgive them if they're late.'

'Posh do, isn't it?' Meggie asked. 'Not that we'd expect anything else from Sophie, mind.'

'My Meggie made the flower girl frocks,' Ben said proudly. 'Done a grand job, hasn't she?'

'Meggie! Did you really?' I'd completely forgotten Sophie had asked her. 'They're so pretty. Then again, I shouldn't be surprised. I remember when you made Lexi's dress for the ball that time. It was incredible.'

'Oh, aye.' Meggie nodded in satisfaction. 'The replica of Lady Eleanor Kearton's dress. That took some doing. Mind you, worth every second of work. Can you believe it's on display in the Hall? I'm ever so proud.'

'So you should be,' I said.

'Have you seen the cake?' Chrissie asked me. 'Eliza made it. It's proper gorgeous. Sophie was a bit demanding and knew exactly what she wanted.' She jerked a thumb in the direction of the back of the marquee, where all the food was laid out in preparation for the buffet afterwards.

'Goodness, that does look good,' I said, seeing the ivory three-tier creation with pale pink roses cascading down the sides. 'Eliza is so clever.'

Eddie tugged at his collar. 'Any idea when this is going to start?' he muttered. 'Feel like I've been here forever already.'

Darcey glanced at her watch. 'They're running a bit late,' she said. 'I wonder what's keeping them?'

Will had taken his place at the front of the marquee, where an arch of pink roses marked the spot where the happy couple would be renewing their vows. He chatted with Joe and Archie, but I could see how nervous he was, even from my place about eight rows back.

I wondered where Derry was. Presumably still with Tally, who was running over things one last time with her mother and Charlie. I couldn't help but wondering what he was going to tell me as we walked home. How soon was he leaving? I hoped he'd be here for a few more days yet. I wasn't ready to say goodbye to him already, not when I'd only just got him back.

As if thinking about him had conjured him up, I saw him enter the marquee with Tally. They took their seats close to the front and I thought it was a good thing that at least he would have her by his side, wherever they ended up. I wished them nothing but happiness.

Sophie and Charlie finally made their entrance ten minutes late. Sophie looked flushed and excited and beamed at us all as Charlie took her arm. Followed by the three children, they made their stately procession down the central aisle towards the rose arch, to the uplifting accompaniment of Pachelbel's Canon in D Major.

I saw Will swallow and knew he'd be shaking with nerves. Even so, he'd do a good job. He was a much better public speaker than he realised. He just needed to believe in himself. A bit like Harry.

I craned my neck, looking for a glimpse of him, but he was hidden from my view by Archie's sister-in-law, who was wearing a hat almost as big as the ones Sophie usually wore to these events.

Will cleared his throat and the buzz of conversation in the marquee died. 'Good afternoon, and welcome to the—'

'Sorry, Will. Can I stop you there?'

We all turned our heads at the astonishing sight of Will's housekeeper, Woody, hurrying up the aisle.

Sophie turned puce. She stared at Woody, then at Archie, then at Will, as if willing him to stop his housekeeper from devastating her precious ceremony. I knew Woody well enough to know that she would never have interrupted without good cause. There was some muttering at the front, and we all strained our ears to hear what was being said, although I had a sudden realisation what it might be about.

Sure enough, Sophie let out a yelp and Archie looked rather dazed.

'What do we do? What do we do?'

Gabriel made his way to his sister's side. 'What is it? What's happened?'

'It's our Fuchsia, isn't it?' Rose leapt to her feet. 'I had a feeling all day something was wrong. Is it our Fuchsia?'

'There's been an accident,' Archie said, his brow furrowed with anxiety.

'It's all my fault.' Sophie wiped away tears.

'Why is it your fault?' Woody said. She put her arm around Sophie. 'Now come on, lovey. None of that. This was no more your fault than mine.'

'But I made such a big fuss about this bloody ceremony.'

'Will someone please tell me what's happened?' Rose demanded.

'It seems,' said Will, 'that the taxi was running late picking up Pandora and Fuchsia, so they decided to walk to the top of Bay Street to meet it, but Fuchsia somehow fell over.'

I put my hand to my mouth. Oh, please let Fuchsia and the baby be all right!

'Is she okay?' Rose had gone pale, and Flynn hugged her tightly.

'They've taken her to hospital. It looks as if the baby's on its way.'

'But it's not due yet,' Rose whimpered. 'It's too early.'

'Only by two weeks,' Flynn reassured her. 'Perfectly normal. Try not to worry.'

I detected a tremor of anxiety in his voice, and knew he was worrying as much, if not more, than she was. If a fall had started Fuchsia's labour, anything could be happening.

'Sorry, Sophie, but I'm going to the hospital,' Rose said, turning to leave.

Sophie looked around at us all, her face stricken, and I waited, realising this was Sophie's moment. She'd dreamed of this ceremony all year, and she'd had such mixed feelings about her forthcoming grandchild. I knew, without doubt, where her priorities lay, even if she hadn't realised herself, and I smiled, knowing exactly what she was about to say.

Sure enough, she did.

'I'm so sorry,' she said. 'I'm afraid the ceremony's off. Please, help yourselves to the food and drink. I have to be with my family.'

Rose paused and turned round, clearly astonished. 'You're coming to the hospital?'

Sophie handed her bouquet to Will. 'Of course I'm going to the bloody hospital. That's my grandchild and my daughter-in-law in there. Come on, Archie.'

'I'll give you a lift,' Flynn said.

'We'll take care of Violet if Cerise wants to go with you,' Eliza said. 'Give them our love.'

There was a scraping of chairs, then Rose, Flynn, Cerise, Sophie, Archie, Tally and Derry shot down the aisle.

'Tally wants me to go with her, Mum,' Derry said, 'so we'll have that talk when I get back, okay?'

'Of course,' I said. 'Let me know how they are, won't you?'

He hurried out of the marquee after Tally. A buzz filled the room as people worried and fretted about Fuchsia's condition.

'We may as well have something to eat then,' Meggie said, seeing some people already making their way to the buffet table.

Joe, Charlie, Eliza, Harry and Gabriel flocked around the children, no doubt consoling them that their big moment had been — what? Postponed? Or cancelled for good? I had no idea. I only knew that as I watched them, I felt so alone suddenly. I was glad for Harry, but I couldn't help but feel surplus to requirements. It seemed he had no need of me any longer. With Derry happily attached to Tally, and clearly about to head off to pastures new, I felt adrift, alone. Thank God for Jack. At least I always had him around.

'I don't know,' Meggie said, as we made our way to the back of the marquee. 'What a day this has been.' She glanced around, as if checking she wasn't being spied on, then leaned towards me. 'I take it you've heard about that Harry Jarvis?'

My heart thudded. 'What about him?'

She rummaged around in her handbag and pulled out a rolled-up magazine. 'You don't know about the interview? Oh, you'll never believe it. I get it delivered, you see, and I had plenty of time to read it this morning before I got ready, and I'm ever so glad I did. That awful woman! You know, Melody Bird. The one who pinched Harry from Eliza. She's been dishing the dirt on him, and I'll tell you now, it's not a pretty story.'

She pushed the magazine into my hand, and I looked at the picture of Melody on the cover and read the tawdry headline, my heart aching for Harry. I glanced round and stilled as I saw him staring at me. By the look on his face, I could tell he was all too aware of which magazine I was looking at. I opened my mouth but closed it again. I wasn't going to call across to him in front of all these people, and besides, he was already moving away.

Hemmed in by villagers eager to attack the buffet, I was powerless to stop him as he practically shot out of the marquee, followed quickly by Gabriel.

I fought my way through the milling guests, only to be stopped at the entrance by a concerned looking Eliza.

'Gabriel's taken him home, Rhiannon,' she said softly. 'It's what he wanted.'

'What's going on?' I asked, feeling wretched and hurt and utterly bewildered.

'It's not my business to explain,' she said. 'You're going to have to talk to Harry about it.'

'But that's what I want to do! Why do you think I was going after him?'

'I know, but he needs a bit of time. I take it you read the article?' She nodded at the magazine that I hadn't even realised I was still holding. I would have to return it to Meggie.

'No,' I said. 'I haven't. Whatever it is, I'd rather not know. I don't care about gossip.'

'I think you'll have to know,' she said mysteriously. 'It's not gossip, it's important. But it's probably best coming from Harry.'

'You know?' I asked uncertainly. 'About...'

'You and Harry?' She smiled. 'Yes, he told me all about it. I couldn't be happier for you both.'

My heart leapt in relief for a moment, but then I realised that whatever Harry and I had once been, it seemed we were no more. Why was he behaving this way?

Clearly seeing my confusion, she put her arm around me.

'Come on, let's go back to the party shall we? I know you won't be in the mood for it, but there are two little flower girls who desperately want people to fuss them, a whole stack of food to be eaten, and let's face it, if you do go home, you'll only brood. All in good time, eh?'

I wanted to protest, to run to Eight Bells without stopping and get to the bottom of this mystery. But something in Eliza's face told me to listen and take her advice. She was my dear friend and I trusted her.

When Harry was ready to explain, he'd be in touch. And I'd be ready to listen.

****

I arrived home a couple of hours later, to discover that Jack, Kerry, and Aidan had already heard about Fuchsia.

'How is she?' Kerry asked anxiously. 'Any news?'

I shook my head. 'Not yet. Derry's at the hospital with Tally, so he'll let me know as soon as he hears anything.'

'You're back early,' Jack said. 'I heard the party was going ahead, even without the happy couple.'

'It is,' I admitted, 'but it didn't feel right, hanging around. Besides, I wanted to get home. I wasn't in the mood for partying so I might as well give you a hand.'

'Well, it's not that busy in here,' Kerry said. 'You go upstairs and change. We can manage in here. We weren't expecting you in so take the day off anyway.'

I wanted to argue, but the desire for time alone outweighed my noble aspirations. 'If you're sure,' I said gratefully.

'Quite sure.'

I made my way upstairs, thinking what a strange day it had been. I'd gone to the Hall expecting a beautiful wedding vows renewal ceremony. Instead, I'd got the terrible news about Fuchsia and the shock of seeing Harry's name on the front cover of a magazine. What was all that about? Eliza had said it wasn't gossip, so what was it?

Somehow, I wasn't at all surprised when Jack appeared in the doorway. Wasn't he always around when I needed someone to talk to? Wasn't he the only person I could always rely on to be there for me?

'I was going to make tea,' I told him. 'Would you like one?'

'Rhiannon, may I talk to you?'

I saw his expression was serious. His dark eyes had no twinkle of amusement in them, and his mouth turned down at the corners. I noticed, for the first time, how lined and drawn his face was. When, I wondered, did he get so old? How had all that time passed so quickly?

'Sit down,' I said, thinking, *please don't tell me you're ill. I couldn't bear it.*

He sat, and for a moment or two he stared at me, as if struggling to find the words.

'Is it your health?' I asked, unable to stand the waiting any longer.

He gave me an understanding smile. 'No, my darling. It's not my health. I'm fine. Well, as fine as anyone my age can hope to be. No, it's not that.'

'Then what?'

A thought occurred to me and I groaned inwardly. 'Is this about Harry? You've read the magazine?'

Jack frowned. 'Harry? What magazine?'

I shook my head. 'Nothing. It doesn't matter.'

'He's not done anything to hurt you, has he?'

There it was again. Jack's every instinct was to protect me. To always be on my side. With Derry about to leave and Harry seemingly as out of reach as ever, I was so grateful to have him around.

'No,' I said, not strictly truthfully. 'There's been some interview published in a magazine. You know his ex-wife, Melody Bird? She's apparently done a hatchet job on Harry. I haven't read it, but I gather it's not good.'

'Poor chap.' Jack rolled his eyes. 'They'll have a field day with that around here. Are you prepared?'

'It doesn't affect me,' I said.

'I should think, if it affects Harry, it affects you deeply,' he said. 'I know you. You'll feel his pain every bit as much as if it were yours.'

'Perhaps,' I admitted.

'Why haven't you read it?'

'Because, if Harry wants me to know what's in it, he'll tell me,' I said. 'I'm not about to start reading anything by that odious woman.'

'Good for you.' Jack nodded in approval. 'You were always a classy lady.'

'Hardly. So, if it's not about Harry, what is it?'

The light in Jack's eyes dimmed. 'I wouldn't hurt you for the world, you know that don't you? And I wouldn't want to make things difficult for you. Not ever.'

'Jack, what's this about?' I asked, a terrible sense of foreboding attacking me. 'You're scaring me now.'

'It's nothing bad,' he said. 'In fact, you'll probably approve. The thing is, I've decided you were right. It's time to hang up my apron. I'm retiring, my darling.'

'Retiring?'

Yes, I'd urged him to do so after his stroke, but even so, it was a shock to hear that he'd finally decided to do it. What would life be like without Jack? How empty would The Hare and Moon feel without him in it? Who would I talk to? Who would console me, comfort me? Derry would be gone soon, and then it would be just me, with Kerry and Aidan downstairs. They were lovely people, but they were young and wrapped up in themselves and, lately, in each other. I could never express myself to them.

'Rhiannon, say something.'

'I'm — I'm so sorry. Yes, yes of course. That's wonderful news, Jack.'

'Is it?'

I bit my lip, not wanting to burden him.

'Rhiannon,' he said softly, 'you can tell me the truth.'

'I'll miss you,' I burst out. 'It won't be the same without you here.'

'I know.' He sat beside me and put his arms around me. 'I'll miss you, too. But you can come and see me whenever you like, and I'll pop in here when I can. I'm not that far away after all.'

'You're in Helmston,' I protested. 'It's miles away.'

'It's a bus ride away,' he said, laughing. 'Maybe I'll get myself a little car. I haven't driven in years, but they say you never forget.'

'Jack, are you sure about this?' I asked.

'Quite sure.'

'Why don't you move in here?' I said, on impulse.

He looked at me, rather quizzically. 'In here?'

'Why not?'

'Give up my flat you mean?'

'Yes. You could have the best room in the place. I don't mind moving into another bedroom. That way, I know you'll always have company, and I can keep an eye on you. Make sure you're okay.'

He shook his head. 'Darling, it's kind of you, but the truth is, I'm struggling with these stairs. It's an old and twisty building, and the stairs are quite steep. They've been giving me some difficulty for a while, but I didn't want to tell you. My old bones aren't what they were. I can manage them now, but in a few years' time they'd be impossible, and what would I do then?'

I hadn't even thought about it, but of course he was right. This building, beautiful as it was, was hardly suitable for an elderly man with arthritis. I slumped, knowing there was nothing I could do.

'Perhaps you could give up your flat and rent somewhere in Kearton Bay?'

Even as I said it, I knew it would be near enough impossible to find somewhere affordable round here. Most rentable properties were let to holidaymakers. Jack would never be able to afford to pay that sort of money.

'Hmm. Now look, Aidan's doing well, though I think he may need an assistant of his own,' he said kindly. 'And I think you should take on more bar staff. I want you to promise me that you're going to do something about these tarot classes and all the other things you want to do with your life before it's too late. Will you promise me?'

'I will,' I said. 'I know I need to do something about this. Life can't be all about running a pub, and the other things are calling to me louder each day. I'll sort something out, Jack. I promise.'

'Well then, it looks like we're both making fresh starts,' he said. 'You'll be all right?'

'Of course,' I said. 'When were you thinking of leaving?'

'Oh, I'll hang on until you've got an assistant for Aidan,' he promised.

'Then I'll place an advertisement this week.' I tried to inject some enthusiasm into my voice. 'I won't keep you hanging on, don't worry.'

'I'm not worried,' he said. 'I'm sad to be saying goodbye to this place, and sad that I'll be seeing so much less of you. If there was any way… Well. It is what it is. I'd better get back downstairs. Got some hungry diners due to arrive any time now. You'll be okay? You're sure?'

'I'm sure,' I said.

He nodded and left the room, and I sank back in the sofa and blinked away the tears. Now what?

I'd hardly had time to process it when I heard footsteps running up the stairs and Derry entered the living room.

'Well?'

'A boy!' Derry beamed at me. 'A bouncing baby boy. Eight pounds two ounces.'

I clapped my hands in delight. 'And Fuchsia?'

'She's absolutely fine. A bit shell-shocked I think but doing well.'

'Oh, thank goodness.' I breathed a sigh of relief. 'I was so worried, after her fall.'

'We all were. Sophie and Rose were frantic. You should have heard them in the waiting room,' Derry said, grinning.

'Were they arguing a lot?' I asked.

'Arguing?' He burst out laughing. 'Honestly, Mum, you'd never have believed it. They were like best mates in there. It's funny, they seemed to draw comfort from each other, more than they did from either Flynn or Archie. Me and Tally couldn't believe it.'

'And did they see the baby?' I asked, smiling.

'They did. They said he's absolutely gorgeous, with dark hair and big blue eyes, and both agreed he's the most beautiful baby that was ever born.'

I closed my eyes for a moment at the sheer wonder of it all. The universe never ceased to amaze me.

'That's wonderful,' I said at last.

Derry sat down next to me. 'And now, may we have that talk?'

I felt cold suddenly, the sense of wonder seeping away as I realised the time was upon us. Derry was about to bid me farewell, as Jack had moments earlier.

'Go on,' I said. 'I'm ready. You're moving on, aren't you?'

'Mum,' he said. 'There's something I have to tell you, and I wish I didn't. I've put it off for so long, and I've dreaded this day, but Tally says it's the only thing to do and I know she's right. But I'm sorry, Mum.' He took my hands in his and gazed steadily into my eyes. 'This is going to hurt.'

31

By the time Derry had finished I was in shock.

'Will you be okay, Mum?' he asked. 'I know it's a lot to take in but—'

'How could he do that to you?' I murmured. 'The cruelty of it! Why didn't you tell me sooner? Oh, Derry, I'm so sorry you got caught up in all this.'

Derry shook his head. 'It was my own doing,' he insisted. 'You warned me, and I took no notice. You can't blame yourself for this, Mum. I knew you would, that's part of the reason why I didn't tell you.'

'Only part?' I buried my head in my hands, agonising over everything Derry must have been through. 'What other reason could there be?'

'Do you have to ask?' Derry's voice was thick with emotion, and I raised my head, staring at him through blurry eyes.

'I know what it's like to find out something about your parentage, remember?' he said. 'I wouldn't wish that on you. Not for anything.'

'My father and I were hardly close,' I protested. 'Finding out he isn't my real father is nothing but a relief.'

'But is it? All your life, you've known who you are. Rhiannon Bone. Except you're not Rhiannon Bone, because that man is no relation to you. And I know how that feels. When you think you're someone, but then your world gets tipped upside down, and suddenly everything you thought you knew about yourself is in doubt. I didn't want to put you through that. And then there was your mum to think about.'

'My mother?'

'She wasn't who you thought she was either. All these years you've drummed into me that your mother was a saint to put up with her husband, who was loyal and faithful and a paragon of virtue. Well, clearly, she wasn't. She had an affair with someone, got pregnant with you, and tried to pass that child off to her husband. She stayed with him, even though he was horrible to you, and she knew why. And she kept it all from you, never said a word about your real father. For her to do all that, and then have the hypocrisy to turn her back on you when you got pregnant with me! How could I break that to you, knowing how you felt about her?'

'Why now?' I asked him. 'You've known all this time. Why are you telling me now?'

'I wanted to tell you as soon as I found out,' he admitted. 'That was some day. But since Tally and I made up, she's made me see I can't keep this from you. It's not fair.'

I leaned back in my chair, totally dazed. 'I can't take it all in,' I admitted.

'I'm going to leave you now, let it sink in,' Derry said. 'I'll see if they need a hand downstairs. Will you be all right, really?'

'I'll be fine, Derry. I just need to think it through,' I said.

He kissed me and went downstairs, and I sat, gazing into the middle distance, thoughts and memories jumbled in my mind as I processed what he'd told me. The fact that Stanley Peter Bone wasn't my father didn't distress me in the slightest. In fact, it came as a huge relief. To know that none of his blood flowed in my veins freed me. In a strange way, it was as if everything I'd always hoped for, and secretly believed had come true. No, that didn't sadden me at all. It was everything around it that occupied my mind. All those unanswered questions, all the confusion, the guilt, the grief…

It was around half an hour later when I heard footsteps on the stairs and turned, expecting to see Derry had returned to check on me. I gave a weary smile upon seeing Jack. Judging by his face, Derry had filled him in on at least some of it, so I wasn't surprised he'd come to make sure I was okay.

'Derry says you've had a bit of a shock, my darling,' he said, sitting opposite me. 'I came up as soon as I could. How are you feeling?'

'I don't know what to feel,' I admitted. Then I ground out, 'Furious! That's how I'm feeling. More than anything, I'm furious. Do you know what he did to Derry? That — that creature?'

'I don't know anything much,' he said. 'Derry said he had to tell you something shocking about his time in Cornwall, that's all. I suppose he thought it was up to you to tell me if you wanted me to know. Do you want me to know?'

'Of course I do,' I said. 'I tell you everything. But I warn you, Jack, it's horrible.'

'I'm sure I can cope,' he said. 'Go on.'

'Remember Derry told me that he and my father had argued because Derry had told him he didn't want the estate? Well, he wasn't being honest with me. Oh!'

I shuddered, feeling a depth of anger that was unfamiliar to me, even when it came to my so-called father.

'That man! He was clever, Jack. Really clever. He was careful not to criticise me or condemn me in any way. He made Derry believe that our feud was all in my head, that I'd been the one to treat him badly. Derry was all too willing to believe it, especially when it came to my short affair with Paul. He was told that my mother had begged me to stay and let them help me care for the baby, but I'd refused her help. Can you imagine? And Derry believed that because, well, why wouldn't he? He already thought the whole episode disgusting, and hated the fact that Paul was his father, so he lapped all those lies up.'

'Well, I suppose that's understandable, yes.' Jack sighed. 'Derry never stood a chance, did he? A lamb to the slaughter.'

'Exactly,' I said bitterly. 'That man used Derry to spite me. He knew Derry meant everything to me, and he knew that keeping him away from me was the surest way to hurt me. I mean,' I said, wiping away tears, 'I understand that. I do, really. But to use Derry and hurt him, humiliate him! It's barbaric.'

'What happened?'

'As we know, he started training Derry to run the estate. He had him working there, basically as unpaid labour, learning all the ins and outs of running the house and grounds, managing the staff, the finances, everything. Derry worked seven days a week from what I can gather, and that man assured him it was necessary, because one day the whole thing would be his, and he needed to understand what went on, what was involved.'

'So when did Derry decide it wasn't for him?' Jack asked.

'That's just it! It was all a lie,' I said. 'The worst of it is, he allowed Tally to visit Derry. He positively encouraged Derry to invite her over, show her around, let her see his future.'

'Tally went there? But I don't understand. What was a lie?'

'Not long after Tally went home, nicely convinced that she and Derry would one day be running the estate together, that pig of a man introduced Derry to my cousin, Crispin, and announced that Crispin would be inheriting the entire estate when the time came. Derry was totally confused and bewildered by the whole thing and, naturally, he wanted to know what was going on. Which was when my father revealed that he wasn't my father at all, that Derry was no relation to him, and that he had no intention of leaving either Derry or me a penny in his will, and never had any intention of doing so.'

Jack looked as sickened as I felt. 'The poor boy,' he murmured. 'Even I never thought that man could be so cruel.'

'A year ago,' I muttered. 'For a whole year Derry's had to live with that humiliation. It kept him from coming home, and it cost him his relationship with Tally, too.'

Jack looked devastated. 'He could have come home! Didn't he realise we'd have welcomed him back, understood?'

'He thought he'd pushed it too far. I think, deep down, he thought he deserved everything he got. And he was worried about telling me. He didn't want to upset me — about my mother more than my father.'

'Your mother?'

407

'Yes, because she wasn't the saint I thought she was.' I twisted my hair between my fingers, remembering how many times I'd cried over my mother, worried about her, grieved for her. 'All that time,' I murmured, 'and it seems she never really cared about me at all.'

'I don't know what to say,' Jack said. 'I'm so sorry, Rhiannon.'

'It is what it is,' I replied, not wanting him to worry. 'I'll be okay. And I can't say I'm sorry he's not my father. It's the best news I've ever had.'

'Did — did Derry say if he knew who your father was?'

I let go of my hair as it occurred to me that I hadn't even thought about him.

'I never asked,' I said. 'But I shouldn't think Derry knows. If he did, he'd have told me. No, I think, if my so-called father does know, he'll go to his grave taking that little secret with him.' I gave a short laugh. 'No doubt he thinks that will be his final revenge. Leaving me to wonder for the rest of my days.'

Jack cleared his throat. 'But you have one advantage that Stanley Bone knows nothing about,' he said.

I lifted an eyebrow in surprise. 'Do I? What would that be?'

He was silent for what felt like forever, then he said, 'Me.'

We stared at each other, and it felt as if my stomach had suddenly hitched a ride on a fairground waltzer. 'You?'

'I've wanted to tell you so many times,' he said quietly. 'I just never knew how.'

'Jack.' I shook my head, as if trying to clear away the confusion. 'What are you saying?'

'I'm trying to tell you, my darling, that it's me. I'm your father. Your real father.'

I couldn't think straight. How was that even possible? Jack didn't know my mother! How could he?

'Are you all right?'

'Do I look all right?' I said faintly. 'I don't follow this. How can you be my father?'

'It's a long story,' he said.

'Well, I've got nowhere else to be, and nothing more important to do. Have you?'

He eyed me steadily. 'There's nowhere more important than here, and nothing more important than you. There never has been. You must believe that.'

I was shaking and couldn't seem to stop. None of this made sense.

'Rhiannon,' he said, and I heard the plea in his voice and met his gaze. I saw the fear in his eyes and something inside me crumbled.

'Please,' he said. 'Don't hate me. Let me explain.'

'I could never hate you, Jack,' I said. 'I love you. That will never change.'

Before I even stopped to think about it, I was in his arms, and he held me tightly as we both cried. It's odd, but even given the confusion and the upheaval, all I could think was, *my father loves me*. It was a strange feeling, but it gave me strength, and filled me with joy. Whatever Jack was about to tell me, nothing would alter how I felt about him, other than to deepen my love for him.

'I'm so sorry,' he murmured at last.

'You have nothing to be sorry for,' I said, already sure of it. 'You came here when I needed you most, and you stayed with me, asking nothing from me. I would have been lost without you. So would Derry. Please, don't ever apologise. It's me who owes you everything.'

He shook his head. 'I should have been honest, but I promised her — your mother. And I knew how much you idolised her. I didn't want you to know the truth. You already felt neglected by one parent, I didn't want you to see…'

'That my mother wasn't interested either?' I asked. 'Tell me, Jack. I want to know everything. Unless — unless it hurts you too much.'

He let out a strangled sob. 'Only you could worry about *me* being hurt! Rhiannon, this is about *you*. This is your time. You've been kept in the dark too long. It was a long time ago for me and can't hurt me now, but I would never want to upset you. Are you sure you want to know?'

'I want to know it all,' I said. 'Please don't hold anything back. It's time.'

He nodded. 'Very well, my darling. I owe you that much. You remember I told you that most of my family disowned me when I decided to be a chef?'

I nodded. 'And that was true?'

'Oh yes, every word. My family thought it was a joke. To them, chefs, cooks, they were servants. I was letting them down, and they wanted nothing to do with me. My sister was more forgiving. She wasn't happy about it, but she still spoke to me, and tried to help me. It was through her that I met your mother. They were friends, you see. Had been for years, ever since they were at boarding school together. Your parents — sorry, I don't know what else to call them yet — were giving a big party to celebrate their fifth anniversary, and were looking for high class caterers, and my sister suggested me.'

'So that's how you met?' I asked. 'You were working for them?'

'Strictly speaking, we'd met a few times prior to that over the years,' he admitted, 'but we'd never had much to do with one another. But this time, it was different. Esme and I — we worked together on the menu, and there was a spark. A real spark. I fell for her, I admit it. And it seemed quite clear to me that she felt the same.'

He hung his head, clearly embarrassed. 'Well, one thing led to another. I'm sure I don't have to draw you a picture.'

'And I was the result.'

'Yes, you were.'

'But why didn't she leave her husband?' I said, puzzled. 'Was it because of the scandal? Because she was afraid of him? She must have had her own money, surely? I know her family weren't as wealthy as he was, but they were wealthy enough. Or was it because she wasn't sure whose baby it was?'

Jack rubbed his face, looking as if he wished he were anywhere but here right now.

'None of those things,' he said at last. 'She didn't leave Stanley Bone because she loved him. And the simple truth was, she didn't love me.'

I hadn't expected that. 'I don't understand. If that were the case, why did she have an affair with you?'

'Because she wanted a baby. Desperately. And her husband was, it transpired, unable to father one.'

'So he knew from the beginning I wasn't his?' I gasped. As the implications sank in, I gripped his hand. 'She used you?'

'She did,' he said sadly. 'Once her pregnancy was confirmed, she told me in no uncertain terms that I meant nothing to her, and I'd simply been a means to an end.'

My mother had treated him like that! I could barely believe it, yet I had no reason to doubt Jack. The sad truth was, if it came to a choice about who to trust, he would be top of my list every time.

'She was more like him than I realised,' I said sadly. 'Willing to use people to get what she wanted, no matter how much it hurt them.'

'I'm sorry,' he said. 'I never wanted you to think badly of her, but with Derry already telling you something to make you doubt her, and with you wanting the whole unvarnished truth…'

'I do,' I said. 'And I understand. I'm just sorry you got caught up in all this.'

'I'm not.' He smiled and ruffled my hair as I sat at his feet, staring up at him. 'If I hadn't, you wouldn't be here, would you? And the world needs you, Rhiannon Bone.'

'I'm not Rhiannon Bone,' I said defiantly. 'I'm Rhiannon Penhaligon if anything.'

'Don't set me off again,' he said, wiping his eyes.

'But Jack,' I said, 'how did she hope to get away with it? If her husband couldn't have children, how did she think she could keep him? What was she planning to do? Declare a medical miracle?'

'I don't think she planned anything,' Jack said. 'Her only thought was having a baby. When I found out she was pregnant, I wanted to take care of her, and of you. But she was having none of it. She told me she loved Stanley, and he loved her, and that she'd done it as much for him as for herself.'

'But he never wanted me!' I gasped. 'She can't have believed he'd welcome another man's child?'

'The funny thing is, at first he seemed to. When he found out, he was furious. She didn't hesitate to tell him who the father was, and I got a punch in the face — well, I got several.'

'Oh, Jack, you didn't!'

'No more than I deserved, and certainly no more than I expected. I had slept with his wife, after all. I hardly expected him to shake my hand. I honestly thought he'd kick her out, and I refused to leave, certain she'd need me, despite her assurances that I meant nothing to her. But strangely, he never spoke of ending their marriage.

'The thing I came to realise was that, as odd as it seemed from the outside, their relationship worked. Yes, it had been about her family name and his wealth to start with, but they understood each other, and they loved each other. She persuaded him that they needed a baby to inherit the estate, and that it was no different to adopting a child. I came from a good family, and with her genes and mine, I think she thought it would be more sensible than adopting a baby who could come from any background.

'I know that sounds shocking, my darling, but I've had a long time to think about this and to try to work out what was going on. I don't think he was ever thrilled about it, but I think he accepted it, and I do know he'd wanted a son for a long time.'

'But instead he got me,' I said wryly.

'Indeed. And instead of thanking God and realising how lucky he was, he rejected you outright and treated you like dirt,' he said sadly.

'It can't just have been because I was a girl,' I said.

'No, I think the truth was when you finally arrived, it all became frighteningly real. I think he was faced with the product of his wife's betrayal and couldn't accept it. He was trapped, because he loved her and wanted to stay married to her, but I think he'd have given anything not to have you around.'

'And where were you?' I asked tentatively. 'When I was born, were you in the area?'

He shook his head. 'I was working in London. He made it clear I wasn't welcome, and if I stayed in Cornwall I'd never work again. I would have stayed anyway and taken my chances, but your mother...' He sighed. 'She didn't want me around. She told me the baby was nothing to do with me, and as far as she was concerned, I'd served my purpose, and she never wanted to see me again.'

'I'm so sorry, Jack,' I said.

'I'm sorry for both of us,' he admitted. 'I could have been a comfort to you, but I couldn't get near.'

'But your sister,' I said, remembering. 'She was my mother's friend, wasn't she? Couldn't she have helped?'

'She knew nothing about it back then,' he told me. 'Your father was adamant I kept it to myself and said if I spoke to anyone I'd be sorry, and that included my sister. I had an awful feeling my sister would back them, rather than me, so I kept my mouth shut.'

'All those years,' I said. 'I knew I didn't belong. I never fitted in with them, not at all. My mother was kind to me, affectionate really, in comparison to him, but she kept all that from me.'

I realised suddenly that my face was wet with tears. 'She used you to get pregnant with me, but when I went to *her*, when I told her *I* was expecting a baby, she didn't want to know! The man I thought was my father ranted and raved at me, called me the most vile and disgusting names, and she sat there and let him! She said nothing to defend me, and when he told me to leave their house, she didn't try to protect me. She just let me go. I never heard a word from her after that. I wrote to her, Jack! I wrote to her and told her about Derry, and she didn't even reply. How could she do that after the way she'd behaved?'

He put his arms around me. 'I know, my darling, I know. I'm so sorry.'

'How did you know where I was?' I asked, confused. 'You knew I was at The Hare and Moon. How?'

'Your mother confided in my sister that you'd got pregnant to Sir Paul Boden-Kean at Kearton Hall, and that she didn't know what had happened to you once you left Cornwall, because of course, Sir Paul was a married man and probably wouldn't take care of you. My sister agreed to make enquiries, find out where

413

you were. She knew someone who knew Lady Boden-Kean at the time — Elisabeth. She let your mother know you were all right. So I think, deep down, your mother must have cared about you and about what happened to you, or why would she ask my sister to find out?'

'But why did your sister tell *you* where I was? She didn't know I was anything to do with you, did she?'

He looked at me with obvious reluctance.

'Go on,' I urged. 'I need to know.'

'When she found out where you were, your mother was — er — disappointed. She decided you were taking after me in being irresponsible and rebellious, with no sense of family loyalty or duty. She felt we were far too alike, with you running a pub, and me turning my back on my family to be a cook. She was clearly so irate she couldn't keep her secret any longer from her friend and blurted it out to her.'

I closed my eyes in despair. 'And that's when your sister turned her back on you,' I said heavily.

'Sadly, yes. Until that point, she was the only person in my family who still spoke to me, but once Esme had revealed the truth about you and me… Well, she was furious. She said she'd given me the benefit of a doubt all these years, had defied the family to stay in touch with me, and all the time I'd been hiding my dirty little secret. I don't know exactly what version of the truth Esme told her, but it was me she cut off, not her friend. It was the end for us. I never saw her again.'

'Oh, Jack. This is awful. So much loss and pain!'

He cupped my face in his hands and stared into my eyes with a fierce expression. '*Their* loss!' he said. 'You were worth every moment of these last fifty years. I wouldn't change a second of it.'

'But you gave up everything to come here, to work in some insignificant pub!'

'To work with *you*. To be near you. To get to know you, and my grandson. I've been grateful every single day that I got the chance to be with you both. As soon as she told me where you were, nothing else mattered, and I've not regretted a minute of it. How

414

lucky am I that I got to be with my daughter every day of my life?'

'But I never knew you were my father,' I said sadly. 'All that time wasted!'

'How was it wasted? We built a relationship from scratch, and it's flourished. You know I love you; I know you love me. We never needed labels to make that real, did we?'

I smiled through my tears. 'No, Jack. We never did.'

'And now you know,' he said. 'Will it change how you feel about me?'

'Only that I love you even more,' I assured him. 'Because you're the bravest, most loyal, unselfish man I've ever met. I'm blessed to have you in my life, and I'm honoured to call you my father.'

There was nothing else that needed saying. As we hugged each other and cried all over again, words no longer seemed to matter.

32

Harry pushed away the plate bearing the remnants of his meal and wondered why he'd bothered to cook anything. He'd known, even as he switched the oven on, that he wasn't hungry. It was more a habit than anything. He wondered idly how many other people automatically started chopping and peeling and cooking just because the clock told them to, rather than their stomachs. What a strange world it was.

He walked over to the French doors, gazing out over what was undeniably a much-improved garden. Lewis had done a good job. The lawn looked huge now and he wondered what he was going to do with it.

'How about a seating area for your guests?' Lewis had suggested. 'A patio perhaps? Or a decked area. And perhaps a gazebo would be good, and a barbecue.'

He'd gone on and on, but Harry had barely listened. It all seemed a bit dull to him. Besides, it was his bloody garden. He didn't want to think about sharing it with a bunch of guests. It was for him and his children, no one else.

Except of course, it wasn't. No matter how much he tried to push away the inevitable, he was going to have to open the house up to paying guests. There was no way round it. His bank account was almost empty, and he had no other source of income. Besides, he'd spent all that money making Eight Bells the sort of place anyone would be happy to stay in. He could hardly let all that go to waste.

There were only two things he'd been clear on.

'I want a herb garden,' he'd told Lewis. 'And a wildflower patch. For the bees and butterflies.'

Lewis had looked astounded, as if it were the last thing he'd expected Harry to say but had quickly recovered his composure and agreed that both things would add a certain something to the garden.

He scowled as his phone rang yet again. He didn't even bother to look at it. It had been ringing from the moment he'd switched it back on, after leaving the wedding vows ceremony at Kearton Hall.

He'd taken two calls from journalists, eager to tell his side of the story. They'd been terribly polite at first, enquiring after his health and saying how shocked they'd been to hear of his illness, but they'd soon shown their true colours all right.

They wanted a revenge piece on Melody. Wanted to stir up trouble, launch a transatlantic slanging match between the two of them. Well, they could whistle for it. He didn't have the energy.

Besides, how would that look to Rufus? One day he'd be old enough to understand, and he might read all the stuff that was being written right now. Bad enough that he'd know how his parents had got together in the first place, but Harry was damned if he was going to let his son read a whole stack of articles featuring his mother and father dishing the dirt on each other. It stopped here and now. He wasn't going to let the journalists play this game.

He should never have turned his phone back on. It was another habit, like cooking because the clock said to. No one of any note ever rang him anyway. Rufus, Amy, and Rhiannon were the only people he wanted to talk to, and Amy, despite her assurances that she would use the iPhone to keep in touch with him, rarely bothered to call him. She sent him the odd photo or gif, but that was it. Rufus had probably forgotten all about him, and as for Rhiannon…

Harry scraped the remnants of his meal into the bin and put the plate and cutlery in the dishwasher.

Maybe he'd have an early night. It had been an endless day, what with the visit from Eliza and the shock of seeing that magazine interview, then the events at Kearton Hall. You'd never think he'd only got up at lunchtime. He felt as if he'd been awake for days.

He leaned on the worktop, gazing out of the kitchen window. The wedding vows renewal ceremony may not have taken place after all, but the event had certainly been extraordinary, just the same.

He remembered how he'd felt, arriving outside the building, feeling sick with nerves as he wondered how many of the waiting guests had read the interview. He'd been touched that Eliza had offered to take him and delighted that they were picking Amy up on the way. It felt as if he had his own little shield to protect him. Amy was thrilled to see him and did quite a few twirls in her flower girl dress, making sure she was the star of the show.

Harry had done his best to ensure he praised her little sister, Hannah, who, he had to admit, looked cute in her dress, as much as he had Amy, and he'd offered encouragement to Hannah's twin, Michael, who was clearly reluctant to be page boy and uncomfortable wearing the outfit Sophie had chosen for him.

Amy had chattered nonstop on the way to the Hall, so he hadn't had much time to dwell on what lay ahead, but stepping out of that car, to be greeted by Gabriel Bailey, of all people, along with Joe and Charlie, had been a test of nerve. Yet they'd all been so kind and welcoming. Yes, even Gabriel, who'd spoken to him as if they were old friends. Harry had initially felt resentment. He didn't need pity! It was the one thing he'd dreaded.

But then Gabriel had murmured to him, 'I think it's time all this animosity ended, don't you? It seems to me you have enough to deal with, and all I want is a quiet life. Amy needs us both, and we both want what's best for her. What do you say to a clean slate?'

Harry had been about to make a sarcastic retort, but then something had stopped him. He'd had a sudden realisation that, actually, that's all he wanted, too. A clean slate. A fresh start. He'd had enough drama to last him a lifetime. Gabriel was offering him a way forward, a path of peace. He'd be a fool not to take it.

So instead of making a sarcastic comment, he'd nodded and said, 'I'd like that very much. Thank you.'

Then Joe had said to him, 'If you ever want to talk, you know where I am. I know how it feels, what you've been through, so you'd be welcome to come to Whisperwood any time you like if you need to chat.' He'd hesitated, then added with a grin, 'And I promise not to set the dog on you.'

Harry had been so stunned he'd hardly known what to say, but then he'd remembered what both Eliza and Rhiannon had told him.

'Joe,' he said, 'I want to say thank you.'

'Thank you?' Joe and Charlie had exchanged surprised glances. 'What for?'

'For taking care of Eliza and Amy when I failed them,' he said honestly. 'For always being there for them, and for doing such a bloody good job of raising Eliza in the first place. You're one hell of a bloke, and you put me to shame. If I ever become half as good as a father to my kids as you were to Eliza, well, I'll be over the moon.'

Joe had blinked, clearly astounded. He'd glanced at Eliza, who'd given him a warm smile and said, 'Well said, Harry. I totally agree.'

There was a moment when Harry wasn't sure what was going to happen and was rather regretting his show of weakness. Then Joe held out his hand.

'Let's start over, shall we?' he said. 'Welcome to Kearton Bay, Harry.'

Harry shook Joe's hand, but found, to his embarrassment, that he couldn't speak, due to the huge lump in his throat. Luckily for everyone, Amy filled the silence by demanding that everyone look at her and admire her dress, which everyone gladly did.

So it had been an eventful day all round. When he'd realised Rhiannon was holding the magazine, and that she'd either read the interview or was about to, he'd fled the Hall, not wanting to see how she reacted.

Gabriel had followed him and had urged him to go back inside and talk to her, but Harry decided he'd done enough for one day, so Gabriel had kindly driven him home and had generously not said a word about anything too personal, expressing only his anxiety for Fuchsia and the baby. Harry had been appreciative of his thoughtfulness.

Rhiannon had probably been glad he left anyway, he thought. She would need some time to think about how she was going to let him down gently. Not that she needed to end their relationship. He'd done a rather good job of that himself. She owed him nothing and was no doubt glad he'd done her such a big favour.

'Do you never answer your phone?'

Harry nearly had another heart attack as the voice came from a few feet away. He spun round, shocked to find Rhiannon standing in his kitchen, of all people.

'I did knock,' she said, 'but no one answered, so I thought I'd try the back way.' She gazed out of the window. 'The garden looks amazing,' she said. 'Very tidy. What you need now is colour, lots of colour, and scent of course. You need to attract the bees and the butterflies, so you need to plant bushes and flowers they'll be drawn to. Have you given any more thought to that herb garden I suggested?'

Harry swallowed. 'What are you doing here?'

'I needed to talk to you,' she said simply. 'You didn't answer your phone and it was obvious you weren't going to turn up at The Hare and Moon any time soon, so I came here. What else was I supposed to do?'

He groaned inwardly. 'I don't want to talk about it, Rhiannon. You needn't worry about it. I get it, okay? Just don't — don't look at me the way everyone else does. I couldn't bear it.'

She frowned. 'What way would that be?'

'With pity,' he said. 'I don't need it. I don't need anyone's sympathy.'

'Why would I pity you?'

'Don't pretend you don't feel it. You read the article.'

'No,' she said. 'I didn't.'

Harry groped for the worktop and some support. 'You didn't? But I saw you holding the magazine.'

'Yes. Meggie gave it to me. I chose not to read it.'

'Why?'

'Because I decided if you wanted me to know what was in it, you'd tell me yourself.'

Harry's mouth opened and closed again. She was extraordinary. He couldn't believe she'd done that, and yet he knew she was telling the truth. He had to admit, if the situation had been reversed, he'd never have been so noble.

'Right,' he said, 'so is that why you're here? To ask me what was in it?'

She shook her head. 'May I sit down?'

'Of course. Sorry.' He pulled out a chair for her. 'Would you like a drink?'

'No thanks. I'm awash with tea,' she admitted. 'It's funny, isn't it? Whenever there's a crisis, we put the kettle on. I must have drunk gallons of the stuff today.'

'What crisis?' For the first time he noticed how pale she was, and how red her eyes were. She'd been crying. 'Rhiannon, what is it? What's happened?'

To his horror, she buried her face in her hands.

'Rhiannon?'

'I'm sorry to bother you,' she sobbed, 'and I know you wanted to be left alone, but, Harry, I need you!'

She needed him? Harry felt a sudden surge of love for her that overwhelmed him. His own problems were forgotten. All he could think was that she was here, she was hurt, she was desperate, and *she needed him*.

He put his arms around her and held her as she cried, saying nothing as he stroked her hair and let her sob until she apparently had no tears left.

At last, she shook her head and pulled away from him slightly, wiping her eyes.

'It's silly,' she said. 'Nothing's wrong as such. It's been such a strange day, and I didn't know what to think or do with all this new information, and — oh, Harry, you won't believe what I found out.'

'Tell me,' he said gently, pulling a chair close to hers and sitting down, never letting go of her hand. 'I'm listening.'

He sat there, saying nothing but thinking plenty, as she poured out what had happened to her that day. He could hardly take it all in.

'Fuck me,' he breathed at last. 'I thought I was a bad father, but that bastard takes the cake.'

'But he's not a father,' she reminded him.

'Always a silver lining,' he said. 'And Jack! I mean, you love Jack already. He's a good bloke and he's looked after you all this time. I call that a result really.'

To his relief, she burst out laughing.

'Sorry,' he said. 'I never say the right thing on these serious occasions.'

'Oh, but you did,' she assured him. 'You put it all in perspective somehow. It *is* a result. I have a father I love, and Derry has a grandfather he's always loved and looked up to. I'm not unhappy about it. It's all a bit overwhelming. For all these years I've thought my father hated me, when in fact, my real father has loved and cared for me all along. He's been right by my side, and I never knew. I — I'm a bit shocked I suppose.'

'Well, no one can blame you for that,' he said. 'I can't believe the way that man treated Derry, too. Leading him on like that. No wonder Derry pushed Tally away. I can't blame him at all. I'd have done the same thing.' He paused, suddenly ashamed. 'I *have* done the same thing.'

Rhiannon raised her head and peered at him. 'You have?'

He ran a hand through his hair, feeling awkward. 'Bloody hell, yes. I've just realised. What Derry did to Tally I did the same to you. He didn't want sympathy. He didn't want to see that look in her eyes. He didn't want her to have to settle for second best after he'd promised her the world. That's me, Rhiannon. That's exactly me.'

'I don't understand.'

'That's because you haven't read the article.' Harry took a deep breath. His turn to explain.

And just as he had moments before, Rhiannon sat in silence, listening intently as he poured out the truth to her. How his career in America had crashed, how Melody's had soared, how she'd paid for the house in Malibu while he'd been reduced to staying at home, taking care of their son.

Slowly, falteringly, he told her about the heart attack, and the long road to recovery that had been made so much more painful by the realisation that Melody had no time for him any longer but had found new love with baseball star Chuck.

'I felt as if I had nothing left,' he admitted. 'Rufus was besotted with Melody's toy boy, and I felt so unwanted. I was hurt, and I couldn't stop thinking about how badly I'd treated Eliza and Amy and thinking this was karma and I deserved it all. That's when I knew I had to come back to England, to try to make it right with them, and to rebuild my relationship with my little girl. I'm sorry, Rhiannon. You must be so disappointed.'

Rhiannon looked dazed. 'Why on earth would I be disappointed? You went through all that alone, Harry, and at the end, rather than stay there and wallow, you came back here and fought for what you believed was right. You put yourself in the path of all that anger and bitterness to make amends to Amy. How can I be anything but proud of you?'

'But I've got nothing to offer you,' he explained, anxious that she understood the full extent of his situation. 'My television career is dead in the water, I'm a laughing stock with anyone who's read that bloody interview, I've got no money, and I'm about to go into business running a bed and breakfast of all things. It's hardly an attractive prospect, is it?'

Rhiannon smiled. 'You really don't want to run a bed and breakfast, do you?'

He pulled a face. 'That obvious?'

'Pretty much.' She leaned forward and kissed him. 'You do know I don't care about money, or a television career, or what anyone else says or thinks — least of all people like Melody Bird.'

'You deserve so much more,' he murmured.

'Harry, all I want is you,' she told him, and he saw in her eyes she meant every word and knew he had to tell her the rest.

'I don't think I can be what you need,' he admitted. 'I haven't — I mean, since the heart attack, I haven't had a physical relationship. I'm not sure I can.'

'Did the doctors say anything about that?' she asked him gently.

'Only that I should be okay to resume normal relations after around six weeks,' he confessed. 'Bit tricky when you know your wife's at it with a baseball player. And it never took off if you know what I mean. I just…couldn't. I was afraid. I still am.'

'That's quite understandable,' she said.

'But I know you,' he told her, cradling her face in his hands. 'You're a woman of passion, you're so full of life. And sex has always been so important to you.'

'Harry,' she said, her eyes glistening with tears, 'I don't care about any of that. I don't want an Olympic athlete in bed. I want a gentle man, who loves me, and who wants to make love with me. And I know that's you. And I know it will happen. And I know it will be perfect.'

He wanted to believe it, so badly. And she was right. He did love her, and he did want to make love to her. It wasn't just about sex. It was about so much more than that. He wanted to be with her, he wanted her to live with him. He wanted them to have a future together, more than anything.

'But what if—' he began.

Rhiannon kissed him gently and smiled at him. 'Trust me,' she said. 'I am a witch after all.'

33

Derry could hardly take it in. His face told me he was shocked and stunned by my proposal, but I was quite certain about my offer.

'Mum,' he gasped, 'you can't do that! Seriously, it's too much.'

'Not at all,' I said. 'I've thought about this long and hard, and it's what I want. It's what I want more than anything.'

'But — but The Hare and Moon is your life!'

'The Hare and Moon is part of my life,' I corrected him. 'A big part of it, and a part that I've loved and cherished. But it's time to move on. I have other things I want to do with my life now. I've known for a long time that my days here were coming to an end. I suppose I was afraid to take that final step. And the truth is, I didn't want to say goodbye to it. I didn't want to hand it over to strangers. But now I know you're staying here in Kearton Bay, it's clear to me that this is what I'm meant to do. This is your home, Derry. I can't think of anyone who deserves this more.'

Tally squeezed his hand, clearly excited. 'It's brilliant news! You've always loved this place, and you enjoy working here. You'll make a great landlord.'

I smiled, seeing how thrilled she was. I knew how much Tally loved The Hare and Moon, and I was quite certain that, one day, it would be her own beloved home, too. And nothing would make me happier.

'Jack,' Derry said, clearly dazed, 'what do you say to all this?'

'I think it's a great idea,' Jack said. 'Think about it. With me gone, and your mum off to pastures new, this pub will get a new lease of life. Aidan's a good chef, and I'm sure he and Kerry will continue to make sure this place runs like clockwork, and with you in charge and, no doubt, Tally helping too, it will be fresh and new. You'll probably have ideas of your own, and that's what a good pub needs. Fresh blood now and then. I have every faith that you can do this.'

'Maybe the lads would like to play here one night a week?' Derry mused. 'We could reform. Do you think live music would work here?'

'I don't see why not,' I said smiling.

'You could learn sea shanties,' Jack suggested. 'That'd go down a treat with the tourists.'

'You're right,' Derry said eagerly. 'We already do a couple — I mean, we *did* a couple. We could expand our repertoire. Play to our strengths.'

His eyes were bright with excitement, and if I'd needed any confirmation that I was doing the right thing, his obvious enthusiasm was it.

'I should tell you, though,' I said, smiling, 'that the painting of the pub that Jack got me for Christmas is coming with me, wherever I end up. That way I'll always have The Hare and Moon with me, no matter what.'

'Wherever you end up? You're moving out, too?' Derry looked concerned. 'You don't have to do that, you know. You'll always be welcome, no matter what.'

'What are you going to do, Rhiannon?' Tally asked.

'I have plans,' I said. 'I need to think about how it would all work. Don't worry about me. I'm excited, too, and looking forward to this next phase in my life.'

'And you'll finally have time to do all the things you've wanted to do for so long,' Jack said, taking my hand. 'It's going to be amazing, Rhiannon. For all of us.'

'But there is one thing I have to make clear,' Derry said, suddenly serious. 'I can't accept The Hare and Moon as a gift, Mum. It's not right.'

426

I held up my hands in protest. 'I won't take a penny from you,' I said. 'I don't want you saddled with debt and a mortgage. Just take it, please. After all, it cost me nothing.'

Derry shook his head. 'But that's just it. Don't you see? The Hare and Moon was Sir Paul's gift to you. He didn't pay a penny towards my keep and he didn't lift a finger to help you when I was born. The only thing he ever did for you was hand you the keys to this place. You've earned it, Mum. You've earned every brick, every stone, every tile of this pub, and I'm not going to take it from you.'

'I want you to have it,' I pleaded.

'And I want it,' he said. 'But not like this. It's not right.'

'I don't want you to get into debt,' I repeated. 'It's no way to start a business, up to your neck in repayment demands.'

'I don't need a mortgage,' he said quietly. 'I can buy the pub outright. Cash.'

We all stared at him.

'Are you saying…' I hardly dare put it into words.

'Yeah. I think it's time I used the money Sir — my father — left me in his will, don't you? It's been sitting there, untouched for years. I can't think of a better way of spending it. Let me buy The Hare and Moon from you, fair and square, for the full market price. That way, we both get what we want.'

'Derry.' I covered my mouth with my hand, hardly able to believe he'd finally called Sir Paul his father, and that he was at last willing to move forward, acknowledging the existence of the inheritance he'd shunned for so long. But how could I take money from my own son?

Then I realised that the final piece of the jigsaw had slotted into place, and I closed my eyes for a moment, appreciating the gift that I'd suddenly been given.

'Thank you, Derry,' I murmured. 'I accept your proposal.'

There was a squeal of delight from Tally, and then we were all hugging each other and laughing and crying. It was the end of an era, but I had a feeling it was going to be the start of something amazing. For all of us.

427

****

'Car keys. Where are my fucking car keys?' Harry frantically patted his jacket pockets, then began lifting newspapers from the table, opening and shutting drawers, checking cupboards, even peering inside mugs, as if his keys would somehow appear magically.

Where had he last had them? He tried to remember, but it seemed like ages since he'd driven anywhere. The supermarket, he thought. Was that the last time? So that would have been over a week ago, and he'd have come in, carrying bags, no doubt in a foul mood because he still hated supermarkets, and he'd have thrown his keys… Where?

Exasperated, he stood in the centre of the room, looking around him with no clue where he'd put them. This was great. He was supposed to be picking Amy up to take her to Kearton Hall. She was going to have a riding lesson, and he'd promised to stay and watch. She was getting on well with Crackerjack, her pony, and couldn't wait to show him how well she was doing with him.

She also wanted him to call into Wychwood first, so she could show him how much Lyra had grown. She'd wanted to take the puppy with them to the Hall, but thankfully, Lyra had yet to have her second vaccination, so wasn't allowed out yet. He couldn't deny he was relieved. The thought of a puppy piddling — or worse — in his car was hardly a cheering one. He wouldn't get away with it much longer, as she'd be having her final injection in a few days, but he'd cross that bridge when he came to it.

Right now, all he cared about was finding his keys.

His phone rang, and he answered it without even checking who was calling, his mind still preoccupied with trying to remember his exact movements upon returning from the supermarket.

'Harry?'

Harry sank onto the chair and pulled a face. Bloody hell, that was all he needed. Martin! What the fuck did he want?'

'Martin. How are you, old chap?'

428

'Well, a lot healthier than you by the sounds of things.' Martin let out a burst of laughter, and Harry glared at the phone. Well, that was charming. Still, at least he wasn't oozing sympathy, which he had to admit would have been a lot harder to stomach.

'Nice one,' he said grudgingly. 'What can I do for you?'

'It's more like what I can do for you,' Martin told him mysteriously. 'So, I've read the interview with Melody.' He whistled. 'She's a real bitch, isn't she? You can't say I didn't warn you, Harry.'

'Yes, thanks for reminding me. Is there any point to this phone call, or are you just ringing to gloat?'

'Harry!' Martin sounded deeply offended. 'Would I do that? Now look, pal, we've had a meeting about this vacancy we've got on *Twice as Nice*, and the upshot is, we'd like you to consider coming back.'

Harry moved the phone from his ear and stared at the screen, as if he'd be able to see Martin chortling away with his colleagues, as they took bets on whether he'd be stupid enough to fall for it.

'Is this some sort of joke?' he demanded. 'Because if it is, it's not very funny.'

'No joke, Harry.' Martin's tone had changed, and Harry realised, with some shock, that he was serious. 'Feedback suggests that you've won our target audience over. Melody's scored a bit of an own goal I'm afraid. People see her as unsympathetic and cold. She's switched in their minds to being a heartless marriage-wrecker, and since she abandoned you in your hour of need to shag that American kid, they're seeing you as the victim now. We've heard from a whole coven of old bats who want to mother you.' He chuckled. 'You're flavour of the month, and we think you'd be good for ratings. And let's face it, you've not had a better offer, have you?'

When Harry didn't answer, Martin said suspiciously, '*Have* you?'

'No,' Harry said honestly. 'I haven't. But that doesn't mean I should jump at this one. I need time to think.'

'What is there to think about? Seriously, you'll be back in the black before you know it. A big pay increase since the last time you worked for us, and you can't deny the co-presenter's a lot more what you wanted. Remember how you kicked off when we hired Melody, because she knew nothing about property and was only there as eye candy? Well, we've struck gold with Fiona, and you can't deny it. Attractive woman, but she knows her stuff. She'll keep you on your toes, Harry. What do you say?'

'I don't know what to say.' Harry could barely believe it. It was all floating there before his eyes. The house in Chiswick, the new car, the magazine covers, the adoring fans, the awards ceremonies… everything he'd had and had thrown away for a fling with Melody. This was his chance to take it all back. To show the world that he wasn't finished yet. He could start again. Get his old life back.

His old life. He remembered the nights away from home — long nights without his wife and daughter when temptation had proved too much for him. He remembered the dinners and drinks with people who hadn't so much as called him since his fall from grace. He remembered how life had become something unrecognisable. How it had cost him his marriage. His child.

'I — I'm not sure,' he said.

Martin tutted. 'Are you for real? Harry, this is just the start. You do realise that? We have other shows going into production. You could be the face of the channel. I've heard mutterings, you know. Between you and me, they're looking for their own Philip Schofield, an Ant or Dec. You apparently have sex appeal. Can't see it myself, you understand, but to our target audience… You could end up on everything, God help us! Why are you even thinking about it? I get it. This is stage fright, isn't it? I understand. Look, come down to London. We'll have a chat. There's plenty to discuss, and we can show you what we have in mind. I promise you, once you've seen the possibilities you won't have any doubts at all.'

Harry gripped the phone. He wouldn't have to run a bed and breakfast after all. He'd be back doing property shows, which he enjoyed. He wouldn't have to throw everything away this time. Yes, he'd be away from home a bit, but he could still fit filming in around home life. He'd still see Rhiannon and Amy regularly, and this time he'd have something to offer them.

What was the alternative? Frying eggs and bacon every morning for a bunch of holidaymakers? Sitting in the living room, playing snakes and ladders with them on rainy days? Handing out leaflets telling them which tourist attractions were cheapest for a family of four, or where in North Yorkshire served the best cream tea? Jesus, was that what he wanted from his life?

He'd never wanted to run a bed and breakfast. That had all been Gareth's idea. Who could blame him for turning his back on it?

But... He wanted a home. He wanted Rhiannon. He wanted to spend every evening with her. He didn't want to have to call her from some hotel room. He knew she would trust him, and she'd be right to, because however many beautiful women he met, he knew they would be no temptation. No one could compare to her. He wasn't worried about throwing her away, it wasn't about that. He just wanted to be near her.

And he wanted to be there for Amy. He wanted to be able to drive her to the Hall to ride her pony, to moan about having her puppy in the car. Hell, he'd even eat the odd cheeseburger if it made her happy. No television career could compete with that.

He remembered the tarot reading Rhiannon had done for him. The Knight of Swords: *You may find that what you thought you wanted wasn't what you wanted at all.* Judgement: *Use the lessons you learned from your mistakes to make changes for the future.* The Devil: *You're on your way to finding who you really are, what you really want.*

Every moment is a chance to start again, Rhiannon had told him. He didn't want his old life. He wanted a brand new one. His chance to start again.

'I'm sorry. There'd be no point. I'm not interested,' he said.

Martin spluttered. 'Are you for real? Do you realise what you're turning down?'

'I do, Martin. But more than that, I realise what I've already got, and nothing, *nothing* can compete with that. Sorry.'

He ended the call and smiled to himself. He'd made the right choice, even if it did mean a lifetime of serving bacon and eggs and making sodding beds. All those doubts, all that festering disappointment, had suddenly vanished. He realised it had been at the back of his mind this whole time, spoiling things for him without him even realising it.

He supposed it was because he'd been craving a life he thought he could no longer have. Now he knew it was all possible again, he no longer wanted it. The longing had vanished. He knew where his heart lay, and he knew what mattered. It was over. Thank God for that phone call.

He jumped as the phone rang again. Rhiannon!

'Hello, Harry.'

He beamed as he heard her voice greeting him. 'Darling, it's so good to hear from you. I've missed you.'

She laughed. 'Since yesterday? I've missed you, too. Is there any chance we can meet up? I have a proposal for you.'

'So soon?' he joked. 'Well, maybe it's time someone made an honest man of me. Thing is, I'm about to go to Whisperwood to collect Amy. I'm driving her to the Hall for a riding lesson. She wants me to see her on her pony.'

'Would she mind if I tagged along?' Rhiannon asked. 'You could watch her riding while I catch up with Lexi and the children, and then perhaps you and I could have a chat. I really do have something important to put to you. I think you'll be interested.'

'I'm interested in anything you have to say,' he said, meaning it. 'Actually, I have something to tell you, too. You'll never believe what's just happened.'

'Ooh, intriguing. So you'll pick me up after you collect Amy?'

'Meet me at the top of Bay Street in fifteen minutes,' he said. 'I love you.'

'I love you, too, Harry.'

The call ended and Harry shoved his mobile back in his pocket, hardly able to wipe the smile off his face.

'Well, fuck me,' he said, staring in amazement at his car keys which lay, as they must have lain all the time, on the coffee table next to him. 'How the hell did I not see those?'

Anyone would think the universe had deliberately delayed him.

34

As the drumbeats grew louder and more insistent, the May Queen ran around the bonfire, her long, dark hair flying, as with one hand she held onto the crown of flowers she wore. I could see her radiant face and almost heard her giggles as she ran, accompanied by the claps and cheers from the crowd.

Behind her, the Green Man seemed to have decided he'd wasted enough time. His steady jog became a sudden sprint, and he grabbed the May Queen, pulling her to a halt.

I watched, delighted, as he lifted his mask a little and kissed her with a lingering passion.

Around them, the onlookers whistled and cheered, and the Green Man replaced his mask and took a bow.

Laughing, I stepped forward.

'Thank you so much to our Green Man and May Queen, who have, I'm sure you'll agree, thrown themselves into their roles. With their union, good harvests are guaranteed, and happy times are ahead for Kearton Bay.'

'You can say that again,' the Green Man said, his voice slightly muffled behind his mask. 'Can I take this off now please?'

'Of course,' I said. 'I think you've done your bit.'

Derry heaved a sigh of relief and removed his mask, then pulled his May Queen to him. Tally put her arms around him and hugged him, and I remembered the day, all those years ago, when Derry had first been the Green Man at our Beltane ceremony, and it was Lexi who had been chosen as his Queen. How much had happened since that day!

I glanced around me, taking in the scene in Gray's Field. Every year we held our Beltane ceremony here, and every year marked differences in local life. Nothing was the same from one sabbat to the next. Life didn't stand still, and each time I saw new alliances, new babies, new arrivals. Each year someone else was sadly missing, but that was all part of life. It was never static. Who knew what I'd find when I looked out over the crowd next Beltane? How many new faces would there be? Whose dear face would be missing?

'May we all please bow our heads and give thanks to the god and goddess?' I asked, as I did every year.

Most people duly obliged, and I bowed my own head, knowing I had such a lot to give thanks for. So many of us did, in fact. Our village had been blessed, and I hoped that those who had benefited from the gods' blessings realised that. Of course, many of the villagers didn't share my beliefs, and some of them had no faith in any higher power at all, but that was all right. They still took part, and I appreciated that very much, although I could imagine that newcomers to the village would find it all rather strange.

The year that Derry and Lexi had played the Green Man and May Queen, I recalled, was the year Eliza had arrived in the village. In fact, I believed it was the very same day. She hadn't known what to expect and had looked scared stiff as she watched us celebrating the sabbat. But then, she was already in a heightened state, having left Harry and arrived here in the village, looking for the father she'd never known.

She hadn't found him. Instead, she'd been reunited with the grandmother she'd had no idea existed. Hannah had taken her in and loved her, and Eliza had found a home at Whisperwood Farm. There, she'd rediscovered who she was, and she'd found true love at last.

As we all raised our heads and people resumed conversation, I looked for her and saw her standing arm in arm with Gabriel, surrounded by their children and grandchildren. My heart swelled with love for them.

Beside Eliza stood Lexi and Will, their faces a picture of contentment and fulfilment, their son and daughter in their arms. Theirs had been a long journey to happiness, but they'd found the treasure they'd been seeking, and no one could deny they deserved it all.

I turned my head and laughed to myself as I spotted Rose. She was unmissable, not only because of her pink-streaked hair, but because she was clearly having a bit of a tiff with Sophie over who was going to take the baby for a walk. They were both holding onto the handle of their grandson's pram, and it was obvious that neither had any intention of letting go.

Both Rose and Sophie, according to everyone who knew them, must have entered some imaginary grandmother of the year competition, as they'd done nothing but try to prove which of them was the best granny since Atticus had left the hospital.

Tally had told me they were falling over themselves to babysit, and Fuchsia and Pandora were having to metaphorically beat them off with a big stick, so they could spend some alone time with their baby boy.

At least, I thought with some amusement, it had distracted Sophie from suspiciously eyeing my friends from the Whitby Goth Festival, as she usually did.

Archie and Flynn stood a little way away, having what appeared to be a relaxed conversation, and taking no notice whatsoever of their wives' bickering. I remembered the days when Flynn avoided all events like this, preferring to stay at home alone, shunning company. Such a beautiful soul, but so lonely. Rose had changed all that. Once she'd set her cap at him, he'd had no choice but to step out into the world and take his place as a much-loved member of our community. I knew, for certain, that he wouldn't have it any other way. Rose had saved him, and I would love her forever for that.

Pan and Fuchsia were standing a few yards from their bickering mothers, chatting to Cerise, Oliver and Stephanie. It seemed Stephanie had already fitted right in with the Crooks, and with

Kearton Bay. She didn't seem in the least bit fazed by her mother-in-law's behaviour and had seemed to thoroughly enjoy the Beltane ceremony.

Judging by the laughter on their faces, the five of them had clearly struck up quite a friendship. I had a feeling Oliver would be bringing his wife to the village for regular visits, and maybe at last, he'd be inviting his parents to Bristol. I hoped so. Sophie had missed him so much, and now that she had Atticus in her life, maybe Oliver wouldn't feel quite so smothered, and would be happy to be part of the family again. And luckily, there was no chance she'd get to rule Atticus's life. Rose and Fuchsia would see to that.

As for Tally… I turned and smiled as I saw that she and Derry had found his bandmates and were deep in conversation with them. Maybe they were already planning their live events at The Hare and Moon. It would all be hugely different from now on, but I knew they would breathe new life into the place, and I had no doubt it was for the best.

'No regrets?'

I gave Jack a hug. 'None. You?'

'None. Aren't we the lucky ones?'

'We are,' I said. 'Are you ready for this?'

He grinned. 'As ready as I'll ever be. How about you?'

'Oh, I'm ready,' I said. 'It's just…'

'No Harry?'

'No,' I confirmed. 'I've been looking for him, but he's not arrived yet. It's strange. He promised he'd be here.'

'You don't think he's had second thoughts?' Jack asked, looking suddenly worried. 'About that offer from his old boss, I mean.'

I laughed. 'No, Jack. There's no chance of that. Harry doesn't want that life any more. He knows what he does want, and it's the life we're going to have.'

He nodded. 'Yes, you're right. Weird he's not here, that's all.'

'He'll be along in a minute, I'm sure,' I said. 'Just give him time.'

'Back to yours for the grub, Rhiannon?' someone called.

There was an eager murmuring and I looked at Jack. Usually, after the union of the Green Man and May Queen was complete,

436

I immediately invited everyone to The Hare and Moon to enjoy a feast especially cooked for them by Jack. This year, Aidan was doing the honours, allowing Jack to be with me at this special moment in our lives. The crowd would be moving off any minute, I realised, and I didn't want them to go just yet.

Derry appeared beside me. 'I think you're going to have to make your announcement now, Mum, with or without Harry.'

I sighed, seeing he was right.

'Where is Harry?' Tally pondered, gazing around. 'He said he'd be here.'

'And he will be,' I said, certain of it. 'I suppose I'll have to make the announcement without him. Or part of it at any rate.'

'Good luck, my darling,' Jack said, squeezing my hand.

I cleared my throat. 'Ladies and gentlemen!'

Everyone turned to face me, and I glanced at Jack. He gave me a reassuring smile, and I held up my hands, gesturing to the crowd to quieten down.

'Ladies and gentlemen,' I repeated. 'You are, of course, most welcome to come back to The Hare and Moon for our annual Beltane feast. However,' I shouted, as they began to move off, 'before you do that, can I have your attention please?'

I could see some puzzled looks in the audience. I'd never delayed the feast for a second before.

'I should tell you that this year will be the last Beltane feast at The Hare and Moon with me as the landlady. I've sold the pub.'

Honestly, if I'd told them I'd cast a spell and plunged the pub into the sea they couldn't have looked more shocked.

'But — but you can't have done,' Eliza gasped.

'You never told us!' Rose said indignantly. 'What have you done that for?'

'Rhiannon, you can't,' Lexi pleaded. 'It won't be the same without you.'

I took Derry's hand. 'Don't worry. The Hare and Moon is in safe hands. The safest. I've sold the pub to Derry.'

'To Derry?' There were some gasps and some surprised looks, but then, to my relief, everyone began to smile and clap.

'Well, thank God for that,' someone called. 'Thought I'd have to brave the bloody Mermaid.'

'There's nothing wrong with The Mermaid,' I scolded. 'As well you know, Bobby Jones. I've heard you've been seen staggering out of there many a night.'

He had the grace to look embarrassed and I laughed as his wife nodded and said, 'You're not wrong there, love. And wakes me up every time when he gets home singing *Brown Eyed Girl* to me. I wouldn't care, but my eyes are green.'

'But what about you?' Gabriel asked. 'Where will you live? What are you going to do?'

'Are you moving out?' Flynn sounded appalled. 'Where are you going?'

'You're not leaving the village?' Will's eyes were full of anxiety. 'You wouldn't. Would you?'

I opened my mouth to speak, but instead let out a sigh of relief as I saw Harry sprinting across the field towards me.

'I'm so sorry,' he called, and everyone turned to look at him.

He arrived at my side and bent over, hands on knees, as he took a moment or two to get his breath back.

'That bloody hill!' he gasped. 'I'll never get used to it. What have I missed?'

'Rhiannon's sold the pub to Derry,' Sophie wailed. 'Have you ever heard the like?'

'What took you so long?' I murmured.

'I'm so sorry.' Harry straightened and put his hands on my shoulders, and I saw his eyes were shining. 'Rufus rang me. Well, Melody rang me, but she put Rufus on the phone. She wasn't happy about it, but Rufus has been nagging to talk to me. Rhiannon, he wants to visit! He actually wants to come over here and stay with me.'

I threw my arms around him. 'That's wonderful, Harry.'

'Did you hear that, Amy?' he asked, looking round, and finding his daughter in the crowd. 'Rufus is coming over to stay for a while.'

'Cool,' Amy said. 'I'll let him ride Crackerjack.'

'Maybe Frosty would be a safer bet for a beginner,' Will suggested. 'Assuming he is a beginner?'

'No idea,' Harry said cheerfully. 'But I'll find out, won't I?'

'There's always a donkey,' Joe said.

'Ooh, good idea,' Charlie agreed. 'Eddie won't mind, will you, Eddie?'

'Of course not. My donkeys are safe as houses with kiddies,' Eddie said.

Sophie had clearly had enough of this conversation. 'All right, all right. I'm happy for you, Harry, but Rhiannon still hasn't answered our question. Where are you going to live, Rhiannon?'

Harry and I smiled at each other, and he put his arm around my waist, while I held out my hand to Jack and pulled him to us.

'I'm going to live at Eight Bells with Harry,' I announced. 'And with my father. Jack's moving in with us, aren't you, Jack?'

There was a stunned silence.

'Jack? Your father? You're living with Harry? You and Harry? You and Jack?'

There was an outpouring of questions, and between us, Jack, Harry, Derry, Tally, and I managed to answer them all.

'Well, I never did,' Rose said. 'How have I missed all this?'

'Too focused on becoming a grandmother,' I said. 'And quite right, too.'

'I call that bad timing,' she grumbled. 'Any other year I'd have been onto you and Harry like a flash. I can't believe Jack's your dad, though. That's weird.'

'It's wonderful,' I said. 'I couldn't ask for a better father.'

'So you're not aristocracy after all,' Sophie said thoughtfully. 'Just shows you.'

'Actually,' Derry pointed out, 'she is. The titles are on her mum's side, not her father's.'

'Oh, bugger,' Sophie said. 'Still,' she added, cheering up suddenly, 'that means my Tally will be married into the aristocracy, through you, Derry.'

Tally's face went pinker than Rose's streaks, and she shrieked, 'Mother! For God's sake!'

Derry merely laughed and called, 'Give me a chance, Sophie, eh?'

Sophie looked sheepish. 'Sorry. You know what I mean.'

In the crowd, I searched for Will and met his gaze. He nodded slightly and, as we smiled warmly at each other, I knew he was giving me his blessing, and that no one would be happier for me than he was.

'Well,' Bernie said, 'this has been an evening of revelations all right, and I'm right happy for you all. Derry, congratulations on the pub. Tally, congratulations on being with Derry who is, after all, aristocracy. Rhiannon, congratulations on finding love at last, when we'd all given up hope. Harry congratulations on snagging Rhiannon, because by God, talk about punching above your weight, and I should know,' he added, nodding at Darcey, who laughed and shook her head. 'And congratulations to you, Jack, on finally being able to claim your daughter as your own. I think I speak for all of us when I say, you've always been the father she needed, and nothing's going to change that I can see, apart from the rest of us knowing what you've known all along.'

Everyone clapped in agreement.

'And with that all sorted,' he continued, 'can I ask one more thing? Can we get to the pub and start on the grub? Because the missus hasn't fed me and I'm starving.'

As I happily gave permission, the largest part of the crowd began to drift away, leaving Harry and I standing amid our closest friends and family.

'I'll see to the bonfire,' Derry offered. 'Make sure it's safe to leave.'

'I'll help him,' Tally said. 'We'll meet you all back at the pub, okay?'

We agreed, and slowly walked out of the field, through the archway between two bungalows, and onto Whitby Road.

'So, the B&B isn't going to happen after all?' Eliza asked as we passed The Kearton Arms and began the long walk down Bay Street.

'No, thank God.' Harry gripped my hand. 'I would have hated it, but thanks to Rhiannon, I don't have to go through that ordeal.'

'And you get to start a whole new venture,' Flynn said, smiling at me. 'I think you'll love it. I'm sure you'll both be incredibly happy.'

'We will,' I said, 'because we'll be doing what we love best.'

It had all worked out beautifully. It had taken Harry a bit of persuading, but he'd finally agreed to accept the money I offered him for Eight Bells. It was enough for my share of the living accommodation, and for the entire business premises, which we'd estimated with the help of my accountant.

I was going to turn Eight Bells into a retreat for people who wanted to learn about my way of life. I'd teach them about the sabbats, about the gods and goddesses, about the rituals that marked the Wheel of the Year. I'd teach them how to read the tarot cards, and how to meditate, and help them to understand the power of crystals. They could stay in one of the rooms or, for those living locally, they could simply come to classes, which I'd hold daily.

Jack had leapt at the chance of moving in with us, once he'd been assured by Harry that he was welcome. The house may be old, but it had been thoroughly modernised now, and the stairs would present no problem for him. And, as we'd told him quite truthfully, there was an annexe outside that we would, over time, renovate for him, so he would have his own little bungalow in the grounds.

In return, Jack had insisted that he cook the meals for any guests I had staying. I didn't want him to, but he pointed out that having something to do would keep him young. It wasn't like cooking for a pub full of hungry diners. There would only be a maximum of eight guests staying with us, even at the busiest times, so it wouldn't be a problem, and he'd promised me that if it ever became too much, he would step down.

He was excited and relieved to be living with us, and I realised his big speech about being quite happy at his flat in Helmston had been purely to ease my mind. He hadn't been looking forward to living so far away at all, and I was delighted that I could make his wish come true after all he'd done for me.

As for Harry, he was going to use the money I'd paid for Eight Bells to invest in property. It was, after all, what he'd loved best. Even before the television career had come along, he'd enjoyed buying rundown houses and renovating them, selling them on for a profit. His dream was to build a property portfolio, eventually making a good living from selling or renting out properties.

'And all to locals,' he assured Gabriel, as we headed over the little stone bridge across Kearton Beck. 'Or at least, to people who'll be living in Kearton Bay all year round. No holiday lets, I promise you that.'

Gabriel grinned. 'I'm delighted to hear it,' he said. 'Spoken like a true Kearton Bay man.'

'I knew it would happen eventually,' Eliza said smiling. 'It's worked its magic, Harry. This village. Just as it did to me. It was exactly what I needed to heal me, and now it's done the same to you. You're going to be so happy here. It's that sort of place, isn't it?'

Harry nodded. 'I think you're right. Though if you'd told me that I'd feel this way that day I arrived at Whisperwood Farm, intent on whisking you off to Italy, I'd have laughed in your face.'

'Hannah would never believe this, you know.' Lexi giggled. 'I'm just picturing her face in heaven right now. Can you imagine? She'll be looking down on us and shaking her head in amazement.'

'And telling Albert to put the kettle on, no doubt,' Gabriel added, as we rounded the final bend in the road. 'Life's a funny thing, isn't it?'

'The universe always unfolds as it should,' I reminded them. 'Oh!'

I stopped dead, and they all stayed with me, as we stared ahead of us at the sunset over the North Sea. The sky was streaked with orange and yellow, and a path of gold led from the horizon to the shore.

'We're so lucky,' I murmured.

Harry took my hand. 'I love you,' he said.

'Yuck, Dad!' Amy pulled a face. 'You're *old*!'

Hannah and Michael giggled, and Eliza cleared her throat. 'Right you lot, let's get down to the pub and get some food before it's all gone, shall we?'

They all hurried off, clearly deciding Harry and I needed a moment alone.

'I love you, too,' I told him, gazing into his eyes. The weariness, I noticed, had left him. There was a sparkle there, a shining hope as bright as the sunlit path across the ocean. 'It's all going to be all right, Harry.'

'It's going to be more than all right, Rhiannon Penhaligon,' he said, kissing the tip of my nose. 'It's going to be perfect. You just wait and see.'

'Come on,' I said. 'Let's go and join our friends.'

Arm in arm, we headed to The Hare and Moon, as the sun sank below the horizon, and another day ended in Kearton Bay.

The End

To find out more about Sharon Booth and her books
visit her website

www.sharonboothwriter.com

where you can also sign up for her newsletter and get a free and
exclusive novella.

Acknowledgements

So here we are at the end of the final Kearton Bay book. I knew it would be emotional, but I really didn't know how emotional it would be!

My journey as an author began with this pretty village on the North Yorkshire coast, all the way back in 2011. That's ten whole years ago, and a lot has happened to me since.

It took me four years to finally write and publish the first in this series, *There Must Be an Angel*, and I learned such a lot in that time. It seems fitting that my twentieth book — yes, twentieth! — is the final Kearton Bay novel. The end of an era.

Readers who have followed me from the beginning will know that there was a long gap between the third in the series, *Once Upon a Long Ago*, and this final story. It was never intended to be such a long break. Life and other novels got in the way, and if I'm honest, I think I kept putting it off because, deep down, I didn't want to say goodbye to Kearton Bay.

When I finally began typing the first draft of this story, I realised that what had been so clear in my head just wasn't translating to the page. Writing this book was a struggle, not helped by the anxieties of a global pandemic which all but destroyed my writing mojo.

Usually, I visit the places I'm writing about, and with my other Kearton Bay novels I'd enjoyed jaunts to Robin Hood's Bay, the inspiration behind my fictional village. This proved impossible for obvious reasons, and that meant I was relying on memory and photographs. Easy to visualise, but not the same as being there, as you can imagine.

Frustrated, I stopped writing and instead wrote *Christmas with Cary*, then *The Other Half*, a novella for my newsletter subscribers.

But *The Whole of the Moon* kept nagging away at me, and I knew I needed to complete Rhiannon's story. She'd been with me a long time, and it was her turn to shine. She deserved this. It was time to give her my full attention.

Without the support and encouragement of some incredibly

special people I might never have made it, so I'd like to say a massive thank you to my husband, Steve, for being there for me, giving me the space to write, and providing me with much-needed hugs, cups of Yorkshire Tea, and stern pep talks when I needed it most and was at my most pathetic.

My friend Julie is always there when I call for help and is my biggest cheerleader. She writes as Jessica Redland, so knows what she's talking about, and her advice and support is invaluable.

My writing group, The Write Romantics, are an incredible bunch of women who always pick me up when I'm down. Massive thanks to them all: Jo Bartlett, Jessica Redland, Alys West, Rachael Thomas, Helen J Rolfe, Helen Phifer, Jackie Ladbury, Deirdre Palmer, Lynne Davidson, I couldn't be without you, and I wouldn't want to be!

Thank you to Julie for working with me on this book, helping me to transform it from a jumbled mess into the story it became, and to Pat Posner and Liz Berry for their proofreading skills.

Huge thanks also to Berni Stevens for her amazing cover, which I absolutely love. Berni is lovely to work with and so talented. You can find more about her work at www.bernistevenscoverdesign.com

Finally, a huge, huge thank you to you, the readers. You've been wonderful, buying, reading and reviewing this series, sending me the most encouraging and uplifting messages, and generally being fantastic. I hope you feel this book has been a fitting end to the series, and that you've enjoyed your last visit to Kearton Bay.

It's sad to say goodbye to my pretty coastal village, but I'm off to a gorgeous market town next year, and I hope you're going to love it just as much.

Until the next time!

Love Sharon xx

WELCOME TO KEARTON BAY

There Must Be an Angel (Kearton Bay 1)

When Eliza Jarvis discovers her property show presenter husband, Harry, has been expanding his portfolio with tabloid darling Melody Bird, her perfect life crumbles around her ears.

With her marriage in tatters she flees to the North Yorkshire coastal village of Kearton Bay in search of the father she never knew, with only her three-year-old daughter and a family-sized bag of Maltesers for company.

Ignoring the pleas of her beloved uncle, Eliza determines to find the man who abandoned her mother and discover the reason he left them to their fate. All she has to go on is his name – Raphael – but in such a small place there can't be more than one angel, can there?

Gabriel Bailey may have the name of an angel but he's not feeling very blessed. In fact, the way his life's been going he doesn't see how things can get much worse. Then Eliza arrives with her flash car and designer clothes, reminding him of things he'd rather forget, and he realises that if he's to have any kind of peace she's one person he must avoid at all costs.

But with the help of a beautiful Wiccan landlady and a quirky pink-haired café owner, Eliza is soon on the trail of her missing angel, and her investigations lead her straight into Gabriel's path.

As her search takes her deeper into the heart of his family, Eliza begins to realise she's in danger of hurting those she cares about deeply. Is her quest worth it?

And is the angel she's seeking really the one she's meant to find?

A Kiss from a Rose (Kearton Bay 2)

Rose MacLean's new beginning in Kearton Bay didn't go quite as expected, but now she has a new career and things finally seem to be improving.

But Rose's life never runs smoothly for long. With money tight, space in her tiny flat at a premium, and her eldest daughter, Fuschia, behaving even more strangely than usual, the last thing she needs is to spend more time with her mother. Mrs MacLean is straight-talking and hard to please, but when she becomes the unexpected victim of a crime, Rose has no choice but to take her into her already cramped home.

Reduced to sleeping on the sofa, dealing with her mother's barbed comments, and worrying endlessly about her teenage daughters, Rose is desperately in need of something good to happen.

Flynn Pennington-Rhys is the quiet man of Kearton Bay. He lives alone in a large, elegant house, and works as a GP in the village. Thoughtful, reliable, but a bit of a loner, Flynn is the last person Rose expected to fall for. Then a drunken kiss at a wedding sets them on a path that neither could have predicted.

But Flynn has his own issues to deal with, and when events take an unexpected turn, it seems Rose may not be able to rely on him after all.

Will the quiet man come through for her? Will her daughters ever sort themselves out? And will Rose ever get her bedroom back from her mother, or is she destined to spend the rest of her life on the sofa?

Once Upon a Long Ago (Kearton Bay 3)

Lexi Bailey doesn't do love. Having seen the war zone that was her parents' marriage, she has no interest in venturing into a relationship, and thinks romance is for fairy tales. As far as she's concerned, there's no such thing as happy ever after, and she's not looking for a handsome prince.

Will Boden-Kean has two great loves: his ancestral home, Kearton Hall, and Lexi Bailey. But the future of the first is in real jeopardy, thanks to his reckless and irresponsible father, and the chances of Lexi seeing him as anything except a good friend seem remote.

While Lexi gazes at the portrait of the third Earl Kearton, and dreams of finding the treasure that is reputed to be hidden somewhere in the house, Will works hard to turn around the fortunes of his home. When he goes against Lexi's wishes and employs the most unpopular man in the village, she begins to wonder if he's under a spell. Will would never upset her. What could possibly have happened to him?

As plans take shape for a grand ball, Lexi's life is in turmoil. With a secret from Will's past revealed, a witch who is far too beautiful for Lexi's peace of mind, and a new enchantress on the scene, things are changing rapidly at Kearton Hall. Add to that a big, bad wolf of a work colleague, a stepmother in denial, and a father who is most definitely up to no good, and it's no wonder she decides to make a new start somewhere else.

Then she makes a discovery that changes everything — but time is running out for her. Is it too late to find her happy ending? Will Lexi make it to the ball? Will Buttons save the day?

And where on earth did that handsome prince come from?

Milton Keynes UK
Ingram Content Group UK Ltd.
UKHW011818130923
428619UK00004B/146